Return
to
Fourwinds

Elisabeth Gifford studied French Literature and World Religions at Leeds University. She has written articles for *The Times* and the *Independent*, and has a Diploma in Creative Writing from Oxford OUDCE and an MA in Creative Writing from Royal Holloway College. She is married with three children. They live in Kingston upon Thames.

Also by Elisabeth Gifford

Secrets of the Sea House

Return
to
Fourwinds

ELISABETH
GIFFORD

CORVUS

First published in trade paperback in Great Britain in 2014 by Corvus, an imprint of Atlantic Books Ltd.

Copyright © Elisabeth Gifford, 2014

The moral right of Elisabeth Gifford to be identified as the author of this work has been asserted by her in accordance with the Copyright, Designs and Patents Act of 1988.

10 9 8 7 6 5 4 3 2 1

A CIP catalogue record for this book is available from the British Library.

Trade paperback ISBN: 978 1 78239 114 2
E-book ISBN: 978 1 78239 115 9

Printed in Italy by 🦌 Grafica Veneta S.p.A.

Corvus
An imprint of Atlantic Books Ltd
Ormond House
26–27 Boswell Street
London
WC1N 3JZ

www.corvus-books.co.uk

To Josh, Hugh, Kirsty and George

CHAPTER 1

Derbyshire, 1981

As Ralph Colchester reached the foot of the hill and began to drive up towards the village, he thought wearily of Fourwinds, the large Georgian house that was waiting for him at the top, of the chaos that would be eddying through the rooms with the Donaghues already there to help, the noise of hammering from the marquee going up on the lawn. It was late afternoon, the air warm. The simmering green fields stretched away under a sky of unimpeachable blue.

On impulse he took a left turn into the longer route home, Draycott Lane, an ancient way deeply embedded between banks and hedgerows. Barely the width of a cart, it had been tarmacked over decades ago, but two rows of weeds persistently broke through to mark the old wheel runnels. And there was the cottage, hidden away in a bend, a huge elm rising up from the opposite bank, spreading its massive branches across the lane.

He stopped the car. The cottage was looking a little dilapidated. A pile of cement bags in the garden spoke of renovations. He'd heard a young couple had taken it on recently. The upstairs curtains were still drawn. Looked like they were commuters then, not yet returned from town.

He thought back to the day when, still in uniform, laughing, he'd carried Alice over the threshold. They'd hardly noticed the damp walls and the soggy thatch at first. They'd seen a glass moon rising over the black silhouette of the hills, heard the scream of the fox in the darkness. In the morning, blue woodsmoke rising through the winter trees. The splash of the stream sounding through the cottage rooms.

No space in there to be anything other than close, to be together. One frosty and moonlit night, Alice had gone out with a handful of salt and sprinkled it round the border of the frozen garden, a shining barrier to stop any harm from reaching them, she told him, an old country custom for newly weds, half done in jest. They had lain in bed, the salt sparkling on the frosty ground outside. Inside the circle, she said, they would always be open and true with each other, intimate and secret from the rest of the world.

And then, in time, came the children, and with them the great romance of moving up to the large Georgian place and renovating it as their home. A stream of purposeful years followed, building a family life together.

But now, the children gone from the echoing rooms, he had turned round one morning and realised that they were not so much a couple as two people with interconnecting schedules, their lives glancing off each other like two balls bouncing around an empty room. He was forever busy with the law firm in Uttoxeter, Alice absorbed in lecturing in social studies at the college. In the evening they came home, listened to music, read through books or papers from work, watched the news at ten, always polite and agreeable.

Last winter, with all three boys absent, he'd been aware for the first time how terribly silent the village was. Late one night, with snow covering the countryside, he'd looked out of the window and seen the empty glow blanketing the land for miles. The trees were thickly gloved and weighted down with white, the church tower a black shape against a pewter sky. The silence almost bruised his ears. He had moved his lips, made a sound, just to check his voice still worked.

God he felt weary. He wound down the window further and the birdsong bubbled in from the hedges and the treetops. He caught a rich and dank smell of leaf mould.

He had thought that the bustle and excitement of Nicky's wedding would bring some kind of change, flick the tracks and send them into a project they would tackle together. But he'd been firmly demoted to carrying out orders, mostly to do with opening the chequebook.

It was only a year ago that Nicky had turned up at Fourwinds with Sarah and announced the engagement. They had met the girl a few times before, but even so, it was hard to suppress a pause of evident surprise before jumping up to hug the children and say how thrilled they were.

Of course, Nicky hadn't got as far as thinking about an actual ring. Alice said that he should let Nicky have the Colchester family ring. Ralph had fetched it from its hiding place. It was still in the small red box with the name of the jeweller imprinted in faded gold letters, the velvet inside fragile and silky.

The young couple had loved the idea of keeping a piece of family history alive, passing it down the generations. His mother's engagement ring from his father now semaphored tiny flashes from Sarah's finger. He'd watched her moving her hand to set the little colours flaring up in the light.

He'd almost blurted something out. 'Thing about that ring is . . .' genial, laughing a little. But he'd remained silent.

Hard to comprehend now, the way that sort of thing stained the fabric of a life, how it could seep through the layers and leave an odour trailing – make you seem worthy of suspicion and questionable. That was simply how things were, all those years ago. And it was too hard now, to crack open the silence and let the little lies spill out, pale misshapen things, grown into their confined spaces.

As a child, the weight of carrying his mother's half-understood, necessary little untruths had always left him exhausted. 'Two wrongs don't make a right, Ralph.' That's what Mama had always taught him, her face serious and sincere, her soft hands pressing his cheeks.

He started up the car. The house on top of the hill felt miles away. Everyone remote in their all-consuming business. Everyone happy. And that's how he should leave it. But the sense of unease refused to leave him.

He had the oddest feeling that Nicky's Sarah had picked up on something, as if she had rumbled him in some way. What a funny little thing she was, sweetness itself, but there were moments when she could be quite fierce. She flinched away from any hugs. Looked at him sideways. He could think of nothing he had done to merit such a reaction, and yet there it was, slight but perceptible; she didn't trust him.

The car arrived at the end of the drive, the afternoon sun deepening the colours of the bricks as Fourwinds came into view, the cedars in front stirring in the wind. Home. He felt a twist of longing for the place, as if he were already gone.

★ ★

Alone in the guest bedroom Sarah had that thing you get in other people's places; she was hungry but she didn't feel she could waltz into the cavernous kitchen, rummage through their bread bin and get the butter from the fridge. Her stomach turned over, tight and empty. But then she never felt like herself at Nicky's parents'. The house was pervaded by a faint smell of wood ash and old polish, and a breezy tone from the air that circulated through the tall sash frames, sometimes making them thump when the wind got up. She wished Nicky were there, his old denim shirt against her cheek, and she'd be fine again. His brother had organised the stag do and had kept the location secret. Knowing Mark, they'd probably be in Scotland, shooting something. They'd even taken her brother Charlie with them, looking like a hostage as they drove off in the car.

Sarah and her parents had driven over from Birmingham to help with various tasks before the wedding, although really there was little left to do according to the schedule on the kitchen wall downstairs. She moved to the bedroom window. The Colchesters' house was famous for its views. Standing on the brow of the hill at the edge of the village, the house with its gracious symmetry looked out over miles of fields and the intermittent shine of the Dove River, the wind stirring the trees into constant motion.

Behind the house was the bulwark of the medieval church. On Sunday mornings there was an incredible noise from the bells, like hammers in a foundry. The Colchesters seemed surprised when Sarah mentioned the din booming through the house.

She closed her eyes against the sun. They felt itchy and sore. For the past few nights she'd been afraid to fall asleep; lately sleep dragged her back into days she thought she'd forgotten, dredging them up again in dreams. She would wake in the dark, soaked in sweat, casting around for the light switch. In the morning it was gone, the room filled with the clear summer light. Nothing to do but let the memory fade.

She'd almost told Nicky once, tried to explain to him what had happened. What she'd done. But the words didn't exist. She leaned her forehead against the window glass.

Down in the garden she could see the marquee and the men who'd spent all day raising it. In just over two days' time she'd be married. Her stomach did a little flip again. She saw herself walking down the aisle of the village church. Heads turning, faces smiling. The insistent smell of freesias.

The evening before, the vicar at Nicky's village church had been taken ill. Impossible to find a replacement at such short notice, Alice had said in dismay. But as a fellow man of the cloth Dad had been able to trawl through the Crockford's directory and had come up with a solution, an old friend called Cyril.

'You remember him, don't you?' Dad said, as he came into breakfast with the news that morning. 'Canon Cyril now. Haven't seen him for years.'

She'd nodded her head. Smiled at the good news. Then she'd realised that the milk in her coffee tasted oddly sour. A lingering smell of burned bacon fat in the room. She'd stood up to take the cup out to the sink, pour the coffee away discreetly, but halfway across the kitchen she'd heard a crash. She saw the cup in pieces on the floor, yellow coffee stains splashed across the hem of her jeans. She'd forgotten to keep holding it. She'd knelt down to clear up and had to let her head drop, feeling suddenly faint.

A few moments later, and it had cleared. The cup swept up, the floor wiped. The day slotted back into gear and moved on.

Now the men down in the garden were packing up for the day. She watched them slamming the van doors and driving away towards the village.

She slipped down the stairs and went out into the garden. The flagstones around the house were warm through her sandals. The hems of her jeans brushed the lawn as she went to peer inside the marquee.

Somebody else's wedding. There were stacks of boards piled up on the crushed grass, ready to go down as the dance floor. And there was Nicky's mum at the far end, talking to Alan, the caterer. Too late now to step back outside and remain unseen.

'Sarah, darling.' Alice waved her over. 'Just in time. We have to make a decision.' She opened the brochure at a photo of circular tables and gold chairs, a sea of flowers and gleaming glassware. 'Do we think it's too much to have the gold chairs after all? Alan says there's a problem with the white. We're going to be short. Do you think it's too much? I think it will look rather smart.' An anxious frown on Alice's petite face, the fair perm and neat lipstick.

'Yes.'

'Too much, or you think it will work?'

A slight pause. The Colchesters spoke English, but it was a different English, the words weighted and given different values. No serviettes at the wedding. Napkins. The wrong answer could be tricky. In a way it was easier to simply think of all this stuff as belonging to Nicky's mum, nothing to do with the real wedding, not really.

'It will work.'

'Marvellous. There's your answer then, Alan. Sarah would like the gold chairs.' She folded the brochure against her chest, smiling.

'It's you, Sarah dear, who matters. This wedding is your big day. We want everything to be right.' Alice patted Sarah's arm ruefully.

'Of course, it's our fault entirely for having so many guests to seat,' she continued.

'Two hundred and fifty,' said Alan, nodding. 'It is a big wedding.'

Sarah left the marquee and its sad odour of crushed grass. At the edge of the lawn was an old apple tree, grey bark with green moss on the weather side, luminous in the evening sun. A climbing rose had grown up and spread through the branches, simple and beautiful. A few weeks ago she had sat out here late in the evening with Nicky, a huge butter moon resting on the horizon, a white owl crossing the garden silent as a moth, Nicky's arm solid round her shoulders. It had seemed impossible to be any happier; Nicky and his kisses the only thing that mattered as they sat alone, whispering in the dark. She longed to see his tall shape now, loping across the lawn towards her, that wide grin that made everything turn out right.

She walked over to the tree and took one of the blooms in her hand and sniffed in the sugary smell. A petal cool as skin.

What Sarah had wanted was to get up early on the morning of the wedding and pick a bunch of roses and orange blossom and lady's mantle from the summer garden. Alice had smiled; actually she had laughed. She thought it was more suitable to order a proper bouquet from the florist's, the kind of stiff and pointless floral arrangement that Sarah hated. To keep the peace she'd gone to the florist's and picked out peach roses and cream freesias and baby's breath.

They'd be left behind when she and Nicky left.

Mum had said Alice was right about the bouquet. Sarah could see that Mum and Dad felt, if anything, even less comfortable than she did about being here. But Fourwinds was so much more practical for a wedding, plenty of room for a marquee, as Alice had said, quashing any objections.

It was so kind of Alice. Her energy was limitless. None of this would have been possible if they'd tried to do it on Dad's salary. It would have been a much smaller affair – sandwiches in the church hall.

And there was something else, something that wasn't being explained to Sarah, an uncomfortable undercurrent to do with how her dad had known Alice Colchester in the past. Turned out that he'd been evacuated to Alice's parents' house briefly during the war. That was as much as Sarah knew. She would have liked to ask more, a lot more, but no opening was offered. But then anything to do with the war years and her parents' childhood was only ever mentioned in snippets of information. It was maudlin to want to go back over those years. Asking for more might dredge up a fact here and there, but never resulted in a cohesive whole that you could really grasp and understand.

Sarah carefully detached a rose stem from the main shoot, leaving a trailing thread of bark. She picked another couple of pale roses, and then she broke off a few sprays of the orange blossom. The combined smell was delicate and clear. She began to walk back to the house. These would be the flowers that she would carry at another wedding, the one that she would hold in her head, just her and Nicky there, and everything else blanked out – even as he asked her to repeat the words. Thinking about that moment, her hands were sticky with sweat, the rose stems slipping and turning sideways, the thorns pricking. She put the flowers down on the bank at the side of the drive.

Ages before tea. Not tea, supper; that's what it was called here.

She looked at the large house, the shadow of someone behind a window, a flickering shape that reappeared and then was gone. She turned away, taking instead the path round the back of the garage with the shingle roof. She headed towards the gate in the yew hedge and went through to the churchyard.

Here at the boundary with the fields someone had been burning old bouquets of flowers cleared from the graves. The ashes still smoked and a faded spray of silk blooms stuck out of the debris, the petals darkened with soot.

She carried on along the gravel path. In front of the church she paused. She slipped into the porch, pushed on the heavy oak door. The warmth of the afternoon had not registered in here, the air cool on her arms. She sat down in a pew at the back and tried to let the calm of the thick-walled building spread into her body, let the silence absorb and still the odd spinning feeling inside.

If anything, here in the church, she felt the worry rising. She took a laboured breath.

She should say something. That's what she ought to do. She tried to imagine forming the words.

Sitting in the silent church she could feel a pain in her throat. Alarmed, she rubbed at the tight ache. The muscles felt constricted, her breathing shallow and short. She tried to make a noise, form a word in the air. Only a breathy sound came out.

But it was years since she'd had that trouble, all those months and months when she couldn't say a thing, the panic of a painfully closing throat each time she'd tried to speak – afraid that her breathing would shut down completely. She'd spent a week in the children's hospital, which had made it worse. The doctor gave her sedatives; she'd slept a lot. Then they'd gone away on a family camping holiday. The warm sun, the freedom to curl up and read, and when they came back they'd moved to a different place. The problem faded.

She stood up, her hand clutching the tightness in her throat. It simply couldn't happen now. But all this past week she'd woken up, trapped in a slippage of time, the past raw and inescapable all over again, hot with guilt, dizzy with fear and relief that it was over.

And now this.

If she could just carry on walking along the lane, walking towards the wood, out in the open where there was less pressure.

★ ★

Sarah's father, Peter Donoghue, listened as the grandfather clock in the hallway sounded ten o'clock. He had been outside, called her in, looked everywhere in the Colchesters' darkening garden and then walked up through the village, but there was no sign of her.

He and his wife Patricia had been more dismayed than worried. Sarah was known for her long, solitary walks; she would disappear for hours and come back red-cheeked and satisfied. But now supper had been eaten in embarrassed silence and cleared away. They had helped the Colchesters wash up, and still no sign of Sarah.

So he had taken the car out and driven around the surrounding lanes to see if he could spot her. Now they were standing in the kitchen, discussing whether they should phone the police – the awful moment when all imagined things begin to tip over into reality – when they heard the sound of the back door opening.

Sarah was slipping off her sandals among the wellingtons and boots lined up in the back porch. She looked shocked as they all crowded in through the door. There were two high points of colour on her cheeks.

'Really, Sarah,' began Patricia. 'We waited for you. We were worried. And poor Alice who's gone to so much trouble.'

'Perhaps a small sorry would do it,' said Alice. 'One doesn't like to see food wasted.'

Sarah's lips moved, but she didn't speak. Her eyes fixed on her father. He took her arm and studied her face.

'Sarah, what's the matter?'

'Lost her voice,' said Alice with a little laugh.

Tears began to run down Sarah's cheeks.

'Oh no,' said Patricia. 'Sarah, is it that? Your voice? But it went on for weeks last time. Listen, darling, you can write things down, can't you? Till it gets better. That's all right to do, isn't it, when you're getting married?'

'This has happened before?' asked Alice.

'But it was years ago. When she was small. Never since.'

They steered Sarah back into the sitting room. A scent of cold wood ash from the fireplace. Ralph unstoppered a bottle of whisky. Poured a dram and gave it to Sarah, but she shook her head and pushed it gently back towards him.

'Never mind, old thing. I expect by tomorrow you'll be your old self, singing at the top of your lungs.'

'How long did you say it went on the last time it happened?' murmured Alice.

'It was several weeks. Then it just disappeared of its own accord, didn't it? Oh Sarah, it's probably just nerves, dear.'

Alice fetched paper and a biro from the writing desk. 'There we go,' her tone cheerful and calming. 'Now you can tell us whatever you'd like us to do, dear. It's not the end of the world after all. Just one of those things. Too much happening.'

She nodded encouragingly as Sarah wrote on the paper in swift block capitals.

Alice took the paper, paused. Her mouth slack, she checked the words over a couple of times.

'No wedding. It says "no wedding".'

'Sarah . . .' Patricia moved to fold Sarah in her arms, but Sarah brushed her off and stood up. She began pulling at her left hand. With a small, hollow clatter she let the ring drop onto the desk: three brilliant cut diamonds, cold under the electric light.

CHAPTER 2

Valencia, 1931

Eight-year-old Ralph Colchester sat in the sun on the kitchen steps next to a box of oranges, peeling and eating them one by one, and trying hard not to get his white shorts and shirt dirtied. None of the maids came out to stop him.

He was thirsty after a hot, stuffy siesta. Solid and full of energy and little boy muscles, it was torture to lie still and wide awake for what seemed like hours, nothing to do but look up at the slatted shutters closing out the garden and listen to the sound of cicadas. He was sure the maid had forgotten to tell him it was over. It was a relief to be out in the sun now, working his way through the fruit, the juice starting to sting the skin round his mouth. He saw Mama coming through the courtyard garden and hastily put a half-opened orange back on top of the box, then rubbed his hands on the sides of his shorts.

She seemed so small beside the fountains of palm trees. She was wearing her going-out hat, like a soft bell shading her eyes.

She sat down on the step beside him. Taking a comb from her bag, she parted his hair to one side. Then they went through the big hallway that ran through the middle of the cool house. She opened the door onto the glare of the streets of Valencia and they walked down the boulevard of calle San Vicente.

The Café de Paris was a big room with rows of small tables across a shiny floor. Mr Gardiner was alone at one of the marble tables, drinking coffee and a large amber brandy. A background of voices echoed off the green tiles on the walls. The ceiling fans high overhead added their clicking whirr. There was a scent of chicory and cigars. Mr Gardiner ordered him a cup of hot chocolate and a long fried pastry to dip in it, even though Ralph wasn't very hungry. Mama tied a big starched napkin round his neck and watched him, both her hands holding on to the bag in her lap.

She opened the bag and took out a letter, handed it to Mr Gardiner. He leaned away and studied it, looked it up and down two or three times.

'He's divorced me,' she whispered, glancing at Ralph, who pretended not to hear. 'He's got a divorce in Chile. He says he's got a new wife. Can he do that?'

'He can in Chile, evidently,' said Mr Gardiner. 'Extraordinary thing to do.'

'I've nothing. He's stopped sending anything back for months now, nothing, and then this.' Mama began crying quietly and sadly.

'Shh, shh,' said Mr Gardiner. 'Come on now, old thing. Chin up. You know you're not alone. Silly Mummy, eh Ralph?'

Ralph nodded hard, Mr Gardiner and he restoring the world to rights again for dear Mama. Mr Gardiner was drumming the fingers of his left hand on the table. He held up the other hand to get the bill.

'Aren't we meeting up with everyone for a picnic, old thing?'

She sniffed and made an effort to rally herself, and got out her small mirror to check her face, then they went out into the hot street to find Mr Gardiner's car for the drive to the river.

'Come on, old Ferdie,' Mr Gardiner said, holding the door of the Austin open so Ralph could jump in the back.

He had an English name and a Spanish name, Ralph Ferdinand Colchester. He was born in Valencia, but Mama said he was English, because his father and she were English. He didn't know what his father had to say about it since, a couple of years ago, his father had had to leave them in Spain and go away to build railway bridges through the wild parts of South America. He had been away so long that he had forgotten to send them any money, and Mama had been forced to take a job looking after dear Mr Gardiner's house. Ever since Ralph could remember Max had been there in the background at picnics and parties with the other English expatriates. And then Papa was gone, and Max had come up with his offer to help Mama.

And now Ralph could play in the gardens and the orange orchard, and talk with the Spanish maids in the kitchens at Mr Gardiner's house, but he was not to disturb Mr Gardiner. Although the truth was that Mr Gardiner didn't mind being disturbed a bit, it seemed to Ralph, and let him come into his office where the spidery pot plants criss-crossed the light slanting in through the Venetian blinds. He liked Mr Gardiner's silly jokes and funny faces that were just for him, and he liked the heavy smell of cigar tobacco that soaked into the fabric of the room. Mr Gardiner bought Ralph tin train sets with clip together tracks from the city shops, and once a wooden boat that he helped him sail at one of the summer picnics in the Valencian parks, picnics where Freddie Marchington or someone from the British Embassy crowd always brought along a gramophone, and someone's maid brought baskets of food, and there was always fizzy champagne and little bottles of cola in a bucket of melting ice. The grown-ups were sunny and giggly and had time to play with him while Mama, with her soft straw hat shading her eyes, sat up straight at the edge of the picnic rug, cutting Manchego cheese into neat squares and arranging them on a plate from the hamper.

Tippy Marchington, with her smudgy red lips, would be lying across the rug with her head on someone's leg, telling stories about people, and making the others put their hands over their mouths and say, 'No, I can't believe that,' or shriek with laughter. But Mama always looked sensible with her serene half-smile; much more good and lovely than Tippy with her blotchy face, especially when Tippy began crying – only because she had been drinking wine all afternoon, Mama said to him later.

★ ★

When they got to the park Tippy was already there, holding court. Mr Gardiner flopped down on the grass and placed his panama across his eyes. Mama folded herself neatly at the edge of the rug, tucking the hem of her dress round her legs. Tippy had a man's booming voice and a cigarette in a holder. She was actually drinking from the wine bottle, as a joke. 'So I had to let her go,' Tippy was saying to them. 'What else could I do? Maids from the country are so silly. I told her when he started to call for her that she should drop that man. I could see he was married. You can smell it, but she just wanted to let herself be sweet-talked. She swore she'd dropped him but I could tell whenever she was going to see him because she'd be all red in the face and fired up and cross. Honestly, can you imagine? And now she's as big as a watermelon, and I can't have the shame in the house. He'll never marry her. And she was so good with needlework. Her poor little *bastardo*.'

Later, as Mama was helping pack away the picnic, Ralph asked her what a bastardo was. Mama said no, she didn't think it might be a type of mule in the villages. She wasn't sure, but it was a common sort of word, not nice. He should never say it again.

Sometimes they all went out in the cars for the drive to the beach, the wind blowing into Ralph's eyes. He'd turn round and kneel up, looking through flickering strands of hair as the wind blew it into tangles, and the legendary road disappeared behind them, the small donkeys and roadside villages retreating into the past. He liked to imagine stories; his best one was how he would see his papa one day, see him walking along the road, and they would stop the car, and then his papa would jump in and say how he had been looking everywhere, looking everywhere for him and Mama.

After a day of being dazed by the beach and the sun and the wind they would make the journey home, and he would go to sleep in the back of Mr Gardiner's big car as they drove through miles of empty coastland. He'd hear the murmur of Mr Gardiner's voice, and Mama's voice, and the long note of the engine as if it were waiting to begin a song and then Mama would be lifting him out with Mr Gardiner's help and he would wake up in his room next morning.

There was a photo on Mr Gardiner's desk of a lady in a straw hat. By her side were a boy and two little girls, in a garden full of roses. For a long time Ralph had thought it was a photo of him, at some picnic he had forgotten. But when he asked Mama she said, 'Don't be silly, dear. All little boys look the same. That's Mr Gardiner's little boy who lives in England with his mama and sisters.'

He wanted to know all about the boy. Mr Gardiner said he went to a school in England – because an English education made you a gentleman. Mr Gardiner looked very lonely when he looked at the photo.

Looking at the picture gave Ralph a funny feeling, that somewhere, far away in England, there might be another Ralph, with two sisters, who went to a school for proper English gentlemen.

CHAPTER 3

London, 1932

Ralph had lived on a big boat for two days, and now he was a long way from Mr Gardiner's house in calle San Vicente. He was standing at a window with a yellowy net curtain, watching the traffic go by in Westbourne Grove. They had been in this house for a week. It was cold, and outside it was foggy and when you walked along the pavements it was hard to see anything till it loomed up in front of you out of the mist. He wondered when they would go back. He missed Mr Gardiner.

Mama came into his room and took his hand. She was dressed in black, because Papa had died, a brave and good man, working hard to bring the railroad all the way to Chile. Ralph understood perfectly well that he would never see Papa now, and he knew it was silly, but he worried that when his papa returned to Valencia he wouldn't know how to find them.

'Come down and have tea with your aunts, dear. And you'll remember won't you, not to talk about the funny old grown-ups in Spain? Aunt Flora and Aunt Cecily, well, they are quite old; they wouldn't be interested, you do see?'

In the drawing room the aunts were sitting either side of a marble fireplace where blue flames appeared in gusts across the red coals. Flora was small and plump with smiley wrinkles. Cecily was dark and stiff, with a sweep of grey hair each side of her forehead; Ralph thought Mama might be afraid of her.

Mama was in a shiny green silk chair with no arms. She was sitting up straight. There was a table with tea and cakes set out next to Aunt Cecily, but he knew not to ask. As soon as she saw him Aunt Flora held out her plump arms.

'Here he is, our own dear Ralph.'

He went over and put his head on her big solid shoulder for a hug, the heavy lace on her dress imprinting his cheek. She put a stool by her chair and they gave him a plate with a teacake, sliced and toasted. He ate it, trying to keep the yellow butter drips on the plate.

His mama twisted the ring off her finger, the one with the three little diamond chips that came from a mine in Argentina.

'Perhaps I should let you have this,' she said. 'I don't know what's correct.'

The aunts began talking at the same time, Flora all fluttery and anxious. 'There's no need,' she said. 'No need. Really, it's yours.'

'After all,' Cecily pronounced, 'that is the purpose of a diamond ring, an investment, for times of trouble.'

'And we are so very, very sorry, dear,' Aunt Flora said. 'We feel so guilty, on his behalf, that he should have abandoned you in that way.'

'The divorce was quite final, with the solicitors you spoke to in Spain?' Aunt Cecily asked.

Mama nodded, pulling at her lower lip with her top teeth. She swallowed and tried to speak, then shook her head.

The aunts looked at each other.

'But Robert remembered the boy? He left funds to support the boy?'

'It appears not. For the last few years I have relied on myself. I found a place with the Gardiner household, as a housekeeper.'

'That must have been such a help to Mrs Gardiner.'

'And really, there's no shame in acting as a housekeeper, it's almost like acting as a companion. Perfectly genteel,' said Cecily.

'Oh indeed,' said Flora. 'Most respectable.'

'But it's so good of you,' said Mama, 'to let us stay here while I look for a school for Ralph, when I'm hardly related to you any more.'

'Lily, I never want to hear you say such a thing again. You have brought our nephew home to us, and such a very dear child.'

'Thank you. And for making it possible with his school.'

'Don't mention it again. And you must tell us if there's anything he needs, that you need.'

Flora and Cecily exchanged a look.

'We want to give something to you, Ralph dear. With Mama's permission.' Flora picked up a little box from the lace cloth on the bamboo side table. 'Come and see. This was our father's watch. He left it to your father, but he never came home.' She paused and looked sad, stroked Ralph's head. 'So now we have decided that it should be in your keeping, as your father's heir. Of course, it's too big yet, but one day.'

'Say thank you,' said Mama.

He whispered thank you, examining the heavy watch, its thick yellow chain and the black numbers on the dial. He held it against his ear and it became very loud, the secret mechanics inside adding their own reverberations to the solid ticking.

That night he put it beside his bed on the table, and lay and stared at it while Mama tidied around his room. He reached out his hand and stroked it.

Mama bent down to kiss him goodnight.

'I like my daddy's watch.'

But the next day he saw that she had tidied it away. He found it folded inside some of his white summer socks in the top dresser drawer.

He liked to walk slowly around the house in Westbourne Grove. There were lots of things to look at. He recognised some things, English things that had been translated into the houses of Mama's friends in Valencia. Now those houses seemed too flimsy and too pretending to be English, with their pale Spanish marmalade on the marble breakfast table, and tea and dusty sponge cake at four o'clock in the afternoon heat. In calle San Vicente the house had wooden slatted shutters and potted ferns and tiled floors that echoed, but this house had a sombre authority that absorbed disturbing sounds into wool rugs and heavy curtains and thick sofas.

It wasn't as big as Mr Gardiner's house, where he had lived for as long as he could remember now, ever since the night his father came into his room and kissed him goodbye – after the big quarrel that he listened to, when there was so much shouting, his father shouting, his mother shouting, and sometimes he half remembered that Mr Gardiner had been there that night to help Mama beg Papa to stay. But that couldn't be right.

He gave up and went back to examining the ivory boxes and carvings that Flora collected. Above them the dark photographs in their ornate little gold frames of his aunts when they were girls, with long black hair and shiny long dresses, each looking frozen and solemn for the camera. He liked the pictures of his father and uncles, tall young men with straw boaters and high collars, standing by a rose trellis, or boating on the river. Sometimes Flora cried and hugged him when she told him about Papa's brothers who had died in the Great War. She pointed out all the names and histories of the people in the frames on the walls, and she even pulled out a scroll with a family tree. She showed him the ink line that went from Papa, all the way back to a king of England, and pointed out the coat of arms for the Colchester knights. She took an ink pen and carefully drew a new line and wrote Ralph's name on the chart. She waved her plump hand at the walls. 'Of course, one day, dear Ralph, this will be yours. I simply can't understand how your father could have abandoned his own flesh and blood.'

He missed the sunny courtyard garden at the house on calle San Vicente, and the maids who sang in the kitchen; that was home, but he understood that this house was somehow a part of him too, and he had come here to learn that. And because they were his and his father's, he began to love the faces in the photographs, and to love the aunts who seemed so much older and stouter than Mama, and their funny shut-in house, surrounded by the London fog and the noises of motor cars and feet hurrying by outside. He began to feel more a Ralph than a Ferdinand. Ralph Colchester. He thought it was a good name.

'Mama, might we visit Mr Gardiner's boy, in his garden?' Ralph asked her as they walked across Kensington Gardens. She squeezed his hand so tightly that it hurt. She knelt down in front of him. 'We are not going to mention Mr Gardiner again. Do you promise me?'

He nodded, but in his room at the top of the tall stucco house he found that he missed Mr Gardiner a lot, more than Papa even. He had no real memories of Papa, but Mr Gardiner he thought about and missed almost every day, but there was no one to tell about the homesickness that weighed on him in the thick London fog, where you had to be on your guard not to bump into something in the cold, yellow smoke.

★ ★

He was playing with an old board game of his father's in the upstairs lobby, when he heard his aunts talking in the hallway below. He leaned forward to peer through the banisters and saw they were dressing to go out. Over their long English dresses they were putting on long, old-fashioned coats like fitted dust covers. Both had heavy rolls of hair piled up round their faces.

'She does try awfully hard, though,' Cecily was saying.

'But really, don't you find her a little bit eager, a little bit paying-guest? You can tell she's been in service.'

'I hardly think housekeeper to the family of a banker is the same as being a housemaid, Flora.'

'And housemaids have that smell in their room, don't you know, something so very housemaidish. It clings. What did you say her parents were?'

'Something in trade. He was a joiner I think.'

'I see. I never quite understood how she met and married Robert, and yet there it is. But we have Ralph, and Ralph is such a dear. Though not very like Robert to look at.'

'But so like Robert in spirit.'

'So like dear Robert in his manners.'

Cecily was pinning a spike with a big pearl on the end through her hat. Flora was carefully putting on her gloves, working each sturdy finger into place. They took it in turns to check in the hall mirror, and then each took an umbrella from the hollow elephant foot by the front door. They left behind a silence that settled in the hallway. Ralph carried on staring down through the banisters. After a while he stood up slowly and went back to his room.

★ ★

He was turning the pages of a favourite book about steam trains, when Mama came in and said they must go out to the haberdasher's. He needed shirts for school, his father's school. She bustled around the room, tidying, opening and closing drawers, picking up from the floor, scolding his bad habits of disorder. He was aware of her perfume, the smell of lavender soap, and something oily she rubbed on her hands. He had never noticed before; he wondered if this might be the smell that betrayed something bad, something he didn't understand.

The trunk in the hallway filled him with terror, but also excitement. If he got inside, he could shut the lid and be completely hidden. It began to fill with folded trousers and shirts; two pullovers and cricket whites; scratchy woollen socks; two pairs of elastic garters to keep his socks up – which he must do at all times; two long striped ties which he had to learn to knot; six clean and folded handkerchiefs. Every item had a label with his name embroidered in red. Mama sat each evening by the lamp, sewing on the labels with tiny, careful stitches, peering closely at the needle. Finally a large fruitcake was wrapped in greaseproof paper and tucked into a corner. The lid went down and was locked.

★ ★

He had never been parted from Mama before. But it was so kind of the aunts to make sure he could go to his father's old school and learn to be a gentleman. He was lucky to go, and after all he was nine now, old for the first form.

In a tall room with a stuffy smell, the headmaster sat behind his desk and jollied Mama along with stories of tea parties and cricket matches. He said best not to visit for the first few weeks, let them settle in.

After Mama left, Ralph stood in the middle of the enormous hallway with boys clattering up and down the stairs. A big boy slapped him on the side of the head. 'Come on. Wake up, you. Get yourself to your dorm and unpack.'

He hated the greasy mutton lumps that tasted of fat in the evening meal, the dry sponge roll and smear of red jam. At bedtime he put on his fine Spanish cotton pyjamas. They still had a faint whiff of oranges, of hot sunshine and even, he imagined, Mama's familiar lavender smell. Tears began running out of his eyes. He had found a place to stand, hard up against the window, half hidden behind a curtain, letting the cold glass touch his burning face. He heard a noise of clattering feet coming along the corridor, bursting in through the doorway.

He turned to see a gang of boys piling in, clapping and chanting, 'New snoot, new snoot.' Twelve or thirteen big boys. And before he could react he was pulled and knocked onto the floor. The boys began to pile themselves on top of him, one after another, the weight crushing down; he couldn't breathe; it hurt so much, and still the pile grew heavier as boys thudded on top. He felt the room blackening. Then they were up, all stamping on the floorboards, sounding like a train wreck, jeering and cheering. Ralph lay curled up on the floor, shuddering with sobs.

'Look at the cry baby,' said a tall boy in disgust.

That was the first day of the new regime. The boys were systematic. They were dedicated. The masters looked away. The cake wrapped in greaseproof paper disappeared on the first day. He was pushed, punched, and his food was stolen at meals. His compass and gym shoes were taken and he was put in detention for missing kit. In the common room in the evening no one would sit near him. They said there was a horrible smell of farts.

He asked if Mama would come and live near his school so that he could go home at weekends, but Mama wrote to say that she had wonderful news. She was going to marry Mr Gardiner. Ralph would spend the term-time holidays with the aunts, and then in the summer he could come out to Valencia. And although it broke her heart to be so far from her boy, she was willing to bear it for his sake. Wasn't he so lucky to be attending such a wonderful school? Think how much he would have learned by the time she saw him again in the summer. How proud she would be of her big, clever boy.

The days went by slowly. Then weeks and months crept past, cold and windy. The rooms were too tall and lonely, and there was nowhere really to curl up and feel safe. You never knew when a master or a prefect might be standing behind you, where a pinch or a slap might come from. He wrote letters and letters to Mama, but Matron brought them all back. He had to copy them out again, missing out the bits she had put a line through. Did he really want to upset Mama, when she so very much wanted to hear how he was happy and making a success of things?

He folded up the letter that had come from Mama that morning, saying how she thought of him having such fun with the other boys, and put it in his locker. He had to get undressed for rugby.

Ralph stood on the muddy sports field in shorts. The winter air was ice, slowly numbing his body. His fingers were bright red, white at the edges. The leather ball slapped him in the face. Three boys hurtled towards him and he went down in the mud. Next summer seemed a lifetime away. It would never come.

For his half-term exeat he stayed with his aunts in the tall and becalmed house in Westbourne Grove. He wrote a long letter, with pictures, the neat little flames from the time his tormentors set his bed on fire. At the end of the road was a post box. He had a feeling that the letter would never get to Mama.

All too soon he was back in the school dining hall, stranded in a sea of boys. Thinking he had made a friend he spilled out stories of Valencia to a boy with an eager face and a thin smile. He explained how Papa and Mama had got divorced. How Mama was getting married again.

After that, 'Colchester's a bastard, a runty bastard,' followed him round the building. They made a big thing of how no one could sit near him because of the bad, bastardy smell. Something in Matron's manner hardened, as if she were slightly repelled by him.

In the music room he found a baby grand piano, black and shiny as a car, almost in tune. He picked out some of the jollier songs that had played on the wind-up gramophone on the rug in a long summer of picnics with Mama. An hour passed, maybe two, lost in a cloud of homesickness.

The door opened and a prefect came in.

'Whole building's been searched for you. You've missed prep and the head wants to see you, and make it sharp.'

Ralph hurried along the upper hallway. He guessed this was the sort of mistake you could get in trouble for. He looked down and saw a small figure in a cloche hat standing alone in the middle of the tiled floor. Wished it were Mama come to get him. Then he stopped, blinked hard.

Mama was standing down there in the darkening hallway. She saw him, held out her arms.

Mama had got the letter he sent from the aunts' house, a letter with no censorship from Matron. It had made her decide that enough was enough. She would take the very next flight and bring him home.

Ralph waited outside the headmaster's study while Mama's voice, high and indignant, carried through the door's wooden panelling. She came out with her chin raised, the headmaster following, looking rather as though someone had given him an awful lot of lines.

'I can assure you that no one has ever complained before. Not a word. Most parents consider such experiences character building. We raise the sons of gentlemen.'

Mama pulled the hems of her gloves straight. 'If that is your idea of a gentleman, then this is not the place for my child, thank you.'

★ ★

Mama said she was going to see to Ralph's education now. Hire tutors. On the train he sat very close, his head bouncing comfortably against the wool of her coat, the familiar smell of lavender and something sharper and anxious.

'Are we going to see the aunts now?' he asked.

'We're going somewhere much nicer,' she said brightly. 'We're going home see Mr Gardiner in Valencia. Do you remember my letter, how Mama said she was married again, to dear Mr Gardiner? We'll be a family now. A papa for you, darling.'

'But not my real one.'

'No. Not your real one.' A sad smile on her lips.

'What about Mr Gardiner's children, the boy in the picture? Will he be coming too?'

'No, dearest. They will stay in England with their mama.'

Ralph stayed quiet, thinking, swaying to the clacking rhythm of the train.

'I know, darling. It's hard to understand. I can't always understand how things turn out. But we have to do the best we can. And dear Mr Gardiner really thinks the world of you. Look. He sent this.'

She opened her bag and fetched out a tissue parcel. Inside he found a hard black model of a bull covered in sleek black hair, with a set of red darts stuck in its flank. He pulled one out and then stuck it back in a new place.

'Sweetie, you know, we don't go on to new friends in Valencia about Mama and Mr Gardiner being divorced before. People might feel uncomfortable, don't you see, if we were to keep talking about it? All Mr Gardiner's friends at the bank, and our new friends in Valencia, they don't really want to think about all that.'

She put her finger on her lips, her eyes expecting an answer. Something important.

Ralph put a finger over his own lips. Nodded.

'I knew I could depend on my boy.'

And he settled back against her side, just the two of them in the train compartment, the smell of damp upholstery, the winter rain on the black train windows, he and Mama sailing through the dark together. He rocked with the train till he fell asleep and dreamed about his own father; he was dressed as a knight, descended from the kings of England, building bridges across Chile in his silver armour. Ralph was there by his side and his father put his hand on his shoulder and said how he simply couldn't manage without Ralph. He saw that now.

CHAPTER 4

Valencia, 1932–1936

They arrived back in Valencia late the following evening. Not to the old house, but to an apartment in a narrow street. Doors led off a long, gloomy corridor, the walls patterned in browns and greens with dark wood veneer up to waist height. At the end of the passageway Mama opened a door into his new room, his books and model airplanes neatly arranged on shelves. Ralph felt so weary that he wanted to lie down on his bed, but Mr Gardiner was waiting, supper was ready.

The dining room seemed too crammed full with dark furniture. Mr Gardiner was reading in the circle of light from a lamp, but he got up and shook Ralph's hand. Two firm shakes, Mr Gardiner crushing his hand. Ralph felt shy and uncomfortable. Before he had been the housekeeper's son, secure in his place in the world. But now? Mama had turned into Mr Gardiner's wife, but that didn't make him Mr Gardiner's son. He felt a fierce burn of loyalty to his own papa.

Mr Gardiner sat down at the head of the table. Ralph slid into his seat.

'Good train journey?'

Ralph nodded hard, relieved that they had skipped straight to the homeward part and missed out school. Throughout supper Mr Gardiner was at his most jovial, full of hearty stories. But Ralph didn't want to find Mr Gardiner's jokes funny; he was keeping his heart safe and honourable for his real father.

Mr Gardiner's bald patch and his round glasses glinted in the electric light each time he bent forward to his soup spoon. Ralph studied the solid man at the head of the table as if for the first time. Mr Gardiner didn't sit straight to the table; his legs were crossed, the chair pushed out to one side to make room for his large shoe to tap up and down in the air, a gap of skin and sock garter showing.

They finished the soup that had been served in huge, flat bowls and sat in a lull of silence. Mr Gardiner chewed at the edge of a fingernail, those long, narrow eyes quietly spying around the room. The door banged open and a girl he hadn't seen before appeared.

'You want the meat now, missis?'

'Oh yes, we're quite finished. And it's "Mrs Gardiner" not "missis", Consuelo. Please try and remember.'

Consuelo was dressed in an orange crepe dress that stretched over her rounded chest, a white apron tied round her waist.

Ralph could feel Mama not saying things as Consuelo leaned across him to gather up the plates. Consuelo's skin was the colour of an apricot. He found himself wondering if her arms might feel soft like a fruit if he were to press the downy skin. He caught a burst of warm odour, ripe and salty as she stretched over him to grab the empty breadbasket. The scent stayed in the air when she left the room.

'I really must mention washing to her,' Mama murmured.

Mama lifted the lid from the tureen. Mr Gardiner leaned forward towards the thick aroma of chorizo sausage with paprika and beans. Mama ladled it out onto soup plates.

Ralph was not hungry, but the familiar smell of spiced meat and roasted tomatoes seemed to sum up all that he had missed over the past few months, and he felt his throat tighten. He made himself eat, to make sure he did not begin to cry. There was a clatter of knives and forks, the occasional question from Mama, but tiredness had begun to creep up through Ralph's body.

After a dessert of figs and cheese Mr Gardiner got up.

'You're going out?' said Mama lightly.

'Sorry, sweetest. Very boring. Have to see someone at the club.'

'Well then, if you must.'

He made Ralph jump when he passed by and pressed a big flat hand on his shoulder, a gesture that was comforting, but weighted with the man's strength.

★ ★

Mama ran a bath for Ralph, and afterwards, while he was buttoning up his pyjamas, she came in and asked him if he would perhaps like to change his name to Ralph Gardiner now.

'It's your choice, darling one,' Mama said, her face red and moist from the steamy bathroom. His pyjamas felt too damp and clammy. She helped him button them up.

He was horrified by her suggestion: he was a Colchester, related to all the old-fashioned people in the photos in Flora and Cecily's house. His father was descended from one of the kings of England. He was of the same blood as his father.

He shook his head, his eyes wide.

She did not say anything more about it, but he could feel that it was one of those things – like not making a success of school and having to come home – where his mother would not force him, and she would take his side, but still . . . He could feel the disappointment in the humid bathroom, the sense that he had somehow failed.

'Well, at least you might like to stop calling him Mr Gardiner now. He thought perhaps you could call him Uncle Max.'

'If he'd like me to.'

'He would, darling. Very much.'

Ralph fell asleep in the high bed with its hard mattress and thick linen sheets. He dreamed tense, inescapable dreams, a volley of bangs going round and round his head, desk lids slamming down, a class of jeering boys clapping. He woke up gasping, and realised that the bangs and explosions were carrying on.

Someone was sitting on the bed, weighing it down on one side. He saw the bulky shape of Mr Gardiner, a shine of lamplight from the hallway on his smooth head.

'OK there, old thing? You were shouting a bit.'

'But that noise? What is it?'

'It's only fireworks. They show films at the bullring each night and the rockets are the manager's publicity stunt. It's a rum do but I'm afraid you'll have to get used to the din each night at eleven.'

'I'm sorry. Did I wake you up, Mr Gardiner?'

Mr Gardiner wasn't cross. He stayed and chatted to Ralph, told him funny stories about the films at the bullring until Ralph could feel his heart settling back to a normal thump again. He realised that he hadn't woken Mr Gardiner up, he'd only just got home; there was a smell of cigars and night air on his suit, a faint whiff of brandy on his breath. Ralph wondered where he had been.

Mr Gardiner stood up.

'You'll be all right now, old thing?'

'Thank you, Mr Gardiner. I mean, thank you, Uncle. Uncle Max.'

Mr Gardiner hesitated, seemed to be about to say something, then he closed the door.

★ ★

Mr Gardiner was quiet and elegantly polite, but he filled the new apartment with his stocky bulk, his sweet tobacco smoke, with his coats and trilby hats and boxes of shoes, with his rigid meal times and his headaches and the knowledge that the poor dear man had to give all his money to his first wife and her children. Ralph and Mama would need to live very frugally and eke out the small money left.

Mama had a smile all the time now. She was getting thinner and taking up less and less space, and her eyes were big black shadows full of patient worry. She wore plain, dark blue dresses with white collars and went to the church each morning for Mass and was always looking on the bright side. She hired private tutors from the ramshackle edges of the British expatriate community to come in and teach Ralph. Mr Gardiner had a piano winched in through the dining room window so that Ralph could continue his music lessons.

Mr Gardiner took a great interest in Ralph's education. He had lots of tips about the sort of things that a gentleman did or did not do, and about whom a gentleman might play with. Sadly, as a young gentleman, there were a lot of children that Ralph might not play with, such as the son of the concierge, or the boy who sold newspapers, or the cleaner's daughter.

On Saturdays Mr Gardiner led Ralph on long walks through Valencia, through wide cobbled plazas and stands of tall palm trees filled with birds, the strong sun dazzling his eyes. They walked past the cathedral and its bubbling decorations, past the modern apartment blocks and the grand bank building where Mr Gardiner worked, all the while Mr Gardiner imparting information about the buildings, or giving short lectures on the paintings in the museum as they walked through its cool rooms.

Sometimes he recounted stories from his own history, as if Ralph were the one chosen to know his secrets. Sitting in a café in the square while sparrows scavenged cake crumbs from the yellow earth, he told Ralph a long story about his mother, a Jewess who had escaped the Russian pogroms and the soldiers' brutal sticks. Ralph was horrified, his chest filled with indignation. He was thinking about how he would have rescued the old lady when Mr Gardiner dropped some coins on top of the bill and stood up. Ralph jumped as the man took Ralph's shoulder in a hard clinch and stooped down.

'Thing is, family stories, d'you see? Not the sort of thing we tell every one. Just between us chaps.'

Mr Gardiner put his solid forefinger over his closed lips. The skin at the edges of his nails was raw looking. A manicurist came to the flat once a week to buff and file his nails back into shape; but the following week all her neatening was always undone, the nails uneven and nibbled.

★ ★

Following a letter from England Mama was suddenly taut and busy and anxious, getting everything ready for a visit from Mr Gardiner's son.

'You mean the boy in the photo?' said Ralph. 'The photo on Mr Gardiner's desk in the old house.'

'Why yes,' she said. 'What a funny thing to remember, that old photo. Of course, he's older now, quite the young man. So you see, we must do our utmost to put our best foot forward, because, well . . .'

'Because he's Mr Gardiner's son,' finished Ralph.

Being eighteen, Tom was now old enough to take it upon himself to come out and visit. So in the space of a week Mr Gardiner had hurriedly organised Tom's tickets and travel arrangements with great satisfaction, excitement even.

'Of course, his mother will quiz him on every little detail here when he returns home,' said Mama, straightening the chenille drapes round the dining room window as Ralph worked through a page of sums at the table.

By the end of the week Mama had taken to weeping hopelessly over the menus and the maid's inability to dust, and by the time Mr Gardiner left to fetch Tom from the station, Mama had taken to her bed with a nervous headache.

She was still indisposed when Mr Gardiner arrived back from the train. He left Tom in the hallway with Ralph and hurried straight in to see her. Ralph could hear his voice, the high, worried replies from Mama.

Mr Gardiner's boy walked along the dark hallway, peering at the pictures on the walls. He had slicked-down black hair and wide baggy trousers. He took out a cigarette, turned it round and tapped it, then put it away. He gave Ralph a wink. Ralph winked back.

Mr Gardiner came out. Shutting Mama's bedroom door he was a man released, lightened of burdens. He embraced Tom in yet another big hug and Ralph followed them through to the sitting room. The balcony windows had been left open onto the tops of the trees along the avenue and the heady evening song of the birds filled the room. Even when he went over to the drinks table to pour Tom a glass of amontillado, Mr Gardiner's eyes went back to his son, as if making an inventory of all the things that made him proud. He squirted some soda into a glass for Ralph and handed it to him with an absent-minded pat on the head.

Mama had organised a special meal for Tom's arrival, but since the headache had toppled her plans as a hostess Mr Gardiner would lead the men out to eat. Ralph went in to say goodbye to Mama and she asked him to fetch her cologne stick from the dressing table. He rubbed the waxy, blue column over her forehead – almost as waxy as the yellowy bones prominent beneath the tight skin – releasing the fresh sting of perfumed alcohol.

'Thank you, dear. It's so silly of me to be so weak-minded. I shall think good, positive things, and say a few prayers to clear my mind. Then I am sure I will be quite better again,' she whispered.

He left her, feeling guilty, glad to be going out with the men.

They went to a small restaurant that was almost a bar. Tom leaned back in his chair. He gave Ralph the feeling that he found something amusing about him, in a friendly way. He showed Ralph how to flick his lighter into a tiny flame and how to light a cigarette for him.

'Sorry, old chap, I should have offered you one,' Tom said, holding out the packet, man to man. Ralph shook his head hard, thinking of the trouble Tom would be in if Mama were to find out.

Mr Gardiner ordered a table full of dishes, fishy rings of calamari and all the strange and misshapen fried things that Mama hated, the dark sausage dishes bleeding the fragrant oil that she disliked. The waiter seemed to know Mr Gardiner well, and they talked in mutters about recent disturbances near the cathedral.

Mr Gardiner tucked a white napkin in his collar and gave a thump on the table. 'Eat up, boys.' He pushed slices of tortilla omelette and grilled sardines onto Tom's plate – and onto Ralph's.

'So, how's your mother?' he said to Tom.

Tom nodded. 'Well.'

There was a small silence. Ralph had also put a large napkin round his neck and was dipping fried potatoes into garlic mayonnaise. His eyes went from Tom to Mr Gardiner.

Then Tom broke into a string of funny tales about his sisters and him, and Mr Gardiner leaned forward and took them all in, exhaling huge belly laughs. Ralph listened and thought how it might feel, to be there, in the English garden with Tom, playing cricket and rescuing the dog from the water and annoying the old lady next door.

The night was mild. Music was playing over towards the bullring. They walked down the broad avenue past the tall buildings with their flaking plaster and ornate balconies. A sudden volley of harsh cracks exploded above the rooftops, opening out in red and silver flowers. Fireworks from the film show over in the bullring.

'How about going to the flicks?' said Mr Gardiner, happy to prolong the evening.

In front of the entrance to the bullring, a lady in a sparkly evening dress and exaggerated make-up was shouting invitations to come in and see the film. She blew a kiss at Mr Gardiner.

Mr Gardiner brought them each a cone of hot, fried *churros* from a street seller. Shedding white icing dust on their chins, they went in through the grand entrance. Ralph thought how anyone watching them would see a boy with his father and his older brother; he felt a wave of borrowed pride, and an odd sort of homesickness, half wishing it might be true.

The sandy bullring was strung round with a line of electric light bulbs. A large white sheet was pegged up on a wire, faint creases rippling the picture. Loudspeakers were blaring triumphant bull-fighting tunes full of horns and accordions. Above the screen hung a round moon as close and as bright as a lamp.

They sat squashed up in the wooden folding chairs, Ralph bellowing with laughter at the Marx brothers. After a while Ralph realised that Mr Gardiner had gone from his end seat. He looked round and saw that familiar shape standing in the dark shadows at the back. He was talking with a man, his head bent as if listening hard.

Later, while the audience was laughing loudly, Ralph jumped, realising that Mr Gardiner was next to him, speaking into his ear.

'Ferdie, old chap. You can show Tom the way back to the flat when this is over?'

When Ralph next looked round Mr Gardiner was gone.

★ ★

It was up to Ralph to keep Tom company in the afternoons, when everyone else was busy; something he looked forward to each day. They stayed in the apartment and Consuelo joined them at the dining table to play cards and smoke cigarettes. Or they walked through Valencia, and Tom explained how school wouldn't be so bad next time. 'Just a question of knowing a thing or two about people. You just need to take your time, watch how the other fellows work. They have their reasons and their logic for doing stuff, d'you see? And once you understand that you can step round them.'

Ralph nodded, but he was sure he wouldn't ever have to go back to a school like that awful place in the wet English countryside with the boys and their constant small wars. He would stay in Valencia with Mama, with Consuelo's generous stews scented with *pimentón*, and always the bulky but elusive presence of Mr Gardiner.

The night after Tom left Ralph got out the small cigar box with the two letters that his real father had sent from Chile, and his father's gold watch from Flora and Cecily. He put the watch against his ear. The secret clicks and grinds of the mechanism lit up inside his head, keeping their old vigil. He thought of Mr Gardiner's shining happiness when he first hugged Tom at the station, and he wondered what it would be like to have your own father there, not to always have to feel like a guest on best behaviour – that sense of having to earn one's welcome.

He put the letter and the other things away in the box. They slid together with a rattling, empty sound. Just two letters; his own father had sent him just two letters in the years of silence before he died. He switched off his light, but in the dark he felt his cheeks burning; a hot shame through his skin, informing him that he was somehow unworthy: his own father had gone away, only ever sent two letters.

★ ★

By the Easter of 1936, just after Ralph turned thirteen, Valencia was already so hot and dry that Mama's geraniums in the window boxes were wilting and in danger of dying. From first thing in the morning the windows were left open to the tops of the lime trees, where hundreds of starlings and sparrows shrieked from first light till dusk with a sharp, tumultuous noise. People went about their business in the dusty streets, the farmers herding a few goats across the square, the old ladies standing in groups and gossiping about the latest news of fighting in the north, worried women hurrying past with baskets, armed soldiers strolling in twos or threes, ready to uphold the young republican government.

In the dining room of the apartment Ralph was sitting at the oak table, his maths books spread out, waiting for the tutor to arrive. As one hand rested on his exercise book he was surprised to feel a vibration in the table that seemed to grow, rising up through the building, travelling in through the open windows, resolving into a gritty, rumbling sound until the whole room shook. He went out onto the balcony. Below, people were appearing on the earth-baked avenue, shielding their eyes, holding cloths or caps or whatever they had run out with. From between the flanks of trees he saw a huge, industrial-looking tank with a long gun barrel rumbling down the street.

Consuelo appeared on the balcony behind him, squashing him against the railing with her soft weight. She leaned out and punched the air. He could feel her waving and screaming at the soldiers.

'*Viva la República!*' she yelled. The soldiers in their pinched caps and blanket rolls for sashes looked up and waved back. Ralph gave a wave too. 'Come on, shout,' she said. 'Shout no to Franco. When Franco comes he do this.' She motioned someone slitting a throat.

'Please Consuelo!' Mama was signalling for the girl to go back inside. In the wealthy, expatriate part where they lived most people were watching the tank go by in silence, remembering the nuns and priests burned in the monastery.

'But it is the new government in Valencia now,' she said. 'Now we are all republicans. You, me, him, all the same.'

'Please,' implored Mama. 'The lunch?' Consuelo stood on the balcony, looking as though she did not think that she was the one who should go back in the kitchen and peel vegetables for soup. She left behind her odour of soured citron and something that Ralph was beginning to recognise as *Consuelo's smell*: a smell that grew almost unbearably strong and sweet at the end of a hot day.

The tutor didn't come. He sent a message to say he was returning to England. Ralph copied out sums from his primer and filled in the answers. Mama held them out in front of her as if by gazing at them she might uncover some truth. She handed them back with a 'splendid, dear', but no ticks or crosses.

The next night the explosions and bangs from the bullring began early. But this time they did not stop; they thundered on mechanically and relentlessly for hours. The noise multiplied, churned itself out, stuttering on and on violently and spitefully. It echoed through the stone streets, assaulted the houses and vibrated the windows. No one could explain what was happening. There was no question of getting any sleep. Max stuffed Ralph's window with a quilt. He brought the gramophone through and played the loudest music they had, took out a pack of cards and made Ralph concentrate on a game of Racing Demon.

Finally, as the darkness faded into the grey shapes of morning, the gunfire fell silent. They took down the quilt and the first birdsong began to seep in through the shutters. Mr Gardiner pulled on his coat and went down to the bar a few houses away.

He came back white and shaken, and forbade them to leave the house. The soldiers from the barracks and anyone suspected of sympathising with the advancing troops of Franco had been machine gunned to death in the sandy arena of the Valencia bullring. Three thousand people.

Everyone with a British passport was given safe passage to the coast, but Mr Gardiner was staying at the bank. He said the argument was between the Spanish peoples; they would not harm the British. Mama wept and clung to Ralph, but they were only taking children on the first boat out. He was to be met off the boat train by Aunt Flora, and Mama would follow on as soon as she could find a place on another.

But in the days after Ralph's boat sailed the Spanish borders were closed. The civil war that was to tear Spain apart had begun and it would be a long, long time before he would see Mama again.

CHAPTER 5

Fourwinds, 1981

On the other side of the bed Alice had stilled, ambushed by sleep, but Ralph remained wide awake. The ring that Sarah had dropped on the desk a few hours ago had been left on the bedside table. He lay and looked at the pale stones glimmering in the darkness, the strange way they had of gathering and reflecting any small source of light, even at night. He sighed. In a few more hours he'd have to get up and collect Nicky from the train, break the news to him. He'd be alone, his brothers not due back till the supposed day of the wedding.

His eyes dry with fatigue, deeply tired but sleepless, Ralph got up and belted his dressing gown. He made his way softly down the wide staircase to make a hot cocoa.

There was a light on in the sitting room. Pushing the door open a little way he saw that Sarah's father was still up, seated at the desk in a circle of lamplight, writing with concentration. The room around him was shaded away, the aunts indistinct figures in their portraits. No one had drawn the curtains against the summer night, the glass black and polished, reflecting Ralph's form as he stood framed in the doorway.

Peter looked up, startled. 'Oh Ralph. Did I wake you? I'm so sorry.' He showed a couple of fingers of whisky that he had poured out into a crystal tumbler. 'I hoped you wouldn't mind.'

'Think I'll join you with that whisky.' He picked up a second glass from the tray on the chest, glancing over at the paper where Peter had been writing, but didn't like to ask questions. 'Sarah's sleeping?'

'The doctor left a sedative. He thinks there's a chance her voice might come back in the morning. When she's had chance to calm down.'

Ralph sat down in the armchair by the desk and Peter laid down his pen. 'Did you manage to get through to Nicky?'

'No. But I'll pick him up at the station in a few hours, so . . .'

'Ralph, I just wanted you to know that if it should come to pass, if things don't go ahead, I want to cover all the costs.'

Ralph held up his hand, made a hushing noise. 'Bride's nerves. I'm sure she'll be fine in a couple of days. A good rest and then she'll be on top form again for the big day.'

'I hope so. But I have to tell you, the last time she couldn't talk it took a while to fade. Weeks.' He sighed and leaned back in his chair. 'I can't say I understand what's happened. She's been so very happy, so looking forward to the future.'

'Nicky's the same. Never seen a chap more head over heels. You get a feeling, don't you, when people are right for each other? Look, why don't we see what the morning brings? I'm sure when she sees him tomorrow things will sort themselves out.'

Peter got up from the desk and sat in the armchair on the other side of the cold fireplace. The iron basket was piled with pine cones, dusty and brittle.

'What must it be now?' Ralph said. 'Nearly forty years since I first clapped eyes on you?'

'In the garden. They were having tea in the garden and you were there with her brothers. The very first day I arrived. They had wonderful gardens, the Hanburys.'

'You know, Alice was pleased to see you again, Peter. We both were. It was just, after so much time . . . She feels badly about how things ended. She didn't want you to think . . .'

'A different world. It was a long time ago. I was always grateful to the Hanburys.'

Ralph studied the man on the other side of the fireplace. Some seven years younger than himself but already grey-haired, there was an almost professional gravitas about Peter, a man who might absorb a confession into his stillness and give some kind of absolution. For a moment he thought, But yes, I could speak to Peter; Peter, who had known Alice when she was still a girl. Ask his advice.

Ralph rubbed his lips. They felt numb.

Through the window the marquee was just discernible in the fading darkness, slowly billowing with the wind, the flank of a creature breathing in its sleep.

He shifted in his seat, aware of his body feeling heavy and stiff, a man in his late fifties who didn't roll with the punches so well any more.

'Suppose I'd better try and get a bit of sleep. I'm sure it's all going to work out, once he's back.' Ralph padded away in his leather slippers.

Peter clicked off the desk lamp and picked up the paper where he had sketched out a branching family tree. Faces that he hadn't seen for decades swam up towards him in the half-light.

And Sarah, what did she know about them? He'd told her so little. When the wedding had been announced he'd had an impulse to track them down, try and invite them, but in reality it was simply too late to do such a thing.

But now, with Sarah stalled and silent, sleeping fitfully upstairs, it seemed clear to him that it wasn't going to do. You couldn't expect to send a child out into life as an adult not really knowing where they came from. That was the truth of it. When Patricia was awake perhaps he would ask her what they should say. How odd, really, that they rarely spoke of the years before they met, the people they had lost – something they had agreed upon without ever stating it openly.

The first notes of birdsong outside, fluid and clear as water. There was no situation that God couldn't redeem, that's what he believed; no situation that He couldn't turn to good in the end. Peter picked up the piece of paper, made his way upstairs.

Later, as he lay almost asleep at the start of that summer dawn, thinking of Sarah, thinking of the day ahead, Peter thought he heard a door open and close again, somewhere downstairs. He listened out for a moment, but hearing nothing more decided he'd been dreaming, closer to sleep than he realised.

And when sleep came in he dreamed of a child in a ripped mac, following his brother through the streets of Manchester.

CHAPTER 6

Manchester, 1935

'Not you two again,' said Elsie.

There was a boy on her doorstep. He wore droopy shorts cut down from old trousers, a shrunken woolly with his long eleven-year-old wrists gangling out. Next to him was a smaller boy in a very grubby raincoat with a big rip down the front. They were right there on the threshold as soon as she opened the door, smiling like she might be pleased to see them.

'Don't you two have anywhere else to go?'

'We like coming to see you, Aunty,' said the youngest one.

They had shorn hair like little convicts and bare, expectant faces, ready to sit on Elsie's new sofa and be offered a plate of malt loaf slices. They were always hungry.

'Come in off the step then, our Peter. Hurry yourself, Bill,' she said, half pushing them in. She went out, taking off her pinny, and gave a swift look up and down the street.

'We got lost finding it,' said the little one, 'but I asked, I did, at the lady's house down the road.'

'Is that your car, Aunty Elsie?' the big one said, sanding the bottom of his shoes on her doormat, trudging off the street dirt. There was a new Austin Seven in front of the house. But Elsie wasn't listening.

'You knocked on the neighbour's door! You don't just go

knocking on doors around here. What did you say? Did you tell them I was your aunt?'

'I told her your new address: 63 Margaret Road, Manchester.' Proud, because he'd remembered.

'God save us,' she said. 'You're not to do that again. Did you hear me? I said, did you hear me?' She was shouting now. Both the boys nodded urgently, eyes wide at this new sin.

She deflated and sighed.

'Not in the front room, go through to the back.'

Sitting by the fire and fortressed inside a square, brown armchair, Uncle Vernon was listening to the football on the wireless. He smiled at the boys and winked. Peter sat down directly opposite him and stared at him as if something might happen. The fire in the grate gave a crackle and the child jumped. Bill jiggled one leg, making his head nod slightly.

The radio commentary washed to and fro across the room in waves of excitement that seemed hardly contained by the wireless box, and every so often Uncle Vernon would take out his pipe, look at the boys and nod his head towards the box, and the boys would nod back.

Elsie came back in after a while and banged a plate of malt bread on the side table. She pointed to it. She switched the wireless dial to the muted sound of music.

'Eat up then. How's your mother's health these days?'

'She's been out in the sanatorium, for her breathing.'

'Oh aye. So who's been looking after you lot?'

'Our Kitty. She's been doing the cooking.'

'Kitty's got a job in the big shop,' the little one said. 'And she's got,' he swallowed and took a breath, 'a costume from the catalogue, but we're not allowed to touch it.'

Well, at least that's a pay packet coming in for their mam at last, since that father of theirs 'as never 'ad a job in 'is life.' She was saying this to Uncle Vernon now, as if they couldn't hear her.

'He's 'ad lots of jobs, Aunty.'

'Maybe I'll go and see your mam out in the country. Though I don't know, I've got a weak chest myself.'

The boys munched and stared. If anything Elsie seemed to have a strong and substantial chest under her floral pinny, like the breast of a big grey pigeon.

'I'll never know what got into your mam's head, the day she came home and told your grandfather she was marrying. You'd better eat that up now. It's a long walk back. I'll never forget his face. He were standing in front of the clock on the mantelpiece – that clock kept time beautifully – and his face was white as a sheet. You can't stop her when she gets an idea. And she'd 'ad an education, you see. Your grandfather said all along she couldn't go to the grammar school, because it were a lot of money for the uniform, but it were our mother said we had to save up the money because Evelyn must go. And that's how she repaid them. Well, that's marrying the Irish, you see, drink away their money. He went white, your grandfather, because he could see it, and she couldn't. She was marrying a man half blind, from the gas in the war. I remember, he said, "Mother, it's our Evelyn that's blind."'

She shook her head and they sat and listened to the fire crackling and the radio mumbling songs in a small polite voice. The plate of malt bread was empty.

'Well, Kitty'll be making your tea, and it's a long way back.'

''Ave you made some nice umbrellas, Uncle?' said the oldest one.

'Ooh, your uncle's been promoted in the works. He's high up in the umbrella business now is your uncle.'

The boys stared at him.

Vernon tapped the side of his nose. He lifted up his left flank and fished about in his pocket. He brought out a handful of coppers and began to sort through them with a pointed finger. Then he held out two clenched fists towards them.

They had to guess which hand. He handed them a threepenny bit apiece.

'You shouldn't encourage them,' said Elsie.

'I'll never know what she was thinking,' Aunt Elsie told them as she led the boys back down the hallway. 'And mind yourselves now.' She shut the front door with a bang.

The youngest boy jumped down the steps one at a time and shoved his hands into his mac pockets. One pocket lifted right up on account of the tear. He ran to catch up with his brother, who was walking stiff and thin down the road.

'But I liked Aunty Elsie's old house. I thought it were nice. Didn't you, Bill?'

'Her old house were council. It weren't posh enough. That's what our dad says. And she don't want us to come round any more. Didn't you hear?'

Frowning at the way the world kept shifting around, Peter thought about this as he hopped over the lines between the pavement flagstones. Suddenly he wondered if his aunty had seen the rip in his mac, and he felt hot and burning, even though a fine evening rain was making his face filmy with wet. He knew she'd seen it.

'Let's go back across the links,' Bill said, brightening, squaring up to the walk back. The links were always an adventure.

Out towards the end of the new housing, they came to rough open land, scraggy fields of grass like fraying string, colourless and papery from the autumn rains. An old nag was tethered in the mist, stretching out its neck to tear at the grass. Before long Peter could feel the marshy wet seeping in through the joins of his canvas pumps. Bill had boots, passed down from their older brother, John. They had long noses at the front, and they folded across halfway in a deep crease, but they were proper boots.

They ran down to where the land grew wetter and stopped on the wooden planks. A stream appeared in puddles among black mud swamps. This was where you could find sticklebacks in summer. They poked around with a piece of wood in case any were still awake. Suddenly a shudder went through the plank under Peter's feet and he saw Bill throw his arms up and half fall, half slide into the mud with a slopping sound. The plank twanged like a giant ruler. Bill was trying to stagger back towards him, his legs sinking further in, Peter shouting instructions. Bill struggled, twisted and threw himself on the planks and his legs came out, one, two.

'Where's your boot?' said Peter.

They poked around in the deep mud with sticks till it was almost too dark to see.

'It's gone,' Peter said in awe.

'Me dad'll kill us.'

Bill stabbed at the mud some more, and then stood up and wiped at his eyes. They started walking back across the curdled grassland. All the way back, through the streets of Manchester, with the tall buildings lit up and the crowds of people in coats getting off trams, hurrying home. Bill's long muddy sock flapped its tongue along the pavement, the proud hobble thump of his one remaining boot. At least the darkness covered them.

Coming up to the front of their terrace they tried to work out from the look of the house if Dad might be back. Peter had a sick feeling.

Kitty had a soup on the stove, a salty, wet ham-bone smell. Mushy lentils.

'Look at the state of you two. Don't you go near Doris's communion dress; it's all ironed for tomorrow. Out the back and wash that off under the tap.'

They crossed the kitchen in black socks.

'And where the bloody hell's your boot?' she yelled from the hall.

When they sat down to a plate of soup Peter was hungry, but the sick feeling in his stomach made it taste too salty.

'Don't we 'ave no pineapple chunks?' said Peter, suddenly wishing there could be pineapple chunks from a tin, and custard.

'Listen to 'im! Of course we don't.' Then she softened: 'Maybe we can get some soon, eh?'

Kitty took the candle up and helped them search the walls for bed bugs. When she found one she held the flame close and burned the small black dot with a tiny spurt of the flame. In the morning they would find red marks on their legs and arms, left by the ones they could not see.

'What if Bill can't go?' Peter whispered to her in the dark. 'The teachers won't let him go to town hall wi' only one boot.'

'What was you doing anyway, miles out there on the links?'

'We went to see Aunty,' said Peter.

Kitty paused in the doorway as if she might say something, and then she went downstairs.

There was no question of sleeping. They listened out for the sound of Dad coming in, even though it might take half the night. Tomorrow was the school outing and without shoes Bill would not be allowed to go. They'd asked Kitty, they'd racked their brains, but the truth was that they could not make a shoe materialise. Peter lay awake and looked at Bill's one lonely boot sitting mute and resolutely single at the foot of the bed. He could hear the rumble of a brewery cart going past and horses' hooves; boots walking by, shouts and talking; the sound of a car. And worst of all, at the back of their minds, they knew it was a bad idea to tell Dad when he came in, much better to get him in a good mood tomorrow, when maybe they could have a plan. But there was nothing else to be done. Maybe they would tell him and Dad would come up with something.

He thought of Dad's leather belt singing through the air and his stomach clenched.

★ ★

Peter woke up spitting fur. Some of the coats that ma had put on the bed still had fur collars, and sometimes the fur got into his mouth, clumped wet and spitty. He saw that Bill was still sitting up tense beside him in bed. Waiting. The candle had burned down. There was the sound of Dad coming in, banging the door shut, stamping off the rain. Humming as he came down the passageway.

Peter and Bill slid out of bed and went and stood together at the top of the stairs. Peter kept shuddering with the cold. Bill had his hands clasped together like a prayer.

Dad started singing a verse from a ballad about roses and hearts, his cap still on, his arms held up to them. Bill couldn't bear it any longer.

'Dad, Dad, I've lost me boot.'

'Where is it then?'

'It's gone in the mud.'

'Yer what?' he said, the song all disappeared. 'Come here, you. What have yer done with yer boot? D'you think I'm made of money me?'

There was a swift movement and Bill was pinned against the wall. The smell of beer and smoke reached where Peter was standing. He turned and ran.

There were some little whimpering noises and the swishing sound of the leather belt; thuds against the thin wall. After a while Bill came back up and lay down in the bed, pulled up the coats over him. He was shaking. Downstairs it was still going on, thumps and the crash of the doors opened and shut; Dad in a black mood now. He heard Kitty and Doris running up and shutting their door.

— 55 —

CHAPTER 7

Manchester, 1935

The teacher lined the children up to see if they all had clean hands. She had a comb and passed down the line, running it through the children's hair. She looked down at Bill and Peter.

'When I picked you boys for this privilege I thought you would at least try and live up to it. But I see you have no feeling at all for the honour of going to hear Handel's *Messiah* by the Halle orchestra at the town hall. Look at the state of you. Well, I can let it pass with Peter, but Bill you have to go home. Those boots must be four sizes too big.'

'They're me dad's boots, miss.'

'Well, you can't go staggering around the town hall like that. I don't care if your sister is singing, you're not shaming me like that, my lad.'

Peter turned out of the line to follow him.

'I didn't tell you to go, Peter,' she shouted.

★ ★

The town hall had the smell of wet coats and the baked-on paint on iron radiators and was chock full of the backs of people. They found their seats at the top of the top tier with all the other school children, and Peter tried to spot Doris in her white communion dress down in the neat rows of school choirs. He saw her and waved, but the teacher told him off.

Nothing had prepared him for the next couple of hours. Mournful and serious, the singers stood up one by one to announce their plaints. Suddenly there was a rushing sound across the hall as the whole choir stood up in one swoop, and sang straight at him in a huge cloud of sound. He hadn't known. He hadn't known that you could hear something like this. And it went on, and on, not stopping to let him breathe, the music like troops and troops of angels and soldiers all mixed together. A huge pressure inside his chest made him want to cry or stand up and shout.

They came out onto the town-hall steps, back into the Manchester night; people in coats and hats streaming away, brushing past them. The teacher said they could walk home themselves. It had snowed, and the rime of frozen snow lay fresh over the streets and rooftops, the air cold and clear and breathtaking, his toes and fingers stinging. He stared around. Everything was different. Everything had changed.

★ ★

Dad said he would get some boots. He took Bill and Peter with him, but they didn't head for the shops, or even for the market stalls of second-hand clothes. They went to the football ground. They had to wait in a long queue that went round the side of the walls then filed in through the gates, men and boys in scarves and turned-up collars against the cold. Like the long queues in the big building where Dad went to get his dole. A constant chorus of coughing tuning up and down. The man in front of them spat. Inside, the stands were empty, the pitch brownish and muddy. There were big wooden crates filled with pairs of black boots. If your dad was on the dole they were free, from the football club. Charity shoes; shoes worn by someone else first.

His dad queued as if they were going to some important match. When their turn came he sat down in the stands to try the boots on

Bill's feet, examining them as best he could for the workmanship, for the quality of the leather. Their dad was a man who approved of things being done right: it was his particular misfortune that in spite of his appreciation for the finer things in life, he should have nothing.

Dad told them to get on home and they left him standing at the corner of Hulme Road with the other men who stood all day in the street. His collar turned up, his chin down in his muffler, Dad looked like he was waiting for someone.

★ ★

When Peter banged in through the back door he saw Ma sitting there at the kitchen table as if she'd never left. She'd still got her coat on. She'd been too puffed to take it off, she told Peter as he helped her pull it off and went and hung it up in the passageway. When he came back she was unpinning her hat. Her hair was flat underneath. Her arms were wrong, thin, all angles and bones.

'Have you been good, Peter?' she said, smiling at him. He nodded.

'Here you are then,' and she held up a silver sixpence in her fingers. 'If you run, you and Bill can still get in the queue at the back of the bakery.'

They ran through the market stalls to where a line of people waited at the bakery's back door to buy a bag of broken cakes. Standing behind the counter hatch a woman in a white mob cap was filling each bag. Peter stopped breathing while she filled his with a shovelful of misshapen baking, everything covered in a crumbled, golden dust so there was always a taste from all the other cakes, no matter what you had. They saw bits of slab cake and parkin gingerbread and the bread and butter pudding and Eccles cakes all going in together. The bag felt heavy, but they hadn't got to open it till they were home. They marched back, stamping their boots and singing one of Dad's rude army songs. 'The copper took out 'is rusty whistle, *parlez-vous*. Blew a fart from here to Bristol, *parlez-vous*.' Left the song outside the door.

Ma wiped the oilcloth on the table while Kitty and Doris made a pot of tea. They put the best looking of the broken cakes on the cake stand, and Ma told them funny stories about the hospital.

She said maybe she'd shut her eyes, just for a moment, have a sit down in the old armchair by the hearth. Doris patted straight the big cushion that covered the spring that had come through. The moment she was sitting there Ma fell asleep.

Peter stayed at the table, turning the floppy, soft pages of his and Bill's old comic, watching over her. No sounds but for those of the Saturday market clearing up in the square outside, the only light coming from the lamp in the middle of the table. She woke up with a start.

'Is he here yet?' she said. Peter shook his head. She went out the back, looked up and down the alleyway. There were steps running down, but it wasn't him.

She came inside, white and wheezing. Kitty made her sit back down in the chair, unlaced her shoes and put her feet on a stool in front of the small fire.

'He's a disgrace, me dad,' said Kitty. 'He'll be down at the Dog still. How many times have we had to flit because he's drank the rent? I'm that sick of my dad.'

Ma gave a shake to her feet. She held on to the arms of the old chair and leant forward. 'I won't hear you speak like that about your own father, Kitty. He does the best he can. A good man in hard times.'

Kitty simmered her anger inside; had her own opinions.

'I met your dad in a hospital, you know. A bit like the one I've been biding in just now.'

Peter wanted a story. He wanted a story of how she had met Dad, back when Dad was a soldier in the war. So she told him again how he'd worked with the planes till the gas had got him. How she'd been nursing him and they'd fallen in love – although at first she'd been that cross with him when she'd caught him sneaking out at night to the kitchens for a bacon sandwich. She'd caught him and his mates coming back down the corridor, a line of three men hobbling back together with their crutches and slings and bandages, sharing out their good arms and legs and eyes between them. She made Peter laugh and he was satisfied. It was a good story.

★ ★

After they'd gone to bed she watched the flame through the bars of the iron range in the hearth, and she thought of that sweet time, unexpected and tender. The children couldn't really see what she'd seen back then, how their father had set out to be a fine man. But the gas had changed him.

It took them both a long time to understand how much.

The last thing Jim had ever seen clearly was the burst of a shell and a sludge of brown liquid spreading out over the snow – the gas attack on Nancy airbase. He told her it looked like sherry, pools of thick Christmas sherry across the snow. A fog was rising up from the sludge, sickly yellow in the flares. And he was already breathing the gas in, coughing, his eyes burning, scrambling for his mask, his fingers numb and thick; but he couldn't get the strap over his head, the balaclava bunched up and in the way. He'd tried to run to clean air, to cool his lungs down. But he blundered on through the thick fog. Burning his breath. Burning his lungs. The siren sounding too late.

You couldn't tell how bad you'd got it. Not at first. You just had to lie in your bunk and wait to see how bad it would get. When his blisters had dried, when he could get back into clothes again, they packed him in a troop train with hundreds of others like him to go home. Rusty iron in his mouth each time he spat into a cloth. The bandages still over his eyes.

She was there on the ward in the Manchester hospital, the assisting nurse, when the doctor had the bandages taken off. Jim told them the room was all misty, shapes that wouldn't come properly into focus. The doctor said the gas had carried on eating into the surface of his eyes, but given the circumstances he could see fairly well.

Then he showed Jim the grey night-map of his lung X-ray. 'These areas here, they're the permanent damage. I would say you've got half capacity.'

'You mean the rest won't come back then?'

'I'm sorry. You will need to look for less physical employment in future.'

'Maybe I'll get meself a job in a bank,' he said.

But he was still sure he was going to get better. Spring was coming out in swathes of blurred purple and yellow in the hospital gardens. There were nurses to tease and flirt with, and the nurses were game and said, 'Oh Jim, you are a right one.' And how Alf was going to have all the ladies running after him once he got out — as if it never crossed their minds that Jim was half blind, or that Alf had his leg missing. It was a form of kindness really, not taken seriously.

But Jim was different around her, serious, noticing everything she did. She wasn't young, not like a lot of the nurses, and she didn't know how to flirt with a man. When she took his temperature he stared right into her eyes and held her wrist, said, 'How's my gorgeous girl?' She'd try to be haughty then and boss him about, but he'd got her. He saw how she was hopeful in spite of herself, half ashamed of the feelings he stirred up in her.

It was as if he knew her life. Given up on marriage, a sweetheart lost early in the war, the one slice of toast in front of the small gas fire in her small nurse's room, washing with the jug and pitcher in the cold, hurrying under the sheets and knowing tomorrow would be as it was ordained. The visits home in a best coat to be bullied by her father, the small pot of rouge bought to keep her pretty. For what: the withdrawing into hard work and self-sufficiency?

He said she smelled good, of soap and ironing and books. For the first time in years she was aware of all that she was holding back; the way her arm jumped if he touched it when she smoothed his sheets; the feel of his hand suddenly grasping hers, thanking her, his palm warm and calloused.

It was an imposing institutional building, miles of corridors, entrances and stairwells that were forgotten, deserted at different parts of the day. There were acres of dishevelled parkland where gentry had once taken their evening stroll. A damp, heady spring turning into summer. They worked out ways to meet and she thought, I'm courting. She was giddy with the tender pressure of being wanted so much.

One night she sat alone on her nurse's bed in her rayon slip, her hand over her mouth, trying not to wake the girl sleeping in the other bed. She'd missed three times. Three times. She was rocking in agitation, and she held her arms round her narrow stomach and let it come to her gladly, this knowledge, this deep root, this baby, already growing inside her. Nothing would part her from this. She looked around the room. How simple and elemental and wonderful this tiny room and her whole life had suddenly become.

They said another couple of weeks and he could leave. She had to tell him. She knew he would finish with her. She would start to show soon, and then she would have to leave too. In disgrace.

Early one morning she came in to a great commotion going on in the ward. The war was over. The patients were dancing around, Alf hopping and waving one crutch, grabbing the nurses, and even Matron let herself be kissed. Jim grabbed Evelyn and said, 'Marry me then.'

He got hold of a brass ring, with a red glass stone; the sort of ring that left a greenish mark on your skin. He said he would do better for her later. When she told him about the baby he was as excited as if the war had ended all over again.

He was twenty-two when they got married. He was war wounded, but had a fire inside him, determined that he could wrest a living for them. But his lungs were eaten away; sometimes she'd find him gasping and panicked, the small amounts of air claustrophobic in his lungs. His eyes stayed blurred over with cataracts from the gas. Each evening he'd ask her to read the paper aloud to him, because she had such a nice voice.

He took what he could in the way of work, but mostly he went back and stood in line in the dole queue. He brought home a pittance to keep them alive – just. They did what they could to manage. And then the babies came, Kitty and John, Doris and Bill, and last of all, Peter.

They did what they could to manage, and he was still sure then that by his will and his bare hands he could make a life for them, refused to take into account any diminishment caused by the war.

You had to wait to see how bad the damage got while the gas was still burning into the flesh, and you had to wait to see how far the bitterness would burn down into a man's soul.

She got out of the chair to stoke up the coals with the poker and sank back down. Eleven o'clock. She may as well snooze here a little longer in case he was back – unless a lock-in started and he stayed on. He would come home sooner or later, flushed and drunk from holding court in the Irish pubs, half the dole money gone again. A small man in a big suit, bought off a dead man's widow. Always looking for the man who fitted that suit.

Tomorrow she would take the clock from the front room, and roll up the bedding. Most weeks Peter and Bill would carry it to the shop with the three metal balls above a window filled with boxes of rings and piles of old shoes. On Friday, when Kitty's money came in, the clock would be back on the shelf, the cover spread on her bed again.

They ate tripe and vinegar; bruised fruit sold cheap at the market, cracked eggs from Seymour's the grocer's. She'd had a grammar school education. She was a clever girl. They didn't go hungry. Sometimes their dad came home with unlikely things from the pub; rabbit meat that came from no one knew where; once, three gorgeous pheasants that needed plucking of all their gold feathers.

★ ★

With the warm weather Ma improved and her wheezing quietened down. The summer when Peter finished at St Alphonse's school was long and hot and glorious. He'd passed the exam for the grammar, and even the sister who kept a slipper in her pocket to beat them had come out and shook his hand. 'I hope your father is going to put the money by for your uniform, Peter,' she told him sternly.

The old lady teacher with a grey bun and long skirt came out from the infants and smothered him into a hug. 'And look at you now, Peter. What are you going to be when you grow up?'

'A priest,' he said.

He didn't know why he'd said it. He didn't like Father David who came to school to do catechism, and slapped their hands if they didn't know the long second commandment. But he liked his Sunday role as serving boy, saying the magic Latin prayers with the nice old priest who was frail as paper. Everyone watched to see if the old man would make it up the ladder to fetch down the golden monstrance with its sunburst of gold rays and the body of Our Lord suddenly there inside it when the silver bell rang. At the grammar he could find out what the Latin prayers meant.

CHAPTER 8

Manchester, 1939

Music hummed through the kitchen, the windows open to the summer, Tommy Dorsey and his band, 'The Way you Look Tonight', Kitty dancing around with the tea towel to 'Begin the Beguine', knocking over the cups. Not even Dad cross. The wireless sat up on the kitchen shelf. It was Peter's job to go and get the big batteries topped up at the shop. Peter might look skinny, but he could shift all right, that's what Dad said.

They were all sitting round that radio on the day Chamberlain said in his grave and sorrowful and posh voice that they were now at war with Germany.

His dad went out to the backyard. Peter went out after him. Dad was standing up in the corner away from the house, his shoulders shaking, wiping his face. He said, 'Not again.' Kept saying the same two words.

Ma came out and sat on the doorstep and looked very thin, squinting up at them in the sun like some beaky bird as she told Peter and Bill they were down to be evacuated. Every bone in her arms in her legs, thin as sticks: she couldn't breathe again and wasn't getting better. You heard her coughing, coughing at night. Dad, who wouldn't ever admit to being slowed down by his scarred lungs – though he wheezed if he walked even a little fast – turned his eyes away from ma when she had a coughing spasm. The war had done for his lungs, and now the Manchester air was thickening up inside Ma's. Asthma or TB maybe; the doctor couldn't rightly say. So Dad fixed his damaged eyes on a stain at the top of the wall when her shoulders shook, Ma trying to cough quietly, his gaze hopeless and angry and clouded. Waited for her to stop.

Ma put sandwiches in their bags and made sure they had clean underwear. She didn't want people to think that they came from a dirty family. They didn't have any pyjamas to pack. Peter's boots needed mending again but it couldn't be helped. Dad cut a cardboard shape and fitted it inside. She walked with them down to the schoolyard where a woman with a clipboard was fastening labels onto buttons or pinning them onto cardigans. When the ragged crocodile of children set off, Ma walked with them to the train station, clasped the boys into a hard, thin hug.

She stood there gathered up into herself, smiling and waving as the train jerked and then pulled away, holding her coat together even though it wasn't cold. She waved till the steam blocked her out and the train curved away round a bend in the line.

They'd be home soon enough, she'd told them.

★ ★

The bus that collected them from the station had blue paper over the windows to stop Jerry from using the light of the bus as a guide for his bombs, Bill said. The holiday mood and any sandwiches were long gone. No water to drink. The night air was cold, a damp warmth evaporating from the children, their breath condensing on the glass of the windows and soaking into the blue paper. The little boy in the seat in front of them had wet himself adding a salty smell to the fug. Someone was crying, exhausted and resigned.

In the church hall there was cake and hot tea. Women in coats or pinnies got them all fed, and one by one the children were picked out by couples – people with 'making the best of a bad bargain' written all over their faces.

The little ones went first. Then all the girls were gone. The trestle table was cleared and packed away. Bill at thirteen was the oldest. Nobody wanted a big lad, causing trouble, eating you out of house and home.

The woman with the notebook had been writing down names as the children left with their new families. She glanced over to Bill and Peter, came towards them with a frown on her face, but at the same moment the green double doors swung open and a man entered. He wore a long camel coat, a trilby hat and small spectacles with gold rims, large teeth that glinted under the electric light bulbs.

The effect on the woman with the notebook was immediate. She snapped her head up, best behaviour, darted over to intercept him.

'Just the one, May' he said, still moving across the room. 'Dilys won't hear of taking two. Is this all you've got left?'

He stopped in front of the boys. He carried the smell of cologne and cigar smoke and cold air on his clothes. 'A bit old, aren't they?'

May looked at their labels. 'This one's all but fourteen, so he won't be here long. 'And this one's—'

'Ten and a half,' said Peter. 'And I'll be eleven in a few months.'

'Will you indeed?' He didn't look pleased. 'She had in mind a girl, about six.'

'It would be so good of you to take them, or one of them. I said to Joan over there, if Mr Hanbury is taking one of them when he's so busy, then we've no right to complain.'

The man nodded and started to leave. 'You come with me,' he said to Peter. Not him,' as Bill started to follow. Peter gave Bill a look of alarm.

'Go,' Bill told him. 'Get yourself gone.'

There was a car waiting outside the church hall, a sleek black Ford, its shape drawn in glinting lines from an autumn moon rising huge behind the church. Dark shapes of trees in the churchyard loomed around them, moving in the wind. 'Needs must in a war,' he told Peter. 'Bloody chauffeur's been called up.'

Grunting, Mr Hanbury hitched his trousers up over his knees and bent down at the front of the car. The cigar clamped between his teeth, he cranked the starting handle with two hefty rotations. The car juddered. He jumped into the driving seat and slammed the door.

'Well, are you coming then?'

Peter shivered, got the back door open and somehow climbed up. He had to lean out a long way to pull the door shut. He felt the car already moving away as he managed to slam it.

Mr Hanbury drove slowly, no light except for the moon. After a while he seemed to find this tedious and Peter felt the car accelerate through the dark banks of lanes. Mr Hanbury kept the window down in spite of the cold, his elbow on the ledge, singing a song under his breath. Peter recognised the song from the radio, one that Kitty liked. Tears made his eyes itch, but he held his face up to the cold air coming in from the window.

Mr Hanbury didn't speak, seemed to have forgotten he was there. Peter watched him throw his cigar out of the window with a trail of red sparks. Mr Hanbury searched in his breast pocket and held the wheel with his knees while he unscrewed the lid from a silver flask and took a few sips. He held it out to Peter in the back of the car. He shook his head.

Mr Hanbury laughed. 'Good lad, well done.' He took another sip before putting it back in his pocket.

The car turned through iron gates and jolted along a narrow track between banks of glossy leaves. He heard the scrunch of gravel as the car pulled up in front of a building with no lights showing. A tall bulk against a black and watery sky, made even taller by being set on the rise of a hill. Mr Hanbury led the way up a series of brick steps. Still whistling under his breath he turned a handle set into the porch. Somewhere inside the house Peter heard a bell jangling.

A wide woman in a brown pinafore answered, hair in a bun. Mr Hanbury steered him in front of her.

'It's a lad,' she said.

'Aye, needed a place to stay.'

'But what will she say?'

'What will she say about what, Maudey?'

A lady in a brightly coloured wrap, long grey hair in a plait down one shoulder, was coming down the wide staircase across the hall.

'Let me see our little guest.'

She stopped on the bottom step. Looked at Peter with disbelief, then distaste. 'Oh William, how could you?'

'Come on now, Dilys. It was just this boy left there, waiting for someone to take him in when I got there. Do our duty, eh? It's for the war effort. Go shake hands now.'

Peter felt his shoulder shoved firmly and staggered a step nearer to the woman on the staircase. He walked towards her, holding out his hand. Hoped it wasn't sticky. 'Pleased to meet yer, missis.'

Her shoulders and arms flinched away. 'Well, put him in a back bedroom then, under the eaves. Not the blue room.'

She turned, and with a sound of rustling material, hurried back up the stairs.

'Maybe we can get him put up at Thompson's farm.' Maudey looked at him doubtfully. 'They always want hands there, once the potato picking starts.' She shook her head. 'Well, it's a good job I put the copper on in the scullery. This one looks like he's in need of a good bath before he goes anywhere near the sheets.'

Maudey put a zinc hipbath in front of a large fireplace and filled it with steaming water. She draped a towel over a clothes horse that stood round it and handed Peter a bar of yellow coal tar soap.

'I want all your clothes there in a pile, and you're to scrub every inch of you with this. Every inch, mind.'

She left a man's shirt with no collar on the clothes horse. All his clothes had gone. The bath finished, he put the shirt on.

'At least someone's cut your hair short.' She ran her finger over his scalp, searching for something – nits no doubt – but satisfied that he was clean she gave a little push to the side of his head.

'There, you'd best eat that up.'

Over on the table was a bowl of hot milk, soft white bread steeped in it, small yellow beads of butter swimming on top. There was sugar in it. It was gone in moments.

She led the way upstairs, not up the staircase with dark wooden balustrades where Peter had seen the lady coming down earlier, but up a smaller, back staircase with shut-in walls.

Three flights up and Maudey opened a door and switched on the light. A room with one wall sloping down to the floor, a small iron bed, a sink in one corner, a chest of drawers. She pointed out the pot under the bed.

'And when I switch this light off you don't put it back on.'

She took a box of matches from her apron pocket and struck one. Bending over the side table she lit a night light in a saucer.

'It's always nice to have a light when you're away from home, eh? Well, in you get.'

The bed had stiffly ironed sheets, cold and smooth as water. She switched off the electric and shut the door. The room wobbled to and fro in the yellow shadows. He kept very still in the sheets, afraid he might leave a mark. He'd never had a bed all to himself before. He was used to sharp kicks from Bill turning in his sleep, John snoring in the narrow bed under the window. Through the thin wall there'd be the sounds of Doris and Kitty and the murmur of them talking together in the small room, which was just about big enough for two single beds side by side. The house was always crammed full of the people who were an unquestioned part of himself, like his own hands and arms.

He hoped Kitty would take Ma some hot water with a drop of Friar's Balsam if she started up with her coughing.

★ ★

He was caught at the top of the stairs again, trying to tell Dad about Bill's boot, waiting for Dad to come up with his leather belt.

He opened his eyes and looked up at the sloping ceiling, bright sunlight. Relief that it had been a dream. Somewhere downstairs he could hear music.

He opened the curtains. Below, a series of large houses with steeply pitched roofs covered the hillside, each secluded by tall trees and fat hedges. The Hanbury's house stood right at the top of the hill.

His stomach growled. He couldn't see any sign of his own clothes. He quietly retraced his steps down the stairs still wearing the old shirt.

After opening a couple of wrong doors along a back corridor he found the kitchen. His clothes were on a clothes horse in front of an iron range, the red coals glowing behind bars.

'They'll be dry now,' Maudey shouted from the scullery. The fabric felt stiff, the holes in his shorts had blossomed wider, a tangle of threads round the gaps like autumn burrs. 'Happen Mrs Hanbury'll find something that's not falling to bits,' she said, ladling porridge into a bowl and setting it down with a bang. She put a spoon of jam on the porridge, poured a glass of creamy milk. No one but him to eat it all, at a big table set into a window alcove that looked out onto the shady well of the garden. Banks of flowerbeds and stone steps climbed up to the top lawn and a rose trellis, the flowers batting against the wood in the wind.

'Do you know where our Bill is lodging, missis?'

'You may as well call me Maudey like they all do, dear. Yes, he's over at Thompson's farm, not so far from here.'

'Am I going to go and live there too?'

'We'll have to wait and see.'

The back door into the scullery rattled open and Mr Hanbury appeared. He kept on his caramel coat but put his trilby hat on the table.

'Is she up yet?'

'She should be down soon. Shall I take your eggs and bacon through to the breakfast room, Mr Hanbury?'

'And I'll take some of that porridge now, Maudey.'

He ate it standing up, added more jam as he went.

There was the sound of the door opening in a room nearby. Maudey and Mr Hanbury exchanged glances. He went through, shedding his coat.

Peter carried his dishes into the scullery. He began to help Maudey with the washing up and got an approving smile from her old face. They began to hear raised voices coming from the open door of the breakfast room.

'Sweetest, how's it going to look if we're not doing our bit, the snobby Hanburys too good to take in an evacuee from the slums? And with the council elections coming up next month it'll mean an awful lot to me, Dilys, if you'd do this. And Maudey'll take care of him. You won't even know he's here.'

A muffled quiet, then Mr Hanbury breezed back into the kitchen.

'Maudey, I'll take this one out with me today. I have to call by at the factory, and he can give me a hand with some boxes.' He picked up his hat and left by the back door. Peter looked at Maudey.

'Aye well, looks like you'll be staying after all. Go on. He'll be waiting in the car.'

Peter couldn't believe his luck, a ride in the Austin two days running. This time he was allowed to sit up front. They sailed along and soon they were out into countryside that was nothing like the scraggy lands around Manchester airfield. Banks of tall, purple wildflowers lined the road each side, like crowds welcoming a pageant through town.

Derby had the same red-brick buildings as Manchester, but on a smaller scale. A gang of boys played a roaming game of football as they drove down a street walled in by high brick and set with rows of small windows.

The car made its stately way in through iron gates and parked under a glass awning. Mr Hanbury led the way into a vast hangar-like room with rows of iron pillars. The floor space was crowded with women seated round wooden benches piled with parts of shoes, the women working on various stages of finish. A huge clock hung overhead from the central rafter. Mr Hanbury paraded Peter past the benches.

'Our evacuee from Manchester,' he boomed widely.

Everyone bobbed their heads as he passed, called out, 'Morning, Mr Hanbury.'

Mr Hanbury left Peter in the care of a tableful of girls, instructing him to watch and learn; this was a fine trade for a boy to be in. He went up to an office with a half wall of glass windows overlooking the factory floor. Peter watched the girls' fingers pressing and gluing the leather shapes. There was a heady smell of cow gum, mixed in with perfume. The girls' jokes flew as fast as their fingers, teasing Peter about who he was walking out with, teaching him a couple of new ideas that made his ears go red. He was glad to be rescued.

As they left for the car the foreman came out and handed a box to Mr Hanbury. Mr Hanbury flipped back the lid and picked up a red lady's shoe with a slim and elegant heel, ran his hand over the leather.

'Your Alice is going to be the best shod at her parties, Mr Hanbury.'

'Alice? Oh yes, Alice.'

Mr Hanbury drove a little way out of Derby, but in another direction. He parked the car across the road from a butcher's shop. Its front stood open to the street, a dim cave of meat. A fat pelmet of plucked chickens hung across the front of the shop, under a blue sign announcing 'Anderson's High Class Butchers'.

'I have to see someone on business for an hour or so, Peter. Here, buy yourself a comic or some sweets. And don't you wander off.'

Peter found himself on the pavement, a shilling in his hand. Mr Hanbury put the small shoebox under his arm. He hurried away into a side door next to the butcher's shop.

Peter bought a bag of penny sweets and sat on the kerb edge, turning the pages of the *Hotspur* carefully so that it would still look new when he took it to Bill.

A long time later Mr Hanbury reappeared, in a hurry. He pulled out into the road, pumping hard on the steering wheel. A sudden bang on the window and Mr Hanbury braked. A woman with wavy blonde hair had placed her palm on the glass, pressing so hard that the skin looked drained of blood. Mr Hanbury wound down the window. 'Can I help you, miss?'

She glanced across at Peter. 'That thing I told you about, Mr Hanbury, don't you forget next time. He needs it.'

'I'll let the factory know.'

Peter watched her from the back window as the car pulled away. She looked fresh-faced and young. She wasn't so much older than Kitty. She waited on the pavement as they drove off, her cardigan pulled across her chest as if the day were cold.

As soon as they got back to the house a voice called out from the top of the garden.

'Daddy!'

A grown-up girl was running down the steps. She launched herself at Mr Hanbury. He staggered and swung her round in a hug.

'When did you get back?'

'Hours ago. Where were you?'

'Boring meetings.'

'We're up in the garden having tea. Who's this?'

'Our evacuee. Peter, say hello to Alice.'

She folded her arms and looked down at him with amusement. 'Oh dear, poor you. Fancy having to risk being taken over by the Hanbury clan. We are horribly good at simply absorbing people. You'll never get away, I'm afraid.'

Peter didn't know what to say; he had lost the power of speech altogether. He stared at Alice Hanbury. She had fair hair in a roll round her brow like a crown. A tumble of curls down to her shoulders. A slight, pointed face. A frock made of shiny material that shimmered in the sunlight. Slender arms, folded, tapering white fingers grasping the elbows.

'Pleased to meet you,' he managed. She shook his outstretched hand and laughed. He wished he were wearing a pair of long trousers, a white shirt with the collar spread out over a jacket.

She led the way up to the top lawn. 'They're saying that it's a scandal, the evacuees from the cities are almost two years behind in growth compared to country children. How old did you say you were, Peter?'

'Nearly eleven, miss.'

'There. You see, Daddy? When this war's over we have to do something about the awful conditions in the slums. Things really can't go on this way.'

'Yes, Alice,' said Mr Hanbury, sounding like a man used to taking orders from his daughter.

Beneath the rose trellis Mrs Hanbury was seated next to a table covered in a lace cloth. She poured a cup from a silver teapot with a black handle and handed it to Mr Hanbury. There were three young men, or boys perhaps, relaxing round the table in deckchairs. They wore jackets with white shirt collars spread wide. Hair oiled and neatly combed away from smooth, tanned foreheads.

'So, here's all the gang,' said Mr Hanbury. 'What time did you ruffians get back?'

'Train got in an hour or so ago.'

'I'd been back for ages by then,' said Alice, taking her tea from Mrs Hanbury. 'Beat all of you, so there.'

'She looks like a weak and feeble woman, Ralph, but she's deadly. Don't take her on at tennis,' said one of the young men.

'Or an argument. She'll have your guts for garters in no time, now that Alice is at Oxford.'

'I'll remember that.' Ralph had a pleasant, willing-to-fit-in sort of smile, squinting into the afternoon sun with a quizzical look. Dark hair, a squarer build than the other two boys.

'It's utter tosh, you know. You're terrifying poor Peter,' Alice said crossly. 'Peter, these are my awful brothers, Neville, Phillip and their school friend . . .'

'Ralph.'

'Peter is an evacuee, from Liverpool.'

'I'm from Manchester, me, miss.'

'Actually, I was an evacuee once, Peter,' Ralph said. 'Had to leave Spain, all by myself a few years back, on a huge liner.' Peter immediately liked Ralph.

'Where did you get sent to?'

'Went to stay with my aunts in London, then Mama got me a place at Repton with these capital chaps.'

'You were in Spain?' said Alice. 'When the civil war broke out?

Oh, isn't it awful now that Franco's seized power? The awful things done in his name.'

'Terrible things happened on both sides.'

'But you can't sympathise with Franco, surely.'

'I'm not saying I sympathise, but I am . . .'

'. . . a little bit of a fascist?'

'Really, Alice! Must you be so rude to a guest?' said Mrs Hanbury.

Alice gave a cross laugh. 'Peter is also our guest and yet I notice he doesn't seem to have anywhere to sit, and nothing to drink.'

'I've hardly had chance to ask him, dear.'

'Here, old chap. Have my seat. I prefer the floor anyway.' Neville got up out of his deckchair. He spread his long length along the flagstones and rested his back against the wooden trellis pole. Peter wondered if Mrs Hanbury would be angry; sitting on the floor at home meant clothes becoming dirty from the ingrained residue of boots, perhaps a splinter in your behind from the floor planks.

Mrs Hanbury poured a cup of tea, holding back the little dog on her lap who was attempting to lick the stream of milk. She handed the cup to Peter. He carefully blew on the top for a while and then took several aerated sips. Mrs Hanbury looked away, gazing out across the open fields.

Peter followed her gaze. Beyond the garden fence a row of tall poplar trees were turning their leaves in the wind, rivers of sixpences flowing in the sun. The windy fields of Derbyshire faded into blue mist. Up here the air felt big and unimpeded. Peter took big lungfuls. If Ma could be here doing this kind of breathing, he felt sure this kind of air would make her better.

'So what is it that your father does, Peter?' said Mrs Hanbury, kissing the side of the dog's head. The wind lazily ruffled the lace collar on her navy dress.

'Lately, missis, he's started up in a scrap metal business. Before that he were usher at pictures, and before that he were 'stop me and buy one' man. He had a bike with a cart of ice cream and he had to pedal it around town every day.'

'How very interesting. How very nice to have so many choices of career.'

'Mummy, honestly, those aren't choices of career. If you'd only read Orwell. Richard was telling me, and I agree with him, that the working classes—'

'Oh, and how is Richard, dear? I wrote to his mother that she'd be very welcome to visit us, but I haven't had a reply yet.'

'The Veseys are ever-so-ever, don't you know,' said Phillip, with a grin made even wider by a pair of large schoolboy ears.

'Oh Mummy. Must he?'

'Phillip, that is entirely unacceptable and not at all funny.'

'Actually, Mummy, I've been invited to Amforth Hall by Richard's mother.'

Mrs Hanbury gave Alice all her attention.

'So could I possibly go into town and get a few new things I might need?'

'Of course, dear. You must. I saw the most marvellous material in Dempsey's. It would make such a nice dress, and I can get Maudey's niece to make it up for you if you pick out a pattern too.'

'I might need gloves. Oh and Daddy, I so need some new shoes. Cream ones would be perfect.'

'I'll see what I can do.'

Peter waited for Mr Hanbury to tell her about the beautiful red shoes, but he seemed to have forgotten.

Phillip pushed himself up from the deckchair and stretched his long limbs. 'Anyone fancy a knockabout on the courts? We've enough for doubles.'

'Why doesn't Peter come too? It will be such fun, Peter. We always need a ball boy.'

Peter picked his way down the unevenly sized steps in the wake of Alice and the boys. All of them were talking loudly and at the same time, but not so loudly that they could prevent Mrs Hanbury's voice from following them down.

'What are you going to do about the state of that child's clothes, William? Is he going to come to church with us on Sunday, because really? And Maudey says he's brought nothing else with him, not even pyjamas.'

'I thought you might do something about that, dear?' Mr Hanbury's voice irresistibly coaxing; a touch of firmness in closing the matter.

But Peter didn't mind what anyone said. His eyes tracked Alice's bright hair as she led the way between banks of pink geraniums and lilac-coloured daisies, her arms swinging lightly as she argued with the boys. His chest felt tight with a pain that was almost grief. Dazed and alarmed, he realised that from now on all his happiness rested on Alice Hanbury, how often he could catch sight of Alice Hanbury, how worthy he was to be in Alice's world.

Late that evening, after he had eaten a supper of boiled potatoes and lamb stew with Maudey in the kitchen, and then helped her wash up the dishes from the meal in the dining room, he was surprised to hear a burst of brave and thrilling music coming from the big room at the front of the house.

He crept through the hallway and listened, crept closer and watched through the half open door of the drawing room. He could see Mrs Hanbury playing a large, flat piano, her hands making sharp pounces on the keys. He recognised a cello being played by one of the boys. Standing next to the piano Alice was shuttling a bow across the strings of a violin, her hair pulled to one side away from the strings, her slender shape tensing and swaying to the music, her face intent and almost angry.

He jumped. Behind him in the shadows of the hallway stood Mr Hanbury, tall in a double-breasted suit. A cloud of alcohol, not so much like the thick beer smell from Dad, but something finer; the word brandy came to mind. Mr Hanbury's handsome, matinee idol face had a high colour. He drew on a small cigar.

'I see we have yet another music lover among us. Well, go on in then, boy.'

Mr Hanbury took the chair by the fireplace. He struck a match for another small cigar, waved it along to the music, taking sips of smoke. Peter felt like a lemon standing there, unexplained and awkward just inside the door. The others glanced at him but carried on as if under an urgent spell to finish the tune. He let the buzz of the cello reverberate in his chest, felt the thumps of the piano through his feet, Alice's violin bow sawing his heart into slices.

When they stopped Mr Hanbury clapped. Alice came over to her father's chair, leant down over the back and slid her arms round her father's neck. 'You went out again.'

'I see you rotters didn't wait for me for supper.'

'Shall I ask Maudey, dear?'

'No. No. In fact I ate there.'

'And you brought Peter in to listen to our Schubert.'

'I found him outside the door, trying to listen through the crack.'
Peter blushed.

'Oh, it's not nice to listen outside doors, Peter,' said Mrs Hanbury mildly.

'But you enjoyed the Schubert, didn't you, Peter?' Alice came and took his hand, led him to a chair.

He nodded hard.

'You see,' she addressed the room. 'Given the opportunity they don't just want to listen to big bands and George Formby and all that kind of ephemera. It's all a question of educating minds, raising everybody up to the same level.'

'It would certainly help if they would hurry up and find some places in the local schools for these evacuees,' said Mrs Hanbury. 'They are saying we might have to wait until they can organise some kind of shift system to accommodate all the children. In the meantime Peter is going to be wandering around with little to do.' She shook her head.

'Do you read books, Peter?' Alice looked at him, frowning, as if he needed adjusting properly in some way. He brushed a hand across his face in case it had a mark on it.

'I love books, me, miss.'

'Well, that's splendid. There are stacks of them up in my room. Would you like me to pick some out for you, Peter?'

'Yes please.'

'Well, I'm so glad you know how to read.'

'I took exam for the grammar school, miss. I passed it, miss.'

'You were attending Manchester Grammar, Peter?' said Mrs Hanbury.

'I passed, but I weren't going to go in the end.'

'But you should have seized the opportunity,' Alice told him. 'Why on earth didn't you go?'

'Ma saved money in tin, but when it were time to buy the uniform it were empty. Me dad took the money. So we couldn't buy uniform.'

From the expression on Alice's face Peter realised that he had just said something that put him even further away from her comprehension.

'That's awful. How can people live like that? You've got to do something about it, Daddy. Can't you speak to the right people, please? Find him a place here?'

Mr Hanbury shrugged. 'I can try, for you.'

Standing in front of the fireplace Alice launched into a small lecture.

'You see, if we can't educate the masses upwards, then how can we have a society that can work together? I agree with Richard, the only class system now is education, and once everyone has access to that, well then.' With her high-domed forehead and finely cut chin Alice looked far too fragile to be holding so much righteous indignation.

Peter had desperately wanted to go to the grammar; he'd felt sure it was a place where secrets like Latin and Greek would open doors of happiness into a world of rare knowledge. But now, as he watched Alice's face, delicate as one of the Hanburys' china teacups, it wasn't the idea of Latin that was making his chest expand with happiness, it was the knowledge that Alice Hanbury minded about what happened to him.

Glancing around the room Peter realised that he wasn't the only one spellbound by Alice. Sitting on the window seat behind them, the dark-haired Ralph was watching Alice's fiery delivery with his full attention.

★ ★

A couple of weeks later Alice and her brothers were gone from the house, the boys back to their boarding school, Alice to university. A quiet routine of helping Maudey established itself: peeling potatoes; blacking shoes and washing dishes; bringing in the coal; glad to show how he could be helpful.

It was Maudey who found out what had happened to Bill. He wasn't at Thompson's farm but further away at old Mr Garrat's, a good six-mile walk, Maudey said. 'You'll need all day to get there and back. Perhaps on Saturday you could walk over there, eh?'

With Maudey's instructions Peter set out to find Bill at Garrat's farm. He rolled up the *Hotspur* comic and stowed it in his back pocket.

Garrat's farm was a sea of hard, grey mud. Around three edges of a muddy yard were low buildings, streaked with dust and green. Beyond, a rusting barn with a collapsed wall of hay bales. When he opened the gate a dog on a chain began to bark and hurl itself repeatedly in his direction. Peter decided to sit up on the wall away from the dog, wait and see if anyone was about. There was a sharp smell of ammonia and ripe old boots from the earth, the lane up to the gate splodged with cowpats.

It wasn't long before a herd of black cows came lumbering into view, lowing and rolling their eyes at the figure by the gate. At the back were two men in rolled shirtsleeves, one with a stick that he used to shoo away flies or tap the backside of a cow that had stopped to grab at the hedge. With a shock of recognition Peter saw that the man with the stick was Bill. He watched in awe as Bill calmly herded the cows through into the farmyard. He barely nodded at Peter's 'All right then?' as he shut the gate. Peter jumped down from the wall and followed him across the yard.

The cows dealt with, with the briefest of calls and slaps on the behind, Bill led the way into a room that was more of a continuation of outdoors than a habitation. The walls had a cold, wet feel when you touched them. The brick floor had a sheen of slug trails and a sweat of condensation. A sink in one corner with a tap, and a bloom of green up the wall. A table with a tin and a plate, a bed in the corner with a ticking pillow case. A jumble of old blankets. Bill sat down on the edge of the bed. He took a packet of five Woodbines from his pocket, lit one and sucked at the end, holding the cigarette between his thumb and finger. His fingernails were black and the creases of his hands inked in with the same black.

'How you been, Bill?'

A shrug for a reply. Peter got out the *Hotspur* comic and put it on the bed. Bill turned the pages. He seemed to have forgotten Peter was there. Peter looked around at the cold room, a sickly smell coming from the walls that made you keen to leave.

'Bill, I could ask if you could come and live where I am. Maudey there, she's a right good cook. You could do jobs. They can't get no one to help in garden, only me at weekend.'

Bill looked at Peter's smart corduroy shorts, the new jumper.

'Don't be soft. I'll be fourteen soon. Going home in a few weeks. Got a place as apprentice at John's works.'

'You're going home?'

'I am that.'

'I'll ask Maudey to make a cake. You can take it to Ma. A big one, with fruit in it and all. They get given all this food through Mr Hanbury's mates. She'll do Ma the best cake ever. D'you think Ma'll come and see us out here?'

'Reckon when she's better, eh Peter. She's none too clever at the moment. You got a letter from her?'

'And I wrote back.'

'You'll be home at Christmas, see Ma then.'

Peter rubbed at his eyes.

'Shall us go out? There's tractor out there. I got to drive it the other day.'

The right pecking order back in place, the boys left the underground cold of Bill's room and headed off in the more forgiving warmth of the air outside.

★ ★

It was a few weeks later that he found Maudey and Mrs Hanbury at the kitchen table sorting through a pile of folded clothes. The clothes smelled new, dark red bands round the grey jersey and blazer. There was also a grey cap with the same red crest as the blazer pocket.

'Peter,' Mrs Hanbury announced, 'these are for you. We had your exam papers sent through from Manchester. Mr Hanbury had to put his foot down a little, and I don't really know how he does these things, but you'll start on Monday at Buxton Grammar school.'

He had to try the uniform on for size. When Maudey saw him she was a little bit tearful. She put her hands against her doughy cheeks and said he looked that grand.

Mrs Hanbury led him to the large mirror in the hallway. In it was a boy he didn't recognise. Gone was the usual prison cut. He had a fringe, a golden brown colour, a face sleek from good food and good air, a grey shirt and claret tie under a tailored blazer.

On the other side of the glass was the kind of boy who might, if he worked hard – worked really, really hard – grow up to become good enough to be part of Alice's world.

CHAPTER 9

Fourwinds, 1981

Sarah awoke in the dark with a gasp and threw back the sheet that had tightened round her shoulders. She waited for the dream to drain from the room. Her heart was thumping so hard she could feel the skin at the base of her throat vibrating.

She reached for the water, the shine of the moonlight on the glass. A white pill still lay beside it on the side table. She hadn't swallowed it. She hadn't wanted to be trapped in a dream with no way of waking herself out of it. She drank some of the water, tried saying Nicky's name in the darkness.

Nothing. No sound. Only the pain in her throat.

But it wasn't meant to be like this. She'd worked so hard to steer her life away into a new world, just her and Nicky.

When she first met Nicky she'd never liked red roses, sentimental songs crooned by pop stars like Englebert Humperdink. She distrusted lace and frills, hated anything labelled romantic. Holding hands, staring into each other's eyes, wasn't it all a manipulation to an end?

But Nicky had arrived one day and suddenly she wanted to believe.

At the end of the second year at university they bought InterRail tickets and travelled through Europe. They spent the summer wandering through a blur of different landscapes and medieval cities, hand in hand, eating bread and apples or whatever was cheap. They slept sometimes in hostels, mostly on trains, long nights in the clacking rail carriages, always the same bubble of suspended sleep, waking in the dark to see various strangers who lay along the seats breathing and snoring, bringing whiffs of fried chips, hair oil, of citrus and aftershave. But sooner or later the others would be gone. The constant was the small world that they carried between them, always moving towards a new place that seemed to have been created with the moment of their arrival.

In France, after Albi and Carcassone, they headed towards Bordeaux and found work on a vineyard, pruning the unneeded shoots and leaves from the vines so the grapes would warm in the sun and swell. Nicky's hair grew longer and his freckles deepened to shades of dark honey. The plaited leather bracelets on his arm and the beads round his neck slid and danced as he worked down the vine rows, nicking the shoots off with a large curved knife, the lean muscles across his back like a country of subtle hills and hollows that Sarah could now read in the dark like Braille.

They stayed in a half-abandoned cottage by the main farmhouse with the others students and Portuguese labourers. The straw pallets smelled of summer, of hay in sunshine. Outside the open back door of the cottage was a wall of green maize where paths led to the woods.

Sarah's Indian cotton tops and T-shirts faded in the sun. Her dark hair bleached in strands of silver. Her hands so brown they looked like they belonged to a new person formed by the summer.

They travelled on, further south, swam in rivers and lakes, slept in cheap family pensions or out in fields. In Spain they hitchhiked through bone bare landscapes and stayed in white hill towns with long views. They travelled across to Valencia, and walked through a legendary town, where Nicky's dad had once lived as a boy.

Nicky said his father had heard the gunfire on the night of the outbreak of civil war and had to leave for England the next day. It was hard to imagine any such thing now, as they made their way down through tourist beaches bright and noisy with sun loungers and red and yellow umbrellas, with crowds of fair-haired people burned a deep pink.

Reaching the foot of Spain they came to a hot and deserted stretch of coast where the winds blew across from Africa. They slept on the beach, the salt never leaving their hair, the sound of the sea always under the hot wind.

At the beginning of September they crossed over to Morocco. With the last of their money they stayed in a tiny room in Marrakesh and wandered the narrow alleyways of the souks while calls for prayer rang out overhead. Their Indian leather sandals were hard and cracked now, wearing out, and they stopped to buy new ones.

She hadn't thought about the cut-off shorts, the halter-neck T-shirt. A man grabbed her breast and spat at her, shouted words that she didn't understand, but she could feel the scorn in his voice. When she turned back to look he flicked his head at her as if she were something disgusting.

Nicky bought a necklace made of silver and blue stones and she was still shaking when he fastened it round her neck. She gave Nicky a white cotton tunic that he wore almost every day, like a prophet, although the evenings were becoming too cool for thin cotton really. The tourists and the long-haired travellers with their guitars and beads were starting to leave.

It was time to go home to England, to streets swishing with autumn rain, grey skies and wet bricks glistening in the dark evenings, but they made toast in front of the gas fire, decided to continue their journey into the country of each other.

They would get married.

★ ★

She didn't own a dress, just jeans and one old wrap skirt that she never wore. One stick of mascara and some dried-out old eye shadow. To visit his parents she'd actually bought a dress. Which meant she'd had to buy tights. She wore the turquoise necklace Nicky had bought in Morocco. Holding on to the blue stone she hardly recognised herself in the glass, softer and more feminine. She wasn't entirely comfortable with that, but she'd give it a go.

Really, said the reflection, who do you think you're fooling? She went out to meet Nicky and his parents.

From the moment she arrived at Fourwinds Sarah loved the house. Alice had enveloped her in an effusive bear hug, saying, 'Darling, we get to meet you at last.' And Ralph had brushed his unruly fringe back, a shock of grey hair like a professor, and twinkled a smile at her that was full of kindness. She felt welcomed, feted even. How marvellous her Birmingham accent was. Exactly how Shakespeare would have pronounced his vowels.

Nicky gave her a tour of the house, the rooms infused with stories about growing up there with his brothers. Ralph's study, with its walls of old books, was high ceilinged and looked out over the back lawns. In the drawing room was a grand piano scattered with music sheets, and a huge display of delphiniums and peonies. Nearby a cello and a music stand. Silver-framed photos of Nicky and his two brothers as schoolboys, Nicky looking deathly serious and good, arms pressed against his sides and face turned up to the camera. Bleached colour photos of the family on holiday in Greece and France.

It was only later, during a meal at a restaurant for the parents to meet each other and talk about the wedding, that they realised Alice and Ralph had met her father before, years ago.

'Of course,' exclaimed Ralph, beaming. 'Peter! One and the same. After all this time.'

It turned out that during the war Peter had been evacuated to Buxton and had stayed at Alice's parents' house. A wonderful house, her father had added. Alice's mother had been so kind.

Sarah had watched Alice's face register surprise and for a flickering moment, dismay. But then Alice had quickly regained her composure, smiled, pressed Peter's hands, said how wonderful to see you again. She had given her attention to the menu and suggested that they order. And that was it.

Sarah would have liked to ask a few questions, a lot in fact, but the topic seemed to have already slipped into the box marked 'the years in the war which no one wants to talk about'. Sitting at the table, trying to follow the cross currents of conversation, she was left feeling puzzled and uncomfortable.

A few weeks after that, during a visit to Fourwinds to talk about wedding plans – who knew it was going to involve so many things to sort out, lists and lists of things – Nicky had found a box of old photographs, including one of her father. She'd seen so few pictures of her father as a boy; it felt like holding an archeological remnant from another age. She studied it avidly. It was taken in the garden at the Hanburys' old house: a skinny boy standing next to a young woman, Alice. She was in a deckchair, wearing a wide-brimmed sun hat, her face serious and pretty, a book open on her lap. The boy wore a vest and shorts, holding a spade straight up and to attention. It was somehow heartbreaking to see how good that child was being.

'Peter worked so hard in the garden, always busy helping Maudey, our cook. Of course, your stepmother in a way.' Alice had said when shown the photo. She patted Sarah's arm, murmured, 'Dear Peter.'

Looking at the picture again Sarah couldn't help wondering if her father was always going to be the boy who helped the cook in Alice's eyes.

And there it was. The past always intruding into the present.

She'd thought once they were married it would be just the two of them. They would carry on journeying into a newly minted world. That's what she had told herself. But now, as she sat in the rumpled bed in the thick, country darkness that closed round Fourwinds each night, she saw how she had been mistaken. She had not reckoned on the way that dreams brought the past flooding back in. How she would would wake up, gasping for air, struggling to escape the night's slippage in time. In two days she would walk into the church –but the past would come with her, seeping in behind, refusing to leave.

She slid from the bed, the sheets damp with perspiration, shivering even though it was summer. The house was silent except for the hollow ticking of a clock in a wooden case.

If she told Nicky . . . If he really knew her . . .

She made a small groan, a grunt.

Her body had already closed her voice down, every nerve telling her body to go now, to keep moving. Leaving was the only way she could assuage the rising panic. It wasn't a thought so much as a compulsion. Feeling with her hands she found her clothes and pulled them on.

She stepped lightly along the corridor and down the stairs, her hands pressing on the wall and the banister to take her weight. She took her jacket and bag from the hall, slipped out of the house and closed the door quietly. She walked on the grass along the drive's edge, making no noise.

The dawn was pink, tender as a rose. She glanced back at the house one more time, the sunrise deepening the red of the brick, the dark trees to the west stirring in the warm wind, graceful and waiting for the light to touch them. She didn't belong here.

She wanted to see Nicky so much that she wondered if a heart could give out with such longing, but her thoughts were like a high note, a distant warning bell, her palms were greasy with sweat, and all she could do was follow the unbearable need to keep on walking. She left by the side gate, a shadow slipping round the corner of the church.

CHAPTER 10

Oxford, 1940

During the night Alice was woken up by the drone of another convoy of bombers. She was so tired she hadn't even bothered to head down to the cellar with the other two girls. As always the bombers would be heading for Birmingham. If Hitler was hoping to annex Britain then he evidently wanted to arrive and find Oxford intact.

She woke some hours later and was struck by the whiteness of the light, the stillness. Even for February, the room was freezing. She stepped gingerly across the chilly floorboards and pulled back the curtain. It had snowed. The roofs, the streets, the spires, the whole of Oxford had been transformed into fragile planes of insubstantial white.

Outside the air was still, no sounds except for her shoes compacting the snow. She walked as far as Christ Church Meadow. Here the light was all in the land, the fields crystalline. Beyond a line of winter trees the fields merged into the duller sky with no discernible horizon. There was a quick movement and birds rose up from the branches in a cloud. She gripped onto the railings. The cold of the iron hurt her hands even through gloves. There was a sign on the railings: 'These fields are private.'

She thought of Richard's room, the hours spent reading together, sitting on the floor in front of the little gas fire, and Richard would read something out and laugh, or explain a passage written by Toynbee or Beveridge. She might give her opinion, read something out and then he'd smile and nod.

A wet cold was penetrating the leather of her lace-up shoes. Why had she walked down to this empty place? Of course, she knew the answer. The walls of Richard's college ran along the meadow. Richard might come down from his rooms and head towards town or to some lecture.

A light snow began to fall, making her blink. Then she blinked again, stood stock still, because coming along the path she saw Richard, not sure if she'd conjured him up. The fine snow was dusting his tweed coat – the coat he'd scrounged from his father's room of shooting stuff. She could feel the precise roughness of that old tweed under her palm.

He was enclosed in a conversation with a girl. They were almost alongside her before he saw her and drew to a halt. The snow had whitened his hair.

'Hello, Alice.' He was, as ever, charmingly pleased to see her, and impervious and unreachable. A few more words – she couldn't take in what he'd said – and then he was gone, walking away.

She began to walk in the other direction, fast, as if she had a purpose. The snow was coming down quickly, veils of scrim catching across her face, fine as a girl's hair and melting wet on her lips.

She hated that pretty girl next to Richard, that small red smile. Lipstick on already at breakfast – the sort of girl who would feel at home with Richard's mother, who would know all the strange little rituals of a place like Amforth House.

She cut up through a cobbled street past Oriel and was back in town, the busy pavements and the indifference of morning bus queues. Most of the shop windows were criss-crossed with white tape now. In one the glass had been boarded over and painted with scenes of Oxford.

The pensive, magical Oxford of last year had gone; it was hard to recall those groups of gowned men walking in a leisurely, reflective manner through quiet streets. Now heavy traffic rumbled down towards St Giles, lines of lorries carrying troops or bulky machinery under tarpaulins. The pavements were crowded with a host of people evacuated from London; civil servants in bowler hats, servicemen in uniforms with the stripes of various regiments, RAF men in sheepskin jackets, Polish officers and Free French soldiers in sharp-cornered berets or kepis, gangs of girls evacuated from London colleges. A whole year's intake of men had disappeared, and soon Richard would be gone too.

She saw him suddenly, waiting to cross at the Cornmarket.

But it wasn't Richard, only her grief conjuring him from nothing.

Had it really all been nothing, the whole of last year? The breathless moment of sliding up the sash window of her room onto the night garden – her room that was placed so conveniently at ground floor level – climbing out and finding Richard there, waiting in the summer mists, going down to the boathouse, muffled laughter as they slid the punt out onto the water, silent and dreamlike. Then coming back in the morning, the sun golden on the perfectly still water, the boat gliding between the curtains of willows, arms tired after punting all the way out to Eton and back.

Or sitting next to Richard in New College chapel, the light through the east window painting blues and purple on ancient stone, the choir melancholy for the Nunc Dimittis, the whispered prayers together. They had shared that. And the ardent discussions about a better world in the sherry-warmed courts of professors in red cravats, daring them to think like communists.

And then came the journey in his father's borrowed MG, to his country house, the long gravel drive and the butler opening the vast door in the Palladian edifice. Richard's family had been away in

London. A maid in a white apron had served just the two of them at a long oak table in a room where gilt-framed oil portraits of Lyly maidens with their luminous silks and wetly red lips looked down on them. A long evening in the green damask ballroom, changing the record on the wind-up gramophone, emptying bottles of fizz, dancing a little, lying on the same sofa and talking – how they would build a shining future. Their rooms were close together on the same corridor. Perhaps it was being in that house, or simply being so sure of each other and sure of everything; but yes, she'd let things go too far that night; but then it had seemed as though only good and true things could come from being so closely bound to Richard.

And she knew it simply wasn't sensible to be standing in the street under the church tower at Cornmarket, saying his name, but she couldn't remember where it was that she was supposed to be going, or which way she should walk.

She heard her name being called and turned to see her cousin galumphing along the pavement. He was red-faced with cold. A fellow behind him was trying to follow Basil's sudden, erratic path.

'Grief, old girl. What are you doing standing there?' said Basil. 'You look frozen. Come on, we're going to find a cup of tea.'

She started blubbing, and he pulled her into the alleyways of the covered market, past the earthy bags of potatoes, and the sawdust and blood of the meat stall, into a glassed-in café full of steam and wet coats. His friend queued at the counter and bought strong tea. They tried to get her to eat a rock cake, for breakfast.

She thought, I will do this, and she was, after a few loud blows into her hanky, even ready to be impressive, since this was Oxford, and they were Oxford students, even if they were from her younger cousin's rather minor public school. So she rallied and thought of something intelligent to say about the Sheridan play.

'You must come, darlings, both of you. The Drama Soc's putting on *School for Scandal* in the quad at Christchurch.' And then she almost started up again, because last year she and Richard had watched *A Midsummer Night's Dream* there.

The boy Basil had dragged along had been nodding intently to everything she said – was he quite all right? When the tears started rolling again he watched her like a big dog watching the distress of humans, puzzled but mutely attuned. Her handkerchief was now sodden and limp. He fished out a big folded handkerchief that was evidently used to blot his ink pen, but it was dry and smelled cleanly of some strange cologne. Finely stitched little initials were embroidered in the corner. It was made of thick cotton, not an English handkerchief somehow.

'Well, I think Richard's a fool to pass up on a strapping specimen of a girl like you, don't you think so, Ralph? The rotter had all but proposed, he was so smitten, and then his rather grand mother comes along and says Alice here won't do. So then he goes cold and it's all off. Shocking way to carry on.'

'It was a mutual decision,' Alice told him. 'You do say the most awful guff, Basil.'

She was remembering why she didn't spend more time with Basil: he had a way of ploughing on and saying the most excruciatingly embarrassing thing he could – the very thing you should never say – and all with no sense of shame, just stating the obvious. A visit to Basil always risked some cheerful little put-down.

'And she's frightfully cultured, you know,' Basil went on. 'Ever so into music and theatre and all that arty stuff, aren't you, old thing?'

She glanced over at his friend, wishing Basil would shut up now. But now his friend wasn't paying attention. He pulled out a fob watch and looked worried. 'I should be at the station, meeting Mama,' he said. She looked at the wet ball of linen. 'No, keep the hanky. It's not much of a gift. Or perhaps you could give it back to me some time. I could come and get it, if I may?'

'I'm sorry, what did you say your name was?'

'Ralph. Actually, we have met before. In your garden.'

'Really?'

'Don't you remember? I came to tea, at the end of last summer. We played tennis. I used to room with your brothers? We shared a study at Repton.'

She recalled the ring of tall adolescent boys, the pimples and the shirt sweat, the impenetrable school jokes. Gawky and angular they carried the ammonia whiff of chrysalises about to undergo a transformation into some higher element of masculine entitlement. She recalled Mummy pouring tea, a game of doubles on the court under a summer wind, the funny boy from Spain quietly watching them. Was this the same boy? She hadn't paid much attention.

'So you're at school with Neville and Phillip?'

'Not any more. I've just come up to Oxford to do Responsions. Really crossing my fingers that I'm going to get in. Damn, I'd really love to stay and chat some more but Mama's found a flat to rent in Oxford for a while, and oh, she'll be at the station and quite lost until I get there.'

★ ★

He was waiting outside the lecture room again. She smiled and shook her head. He must be rather lonely to seek out her company so much, or else he had some kind of crush on her, which was sweet really because he was so much younger, two years at least. When he saw her coming down the steps of the building he came forward in his awkward way, nothing elegant or refined but like some enormous puppy, waving both of his two large hands at her. Either he didn't know how things were done, or he just didn't care. For some reason, as a greeting, he gave her an enormous hug that almost, she was sure of it, broke one of her ribs.

'I've found a place that does real hot chocolate.'

'Honestly, Ralph, most people drink cocoa at bedtime, not in the middle of the afternoon.'

'No, no, I don't mean that watery boarding school swill. No, this is thick and tastes like heaven, and the café owner will only make it for me because I can talk with him in Spanish. And for you. He says he'll make it for you.'

So she found herself in a tiny upstairs tea room in Turl Street. The Spanish family all thought of some reason to come over to their table one by one and stare at her with interest.

'What have you been telling these poor people?'

He smiled back at her, waiting for her to get the punchline of some joke. She fiddled with the spoon.

'And how is your mother, Ralph?'

'Not so good today. She gets frightful headaches. She's so cheerful and always thinking of me when I go back to the little flat she's rented, but I know she's given up a lot to be here with me. She's missing my stepfather a lot. But his job is back in Madrid, at the bank, so.'

'I'm sure he misses you both too.'

'I think he's quite happy where he is really, quite a cushy number, away from the war, away from the snow. Then today a parcel arrives. The funniest thing. Woollen vests and long johns that he's had made in Madrid. He wrote to say he's worried that I might find it too cold here in the winter.'

'Oh Ralph, I'm sorry, but I can't stay any longer. I have to go. I'm sure your mama is going to be fine, you know. The thing is, it can be lonely in Oxford, but you really have to stop waiting for me outside lectures and so on. You need friends your own age.'

She stood up and slung her bag over her shoulder, but he grabbed at her arm.

'Wait. I get my results in a few days. I don't expect I'll get in, I'm not brainy and stuff like you, but if I do get in will you come out with me?'

'On some kind of date?'

'Yes. No. I don't mind. I'd just like you to come out with me, for dinner.'

Honestly, she'd no idea why she said yes. She was quite frankly nervous about how he would look. Ralph had longish hair that was potentially floppy and arty in the way of a bright young thing, posed and aloof, in a photo by Cecil Beaton, but which always managed to stick out stiffly to one side. His jacket slid off one shoulder in a messy way. He had a long, strong nose. He simply didn't look, well, English.

But she had agreed to go, and now she was taking out the wretched green dress that she and Mary had spent hours sewing on the Singer treadle, ready for the call-up to a New Year's party with Richard. Just looking at it now made her feel sick with something like grief or shame. Yes, that was it, shame.

How naive she'd been. No way back now to that blindly hopeful girl of last term, cycling the roundabout near Magdalen Bridge where the punts clustered under the stone arches. She'd cycled past the shop that sold formal eveningwear, and smiled. Her own dress now hung ready and waiting inside her wardrobe. Richard had mentioned the New Year's ball that was held each year by the Mountfords, old family friends of his who had a pile near Oxford. She'd understood that this year she was going to go with him to the glittering event at Garstang House. She pictured Richard's face when he saw her in the green silk sheath. Another little victory on the quest to be good enough for Richard. Even Richard's mother had to approve of a dress like this.

She could still feel the flush reddening her neck each time she recalled the awful moments of the weekend at Amforth with his mother.

On that second visit with Richard there had been no private, magical dinner in the vast and candlelit dining room, and certainly no secret tryst in the bedroom with the blue silk walls.

It had been early autumn and already cold; the mausoleum of a building sucked all heat towards the ornate plaster ceilings; her room, away at the top of the house, had freezing bed sheets and an icy bathroom.

After a stiffly formal tea with his mother and sisters Alice had gone upstairs to change. Supper was at seven. She dressed, did her hair, twice, pinned a brooch to the ruffles on the neckline of her dress, puffed out the gathers on the sleeves, and then sat and waited, watching the clock. She was too nervous to read. Up in her bedroom on the third floor she could hear no other sounds from the house, and had no idea of what the others were doing. Feeling ready and a little excited she decided to go down ten minutes early. If she was too early she could melt into another room for a while.

She heard the thick noise of raised voices and found a crush of people in the large drawing room that overlooked the park.

'I was just going to send a search party up for you,' said Richard grasping her elbow. 'Papa takes it amiss I'm afraid if people are late, don't you see?'

'But you said seven.'

'And cocktails first. I thought you'd realise.'

But it was a simple misunderstanding. Alice smiled, still felt confident, a strong sense of inner strength that she knew, given time, Richard's people would see and value. After all, all this superficial glamour counted for so little in the real scheme of things.

'And such a very pretty dress,' Richard's mother said carefully when Richard led her over. Alice had glowed at the compliment.

'Alice's people are from Derbyshire,' offered Richard.

'Do you know the Devonshires?' said the woman next to Richard's mother.

'No.'

'Alice's people live in Buxton.'

'Ah.'

'Yes, my father has shoe factories in the area.'

A silence as both women looked at her and smiled. 'How very interesting,' said Richard's mother. 'Richard dear, have you got a drink for your friend?'

He fetched her champagne. It was delicious, the bubbles fizzing as she drank. Two tall and exceptionally slim girls approached.

'So you're Alice,' said the first. The note of surprise in her voice seemed positively rude.

Alice hadn't packed a long dress for dinner. That had been a mistake. She was furious that Richard hadn't warned her. The other girls, friends of Richard's mother, wore long sheaths of bias cut silk that had definitely not been sewn by Maudey's niece from a pattern bought in Dempsey's. They had perfect lipstick and polished hair. She felt the expanses of her nyloned ankles and shins girlish and monstrous. Why had she thought ruffles a good idea?

She left Amforth House wiser. Her accent, her vocabulary, her waist, her frizzy hair, all needed improving; she saw that now. But next time she was invited to Amforth she'd do it all so much better – now that she understood there was another way, the correct way. Sailing along through Oxford on her bike like a questing knight, she'd been humbled but ready for the challenge, happily secure in the knowledge that Richard and she could overcome any obstacle.

She was surprised when Michaelmas term came and went and he stopped speaking of them going to the Mountford's New Year's ball. When she finally plucked up the courage and mentioned it before they went down for Christmas he'd looked surprised. Oh that. Not happening this year, pookums. Not with the war on, he'd told her. And anyway he had to go north to visit a very dull and aged relative. Sorry pookums. There'd be another year, other parties.

When she arrived back after the Christmas break, Richard had already been there for a week, studying hard for exams. He met her at the station and they fell into their old ways of spending every minute they could together. Three weeks after Epiphany, and she was sitting in Christchurch Cathedral where Richard sang each week as a choral scholar. The winter sun was making an effort to penetrate the chill inside the cathedral as Alice listened to Richard's baritone, quite distinct, as the choir sang 'Ave Verum Corpus'. She thought how in Oxford you felt so much closer to God in church, more than she had ever felt in the earnest red-brick services with their plodding hymns in their suburban church. And Richard had agreed with her, that when you both feel closer to God, then you feel so much closer to each other. There was a smell of damp stone, tinged with wine. The Bishop of Oxford was raising his arms before the altar.

'The Lord be with you,' he announced in a deeply polite voice.

'And with thy spirit,' came the echoing murmur from the congregation. The organ boomed into the closing hymn and Alice felt a wave of dizziness and felt herself slipping down towards the floor.

When she came round Richard was sitting next to her as she lay on the bench at the back of the church.

'How long have you been fasting this time?'

'Just for a few days.'

'You are a stupid old thing.'

Yes, she thought, but getting thinner, getting better. When she danced with Richard in her slip of a gown she would be as lithe and thin as that girl in the blue satin sheath at Amforth.

'Come on,' he said, standing up irritably.

Richard's room was hot and the air smelled of unaired bed. The scout did not come in on Sundays. She opened the window, pulled his sheets straight. He made her some sweet tea then he said, 'Why don't you lie down for a bit?'

He came and lay down beside her and they started the same game that they always played with passion, with her belatedly well-defined rules as to which garments could come off and which not. But after a while he sat up and looked at his watch.

'Look, I've got a really dull drinks thing to go to with a fusty old tutor. You have a nap. I'll be back in an hour or so. We'll go to lunch.'

'I'm fine. I'll come with you.'

'No, really, it's ever so dull, and you'd have no one to talk to. It's just my tutors drinking sherry. Really, not your thing.'

He was gone a long time. She was so hungry – and bored. She slid open the cupboard door, his neat row of shirts, his jackets, his cricket jumpers. On a shelf at the bottom of the cupboard there was a box of pink and yellow candies, half of them eaten. A gold box with a ribbon. It was a girl's box of sweets. The sort a man might buy for a girl for a special occasion – and then she eats half of them right away because she's greedy. Alice felt her heart knocking hard inside her ribs. Something made her pull open the little drawer by his bedside and there they were, a pile of little black and white photographs; Richard at a ball in some college, with a girl who was smiling and laughing and waving around a glass of champagne; Richard and the girl kissing and in the corner of the picture a set of fuzzy lights like alien spaceships in a matinee film, or falling stars. She stared at the pictures for a long time, and it slowly dawned on her that she was holding actual pictures of Richard going to an actual ball with an actual girl who was definitely not called Alice. Behind them, a huge Christmas tree at the end of a long ballroom filled with blurred people. The party at Garstang House.

She looked out of the window. Oxford was still there, the delicate towers and spires scissored against the sky, and she watched all the glamour fade from the buildings as if the day was already ending, even though it was barely two o'clock.

When he came back she gave him the photos.

He let out a high giggle and then held out his arms to her.

'I'm sorry, pookums. Ma and Celia insisted. I couldn't say no.'

She saw then how easy his life was, how he fell into things, how he would happily love her, and love any number of people besides, and it would all be easy.

She backed away, and heard herself running down the stone steps of his staircase.

★ ★

She had no idea where they were going, except that it would involve dinner. The dress was probably too much, but she was glad to have a chance to get some use from the thing.

As soon as the girls in her lodgings had heard that Alice was going to wear that dress they wanted to help her do her hair, lend her silver platform shoes and an evening wrap. Even the landlady had got all misty eyed and excited. She had insisted that Alice risk sidling into her stuffy bedroom to see herself in the wardrobe mirror.

The dress was beautiful.

She thought, Richard and all his set, they could go and jump in his wretched lake.

The doorbell rang.

'Ooh la di da,' the landlady said, peering through her bedroom blackout curtains. 'He's here and he's come in a taxi, milady.'

Ralph took her to dinner at the Randolph Hotel. He had a linen suit that was probably the thing in Spain, and looked almost exotically handsome. He pulled out her chair and helped her sit down. Then he opened an enormous menu and ordered for both of them, in French. He even studied the wine list carefully and was quite sure they should have a white burgundy.

'I can't believe you booked a table at the Randolph. It's outrageous. And when did you learn about ordering wine?'

The restaurant was full now; servicemen in uniforms, women in evening frocks, couples leaning close, perhaps saying goodbye at the end of a leave, older couples, grand and silent and carefully dressed.

'It doesn't seem fair, does it, that just because people have money they can come and dine out in a place like this every night and never have to produce any ration books. Not that I mind being forced to spend the evening in style, darling. One could quite get used to it.'

'Well, a place like this suits you. You're the loveliest girl here.'

'Gosh, and he's charming too. But we should make a toast, to you. Basil said you aced Responsions. You got in, with distinction. Well done you.'

'Sadly I'll only have a few terms here at Oxford, and then I'll get my call-up papers. But it makes you realise there's no time to waste on stuff that doesn't matter. So you see, I want to make it all count.'

'A man in a hurry.'

The piano music stopped. A small band of musicians started playing dance music. She noticed that Ralph had become a bit agitated, pleating his napkin and scratching at his head.

'Look here,' he said, 'I don't suppose you'd like to dance? With me, I mean.'

So because he looked so earnest, and because he seemed to want so badly for her to say yes, she stood up, gave him a curtsy. He took her hand and led her to the area of parquet flooring in front of the musicians. She was aware that she looked the part in her outrageous green evening gown that left her shoulders bare, clung over her hips. He held her tentatively in a waltz embrace, did an odd step forward that made them both stumble. Then he got flustered, started again, and with a lunge he began leading her round the little dance floor.

They circled carefully at first, then with more confidence. She realised that he was leading. She began to feel the push of his steps, carrying her a little further than she expected each time, the slight, effortless lift in her body from the compact strength in his torso, following the melody of the music.

And she thought, This feels right; and while she was thinking about how that was such an odd thought, he gathered her up, that was the word for it, gathered her up, and kissed her.

This was nothing like the elegant kissing practice she and Richard had gone in for. This was a revelation, elemental – a sudden response that shocked her.

The music stopped. They stepped apart. She felt small, and suddenly fragile. Disconcerted by the impression of his mouth on hers, she turned her face away to regain some composure and place herself back in charge of things. He took her hand in his fingers; they felt hot and crackling with electricity. He led her back to their table.

By the time she was seated, sipping a glass of cold water, she was resolved not to let things slide into such silliness again.

'I'm sorry. I hope you don't mind,' he said.

She patted his hand. 'You are very sweet, Ralph, but—'

'Wait. Please don't start telling me I'm so young and all that guff. I'm deadly serious, and I know exactly what I want. Alice, I already know I want to marry you.'

Shocked, she blurted out a laugh.

'I know there won't be anyone else for me, Alice. From the moment I saw you in the garden at your parents', the wind ruffling your hair, and you so small and so fierce, I was done for. You're the one. Alice, will you? Will you marry me?'

'You can't just propose at the drop of a hat, because you danced with someone, because of one kiss. Do you even have a ring, Ralph?'

'No, there's no ring, yet, but . . .'

'You see then, you're not really serious.'

'I'm very serious.'

'Maybe we should go.'

'Please don't.'

'I'm sorry, Ralph. I think that's enough this evening.'

He looked stricken with unhappiness. He seemed so much like a boy that she wanted desperately to hug him, just to see him happy again. For a moment she thought, But that's why I love him, because he's so unguarded; because he's so completely himself.

A mad and dizzy moment when she saw how she could leap into a different life, she could say yes. Yes, of course she'd marry him: she was completely in love with him.

But that was ridiculous. How could she possibly ever love Ralph?

It was as if all the stuffy Victorian uncles – who she so despised for their petty litanies of self-importance and their bowler hats and stiff suits – had now crowded round their table in a half-circle; as if Richard's mother were there whispering in her ear, making her look at Ralph and see that he wouldn't do; he wasn't really quite the thing, not really English enough somehow. And the thought of having to bestow all that civilisation on him, and the fear of what might happen if she could not get him safely inside the pale of right opinions, left her feeling too exhausted.

He fetched her coat from the lobby, helped her into it. Silent and looking stunned, Ralph found a taxi and took her back to Iffley Road.

They stood awkwardly on the dark pavement.

'Ralph, I'm sorry. I do enjoy your company, and I really wish you all the best with you going off to who knows where with the army, but really it's time to stop this.'

She held out her hand. 'Goodbye, dear Ralph.'

He didn't take it. 'I am right, Alice. I absolutely know; you are the one.'

She sighed. 'I'm trying, I'm really trying, Ralph, to be sweet about this, but it's only fair I should tell you. I know I'm not in love with you, Ralph. You have to wait for someone who does love you, and Ralph dear, I'm sorry, but I'm not her.'

★ ★

Ralph waited on the pavement until she had gone into the house and shut the door. A blur of movement behind the glass panel as she took off her coat, pulled across the blackout curtain.

A light drizzle was coming down, making the linen fabric of his suit relax with dampness. He turned up his collar and began the long walk back to his lodgings on the other side of town.

He only hoped that Mama would have gone to bed and not be waiting up with cocoa, anxious to hear every detail of the last few hours spent without her.

CHAPTER 11

Fourwinds, 1981

Peter got out of bed, pulled on a dressing gown and quietly let himself out into the corridor. The watch by his bed said seven. Ralph would have left to fetch Nicky by now.

He walked along the corridor and stood outside Sarah's door, head bowed, listening. Not a sound. He was glad she was still sleeping. Then he thought of the sedative she'd been given and he began to feel uneasy. He knocked gently but there was no reply. He pushed the door open a little way. The bed was ruffled and empty. He called her name as he walked in, but she wasn't in the room. By the bed was a glass of water. The white pill lay untouched beside it.

At that moment he recalled the sound of a door opening and closing somewhere in the house as he had fallen asleep – and he knew that she was gone.

A thudding, empty space where his heart should be, he searched through the house swiftly, hoping to find her curled at the end of a sofa, sleeping, or in the kitchen with a coffee. She was nowhere. He ran outside and walked rapidly through the gardens, checked inside the interior of the marquee that held nothing but the cold, grey light. A thought occurred to him and he ran back into the house. He looked in the hallway. Her jacket and bag were gone.

Where was she? He stood, breathless and dizzy. He held on to the door frame for a moment. He heard the heavy crackle of a car in the driveway, doors slamming.

Ralph was back. Nicky.

The front door opened and Nicky came in, his face white and drained.

'Is she upstairs still?'

The boy began taking the stairs, two at a time.

'Nicky, don't.'

He didn't pause.

'Nicky! She's not here.'

He stopped dead. Turned.

'What do you mean? Where is she then?'

'This morning, before we woke up. Just before dawn. I think she might have left. I can't find her anywhere.'

Nicky shot him an angry, bewildered look, then ran up to check her room. Patricia passed him coming down the stairs, asking Peter where Sarah was. Did he know she wasn't in her room?

After a further search of the house, all of them taking part, Nicky went up to the village and looked for her; no sign of her.

They convened in the kitchen, Nicky distraught. 'Well, where can she be? Tell me what happened. Tell me exactly what happened.'

'We don't know, Nicky,' said Alice. 'She was fine, and then suddenly she wasn't. She lost her voice. We called the doctor. She slept. And then this morning we got up and, well, now this.'

'It doesn't make any sense. You're not making any sense. Start from the beginning, Mum.' He was waving his hands, chopping the air into blocks. His auburn hair was tousled and on end, the blue tinge that could make his lips violet hued was marked now. 'What happened? What did you say to her? Mum?'

'Nicky! I didn't say anything.'

Peter broke in. 'It must be almost six hours since I heard the door closing, and I think that's when she left, last night. If only I'd got up. But what is really worrying at this moment is why she wouldn't have phoned by now, let us know something.' Peter swallowed, looked over at his wife. 'Perhaps we should call the police?'

Patricia began to cry.

The doorbell sounded. Nicky leapt up to answer it. Alice followed, the others gathering in the doorway behind them. It was Barbara with the post, a handful of wedding cards for Nicky and Sarah.

Barbara looked gleeful. 'Maureen says she's bringing the cake round tomorrow morning. She's really done a lovely job. And I'll come by with the others from the village to help with the flowers in church first thing on the big day. And Sarah was up bright and early this morning. Saw her getting on the first bus to Stanford. Off to town to get last-minute things I expect. It never ends with a wedding, does it?'

'The first bus? What time was that?' said Patricia.

'Oh, about six. I saw her from the window. With the birds waking me up I can never get back to sleep on summer mornings, and I thought, Well, there's Sarah, up and about already. I must say she's a keen one.'

Alice waited till Barbara was crunching away up the gravel, waved to her as she went and then shut the door.

Nicky was already gathering up the car keys. 'I'm going into Stanford to look for her.'

'I'll come with you,' said Peter. 'We can both look.'

'Wait.' It was Alice speaking. 'What are we going to do, all the people planning to turn up for a wedding in forty-eight hours?'

A silence. No one wanted to think about it, let alone make a decision.

'Let's give it a little longer,' said Ralph.

Alice pressed her lips together.

As they left, Nicky wound down the car window and called out,

'I'll ring you from Stanford, in case she's called while I'm gone. You'll listen out for the phone, yes?'

The car moved away up the drive, turned into the village. Alice caught a glimpse of Peter's face through the side window and his set and anxious expression. For a moment she saw another day, a much younger Peter, a white face in the back window as the car pulled away, and she felt the shape of old regrets, stored somewhere under her breastbone.

She shouldn't have given up so easily.

CHAPTER 12

Buxton, 1940

Peter wheeled his bike round the back of the house and put it away in the shed. In the kitchen he got a drink of cold water from the tap. He left his books lying on the kitchen table and ran upstairs to hang his uniform on a coat hanger on the back of the door, and then changed into the shorts and shirt that he wore to help Maudey with the chores, rolling up his sleeves. It was stuffy up there under the eaves after a day of unusually warm spring weather. He opened the casement window. Cooler air and birdsong came in from the garden – and music.

Looking over to the top lawn he saw a figure spread out on a rug. Alice was back from Oxford. She was lying on her front, propped up on her elbows, reading a book. She wore a pretty, flowered dress and a cardigan. Next to her was the wind-up gramophone from the drawing room. Her feet were rubbing together in the air as Beethoven sounded out across the lawn – a little swell of pride because he knew the name of the music now.

He went to the sink and splashed cold water on his face, looked in the spotted mirror that hung on a string. He combed his hair, wetting it down, neat and shiny.

By the time he got downstairs Peter realised that he desperately wanted to do the gardening that Maudey had had in mind for him to do for the past week. So far he had sidestepped it with other tasks around the kitchen; but now he really wanted to get out and begin, starting perhaps with the beds in the top terrace.

Maudey had a bowl full of three small lettuces from the greenhouse.

'Be a good lad and wash those out for me, Peter. And you can pat them dry on that tea towel.'

Then there was the dining table to set, potatoes had to be peeled. Maudey was standing over the kitchen table puzzling over her recipe for ham and chicken pie. 'I don't know how I'm supposed to make a nice pie for tonight, with not a shred of ham and precious little chicken. Ah well, there's lots worse off than us. It's a blessing Mr Hanbury has so many friends who want to give him presents.' She picked up an egg and cracked it into a bowl. 'And I don't know what it is in those boxes that come from America, but it's not dried eggs like it says on the cover, I can tell you that.'

Peter left Maudey to her problems with the pie and fetched the trowel and trug from the garden shed. He decided not to put on the hessian apron. Far too hot.

He began digging at the dry dirt round the roses where feeble green weeds had started to appear. Alice turned her head but didn't call out her usual hello.

The last time she had left for Oxford Alice had shown him a shelf in her bookcase where she had collected together the books he should read while she was away: *David Copperfield, Great Expectations, Moby Dick, The Complete Works of Shakespeare*. Peter couldn't wait to tell her that he had read all of them, well, not all of the Shakespeare, but she looked too preoccupied, tapping her foot in the warm air in a way that seemed irritable. The chipping noise of the trowel made her glance over and frown as the music reached the third movement, the bit he liked best. He was dying to tell her that he knew the name of the one she was listening to now; he had sat in the school room and listened to a record of Beethoven's 'Pastoral', trying to identify the feelings that swept over him in waves – or trying sometimes to feel a little more noble in the long sleepy passages where the feeling he identified was very like boredom. In the evening, doing his homework at the kitchen table, he liked to leave the door open so that he could hear the Radio Three broadcasts that Mrs Hanbury listened to in the drawing room.

He'd popped into Alice's room to change his book quite often. He felt like a thief each time, even though her instructions to borrow the books had been clear. He knew that if he were caught he'd be in trouble; they'd forget what Alice had said. He would stand carefully on the Chinese silk rug by her bed, reading the book spines, easing one out reverently, putting it back, repeating the process several times with various books, taking a long time to make his choice.

The smell of the room would assert its presence, faded perfume and aired cotton and something a bit sad and musty. He couldn't help glancing around. He knew by heart every item on her dressing table, the glass candlesticks, the china rabbit in a blue coat, the silver hairbrush set on the glass top of the table, the curtain of flowered material where the stool was pushed against the cloth. He liked to admire the swirly reproduction of trees by Van Gogh – he'd seen the picture in a book of prints in the school library.

He hacked down round an embedded dandelion root. Alice had been turning the pages of her book abruptly, flicking her foot faster. Now she glanced over at him and frowned again. Peter got up and carried away his trug filled with weeds.

Over the next few days there was still no opportunity to ask Alice all the questions he had about her books. Alice seemed to have returned home caught in a black mood, angry and distant. Carrying the breakfast through to the table one morning, Peter found Alice explaining to her mother why the ballet – her father had taken them to see *Coppélia* in Manchester as a treat – had in fact been lacking in many ways. Her mother burst into tears as he set the plate in front of Alice and said she didn't know why Alice always had to find fault with everything.

'Honestly, Mummy,' Alice insisted. 'If one can't give a perfectly sensible and intelligent critique.'

But Mrs Hanbury wasn't listening; she said that since Alice had been at Oxford, none of them were clever enough any more and she was always having to be horrid about something. Mrs Hanbury left her kipper unfinished to go upstairs and lie down.

Alice sat at the table, crossly buttering toast with a scraping sound until she let the butter knife fall with a clatter on her plate, saying, 'Oh, but she always manages to make me feel so wretched,' to no one in particular, or Peter perhaps. She left with arms folded across her chest to follow her mother upstairs.

It took Peter a couple of days to understand that a disaster had happened. Richard had dropped Alice.

Peter carried the tea tray into the drawing room and Mrs Hanbury smiled a thank you. Not particularly quickly, but very carefully, Peter set the tea things out on the table.

'Do pour, Peter. Thank you, dear.'

Mrs Hanbury took a sock from the basket of mending by her chair and spread the wool out with her hand to show a gaping hole. 'It's not as if they're an especially grand family really. Nothing like the Devonshires. I hear his money was from Mustard.'

'Oh Mummy, can't you leave that mending for Maudey to do? Really.'

'But it's hardly fair on Maudey, darling, when she has to spend so much time queuing and it's quite impossible to find extra staff to help out now. With a war on, one would need to consider oneself terribly grand to be above darning a sock and spend all day doing needlepoint. She sniffed, no doubt remembering how Alice had praised Richard's mother's needlepoint cushions. 'Here, darling, if we can match the colour then these cotton stockings could be mended quite nicely. So hard to get new ones.'

With a look of distaste Alice slid her hand inside some dun-coloured hosiery and spread the hole in the toe with her fingers. She took the needle and thread from her mother and began to stitch angrily, her fair hair hiding her face as she bent over her task. Some dark drops fell on the cotton. Peter was horrified to realise that Alice was crying. Who was this Richard? He felt sure, if he were to appear right now, he could lay him out with a right hook. He might be skinny, but he'd stood up for Kitty before now when a boy was calling her names in the street.

He carried the empty tray out of the room, pausing quietly outside the door, as if he should stand guard in the hallway. At least Alice would cheer up once he told her how he'd read tons of her books. 'Oh Peter,' she might say, 'I knew you had it in you. Not all men are like Richard,' she'd say, happy and grateful.

He heard nose-blowing. Cooing from Mrs Hanbury. 'I don't know what I'm crying about, Mummy. I don't even care about Richard any more. I just feel so angry, looking such a fool.'

'I'm sure you've met lots of nice men in Oxford. Someone else who's special in some way?'

'No, Mummy. And honestly, that's not why I'm at Oxford. Anyway, anyone half decent has already been called up.'

'Oh darling, the right person will come along. You'll see. One has to wait for these things.'

Peter carried the empty tray back to the kitchen, holding it out in front of him as if it held a scroll with his entire future written on it. When he grew up he was going to look after Alice; nothing would stop him becoming worthy of the task.

When he went back later to collect the cups and cold teapot, it was just Alice in the room. She had pink patches on her cheeks.

She had evidently decided to work through the whole basket of mending.

Now would be a good time to speak.

'Read all them books, miss, on the shelf.'

She flinched and tutted. Sucked her finger where the needle had jabbed it. 'Gosh. All of them? You do read a lot, Peter. Oh and leave the plate.' There were a couple of Rich Tea biscuits still left on it. She took a snuffly bite at one of them, carried on stabbing the darning and chewing the biscuit mournfully. She sighed. 'And look, well done. It's splendid of you, really it is. I'm sorry I'm in such a rotten stew just now.'

If that Richard ever turned up he'd definitely thump him, good and proper.

★ ★

Perhaps it was the spring weather blowing in over the countryside beyond the garden fence, or the effect of being home once more, but Alice slowly cheered up. And she began to take an interest in Peter again, giving him a whole new list of books to get through.

One morning she came into the kitchen with her hands clasped and a smile on her face.

'Buxton theatre's opened again,' she announced.

'Oh aye,' said Maudey. 'Maybe they'll open the Picture Palace up now. I'd love to see that film again, with Fred Astaire. He's got lovely feet.'

'Well, yes, but the thing is, Peter, we're going to take you to see *Swan Lake*.'

'If you like that sort of thing,' said Maudey, sounding a bit peeved that no one had asked her.

'Obviously, it's only a provincial company, but it will be such a good experience for you. Have you ever seen a ballet before?'

Peter shook his head.

'Well then. Splendid. We'll leave at seven.'

★ ★

They sat in the stalls. Alice passed him a pair of tiny pearl binoculars so he could see the dancers' white powdered faces; although they were in fact close enough to hear the click, click of the satin shoes on the stage floor. He tried hard to look out for the things that the dancers were doing wrong, as Alice did, but to him it all seemed equally unlikely and wonderful: the sad girls dressed in white veils for skirts; the man who leapt as high as the music. After taking a long time to die the swan lay very still on the stage floor, and once they were sure she wasn't going to move again the audience burst into applause.

It was hard to imagine himself almost a year ago, that faraway summer when he had arrived at the Hanburys' and found them all in the garden, their quick banter and their easy ways with knowing all about how things were done in life. He was a good few inches taller now, shot up almost beyond recognition.

'A right good-looking lad,' Maudey had declared, 'and a good boy too,' as he helped out around the kitchen. 'If I'd ever been blessed with a boy of my own, Peter, a son like you would have done me proud.'

Back then he hadn't yet started at the grammar. Now he was almost always top of the class there. He could conjugate French verbs. Knew pages of Latin words. He had been shown how to use a Bunsen burner. Admittedly he only went to school for half-days since the building was shared by an evacuated school from Salford, and three afternoons out of five they dug for victory in the school playing fields, rows of turnips and cabbages where there'd once been games of rugby. But he seemed to have travelled miles away from the Peter Donaghue with the unashamed Manchester accent and the shorn-off hair.

All through that first winter at the Hanburys' he'd longed and longed to be back with Ma and with Bill. When he'd gone home at Christmas Ma had been proud of him, and a little deferential, as if he were a too-bright lamp, showing up the shabbiness in the room. He saw the defects there now, the limitations in their lives, and there was no way to go back and undo that sadness.

He and Bill were too old to go out in the market square and collect beer bottle tops to fire at each other. Bill had a blue overall that he wore to the tool factory where he was now doing his apprenticeship. He came home and looked at an old newspaper while Peter sat and waited for him to speak. No sign of Dad. Finally Bill had shut the paper and said, 'Shall us go then and get him home?' to Peter.

Peter had followed Bill though a wet sleet to the Queen Alexandra where the tall windows shone with light, frosted and etched with beautiful swirls and garlands. Once through the door they were embraced by a warm din of masculine noise; a smell of malt beer, of bitter tobacco and wet coats. Behind the mahogany serving bar mirrored shelves glinted with bottles and tipsy strands of Christmas tinsel; coloured paper chains hung from the ceiling. Dad had a pint and an audience, so it took them half an hour to get him to come home for Christmas dinner.

Ma, he saw, was thinner than ever, her face carved sharply by the thing that made her wheeze and have to sit down. He wanted to stay home and make sure she was all right. Cried when Kitty hugged him, said she'd take care of Ma for him. And Doris was getting married soon; he'd be home for the wedding, eh?

But once he was back with Maudey in the bright kitchen with the full pantry and the Christmas cake that she'd saved for him, back again in the Hanburys' world, then his life in 167 Albert Terrace had begun to fade into another world. When he talked about walking home after school he saw the Hanburys' house.

Summer came in and Alice was home once more. Her brothers were also back from boarding school and Peter was called on to make up sets for doubles. Proud to be able to return a ball, to own white shorts from his school PE kit, he carried the cotton bag with the lemon barley and the stack of Bakelite beakers. As they sat in the shade of sycamore trees, resting their backs against the wire netting fence after a fierce game, Alice's shins were bare in ankle socks and pumps. Wiping sweat from her top lip she said, 'There's no reason why you shouldn't think of university one day, Peter. I mean why not? Honestly, you're getting such good exam results, better than these two stinkers ever got – and they'll go to university.'

'Not me,' said Phillip. 'I'm sticking with the army once I'm called up. Had enough of schoolrooms.'

'At least Peter isn't a philistine. Imagine you're going to college, Peter. What would you study?'

'Everything, miss. I want to know everything.'

Alice looked immensely pleased.

It was so hot that Alice begged Mr Hanbury to let her take the car and she drove the boys to a place in the Dove River where they could swim. Turquoise dragonflies hovered over the dark green water; long skeins of green weed flowed in the currents like a giant's hair. Alice stood at the edge of the water in a white bathing suit. She tucked her hair under a white bathing cap that made her look like an otter and adjusted the strap under her chin. Shivering, she walked into the water up to her waist and then let herself float out to a pool where the water eddied into a calm stillness. She flipped over like a fish.

Peter watched her white limbs disappear, then appear again, shivers running down his arms. He'd put on one of the boys' old costumes but stayed paddling at the shallow edge, where the clear water ran over the pebbles, nothing but moving light and shadows.

Wearing thick bathing suits with straps that came over their shoulders, the boys ploughed in, churning up the water, splashing each other and Alice, sending showers of drops over Peter, making him risk going deeper to splash them back until he found he was managing a passable sort of doggy paddle, keeping afloat with them.

He didn't think he had ever had a more perfect day. When they got back to the cool of the house Peter headed for the kitchen to get a drink of water from the tap.

'Letter for you, lad,' said Maudey, nodding at the kitchen table.

He saw his ma's neat copperplate handwriting on the front, the writing she'd won prizes for in school. His chest bumped with happiness. They'd not been able to afford for him to take the train back for Doris's wedding and sometimes, in his lonelier moments, he had felt a lowness of spirits, as if floating between worlds. At last here was a letter.

He took it up to his room, opened it to a chorus of sparrows chirping in the larch near the house. Ma was coming to see him; in a couple of weeks' time she'd be here. He almost bounced on the bed like a boy. He'd have so much to show her. And Maudey would magic up a cake and there'd be sandwiches with a lace cloth in the drawing room, and – a slight niggle in his stomach when he thought of Ma's best hat. It had been her best hat for a long time and was a bit defeated-looking. And there was the coat that had been in and out of the pawnshop. It drooped and had a big seam across the middle as if it had once been two different coats, the raggedy wide fur collar she wore for best, even in hot weather. No, she wouldn't wear the coat, surely not in this heat. She'd put on her dress with the brooch at the neck perhaps to visit the Hanburys. And what of the hanky that she always had to discreetly spit into after a coughing fit? Feeling disloyal he pushed those worries away.

He was going to show her all his exercise books upstairs, the writing almost as neat as hers now. When he'd told her at Christmas that he was doing well at the grammar she'd looked that proud and satisfied. Wet-eyed.

'The teachers are a terror, I bet. I remember what it was like,' and she admitted that when she was a girl she could read Virgil in Latin, that she could write equations in chemistry. A far-off ghost of a smile on her face that was soon gone as Kitty screamed that the cat was clawing at the precious Christmas chicken.

Well, he'd get her a chicken from the farm, a right big one, like Maudey did for the Hanburys. You didn't always have to have the ration points. He'd pay for it with his potato-picking money that Maudey was keeping for him so one day he could get a bike. Ma could take the chicken home for Bill and for all of them. And for Dad.

When he'd told Dad he'd passed all his exams at the grammar, his dad's cloudy eyes had looked over Peter's head. In his worn suit, big over a caved-in chest, Dad had swelled up, stood higher, a man with no need to go to any grammar – and with no need for his son to look down on him – that was for sure.

A couple of weeks after the letter and everything was ready for Ma's visit. Maudey had baked a cake, done him proud. He ran home from school, burst into the kitchen, but it was Dad sitting at the kitchen table with Maudey, his trilby on the table. His dad was the last person he'd expected to see sitting there. He swelled with gladness, proud. His dad had travelled all the way out to see him.

'Hello, Dad.'

'Are you well there, Peter?'

Maudey glanced over at him. She looked worried, upset. Something wrong.

'Grand I am, Dad. And yourself?'

His dad looked down. The kitchen door opened. It was Mr Hanbury. Dad got up, standing to attention. They shook hands for a long time.

'I heard from Alice,' Mr Hanbury said. 'I'm so sorry. Why don't you come through to the drawing room?'

Peter followed the men through to the big front room. In the daytime it had a cold feel, looking out onto the dull side gardens. The two men stood in front of the unlit fire and Mr Hanbury took out his gold cigarette case from the folds of his suit jacket. He offered one to Dad.

Dad looked small next to Mr Hanbury, and worn-down looking. His eyes always had a sunk-in look from the gas injury back in the war, and recently his jaw had shrunk after he'd had his teeth pulled. His suit sleeves moulded to the shape of his bent elbows; the brown cloth looked rusted in the daylight.

Mr Hanbury was elegant in navy cloth cut to fold neatly round his tall shape, his black hair shining like it had been done with boot blacking and given a good polish. But Dad stood tall, seemed unaware of being anything but Mr Hanbury's equal. Excited even, to be able to show how he could hold his own in a room like this, next to a Mr Hanbury.

'I'm very sorry for your loss,' Mr Hanbury said. 'Peter is taking it very manfully.'

'I've yet to tell him the news, Mr Hanbury.' He turned to Peter. He swallowed and looked stricken. 'Lad, I've something to tell you about your mother. She's in a better place now.'

'You mean she's in the sanatorium again?'

'No, lad, you're not listening to me. She's passed away, Peter. Your ma died last week.'

Mr Hanbury slipped out. Squeezed Peter's shoulder as he went.

Peter tried to make sense of it. Heard himself wail. There was

Maudey. She sat him in an armchair. He curled up and hid his face in his arm while he wept. Someone put brandy to his lips. Peter took a gulp at the hot medicinal taste, and it made him feel distant and empty and the room moved away. Maudey put a cool hand on his forehead, stroked his hair back. Dad stood by the fireplace and waited for Peter's weeping to slow to a hiccup. He rose up and down on his toes, looking around the room. Maudey creaked up off her knees. She said to come by the kitchen and she'd make them tea.

Peter sat with his head on his arms on the kitchen table. His tea went cold. Maudey moved around quietly and Dad picked up a paper from the side. Peter could hear the pages turning slowly, as if Dad was trying to be quiet.

'Maybe outside for some fresh air would be good right now,' Maudey suggested.

'Aye, it's nice round here. Why don't we go for a walk, lad, like she said?'

Out in the sun Peter shivered, his face cold and wet. He rubbed his face with his hands to dry it, then followed Dad up the lane. Dad whistled under his breath, walked on ahead with his hands behind his back, approving of the tall banks of laurel hedges with his cloudy eyes, sniffing the clean air.

'Am I going home with you now, Dad?'

He turned. Seemed surprised to see Peter still there.

'Best you stay here.'

'But her funeral.'

'Funeral's done. No, lad, you're best here. Nothing to do for her now.'

'Dad, I don't have a picture of Ma. Can I have a picture of her, Dad?'

'I've only got the one, Peter. Only one we ever had took.'

He stopped and took out his cracked wallet, frayed to canvas at the edges. He slid out a small brown snap. Him and Ma in front of a church. She was young and shining. She had her head bent under a cloche hat and was holding a small bunch of lilies of the valley. She looked away to one side, shy, like she was keeping a secret that made her smile. Dad was standing small and foursquare, legs apart and beaming with a smile to light up all Manchester.

'If you'd but seen her then, Peter. She were best-looking nurse in all the hospital, that's the truth. And clever. Clever in the way you are. Here. You have this.'

'But don't you want it?'

'You have it. It's yours now to keep.'

Peter stared at Ma, the picture blurring over. Then he put it in his pocket carefully. He ran to catch up with Dad who was whistling a tune that sounded sad. He knew the words: 'Let Me Call You Sweetheart'.

After more of Maudey's tea Dad was gone, restored for the journey back, he said, by her bread and butter and cake.

Coming in from waving Dad off he found Alice in the hallway, going back to college early. Her bags were packed and waiting there by the door.

'Oh Peter, I heard. I'm so terribly, terribly sorry.' She leaned in and hugged him. 'We'll look after you, Peter dear. Study hard for me. We're both going to be so busy reading and writing essays. Yes?'

He swallowed, nodded.

Mr Hanbury was calling her from the car.

★ ★

That autumn term he came top in all his exams. He would be a doctor, or a judge, or a vicar. Alice posted him books from a shop in Oxford, with his name written in the front in her very best handwriting.

CHAPTER 13

Buxton, 1940

Peter was going home for Christmas once again – a pang of loss when he remembered that Ma wouldn't be there. But he was longing to see Bill and Kitty; and Dad, when the mood took him, could be matey and funny. With the first couple of drinks in him Dad was still good at stirring up fun. Later it was best to let him be.

Maudey had packed a small cardboard suitcase of clean clothes and fitted in a boiled fruitcake, a jar of damson jam and a greaseproof packet of sandwiches. He was to take the train by himself to Manchester and someone from home would be there to meet him.

'It's a shame you couldn't be here with us for Christmas. I'll be doing dinner for my brother over in the dale. You could've spent the day over there with us.'

'Won't you be here with the Hanburys?'

'I don't live here all the time you know, Peter. I do have a home to go to, over with my brother in Baxendale. Mrs Hanbury makes a big thing of how she does the Christmas dinner, once I've set it all ready for her, but it'll be me who's back here on Boxing Day to clear it all up, right enough. Well, I've put in sandwiches for the train and there's your spare jumper. Aye, I'll miss you while you're away, that I will.'

She gave him a hug that smelled of flour and baking. Since Ma had passed way Maudey had been almost tender with Peter, keeping an eye out for all the little things, if he was hungry or needing his clothes mended, money for something at school. They played cards at the kitchen table in the evening, long games of Gin Rummy, listening to the old set that had been demoted to the kitchen when the new radio was delivered to the drawing room. Maudey liked the big bands and Vera Lynn's hopeful, teary-eyed songs. But she let Peter tune it to the Radio Three concerts while he was doing his homework at the kitchen table. She stood and looked at the radio when he told her to listen to this bit – no, really listen, Maudey – in the middle of a Mozart symphony. Wiping her hands on a tea towel she would stand and wait to get on with something useful. She was so familiar to him now, her soft creased face and grey hair wound back in a bun with wisps of hair curling up in the damp warmth of the scullery; her shapeless pinny with crossover straps and her big red hands with cracked skin round the nails. She would have been a good mum. He was sorry for her: there'd never been a Mr Maudey. Sometimes he was aware of playing a role, standing in for a boy she might have had, in a different life.

★ ★

It was cold on the train. The soldier on the opposite seat was bundled up in a greatcoat. Using his canvas kit bag as a bolster to sleep against, he took off his boots and stretched out along the bench.

At lunchtime the train stopped. The soldier produced chocolate and Peter shared his egg sandwiches and gnarled farm apples from Maudey's cellar store.

'We'll miss Christmas Day at this rate,' the soldier said, as a joke. He went off to find a guard. He came back blustering with anger.

'Going the bloody wrong direction.'

Peter looked at him, alarmed.

'I've only got a two day pass and it looks like one of them's going to be on this effing train.'

With a jolt the train pulled taut and began to move, slowly, stopping in the middle of nowhere, then starting again for a little way. People walked up and down the corridor trying to find out what was going on. It was getting colder. His hands numb. The winter afternoon was starting to turn dark. The dim blue light bulb came on and made the face of the soldier in his compartment look unearthly. Wrapping his coat round like a blanket the soldier huddled back in the corner of the carriage and looked at photographs of his family. Showed them to Peter, a wife with wavy black hair and a baby girl.

He went off to find why they had stopped again. 'Happen we've been delayed because Liverpool got hit last night. Got hit hard, poor buggers,' he said.

It was dark when the train passed Crewe. Searchlights stretched for miles into the sky above the Cheshire plain. Barrage balloons like grazing elephants in the sky. In the distance a strange red dawn over the horizon.

'Ayup,' said the soldier. 'That don't look right.'

As the train drew closer they saw the black shapes of a long townscape spread out along the horizon. Above it the underside of the clouds reflected an eerie red light, their forms sharply defined like a vast, inverted landscape.

'Is that Liverpool?' said Peter, awed and scared by this vision of a world upside down.

'That's bloody Manchester.' The soldier opened the window and craned his head outside.

The train crept into Manchester Piccadilly, an acrid smell of smoke, the din of sirens and clanging ambulance bells. Across the far side of the station the roof had come down in a twisted mess of girders.

Peter got off the train and looked up and down the platform for Dad or perhaps John, but there was no one there. Underfoot the platform crunched with broken glass. Hard to know who to ask, everyone rushing away fast. There was nothing for it but to walk back to the house. It was maybe two miles; he'd done it before.

Outside the station the front of the grand bank building was on fire, a black cut-out with the windows filled with roaring flames. He had to walk past it to go down the main road and kept as far back as he could but the heat made his face prickle. A top corner of the edifice tipped over and crumpled. It fell, exploding on the ground, sending up billowing waves of smoke and black dust. The ARP warden yelled for everyone to get back.

Peter backtracked down a side street in the red darkness and made his way out onto a wider road, picking his way across tarmac rippled into crests of cracked asphalt and rubble. Above him black plumes of smoke boiled up through a sagging net of tramlines.

The end of the road was glowing with fires. He came out on a main road of high buildings filled with more roaring flames. Between them arcs of water met together like the transepts of a cathedral. He had to step carefully, watching for the fat water hoses that snaked across the road.

A man yelled at him. 'What you doing here? You can't go that way.' A loud explosion and the ground shook.

Peter slipped away between two buildings. His heart was beating a tattoo in the dark. He passed three firemen in rubber suits with the hoods down like giant collars. They were ashen-faced and drinking mugs of tea, staring at Peter as if he were a phantom from another world.

The air raid siren began to wail again, but Peter had no idea where to go other than to keep on heading in the direction of home. Singing the 'Our Father' loudly, he walked on and after a long time chanced on a road he knew.

Two hours after he left the station, and feeling sick with relief, he reached the end of his road and saw the familiar terraces of low red-brick houses. A deep bomb crater sat at the entrance to his street, perfectly round, even and smooth as a newly dug grave, the bottom white with a chemical dust. Along one side, houses stood on a precipice, their windows blown out, and the curtains lazily flopping in and out in the breeze.

Walking further down the road he saw with a sob of relief that his own house was still standing. He knocked on the front door. A few moments later Kitty opened it.

'It's Peter. How did you get here? We thought you'd have heard.'

'Is that Peter there?' said his dad. 'I'm sorry you came, lad.'

No sign of Ma. Why had he expected to see her? He knew she wasn't there. But all the same, he wanted to cry.

'So this is Peter then? Let me have a look at him.'

A woman he'd never seen before pushed through into the narrow hallway. She was short and dumpy, already in her coat as if about to go out.

'Nice-looking lad. Hello, Peter. I'm Ivy.' She said it as if he would know who she was and put out her hand for him to shake.

'And just how the bloody hell did you get here?' asked Dad.

'I got on the train at nine this morning.'

'Well, we'd best get to shelter. Siren's already gone.'

Ivy ignored dad. 'Have you had your tea?'

Peter shook his head.

'He should have a bit to eat first, Kitty, eh? You must be starved, our Peter.'

Kitty made him a doorstep of bread and jam. Then they set off for the shelter at Hulme, Peter eating and trying to mind the scattered cobbles and broken glass as they walked. It was dark but there was a red glow across the sky to see by.

'Jerry will know the way back tonight sure enough with this lot burning like a lamp,' said Dad.

By the time they got to the shelter the ARP man in his black steel helmet was turning people away.

'It's packed in here. You'll have to find someone with a cellar or an Anderson,' he said when Ivy asked him if he was happy about them all dying that night.

Ivy took charge. 'We'll go to the Dog and Partridge,' she announced. 'I used to pull pints there before war. Landlord's always had a soft spot for me. Your mother might not have held with doing herself up, but a bit of lipstick goes a long way in this world, our Kitty; you mind me.'

A warning growl of plane engines, an explosion to the south, the ack-ack of an aircraft gun somewhere in a street close by. They walked faster, began to run.

The cellar of the Dog and Partridge smelled cold, of coal and spilled beer. The landlord's wife ignored Ivy, but made a big thing of welcoming Jim and his motherless children. Got the boys to go up to the bar and fetch down chairs. She seemed to know dad well enough.

'And don't put your head against the wall. Shock could knock you out,' she warned. 'Might snap your neck.'

Ivy wanted a sing-song, but the landlord's wife stared her down and no one else had the energy to do anything but sit and try to decode the noise thundering around them. The mechanical drone of planes carrying their heavy load above the city, the whistle of bombs falling, the awful wait until the bomb exploded – somewhere else, somewhere else – then the wait for the next one. The constant thumping of the anti-aircraft guns in the distance. There was another explosion, the nearest yet, and the cellar jumped, the pressure in the air pulsing in a wave. Dad was white as a sheet, his face sweating. He passed a large handkerchief over his forehead.

Ivy led a foray back up to the bar, came waddling back with more bottles of beer. She'd kept her coat and hat on. Set up her own sing-song. 'My old man said, "Follow the van, and don't you dilly dally on the way." Off went the van with me old cock linnet, and I ran behind shouting wait a minute.'

The landlord's wife had her eyes closed now, too terrified to give Ivy a piece of her mind. Peter sat between Bill and Kitty. She held tight to Peter's hand, squeezing it so hard each time a bomb resounded nearby that he winced with pain.

Bill brought out a pack of cards and Peter taught them Maudey's game, Gin Rummy. They all flinched each time the room shook, but carried on playing, arguing over points.

At around three in the morning everything fell quiet. They went up into the pub's backyard and looked up at a dirty red dawn, the light bruised and bloody. The air was thick with the bitter smell of smoke. Dad began coughing. Walking back to the terrace they found the pub on the corner gone. Several houses nothing but a gap and mounds of rubble.

Their house was still there, all the windows had been blown out this time. Inside there was an even layer of brown grit over everything. Ivy stood in the cold kitchen, swaying. She sat down on a chair, not bothering to brush off the dust. Kitty rinsed out the kettle and put it on to boil. She put Peter and Bill on sweeping up glass while she washed out cups. Dad went to see what he could find to board the front windows up.

They'd had no breakfast. Ivy said she was going to do a proper dinner for them all, but she didn't move.

Peter couldn't understand where Ivy had come from. And who had decided she should act like she was their new ma? She was nothing like Ma. But when Jim came back she made him hand over some money. She told Peter to come with her.

On the main road into town was a fish and chip shop with the glass window blown out and a new handwritten sign propped up in front: 'Open for business – just more open than usual.' Ivy carried the newspaper parcels of fish and chips back with Peter and they ate from the paper, sitting round the kitchen table, sprinkling plenty of salt and vinegar on the hot chips.

'I'd eat this every day, me,' said Ivy. 'Don't hold with all that slaving in the kitchen when you can go out and fetch this every day. Did you tell him, Jim? Me and your dad are getting wed, Peter.' Her face was bright pink, the grease of the chips made her lips shine. He felt embarrassed for Dad. Ivy sat with her knees apart and scratched inside her calf. Dad ate on, looked shifty.

He couldn't help it; Peter thought of how Ma would say Ivy was common, not their sort. And if Alice saw Ivy . . .

Christmas Day Kitty cooked a chicken like Ma would have. Everyone gathered round the table. There was a paper lantern hanging from the ceiling. Some straggly tinsel over the mantelpiece. Ivy had bought a slab of pink and yellow Angel cake from the shop. It tasted like the dusty shop cake they used to have for breakfast as a treat, coming home with Ma after the communion fast on Sundays. Ma always made them go to church with her early every Sunday, the priest blessing them all in a row at the communion rail. He swallowed hard to make Ivy's cake go down, his throat tight.

Ivy and Dad went to the pub in the afternoon. No heating in the house but for the fire in the kitchen.

On Boxing Day they went to the pantomime at the Hippodrome and laughed themselves sick at the bawdy jokes and the slapstick Widow Twanky. They all stood and sang their hearts out for 'There'll be Bluebirds Over the White Cliffs of Dover'. Dad had tears running down his cheeks and he gripped onto Peter's shoulder. Peter stood up straight and sang his loudest, because they were together and he belonged to Manchester, and Hitler couldn't beat them. And that was the truth; and he was proud to be Peter, standing here with his people in the dim light of the huge theatre with the spotlight on the girl in the blue dress and bright make-up, holding her arms to them and singing like Vera Lynn.

It was a long walk back. Ivy was complaining her feet were killing her. She said they'd get fish and chips, and then Dad and Ivy argued. He said did she know how much this was costing. He said Evelyn could make a meal from next to nothing. Ivy said she was sure Evelyn could, as if it wasn't something to be proud of.

'Isn't it time some of this brood were fending for themselves?' she muttered. 'Kitty and Peter'll just have to share a bag of chips if you're that stingy.'

They stood around on the pavement over the road from the chippy while Ivy and Dad argued, and the last of the Christmas cheer drained away. John sloped off back to his lodgings. He said Bill may as well come too since they had to get up for work on the morrow. They muttered goodbye to Peter, and then the two lanky, cowed-looking figures disappeared into the darkness. Then Kitty shouted at Ivy that she didn't need to bother about her because she'd be wed soon enough like Doris. She'd stay with her mother-in-law, who wanted her to go live with them.

There was the clanging of an ambulance in the distance. Unexploded bombs were still going off intermittently around the city. Ivy looked at Peter with a sour expression. She held out a palmful of coppers and said, 'Here then, get four lots of chips.'

So he dashed across the dark space to the chippy, heard the clanging of the ambulance bell getting louder, felt an explosion, something slamming into his side and then a weightlessness as he flew up into the air.

★ ★

He woke up in the hospital, his arm wrapped in heavy plaster. It hurt to move it. Dad was standing by his bed looking uneasy, but he smiled and let his eyebrows slide up his forehead when he saw Peter awake. All he wanted was to stay with Dad by him, the way he was now, his father's concern like a lamp, warming and close.

'Best get back to Ivy,' he said. Her nerves were that bad after what she'd been through with the accident and all; she wasn't used to doing a big Christmas. Dad looked shifty again and squeezed the cap in his hand. He gave Peter a shilling.

'I'll come home wi' you now, Dad?'

'Peter, you saw the state of the house now. The state of Ivy's nerves. Best you go back to the country, eh?'

As soon as his arm was set in its plaster they said he could go home. He waited for Dad to come. He thought he was dreaming when he saw Maudey walking down the ward between the ends of the beds, but there she was, her coat buttoned up over her shape like a risen cottage loaf, her round face and smile as plain and good as her own baking. How was the lad? She couldn't believe how he'd walked through the blitz like that.

Maudey and he went back on the train to Buxton. He thought of Ma, telling him stories about Dad in front of the fire, Kitty and Bill listening in. And he thought of the house covered in brown grit, the wind blowing in through the broken glass, Bill sloping off into the dark in his workman's overalls, Ivy's greasy lips and loud voice; and he was homesick, for a place that wasn't there any more.

CHAPTER 14

Derbyshire, 1981

As Sarah walked up into the quiet village she had no clear idea of where she was going, only aware of the anxiety pushing her to keep moving. She came to the wooden bus shelter at the top of the village. The early bus arrived in a burst of diesel and vibration.

It stopped, the engine still rattling. She speeded up her steps, as if the bus had been waiting for her, and got on. And there she was. The bus driver didn't look at her as he took the money, issued a ticket. He scanned the road and swung the bus out. She sat down, listening to the thrumming of the engine, letting it override the din of panic in her head.

She stayed on the bus until it drew into the bus station in Stanford. The engine cut. Propelled by the need for motion, like a vertigo in her stomach, Sarah walked round the dismal place two or three times on a loop.

Over the far side of the station she saw a row of coaches. Above the drivers' windows were the names of distant towns in white letters. She had some money in her account; she had a chequebook in her bag, a comb, some tissues and old receipts. Nothing else. She could take one of the coaches somewhere, stay in a bed and breakfast. After that her thoughts stopped.

She walked over to the ticket office and paid for the bus to Glasgow, because it sounded so far away. She had to write down where she wanted to go. But reading the ticket she realised it was an hour before the coach left. She almost turned round and decided enough was enough, she was being silly, really selfish; she should go back. But what would happen when she got back, and what she would say exactly, left her blank.

She was sitting in the hot and dusty bus station, on a metal bench next to an old man and his large daughter, both of them dressed entirely in black. They were talking about the funeral they were going to, cross because they had to change coaches in the middle of nowhere. He wore a bowler hat and a long coat, like a phantom Edwardian businessman. His large and doughy daughter had a straw basket filled with a picnic and they spread food across their laps, oranges and Tuc crackers, all the while disapproving in very English tones of the various family members they were going to see at the funeral. Nothing malicious, simply correct and censorious, a knowledge of the faults of others run through their fingers like the beads of an abacus, the small elderly man surprisingly final in his judgements, the disappointed-looking daughter salting his words with tight-lipped nods.

They packed away and left, Sarah relieved and almost surprised to find she was no longer annexed to their lives. The dry wind across the asphalt pushed a paper bag, soft and dirty, against her ankle. She got up and bought tea from the van parked near the ticket office.

A little way away was a red telephone box. She could almost smell the air thick with metal and plastic if she were to push the door open and step in. She stared at the phone through the glass, a relic from another age, and then moved back to the metal benches. She was not a good person. Overcome with the need to stop thinking she lay down, curled up with her head on her jacket and waited.

★ ★

It was beginning to go dark as the coach neared Glasgow. Most of the seats were empty. She had turned sideways, her back against the glass window, bare feet pulled up, arms grasping her knees. The feel of her skin on her legs called up for a moment the touch of Nicky's arm against the back of her neck, and a vast hole turned over in her soul somewhere.

Two rows up a man with grubby denim flares and a grey ponytail leaned into the aisle, rolling a cigarette. He angled himself so he could stare at her, pointed at the roll-up, but she shrank back.

The lights in the coach dimmed. Nothing now but the thrum of the engine, the shadow of herself in the window glass, insubstantial, travelling through the dark. Far into the distance an oblique view of the lines of white headlights coded past the bus like a computer read-out, continually moving away.

The traffic thinned out. For a long time they travelled across a dark moor. Then buildings and areas of industrial landscape began to break up the darkness, and they came into the outskirts of Glasgow. A car park, deserted except for tents of light pooling in the rising mist. A stadium with a green glow. Industrial buildings painted with neon, floating in the night mist.

For a moment she saw Nicky in the kitchen at Fourwinds, her parents, and her heart lurched. What were they doing now?

The bus moved relentlessly on. She had no idea really why she had got onto this bus. She turned and leaned her forehead against the glass, felt the condensation against her skin like cold sweat. And then it came to her; but she did know. She understood where she was going. She would find another bus heading further north. The last stretch she would have to walk. And if they weren't there?

That was a question for tomorrow.

She closed her eyes, longing to be next to the quiet sounds of the sea, the uninterrupted dark filled with salt and the sound of waves, silence unknotting the pain beneath the hollow of her collarbone.

Nothing more she could do now except let things fall from her hands. The truth was she was only bringing forward what was going to happen, when they eventually knew. She saw Nicky marrying the sort of girl that Alice had wanted for him. And she saw how Alice was right: Nicky would be happy. He would marry the kind of girl that Alice would approve of. Best this way in the end.

CHAPTER 15

Buxton, 1941

The first thing Alice had noticed when she read the invitation was that Richard would be there. There was his name on the choir list. He must be on leave for the weekend.

Then she was cross with herself: she wanted to go because it was music and it was Yarnton Manor and the weekend would be delicious, and if Richard was there – they had after all met through the Music Society at a college do – well then, she couldn't help that. She'd ignore him and he'd see that she'd completely got over him. She'd chat with him, perfectly civilised and carefree, because, really, she was absolutely fine. She blinked away the smart in her eye that came when she thought about those photos.

'Who is your letter from, darling?'

She folded the typed sheet, as if mother might see her thoughts written out on the paper.

'Oh, it's just an invite for the Music Society. Daniel's organised a Tallis weekend at his parents' place outside Oxford before term starts. Thought I might go along.'

'You'll be going up to Oxford early this term?'

'Yes, Mummy, but only by a few days.'

'Will Richard be there?'

'I really haven't given it any thought.'

Yarnton Manor wasn't huge, but it was perfect. The stone was honey-coloured biscuit with rococo gingerbread decorations of urns and swags of leaves. It stood with a pale golden symmetry in front of a winter blue sky. The gardens leading to the stone portico were laid out in circles and rhomboids of spicy boxwood hedges. The frozen icing sugar of morning frost had paled the colours of the leaves to a silvery green.

Daniel, who had taken on the running of the Music Society, answered the door. He was wearing a baggy jumper with holed elbows and a yellow silk cravat. His hair hadn't been combed and his tortoiseshell specs had slid halfway down his nose. He was holding a sheaf of music.

'Alice, you old rogue. So glad you could make it.'

'It's awfully good of you to have us, of your parents, I mean, letting us tramp all over their place.'

'Oh, they love it. Mama will be sidling in to join the altos, and so long as Papa has his bottle of malt, he doesn't care what noise we make. And well, just because there's a war on doesn't mean the important things should stop. Then we really would be beaten.'

'When are you called up?'

'End of this term. Start training, then get posted.'

'Oh, Daniel. That's so soon.'

'Anyway, hoping for enough people to do the forty part motet,' he said, evidently not wanting to think about anything but the weekend, a rare space of a few days, protected from anything to do with the mess going on in the rest of Europe. That would come soon enough.

She followed him across the threadbare Indian rugs scattered over the flagstone floor, their patterns worn away to an imprint of colours. Even though it was late morning the blackout curtains in the great hall were still drawn. An elderly man in a black suit was slowly pulling them back with a long pole.

One side of the hall was cluttered with bedrolls and sleeping bags and exploded rucksacks. In spite of the fire crackling in the huge fireplace the hall was almost as cold as the garden outside.

'Boys' dorm down here, girls' dorm up in the long gallery. Though we're also using it for rehearsals in the daytime.'

She followed him upstairs, the uneven wooden treads creaking as they went. He paused. 'You know Richard's getting here some time today?'

She smiled broadly. 'How lovely. Haven't seen him for ages.' She held the smile.

'So long as you know. Main thing is, as soon as we have enough voices we can get going. And here we are. Find somewhere to stow your stuff in one of the rooms at the end and then come through to the long gallery.'

The long gallery was full of groups of people talking, half-heard conversations about who was being called up. She didn't know any of them particularly well, but she broke into a circle of backs and listened to an aloof man complaining that the last time he'd heard Palestrina it had been ruined by the soprano being a girl, when everyone knew it had been written for a boy soprano or, best of all, a castrato. They laughed. She scanned the room, but there was still no sign of Richard.

She headed for a cluster of girls she recognised. They were seated on a large sofa, some on the rug, laughing at a young man who was rolling on the floor with a collie pup in a mock fight. He had a lean but sturdy athletic build, and an evident disregard for the occasion and the place.

It was Ralph.

She'd hardly seen him since their disastrous evening at the Randolph a couple of months ago. He'd left a note in her college pigeon hole several times, called her lodgings, but she hadn't replied. A couple of times she had seen him in town; she'd turned and slipped away in the opposite direction. With a sinking heart she realised that she may as well get it over with. She walked over and stood primly at the edge of the rug. He was bunching up the pup's ears and growling as the dog tried to lick his face.

As soon as Ralph saw her he leapt up and enveloped her in a bear hug so entirely comical that all she could do was laugh. Trying to get her breath back she flopped down on the rug. Ralph sat down next to her, beaming broadly. The collie pup leapt over him onto her lap and stretched up to lick her face. She trapped the warm puppy in her arms.

'Oh good save, Alice. I think she likes you.'

'She's wrecking my poor jacket,' she laughed.

'Here.' He took the enthusiastic pup from her while she adjusted her clothes and then her hair. She'd done it up with more care than usual. While it was still dark she had got up to set the rolls of curls in place with pins.

'But I didn't know you were coming, Ralph. I didn't know you sang.'

'I sight read, but this is all a bit new to me. I was always the stinker at boarding school who was sloping off to play the piano instead of getting on with my prep; but then I met Barbara here and she introduced me to Tallis.'

'You like early music?'

'I think some of the nicest stuff you can hear was written in the Renaissance,' he said.

The girl next to him nodded enthusiastically. Small and dark and with an intelligent face, she was paying intense attention to anything Ralph said or did, holding herself in a stiff, self-conscious way. Evidently this was Barbara. She giggled and leaned over to Ralph to brush a strand of hair behind his ear.

Slightly taken aback, Alice stared. Ralph certainly seemed perfectly at one with the world; and apparently quite recovered from his infatuation of the term before. Well, she was glad to see he'd found someone else at last. She raised her head and scanned the room again.

'We're in the same group, you know,' Ralph said.

'Oh?'

Daniel appeared, looking gloomy. 'Just got a telephone call from Richard. He won't be here till tomorrow; and he was giving a lift to a couple of the others so we're still three voices down today. I suppose we could make a start with what we have.'

There was a flurry of people being arranged into small groups. Then they began the work of the first sing-through.

There were eight groups, each with five voices, set around the room in a semicircle so everyone could see Daniel conducting. Alice joined Ralph and Barbara, who spent more time with her eyes on Ralph than on the music. Ralph didn't seem to notice. Absorbed in the music, his baritone voice blended with the others' thoughtfully, with none of the bravado that some of the male singers displayed – Richard would have been clearly distinguishable above everyone else and pleased to be so.

With no Richard there, even in a place as lovely as Yarnton, the day lacked the heart-stopping magic that seemed to follow him around, and yet the moment she'd heard Richard was delayed Alice had felt oddly relieved; for a while she could put aside all the tense scenarios that she had played out on the early train, watching the dark window change into the glare of dawn.

After the first rehearsal she sat with Ralph and his friends at one end of the long, oak table in the Jacobean dining room for lunch. There were trays of baked potatoes and the wartime sausages, all fat and bread – but plenty of them. And it was easy and rather fun being with Ralph now that all that silliness was over. She looked sideways at him, seeing what Barbara might see. His face seemed longer and less boyish these days, although his dark hair was as dishevelled as ever; one had to admit that Ralph was rather handsome really, in his way.

Barbara had taken to staring at her. It was positively rude. Alice wasn't sure what she'd heard about last term, but she was definitely boring into Alice with her eyes as if trying to read what was so special about her. She decided to leave Barbara with her prey.

★ ★

She'd packed the long, satin gown in case there was a formal party that evening, one never knew with the war and all that. But she couldn't be bothered to put it on – have to live up to it – and it was too cold anyway. Nobody else was getting changed. They ate thick barley and vegetable soup down in the kitchens, bread and more sausages, wrinkled apples from trays from the wine cellar.

'If there's a raid we all head down to the cellar,' Daniel announced, waving his apple. 'Not that there's been one out here so far.'

The shadow of a thought passed over faces. Next year, what would have changed? Who would be away fighting? Who would be missing? It made the evening seem intensely sweet and fleeting, already too nearly over.

Up in the long gallery someone put a record on the gramophone and people began to dance to 'In the Mood'. Ralph and Alice sat and watched. Ralph had rolled up his shirtsleeves, leaning back with a half-smile, his hands behind his head.

They roasted small chestnuts from Yarnton woods round a fireplace with a scorched back of heraldic stone arms and enough room to roast a couple of sheep for an Elizabethan banquet. Alice noticed that Barbara had fallen asleep on the end of a sofa, snoring lightly.

There was a tight knot of excitement and apprehension in Alice's stomach as she went to bed that night; tomorrow Richard would arrive. And then an awful thought occurred to her for the first time. What if he was bringing Celia?

★ ★

When Alice went down to find some tea the next morning there was Richard, already seated at the table in the dining room, framed in the garden window. Seeing him there gave Alice a bit of a jolt; he was every bit as handsome as ever, his navy officer's jacket on the back of the chair. He smiled widely at her.

'Alice. Dear. Drove all night to get here as early as I could.' He stood up and indicated the empty chair next to him.

No sign of Celia.

Alice sat down and helped herself to a piece of toast from the rack. The sideboard had large serving platters of beans and eggs, but she felt too nervy to eat any of it.

'Where did you drive from?'

'Ship's stationed at Portsmouth.'

'It took all night to get here?'

'Pretty much. The blackout and all that.'

'Poor you. Well, I'm so glad you managed to get leave this weekend. Being out there on the sea, has it been very awful?'

'You know, rather not talk about that right now. I'd much rather concentrate on you.'

And drat it, yes, she was blushing. She focused on spreading some pale jam on the toast.

'Only wish it were just the two of us this weekend, just you and me,' he murmured, leaning in.

She wondered if she had misheard, then remembered the unattractive piece of toast held to her mouth. She put it down. He laid a hand on the table close to her forearm and she could feel how close he was, a tickling effect from the hairs on her skin tightening.

She couldn't help it; she stared at him. With his blond hair and regular features that were so right, he looked every inch the naval officer, the absolute poster boy. He was staring back at her, strangely intent.

'I've been a fool, Alice. Ma and Celia, they put such pressure on me, don't you see? I should have listened to in here,' and he put his other hand on his breastbone. 'Isn't there some way we can spend some time alone this weekend, talk things over? I've got the car. Why don't we pop out for lunch? Just you and me.' He was whispering.

Blushing ridiculously she glanced at the other people sitting across the expanse of white linen. They were carrying on with their conversation, unaware of the momentous events taking place on the other side of the table.

'I suppose we could, after rehearsals are over this morning. There's quite a long break before the afternoon session. It would be so lovely to talk.'

He squeezed her hand. 'Deal then,' he said. 'And thank you, darling. I've so little time, don't you see?' Wiping his mouth with his napkin he got up. 'See you later then.'

She could hardly concentrate on the music. She was fizzing with nerves, longing for the rehearsal to end – when she would step into the car with Richard. She kept her head from turning to look back to where he was standing. Was he trying to say that it was over with Celia? But gradually the music began to assert itself, and she began to focus and work on her part. Then suddenly it was over. Daniel tapped on the music stand and said they'd break. 'Back for the last rehearsal at three.'

Richard smiled at her conspiratorially as he left the room. It was ridiculous all this subterfuge, but of course it would be so hard not to take half a dozen other people in the car once the idea was mooted about. She slipped away and waited outside on the steps where his car was parked to the side.

When he didn't appear she thought maybe she'd got it wrong, and then he came running out and they were driving away.

The Crown Hotel was a square, sandstone building on the way to Banbury. It smelled of pork pies and beer. They took a table by the window, sitting each side of a chintz-covered corner seat. The table was varnished to almost black, imitating a Tudor relic. The waitress brought ham salad, wet lettuce and a plate of bread and butter, the squares of ham flabby, more tinned spam than ham. Richard looked at the plates, raised his eyebrows so that Alice giggled. He called back the waitress, gave her a ten-pound note and told her to bring a bottle of champagne. He turned his attention back to Alice. Reaching across the table he balled her hand up inside his fist. She winced: he squeezed so tightly.

'Look, is there still a chance for me, Alice? Oh Alice, dear, if you only knew how I still feel about you.'

A boy in an apron came back with the champagne bottle and two glasses on a tray. He struggled to loosen the cork, so Richard took over, eased it out and filled two glasses. They waited in silence till he left.

When she spoke her voice sounded hoarse and tight.

'I still care about you, Richard, of course I do, very much, but . . .'

'I know I'm passionate about you, darling. Don't you feel the same for me still? It's been the only thing that's kept me going really, thinking of us, on the river at midnight, remember, taking out the punt? And in my room, alone together.'

'Of course I do. How could I forget?'

'I've been such a fool. Wasted so much time. I don't ever want to be such a fool again.'

'Really Richard? Because I feel the same about you. I haven't stopped missing you.' She felt tears welling up. 'You're all I think about. All I want.'

He stared at her, the full beam of his focus on her. 'Alice, after lunch, we could go upstairs. They have rooms.'

There was a beat while she took in what he had just said. Her hands on the polish of the table felt tacky and moist, sticking to the surface uncomfortably. It was the war. It was the war that made people so brutal, so honest. She swallowed, felt a clamour in her head, the smell of his hair close to her face as she looked down on his bent head, a sharp almost goaty smell.

'Oh, Richard, I don't think that's a good idea. Everything's happening so fast. Let's eat and then maybe we should get some air, walk along the river. We don't need to rush at things, dear.'

His face when he looked up was suddenly sulky and pinched. They ate in silence, the clink of knives and forks making the silence seem more ridiculous. She drank just the one glass, then almost two in the end. Richard finished the bottle, threw down his napkin and said, 'OK, let's do that walk.'

He stalked out of the hotel. Really, he did always manage to make her feel guilty – when she was the one who had every right to be offended. She ran to catch up with his long strides as they headed across a lumpy field towards the riverbank. The air was flat and frozen, too cold for birdsong; the banks of weeds along the path were papery straw, washed to grey by winter. A sound of rushing water ahead of them was getting louder. He was striding on, slapping at the weeds with the back of his hand.

'It's a bit slippery here,' she called out. 'Do take care.' There was no reply.

She hurried to catch up.

'I've started giving a few lectures at evening classes,' she called out. 'It's great fun. We get all sorts of working people, but they read endless books and they're so keen and ready to discuss them. Of course, they read anything and everything, in quite a disorganised, haphazard way, so they do need guiding, but once I've given the lecture and opened the discussion—'

'Alice. Darling. I don't want to talk about your lectures. You know what I want.' He turned towards her, blocking the path. He was almost shaking, holding her wrists so firmly that she couldn't move. The force of his wanting her so much felt like downing a whole bottle of champagne. All the months that she'd longed for him welled up now inside her throat, painfully; all those hours of trying to understand why he'd stopped loving her; and now, the pressure of his hands on her wrist bones, proof that it had all been nothing but a silly mistake; she was wanted, vindicated.

His arms folded round her waist, pulling her in. He was so close she could smell the familiar almond perfume of his Fortnum's soap; she could feel the small heat coming off his skin as he put his cheek against hers. The sound of the water going over the weir filled her ears.

'Let's forget the rehearsal. I'm so mad about you, Alice. Why don't we stay here all night, just the two of us? Run away from everyone else. Now.'

'But they need us.' She gave a small laugh. 'There's no such thing as Tallis's thirty-eight part motet. Richard, I love you so very much, but this, rushing at everything . . .''

'Alice, if you don't want to come with me now, if you don't really love me any more, I swear, I'll throw myself into the water. I swear, I'll do it.'

'You don't mean that.'

'I will. I'll do it.'

He took a step towards the water. His face was wild but watchful. She was on the point of running forward, pulling him back, saving him, but she didn't move. She felt very calm. Standing there in front of the water, as if about to jump, he looked so very like an actor in a cheap provincial play. And she recognised that expression, the way he would watch her and calculate, his thin face politely bullying.

She'd forgotten just how Richard could throw a tantrum, how he could upset and dominate the whole day with a mood. And then a niggling little thought presented itself clearly at the front of her mind.

'But you wouldn't.'

'How do you know I won't do it?'

'Something you said, about how long it took you to get here. Richard, you didn't drive straight here, did you? You went to see someone else first.'

He looked guilty. Caught out.

'I had to see someone, an old friend.'

'And she turned you down. Celia, or whoever it was, wouldn't let you stay the night, so you thought, give old Alice a try.'

He paced up and down the bank, exasperated, shouting almost. 'Alice, this could be my last weekend. You don't know what it's like out there. I could be dead next week. I love you now, so why shouldn't we share that?'

She blinked. Blinked away tears. She felt cheap and cold and foolish. One ham salad and a bottle of indifferent fizz and he thought he'd talk her into bed for an hour or two.

'No.'

'It's not as if you minded before.' He looked spiteful.

She slapped him. Not bothering to see what he did next she started walking back. She didn't care if he followed or not. Didn't care if he jumped in.

Then, damn it, she realised she'd need a lift back with him. She waited by the car in front of the hotel. When he appeared, leaving just enough time to let her worry that he might have gone through with it, he got into the car and slammed the door shut, and started the engine without once looking at her. For a moment she thought he was going to leave her there. But he waited, revving the engine while she opened the car door and got in.

They drove away, Richard clutching the wheel tightly and staring straight ahead.

After a while she broke the silence.

'Let's just enjoy being together again. Don't let's spoil that. Old friends?'

'Sorry. Not likely to happen really, is it? Not as if we'll be mixing with the same people much.' He took out a cigarette and lit up, driving with one hand. 'Of course, the wedding with Cee will still go ahead. They won't let me get out of that. Just that Cee has this thing, you know, saving herself for the big day and all that.'

She couldn't wait to get out of the car. As soon as they pulled up at the side of the manor she threw the door open and stumbled out. He leaned over and slammed the door shut after her, sat on in the car.

Ralph was sitting on the steps. He looked at her flustered face and struggled to his feet quickly as she ran past.

'Alice, whatever's the matter?' he called out. 'Alice?'

But she managed to escape him.

She hid in the lavatory. She sat down on the wooden lid and clunked the Victorian chain once or twice to hide the noise of her crying. She was more angry than anything. She waited for the hiccupping to stop convulsing her shoulders. Then, feeling totally exhausted, her eyes stinging, she wearily washed her face with cold water. Turning off the heavy tap she stared at the mess in the mirror.

Yes, she looked awful, but quite frankly she didn't care. Beyond the frosted glass of the window she could see the muted shapes of the garden. All she wanted was to be out in the cold air. She looked round at the beautiful Delft tiles on the walls, the pictures of horses and dogs; it was a grand, baronial sort of lavatory, the sort you felt honoured to spend time in, but it was still a lavatory.

After wandering around the garden, the frost already starting to glint on the winter leaves and the stone paths, she came back inside.

She glanced in a mirror and saw a face that looked almost passable. Rehearsals were starting, people clattering up the wooden stairs to the long gallery. Joining everyone else she suddenly felt giddy, reckless and, well, released from something shabby. Had she really ever wanted a whole life with Richard?

'Everything OK, at lunch?' Ralph asked as rehearsals started.

'Incredibly dull,' she said.

He seemed rather satisfied with her answer.

During the afternoon they moved from the hard work of learning the music into a flow of melody and volume, following together the swoops and dives of Daniel's arms. As he urged singers in on cue, raising and lowering the volume with his hand, the music began to breathe and pulse. The sun showed pink through the frosted lead panes of the windows. Alice's toes and fingers, the ends of her nose were cold, but she found herself wrapped up in sound, listening to Ralph as they followed the thread of song, their voices hitting the harmonies with pleasing effects in a way that made them both smile broadly.

She didn't even care when she saw Richard stooping low over a first year, turning her page as they sang. The girl stared up at him like a mesmerised rabbit. Alice took in the girl's escaping hair and inexpert overdone red lipstick. Perhaps she should warn her.

When Daniel finally let them stop the last of a red sun was burning away behind the silhouetted winter trees. She stayed and talked with Ralph and his friends for the rest of the evening, grateful for his easy company. And all evening Barbara stayed close to Ralph, warding Alice off with her eyes.

★ ★

It was icy the next morning. Alice's breath formed white clouds as she shivered in the Victorian bathroom. She had the quickest wash: there was a queue waiting outside, someone rudely rapping on the door.

From the moment she'd woken Alice had been in a bad mood, particularly irritated when she thought of Barbara. Not at all the sort of person she would have picked for Ralph. She couldn't help seeing Ralph through Barbara's eyes. Once or twice over the past couple of days, noticing him across the room, she'd been struck by just how handsome he was; then she'd checked herself, because she didn't think of Ralph in that way. Yet an impression of his solid strength, that evening at the Randolph when he had danced with her, remained. Thinking about him now she found there was a lump in her throat.

But how could that be?

To say 'Richard and I' had always seemed like a badge of honour. In Richard's circles of friends, to say 'Ralph and I' would need an explanation, some sort of qualification. She wasn't proud to think that, but that was the way things were in the world. He lacked that English understanding of what mattered – or else he simply didn't care.

The person rapping on the bathroom door turned out to be Barbara. In the foulest of tempers Alice conceded the bathroom and sat in the kitchen drinking very strong tea. She snapped at Ralph when he said good morning.

All through the rehearsal she didn't look at Ralph, dangerously close to crying at some of the passages. When his hand touched hers as they sang, she felt it like a shock.

★ ★

The session in the afternoon was the final one, and guests were invited in to hear the performance. The hairs prickling on the back of her neck for the solos, floating with the music for the harmonies, Alice didn't want it to end. When the music was finally over and people began gathering their things together to go down for supper, she sat down heavily on one of the hard chairs.

Ralph came over, stooped low and looked into her face. 'What is it, old thing?'

'Oh, I don't know. I don't know what's happening to me.'

He sat down by her. She put her head on his shoulder. Resting there against the warmth of his woollen sweater felt peaceful. The weight of his arm round her shoulders was comforting. The emptied room smelt of old polish, the wood floorboards and panelling creaked in little murmurs. The fire snapped. She had an impulse to tell him that she was sorry; all those months she had wasted, she wanted them back now. She wanted to spend them all over again, but with him. She realised she was blubbing and fumbled for her handkerchief. She must look like a dropped blancmange again.

'Sorry,' was all she managed to mumble. Pushing his arm away she left the room

She found herself standing by the back door, looking out onto the dark gardens, glints of frost on the grass. She could hear the muffled sounds of the diners gathering in the great hall. But Ralph had followed her. He came outside into the cold, pulled the door to and stood alongside her quietly.

'I don't suppose you've got a cigarette,' she asked him after a while.

He nodded. He lit one for her and one for himself. They smoked in silence, tapping the ash every so often, the tips of red against the dark.

'You know, I'm really happy for you and Barbara. I only hope she realises how lucky she is.'

'Barbara?'

'She likes you so much and she's so . . .'

'Good grief. Really? You think Barbara likes me? Oh dear. I was too busy looking at you to notice anyone else. How could you think . . .?' Suddenly decisive he said, 'Come on, let's walk.'

So she walked with him through the gardens, out through the stone gate into the orchard. The winter sky, with no hint of town lights, was thick with stars. 'Looks like frogspawn,' Ralph said. And he was right, the stars were deep and layered and mysteriously suspended, like very beautiful frogspawn. She shivered. He reached out and put his arm round her, rubbed the outside of her arm to warm her up. She could smell the faint musk of his hair, and she thought how deeply right it felt to stand so close to his warmth in the dark. Like home.

He took her chin in his hand, turned her face, and then she kissed Ralph for the second time.

CHAPTER 16

Fourwinds, 1981

Alice rubbed cream into her hands. She could see Ralph's soft bulk in the dressing-table mirror. He was very quiet, his heavy shoulders resting against the bedhead. She tried to picture the young man who had used to sit smiling and mischievous as she got ready for bed.

Time had changed them both. The woman in the glass had a dry look to her skin, fragile like leaves at the end of autumn. Ralph's features had grown thicker and stronger, the bushy eyebrows, the long nose almost hooked. And she loved him more than ever.

A tightness in her throat for Nicky that he should be so alone. How could Sarah do that to him?

But then, when he'd first brought Sarah home, she'd already had a niggling worry that it might not work. Sarah had a way of holding back that had left Alice a little hurt and puzzled; she recalled her own strenuous efforts with Ralph's mother, building a bridge of good intentions and little deeds. Although it was always hard to second-guess quite what it was that Lily had wanted from her. Alice smoothed the Penhaligon's lotion into her forearms and round her neck. She put the stopper back in the old-fashioned glass bottle.

'That was always the thing that worried me about Sarah. The way she didn't talk. I know we sometimes talk too much, it can all be a bit overwhelming if you're an outsider, but at least in this family we talk about the things that matter.'

Ralph gave a shake of his head, or was it a nod. It was hard to tell sometimes if Ralph had actually heard her. Ever since the wedding had collapsed round them Ralph had seemed perpetually preoccupied and absent.

'Don't you think so, Ralph? Sarah, she would never let herself be drawn in? That self-contained air, detached, that's never been our way. Ralph?'

Ralph looked up. 'Sorry? You were saying?'

She tutted. Finished brushing her hair. 'Never mind. Let's get some sleep. We're all a bit under strain right now.'

She folded back the sheet and got in. Ralph wouldn't have a duvet. They still had the antique silk eiderdown that had come from Cecily and Flora's house – as did the bed itself, a wonderful French oak thing, the gilt on the carved wood worn by time and the history of other lives, and the beautiful armoire with the mirrored front. So much of their best furniture had been inherited from the London house. Ralph had refused to part with any of the aunts' furniture when the sale of their house had gone through, something about wanting to hold on to these remnants of his small family circle.

Ralph was still quiet. He looked white, his head leaning against the wooden headboard. He had to take a cocktail of pills for this and that now.

'Are you not feeling well? For goodness sake, what is it?' A flash of anger that Sarah should be putting them through this. The last straw if it made Ralph ill again.

'Alice. Perhaps I should have told you. A long time ago.'

Her heart clenched. There it was, a rustling round the edges of the room, whisperings that she'd spent so many years not listening to, the worries that pressed against the windows at night in the small, sleepless hours.

The silence stretched out, and she waited.

She found herself thinking of the girls at the law firm, a string of lovely secretaries who were always so solicitous – tender even – with her, implying a life they shared with Ralph that she knew nothing about. For years she had wondered about them, those girls who came and went and yet remained remarkably the same – who sooner or later would have a crush on Ralph. Of course, it was all harmless; easy for them to misinterpret Ralph's general enthusiasm and warmth as something intentional, something special for them. She'd seen them each glow and blossom before the penny dropped and they finally understood that the hugs and the praise and the attention – that's just how Ralph was with everyone. She hadn't really worried, although sometimes she'd had to drop a little hint to the dimmer and more star-struck ones.

It was nothing really.

And yet. That girl who'd turned up at one of the New Year's parties Ralph and she held each year. Carole Harker. A horrid name.

Nicky must have been eight years old. She'd let the boys stay up to hand round plates of cocktail sausages and her speciality, mushroom vol-au-vents. She was refilling Nicky's serving platter – he was taking it very seriously and not leaving each group of guests till they'd had one of everything – when the doorbell sounded. A girl was standing on the doorstep. She had a thick, blonde ponytail and powdery blue eyeshadow. She came in, furtive glances at Alice, looking around the hallway speculatively – a prospective house purchaser. Her skirt was very short, the blue polyester material riding even higher as she sat down in the middle of the sofa. Even in tan tights the girl's legs seemed shockingly naked.

Alice had made a special point of talking to her during the evening, casually hinting how affectionate Ralph was by nature, letting her down gently. Carole looked back from under that powdery blue eyeshadow, something set in her eyes – as if no matter what Alice said, she knew better. The silly girl had stayed and stayed, and eventually told them that she'd no idea how she was going to get home so late. No taxis to be had. Ralph had been very cross, uncharacteristically rattled. Swearing under his breath he had got the car out and driven her back. He wouldn't hear of Alice's sensible suggestion of letting the girl stay the night in the spare room.

After they left Alice had sat in the dining room, waiting for the sound of the car returning. Even with the table strewn with the remains of the finger buffet, the room retained its melancholy feel of an unloved place where you wouldn't choose to linger. She could see the hallway obliquely reflected in the mirror, a place she didn't recognise from that angle, the doors opening into unknown rooms.

He'd been gone a long time. Really, he shouldn't have driven. If something happened . . .'

There it was. She let herself look at it for a moment. Had something already happened? She opened the brandy left out on the sideboard and poured a little, sipped at it. Felt worse.

When she'd first met Ralph the thing she'd loved about him was the way he was so open to life, so brave about laughing down any stuffiness. He'd rescued her from the confines of her own snobbery. She knew that. The way those tentacles wound round your heart and stopped you giving yourself to a book, a poem – a person – not until you were sure it was good enough, the done thing – Ralph had saved her from that.

But later she had understood that there was a countermovement in his personality: he was always deeply reticent about his innermost thoughts. Secretive even. He was there, and then he wasn't there, and the harder she pressed him to open up, the more she shouted and complained, then the more he would clam up and slide away somewhere else.

When they got married it was just Ralph and her against the world, always had been, always would be. That was what they had vowed in the little damp cottage on the first night after they had moved in.

Feeling heavy with the brandy she went upstairs and lay down on Nicky's quilt, her head next to his, her stomach so tight that it ached. The child's eyes opened briefly. He smiled and went back to sleep. A long time later she heard the car and Ralph coming in. Making her way out onto the landing she saw his shape down in the dark hallway, his skin white and waxy in the shadows. He pulled off his tie with a sharp movement. One side of his collar was left standing up.

'Bloody stupid girl. She's hopeless in the office too.'

It was his everyday annoyance that reassured her. She felt her worries evaporating, a dream you awake from and instantly forget.

And yet, and yet.

★ ★

'There's something I should tell you, Alice,' Ralph was saying to her now. She heard the dull thud of her heart. She put her fingers over his lips.

'Not now, Ralph. I can't take one more little thing right now. Please? Let's just get some sleep.' She clicked out the light and lay very still, as if by remaining unnoticed the thing that was approaching might pass over her.

It had taken her years to realise she'd never really know what was going on inside that head of his. Not really. And lying in the sudden dark she felt how isolated their house was, perched on the hill at the edge of the village, nothing before them but miles of wind and distant fields under the darkness.

She could feel Ralph silent but awake beside her.

How easy it was to wreck a life, with a careless word, with a lack of resolve; it only took the space of a day to send a whole existence skittering down a path you'd never intended.

CHAPTER 17

Buxton, 1941

Each morning Peter collected the post from the coir mat and looked through to see if there were any letters for Alice. If he recognised Ralph's writing he'd run up to her room, tap on the door and leave the letter outside. Moments later she would appear in a wrap and tear the envelope open, letting the door fall shut again.

When Ralph had arrived at the Hanburys' in his new army greatcoat, dropping his long kit bag in the hallway, Peter had been minded to feel resentful towards him now that he was Alice's official boyfriend. But it was hard to dislike Ralph, and if he had to choose someone to take care of Alice well then Ralph was a pretty good bet, genial and bumbling and evidently surprised to find himself in army fatigues. He always produced chocolate for Peter from his NAAFI rations and was happy to sit in the kitchen playing a game of cards with him and Maudey if Alice was out on some other errand.

Over the summer Ralph was sent away to various training camps and they saw little of him. Alice decided to do her bit by helping Peter dig for victory in the Hanbury gardens.

Peter had turned over the top two terraces to make neat beds of carrots, cabbage and orderly runs of potato plants. The tomatoes on the top terrace were ripening so fast that Maudey had had to start bottling them. She'd declared it was champion, his garden. And even Mr Hanbury had looked at the mounds of produce on the kitchen table as he passed through and said it was splendid, Peter, a splendid effort for the war.

Alice wore old jodhpurs, a cotton turban to keep her hair out of her eyes. Sometimes she brought the wind-up gramophone out, and they dug side by side, Alice humming along to Glen Miller or some show tune, since a taste for love songs had arrived along with Ralph. Or she quizzed Peter on his English texts and spun dreams of him going to Oxford – one day.

He did want to go to Oxford, or at least to university; he wanted to be a doctor or a teacher or a lawyer. Alice thought a teacher, but he might have to do something to correct some of his vowels, she mused, looking at him critically as she rested her hands on the top of the hoe. She stroked the perspiration away from her forehead, tucked some wisps of fair hair back under the turban. 'Just the way it is,' she explained to him. 'If you're a doctor or a teacher people expect the Queen's English, you do see.'

Alice made him practise saying things like: 'The water in my bath is awfully hot.' And they spent some time saying 'gas mask', rhyming the right vowel with 'pass' and laughing at the people who got it wrong, because he could hear it now, it did sound funny if you got it wrong.

They were hoeing around the leeks, leaving a wake of cleared soil, singing along to 'Little Brown Jug', when Peter noticed someone else in the garden, looking up at them from the bottom terrace. He shielded his eyes. It was a woman with yellow hair. She was wearing a striped dress and clutching a toddler in her arms, the child struggling to get down.

Alice straightened. Peter watched her take in the girl's little hat, the tight, striped dress. 'No one I know. Pop down and see what she wants, would you, Peter? See if Maudey's there.'

Peter placed his hoe on the grass and rubbed the grit from his sticky hands. The young woman glared at him as he came down the steps. The child had finally managed to kick free and drop to the ground. She grabbed his arm and held tight.

'Can I help you, miss?'

'I've come to have a word with Mr Hanbury.'

'I don't think he's in.'

'I'll just have to wait here till he's back then.' She looked around for somewhere to sit down. Her face was bright red with the heat. The child had started crying.

'Would you like to wait inside, out of the sun?'

She thought about it for a moment, glanced around the garden and decided that yes, she would like to wait inside. She didn't see why not after all, she said, as she walked in haughtily.

There was no Maudey in the kitchen to ask what to do with her.

'Is it about business?' He wondered if she worked in one of Mr Hanbury's shops. 'About shoes?'

'Shoes?' she echoed. 'I was at that factory right enough, time was. But it's about a lot more than shoes, lad.'

He had a bad feeling that she didn't look like someone who would be shown in to sit and wait in Mrs Hanbury's drawing room. He'd seen tradesmen waiting on the chair inside Mr Hanbury's office, their hat on their knee. He decided, since she was from the factory, that she should wait in Mr Hanbury's study. As he led her through the hallway her head turned to examine everything, and everything she saw seemed to make her displeased.

'And I'm supposed to manage on what I get given,' she said as he left her on the study chair. 'You might offer a body something to drink on a day like this.'

While he fetched two glasses of barley water he tried to think where he'd seen her before. Was it at the factory that day, one of the girls at the bench who had teased him? As he carried the tray through to the study he had it: it was the girl who lived over the butcher's shop. She looked more worn down and sour now, but it was the same girl who had run out and banged on the car window as Mr Hanbury pulled away.

He put the tray on a side table and glanced down at her feet. She was wearing them. They were scuffed, worn-looking round her feet, but it was the same pair of red shoes. He began to feel uncomfortable about having asked her about who she was; there was a horrible worry creeping over his shoulders that he'd done something wrong.

'Is there anything else I can get for you?'

'Is she home, his missis?'

'Mrs Hanbury? No. I think she's having her hair done.'

'Is she indeed? Well, it's all right for some.' She sipped and glared around at the bookshelves. She slapped the little boy when he spilled his barley water on the rug. Peter decided he'd better stay and play with the little boy, save him from causing any more damage.

It wasn't so long afterwards that they heard the sound of the front door opening, and voices in the hallway. Mr and Mrs Hanbury were back. The little boy shouted something and Mr Hanbury stepped directly into the room to see what the noise was.

From where he was, lying on the floor to help the little boy colour in a drawing, he saw Mr Hanbury's face cloud over with fury and panic. He lunged into the room, grabbed Peter by the back of his shirt and hustled him out into the hall. Holding the door shut behind him Mr Hanbury checked along the hallway in both directions. Mrs Hanbury's hat was on the stand, but she was gone.

'What the Dickens is she doing here? Was it you invited her into this house?'

'She said she wanted to see you.'

'Don't let Mrs Hanbury know she's here. D'you hear me?'

He had never seen Mr Hanbury look so furious. Peter nodded, relieved when he let go of his shirt. Mr Hanbury disappeared into the study, closing the door firmly behind him. But Mrs Hanbury was coming back down the stairs.

'Did William just go into his study?' Peter shook his head. She frowned and called out, 'Are you there, dear?' She headed towards the closed study door, turned the handle and half opened the door, peeking inside. 'Oh, we've got visitors,' Peter heard her say cheerfully, and then the room fell silent. He could hear the little boy begin to sing some nonsense.

'Dear, this is Louise, come to ask about . . . about a job.'

'Is that what you call it then?' the woman said.

There was another long silence. Peter stood still, not daring to move. Mrs Hanbury came out of the room, quietly reclosing the door, her face drained of colour.

'I'm sorry. I should have took her in kitchen,' Peter offered. But Mrs Hanbury didn't hear. She looked straight past him and walked up the stairs, like a ghost in her own house.

Peter was glad to get back in the sun. He rejoined Alice and picked up the hoe. He began to chip away at a patch of chickweed.

'Who was it?'

'It were someone from your dad's works, miss.'

'It *was* someone, Peter. I thought so, from the look of her.'

He nodded. 'Miss, I don't think your mam's too well. I think maybe you should go see her.'

Startled, Alice put down her hoe. 'Well, what is it?'

But Peter wasn't sure himself. He shrugged and shook his head.

'Oh, you should have said straight away.' And she hurried inside.

★ ★

A cloud had fallen over the house. Mrs Hanbury stayed in bed, clutching a green satin bed jacket round her shoulders, staring bleakly at the wall. When Peter took up tea she held it in both hands but the cup rattled in the saucer. He wasn't sure what to do. He took it from her and placed it on the side table.

Mr Hanbury was in a foul mood, of a kind that Peter had never seen before. He felt afraid when he came across him in the house, the man's face thunderous, the way he snapped at any question. He stayed in his study, endlessly smoking. But he wasn't working at his desk. Peter could see him walking up and down in front of the lace-curtained bay window, or sometimes standing still, staring out with his hands in his pockets.

On Sunday morning Mrs Hanbury came downstairs. She was dressed and her hair was immaculately swept up in a pleat. She fetched her hat from the stand and set it on her head. She knocked on the study door where Mr Hanbury had retreated to read the paper.

'You need to bring the car round if we're not to be late,' she said.

Subdued and silent, all the Hanburys gathered in the car, as they did every Sunday morning to go to eleven o'clock matins. Peter set out on foot as usual; he would catch up with them in the church and sit in the row behind.

If anything Mrs Hanbury stood straighter than ever that morning, singing the hymns with careful precision, kneeling deeply as she left the pew. She made her way down the church aisle, shaking people's hands, stopping to chat.

Phillip was off to see friends after the service, so Alice said Peter would ride back in the car. On the way the car was filled with an odd silence. Mrs Hanbury leaned against the window with her eyes closed, a sheen of moisture breaking through her face powder. When it stopped in front of the house she seemed to take a while to find the will to sit up and get out as they all filed inside. The family sat round the table for Sunday lunch, still in silence, waiting for Maudey to serve.

Alice and her brother began some banter about a friend, trying to infuse the meal with their cheeriness. Mrs Hanbury got up and left the table and returned to her room before dessert was even served. Peter carried the plates of Apple Charlotte back through to the kitchen almost untouched.

'Well may he lose his appetite after what he's put that poor woman through,' said Maudey.

'Put her through what?' Peter wanted to know. His heart was knocking against his ribs, waiting to hear Maudey confirm what he already knew. Lewd imaginings tumbled in his head: his idol, the immaculate Mr Hanbury, behaving like the barmaid at the Rose and Crown back in Manchester. Famous for her shameful ways she brazened out being the butt of whispered jokes – though she had always been nice to Peter when he and Bill had gone in there to fetch Dad home.

'Never you mind what,' Maudey said sharply.

Later that afternoon Alice knocked on his door. He welcomed her into his room. She walked around examining the prints on his wall, as if this inspection was the reason for her visit.

'Peter, the lady who came the other day, the lady with the little boy, you'd seen her before, hadn't you?'

He nodded, his heart going fast. He remembered Mr Hanbury's threatening tone. But this was Alice.

'I did, miss.'

'Where? At Daddy's factory?'

'Not there, no.'

'Well?'

'It were a while back, when I first came here. Mr Hanbury stopped by to drop off some shoes for her, at her place outside Derby. He was gone a good hour or so, and then she came out after, talked to him through the car window.'

'He went to visit her?'

He nodded.

'Peter, I think I need to talk to this lady. Do you think you can remember where she lives?'

He nodded. Proud to be on Alice's side.

That was the mistake he made: he shouldn't have taken Alice there. Without asking permission Alice took the car and they drove towards Derby. Just as on the day he had first been brought there, the lanes were thronged with banks of wild flowers, the air blowing in hot through the wound-down windows, but this time there was no adventure, just the dread of something bad looming. Alice didn't want to talk other than to ask him what he could remember of the location, trying to work out where it was from what she knew of Derby. She made grinding noises with the gears and hung on to the wheel grimly.

It took a while to locate the small row of shops on the edge of town from his description, but he recognised the butcher's as they drove along the road. Alice parked opposite, stared at it through the car window and then headed over towards the blue door.

She was gone for a very long time. Peter was thirsty, but had no money to buy a bottle of pop from the grocer's. The shops were closing when he saw Alice finally coming out. Next to her was the girl, holding the hand of the little boy. Alice knelt down on the pavement and talked to him. He had the same pale, blowy hair as Alice, the same pointy chin. The child hung back shyly. His mother watched with a hard, satisfied look as Alice walked back to the car.

Her eyes red, Alice drove home in silence. Peter didn't dare say anything. A mounting dread now that he had stepped over a line. She raced into the house. Peter heard a blazing row going on in the study; Alice and her father shouting. Then the house went back to silence. He caught the murmur of Alice's mother talking to her in a low voice, soothing.

But he lay awake at night, listening, waiting for something else to happen. Everything felt out of balance and something was going to fall.

CHAPTER 18

Buxton, 1941

When Alice came downstairs she saw the brown cardboard box on the hallstand with the black cursive writing: Garrets Haberdasher's. She carried it through to the morning room, lifting the cardboard lid. Inside, two grey shirts and a neatly folded blazer with the badge of Peter's school.

She wanted to shout, 'It's not his fault. He shouldn't have to pay for this.' But instead she held her cold elbows and stared at the box.

Mother came in. 'It will have to go back,' she said. She sat down and took a slice of toast, began to pour tea into a china cup. Alice sat opposite her, the sound of mother's knife scraping the butter on the dry bread too loud. Alice pushed back her chair and went out into the garden. She climbed up to the top lawn; the sky washed empty of everything except the thinnest blue. For the first time there was a hint that summer would end. The air felt sad and quiet, unable to reach the energy of a full summer's day again.

Soon Ralph would move on to his last training camp, and then he'd be sent to fight. She couldn't bear to think about it. She looked down at the house. Figures moving in the kitchen. Peter helping Maudey with the dishes.

So far, no one had told him.

She wanted to scream. But scream what exactly? Why did she have the feeling that somewhere in the house, in the next room,

Richard's mother was there, waiting with her opinion? The last word.

There'd been a conversation she'd overheard at Amforth, in the high-ceilinged drawing room that looked out over the park. Gossip about some girl she didn't know. It wasn't that she was eavesdropping, but she couldn't stop listening to the woman's clear, matriarchal tones. 'But darling, the father had a mistress in London. Parents getting divorced. Well, I told him he had to drop the girl, like father like daughter, don't you know. No concept of discretion. Everyone knew about it. She was quite out of the question after that. Now? He's engaged to a lovely creature from Windermere.'

Hidden behind the chair's high back Alice had sat and felt safe and unassailable, thankful that she was not that girl. Thankful that her parents were solid and dependable and boringly respectable.

Even as Alice had shouted at her mother, demanded that they keep Peter at his school, it was really the memory of that voice that made her understand that the battle was already lost. Her mother was implacable, adamant that Peter should now go to a different family, in another town: if Peter had told Alice then whom else might he tell?

As Alice ranted her mother became deeply, deeply calm. She had finally turned to Alice, her face set.

'You are behaving like a naive child. How do you suppose we will live if people know? The boys and you too, Alice, it will affect you. People can be dismissed from their employment for something like this. Your father is sorry, and now I don't want to talk about it ever again. Not a word.'

'Have you told Peter yet?'

'I will speak to him this morning.'

Alice had never really seen the steel that underpinned her mother's softness. She had watched the narrow back as the small woman left to make her way upstairs.

Back in the house, her mother was gone. Alice found Maudey clearing away the chaffing dish from the sideboard. Her eyes were red.

'Oh Maudey. What are we going to do?'

'Your mother's told me to pack Peter's things while he's out on an errand, for him to go home. There's nowt else to do now.'

'But they won't be expecting him at home.'

'A letter was sent two days ago warning them he'll be on the train.' Maudey shook her head sharply and gathered up Mrs Hanbury's dirty plates.

Alice sat and scraped marmalade across the limp toast, thought of the books she would give to Peter to pack in his case, the words she would say to him to encourage him to keep on studying, learning new things. The toast was inedible.

The shrill of the doorbell sounded in the hall, followed by Maudey's raised voice. A low, masculine voice, monotonous in reply. Maudey scolding. Alice went to see what on earth was going on.

On the doorstep was a strange sight: a priest in a long black cassock, a nun in a white wimple. Maudey was blocking the doorway, holding on to the doorpost, the priest poised as if he'd been expecting to enter.

'Ah,' he said, spotting Alice. 'If I may come in a moment, Mrs Hanbury? There seems to be some confusion. I'm here to pick up a Peter Donoghue.'

'I'm sorry. You are?'

'Father O'Carroll. I've been sent by St Xavier's. I've a letter here from his father requesting that Peter be placed in our care now, since Mr Donoghue is not in a position to adequately provide for the child himself sadly, and young Peter's time here is no longer appropriate.'

Mrs Hanbury was now in the hallway. She took the letter and read it through. 'But I thought he would be going to another family, or he'd go home. No one said he would go to an orphanage. We thought . . .'

'If you'd just like to fetch Peter for us,' the nun insisted kindly.

'But no one's told the child he's leaving yet. He doesn't know.'

'We can do that,' the nun said, a smile of great sympathy on her face, as if commiserating a bereavement.

Alice stepped in. 'Well, he's not here. He's gone on an errand. He'll be ages, so you see . . .'

'We can wait.' The priest and the nun were now inside.

'Mother, you can't allow this—' Alice stopped.

At the end of the hallway the door to the kitchen had opened. Peter was standing in the doorway.

'Oh, there he is himself,' the nun said warmly. She brushed past Maudey with her implacable kindness, gliding towards where Peter stood.

'You're going to like it, Peter, at the boys' home. You're going to come home with us. So many boys your own age. You might even get to go out to Australia once this war is over. It's lovely in Australia.'

'Go and get your things now, boy,' the priest said firmly. 'And be quick, mind. We have to drive back before blackout starts.'

'Maudey, would you take him up, get his things?' said Mrs Hanbury.

Alice ran up behind Maudey, fetched an armful of books which she packed round Peter's clothes, drops of water spotting the fabric as she wiped at her nose with the back of her wrist.

Peter looked frozen, uncomprehending as Maudey gathered his belongings.

Downstairs the nun undid the case and began taking out the books, checking the titles on the spines and putting them on the carpet. After passing her hands under the shirts to check there was nothing else to take out, she closed the case.

'But I can't come with you,' Peter said. 'If I'm not staying here, then me dad'll be expecting me back home. You've made a mistake. I'm not an orphan. I've got a dad, me.'

'Could it be a mistake?' said Mrs Hanbury. 'That's what we thought. We thought he would return to his father's care now.'

'It's been signed.' The priest brought out the letter again. 'There, look.' Alice pulled at it so she could read it too.

'But whose signature is this? Mrs Ivy Donoghue. Peter, did your father get married again?'

'I don't know. Ivy was me dad's girlfriend. She don't like me, miss.'

'So you see, it is all in order,' said the priest. 'Best make a start, eh, Peter? This way we'll get back in time for tea. You don't want to miss that, do you, go to bed hungry?'

Alice had grabbed the letter. 'But this is wrong. Look, it's not even signed by his father. Mother, you can't accept this.'

'It's perfectly official now, miss,' the priest said, firmly. 'Peter will come with us now.'

'But you can't. I won't have it.'

'Alice. Stop making a scene please.' Her lips pressed tight together. Alice scanned the wreck of her mother's face and seemed to wrestle with some idea, and then handed the letter back to the priest. She looked helplessly at Peter.

'Peter, I'm so sorry.'

She hugged him, stiff as a dangling piece of card against her. Maudey had gone for a moment but reappeared with cake wrapped in greaseproof paper. He took it, held it out like an offering, a lone wise man, and then let the priest herd him outside and into the back of the car. The nun slammed the door and got into the front seat next to the priest.

Alice could do nothing but watch as the car drove away, Peter's white face looking back at them through the rear window.

CHAPTER 19

Manchester, 1941

They spent the first few days at St Xavier's Home for Destitute Boys, a cold barracks designed to overawe and raise the constant possibility of punishment. Not a place you ever went to, unless you deserved it. It was echoing and empty since the children who lived there had been evacuated to the camp set up over the border in Wales.

Peter joined the handful of waifs and strays being herded together while waiting to move on to the camp in a few days' time. Seven boys of various sizes lined up to do marching drill in the courtyard that evening, their footsteps echoing between the high walls of the building. There was something grey and sloppy with carrots that none of them wanted to eat for supper. The smallest boy spat it out, but was caned to persuade him to get on and eat the mess.

Over the next thirty-six hours they were all found wanting, enough to deserve a caning. The master followed the Navy method, approaching at a run and then leaping in the air before bringing the cane down with maximum force.

They slept in the cellars in a line. Peter could only lie on his front, his back and buttocks burning from four hot welts after his caning, for asking one question too many. A dead-eyed older boy, something in him broken, had been left in charge. If they made any noise he threw his boot over, landing like a wooden brick. Or he lumbered over and clouted the offender in person, hard.

The next day they were all driven out in a van to a vast field with rows of huts beside a large square mansion. Boys in sailor suits lined up in front of a flag. In Peter's hut the boys greeted him with a ritual pelting of blows and thumps and yells, and then went through his belongings to see if there was anything worth taking. The hut leader found the one remaining book that the nun had missed. A copy of *White Fang*.

'You're not allowed this,' he said, holding it in front of Peter's face, and fed it into the wood stove.

It was cold at night. The sheet and blanket not enough to keep him from shivering. Walking between the hut and the latrine pits or the wash tent, lining up with the boys, stripped to the waist to wash, standing in rows for marching drill, Peter felt as alone as a penny dropped on a vast beach. He felt himself drifting out into a silence that made even the master's shouted words seem distant and noiseless.

Lessons were brief and basic. In the afternoon, digging in the surrounding fields. There was nothing too hard about the life there. But the harsh truth, like the cold, autumn wind, picked at his flesh and chilled him through and through: he was unwanted, one of the throwout kids, tidied away into neat lines with hundreds of other destitutes.

Six weeks later – no visit or letter from Dad – he was taken to the principal's office in the main house. He knew it would end in a caning.

He couldn't believe his eyes. There was Maudey, solid and real and smelling faintly as ever of baking and clean tea towels. The principal was reading a letter in silence. Maudey had her hands folded, her face determined. She nodded at the letter.

'There it is. That's his father's signature. So he's to come with me.' She turned to face Peter. 'I've talked to your father and he's agreed. I'm to be your legal guardian from here on. Are you happy for that to happen, Peter? To come with me?'

He nodded quickly.

'Then do you have a coat somewhere?'

'I can't sanction this.' The priest stood, threatening in his black cassock. 'Peter was born a Catholic and as such he should be raised by a Catholic guardian.'

'There's the signature. There. Come on now, Peter.'

All the way, walking out of the camp, he felt a prickling on his back, the ominous waiting for someone to call him back.

'Are we going to the Hanburys' now, Maudey?'

'No, not there, lad. I've quit my job. Mrs Hanbury will have to shift for herself for once.'

He looked up at Maudey's soft face, her mouth set, her eyes wide like the wind that was blowing in them. With a pang of gratitude he saw what Maudey had done. She'd left her job for him.

The bus dropped them off a short walk from the door of the little miner's cottage.

'This is it then, Peter,' she said. 'Your new home.'

Maudey lived with her brother. Gruff and taciturn, disposed to be stern since he could see Peter must have done something wrong. Nobody mentioned his school. It was miles and miles to the grammar, and no bus.

'Time the lad started to pull his weight,' Maudey's brother said.

At the end of the school year Peter was given a job in the office at the mine, on account of his good maths, and shown how to do double entry bookkeeping. Maudey got him a bike to get there each morning, cycling in past the rows of men with creased and caved-in faces, in mufflers and heavy boots, heading for the cage that would take them down into the enclosed world of the pit. And it was reckoned that he was lucky, being handed a job in the office, a boy like him.

It was only weeks later that he learned the price of being with Maudey, of the good food and the job he could go to, of the radio playing Bach so he could carry on getting to know the names of the music.

He asked Maudey when he could go back and see Kitty and Bill. She went very quiet. Hurt. That was the price of her taking care of him so well. His loyalty should be to her. And it seemed there was something shameful about his old family now, best not to mention things like that.

None of them came to see him again. And there was no way he could find the money to make his own way to Manchester and look them up by himself. The names of his brothers and sisters became secrets, words that mustn't be spoken again, in case they hurt Maudey.

And underneath was another thought, gritty and troubling.

In the end it was his fault. He had carelessly wished them all away, because of what he told Alice.

CHAPTER 20

Fourwinds, 1981

The next day Alice saw that Nicky remained stubbornly hopeful, as if everyone else had yet to catch up with his reality. 'Something's happened,' he kept saying, unshaven, in yesterday's clothes. 'This isn't Sarah. This isn't what she wants. It doesn't make any sense.'

When Alice told him that the police were going to drop by with some information – Sarah had been seen a few miles away – he was triumphant. At last, some news, they could begin to sort things out.

A woman police officer called at the house. They gathered in the drawing room. Peter's hand on top of Patricia's, holding tight.

The policewoman told them that Sarah had been seen in the bus station in town the previous day, but after that there had been no further sightings. The woman looked uncomfortable and said that she was sorry, but as Sarah appeared to have left voluntarily she wasn't classifiable as a missing person. There was nothing further that they could do officially, but they were still going to keep a lookout in the area. If they heard anything they would let the family know immediately.

Alice watched as Nicky listened to what she was saying. Sarah had chosen to leave. Voluntarily. The girl had chosen to leave. She could see that he was resisting the words, refusing to let them sink in, stiff and taut and confused.

'She'll probably get in touch herself once she's had time to calm down,' the policewoman offered.

Nicky nodded.

She was terribly sorry, reluctant to go, as if she personally wanted to do a lot more, her eyes resting on the signs of a wedding that would never happen, the row of gifts wrapped in silver and white paper on a side table, and now a cardboard tray of buttonholes, tiny bunches of paper flowers for the men's tailcoats delivered only a couple of hours ago.

After the policewoman had left, Alice said it was time to let people know. Tell them that the wedding was not going ahead. 'Of course, some guests will already be on their way.' She closed her eyes for a moment.

Peter said perhaps it was best for them to move into a hotel nearby for a night or so. That way they could have a second phone line and begin working through their guest list.

Alice didn't object. It was after all the sensible thing to do. Nicky looked from one face to the other, dazed.

Peter and Patricia carried their cases down. There was a horrid feeling of something final as they all stood in the hallway to say goodbye. Nicky stood back, hands in his pockets, stiff and removed, his thoughts seeming to float somewhere above his body, a little absent smile. It was all going to come right.

Peter put down the cases and walked over to hug him. 'Perhaps in a couple of days . . .'

The phone rang. Nicky jumped, moved swiftly to snatch up the receiver. Alice could faintly hear a woman's voice, middle-aged. An accent.

'But could you tell me where that is?' Nicky said. 'Can I speak to her?'

The small voice again, apologetic.

'But would you give her a message?'

Whoever it was rang off. Nicky held the phone, stared at it, then put it down.

'Where is she?' said Patricia.

'I don't know. She didn't say. It was somewhere echoey.'

'Echoey?'

'A school, or a hotel. I don't know. She wouldn't come and speak to me.'

'But who is she with?'

'It was a woman. She didn't say. '

'You should have let me speak to them,' said Patricia. 'Why didn't you let me have the phone?' She began to cry.

'We'd better go.' Outside Peter helped Patricia into the car. Turned to shake hands with Ralph and then Alice.

She hung on to his hand. 'Peter, when you left all those years ago, I've never really forgiven myself. I should have made a fuss.'

'Oh Alice, dear, I've forgiven those days long ago. You see, all things work together for the good in the end.'

'You believe that?'

'And they will for Nicky and Sarah too.' He leaned over and embraced her.

She nodded, not trusting herself to speak.

★ ★

After the Donoghues had left the three of them ate supper in the kitchen, a supermarket quiche warmed in the oven, the onions too sweet.

Suddenly Nicky let his fork clatter onto his plate.

'I just don't get it. How could she go and say nothing?'

He rushed out and Alice half got up to follow him, but Ralph said, 'Let's give him some space.'

She knew he was right, sat down. What could she say that would make things better? They finished eating in silence, Ralph glancing at the door, or folding salad onto his fork, lost in his own thoughts.

There was a time when Ralph and she would have talked it through together, come to a shared position, and there would have been comfort in that. How did all that change? Gradually, almost imperceptibly, in the years after they moved into Fourwinds, even as the house had filled with children and their noise, she had found herself increasingly lonely, Ralph drifting further away. But life had been so busy. It seemed that other things were always more important. When there was time, soon, then they would get back to their old intimacy, their old ways, wrapped up in each other's lives.

She thought back to an evening when she'd rushed to get to Nicky's prep school in time for the singing competition. There had been a late session at the county court and she'd been asked to give her opinion on the family concerned. But in the end it had been cancelled, and so she'd arrived at The Merlin School just as the singing competition was beginning.

She'd spent a lot of time coaching Nicky for the evening. She'd picked out a lovely Cole Porter song, 'Let's Face the Music', and even found a little suit and top hat through a theatrical hire agency. She'd shown him how to do the steps at the end, twirl the cane. It was irresistible. Of all her boys Nicky was the one who could sing. It would be nice for him to win something for a change.

Nicky hadn't really taken to prep school in the way his brothers had. He missed the small village classroom with its array of infants of all ages, boys and girls. He'd been happy there, seemingly doing nothing but crayoning.

She didn't hold with the way the system worked of course, the way it divided people in the village, but if the boys were to go to Repton then they'd need to be at The Merlin first. It was just the way things were. Although Nicky still preferred to play with the boy from the village school, from the row of council houses at the other end of the village, endless games of den-building in the copse at the edge of the garden. Whooping through the undergrowth, coming home smelling of greenery and cold air.

She nodded at Audrey MacKenzie-Riley, a woman with a startled, bird-like face, as she squeezed along the row to find a seat. Like most of the other parents Audrey was from a rather county set, some more some less. Alice was never sure where she stood in the order of things.

There was an air of organised attentiveness in the audience as the first boy handed his music to the master at the piano. He stood in the centre of the stage as if waiting for an execution. The parents focused.

He sang a song with an interminable number of verses about buying a fine horse at market. Alice ran her eye down the programme. Three boys were singing opera arias. Several religious-sounding pieces, boys whose parents had in mind the distant dream of a choral scholarship to Oxford. She saw with satisfaction that there was only one Cole Porter. Nicky.

Dear Nicky. And he'd been desperate to sing something from Disney. Should she go and check with the music teacher that Ralph had remembered to bring everything: the tails and top hat, the little cane to hold out for the final twirl?

The clapping subsided. An anxious child came on and sang the treble solo from Faure's *Requiem*, eyes wide with terror as each top note approached.

Nicky was next. His Cole Porter solo. She glanced round and finally spotted Ralph, standing at the back. Waved, but he didn't see her.

Three children walked onto the stage in very homemade costumes, their faces covered in thick grease paint. It looked like they weren't following the programme order then. No matter. She crossed one neat leg over the other and looked on fondly. Their mothers must have let them fish around for costumes by themselves. Probably rather regretted that now. The seen-better-days, woolly balaclava and mittens on the child on the right for instance. Was he a monkey, a bear?

Mr Bowman at the piano gave them a nod of the head and then rollicked into the opening bars of 'The Bare Necessities' from the *Jungle Book* film that Nicky loved so much. She'd not been the only mother whose child wanted to do something from Disney then.

The child in brown face paint turned towards the audience, held his arms out wide and began to sing out with abandon, the poignant timbre of a boy who only has another year or two before his voice breaks.

An awful realisation was beginning to dawn. The boy was wearing an old brown shirt, very like Ralph's old shirt. And the hat, the terrible old fur hat, wasn't that her old one from the dressing-up box?

It was Nicky. He skipped across the stage in her old brown tights. A monkey in black and a snake in a green dress followed. No, this was wrong. Where was the little suit? Alice felt herself go hot with embarrassment. When, when was it going to stop?

Nicky sang out in his lovely, woody alto, arms outstretched, dancing sideways across the stage with verve, cheerfully advocating that they all forget about their worries and their strife.

She swivelled her head. The audience was clapping, singing along. Finally enjoying something. There was Ralph beaming and mouthing the words along with Nicky.

He knew. He knew Nicky was going to sing this. How could they do this to her?

Nicky finished and took a bow, the audience cheering and applauding enthusiastically, as if they'd just woken from a dreary sleep. The music master stood up at the piano, clapping hard. And of course Alice was clapping loudly, crying because Nicky was so wonderful, so completely himself, and she was overwhelmed by his energy and presence once more, bursting with pride at how amazing her child was.

Another theatrical bow and Nicky looked out at the cheering audience. Finally he caught sight of Alice. His smile was as wide as she'd ever seen it as she stood and cheered him.

'I don't mind a bit,' she told Nicky as they drove home in the car. 'A much better idea. Everyone loved it.'

'I'm sorry I didn't win.'

'It doesn't matter a bit about winning.'

Ralph looked sheepish as the boys went up to bed later.

'Why didn't you tell me?' she said angrily, once they were alone. 'Were you going to tell me? I simply don't understand why you didn't tell me.'

Ralph shrugged. Held up both hands. After a while, after she had covered in quite a lot of detail how she felt about the evening, and how she couldn't see why on earth he hadn't told her, he mumbled, impatient, his shoulders hunched. 'Because you won't let things drop. Because you get like this.'

And she was alone in the room.

★ ★

Had it been her fault? But how did it happen? How had they got to a place where the more she tried to reach him, the more she pushed, the further Ralph had retreated into himself? When, when did it begin? With a painful longing she thought of the night she had sprinkled the ring of salt round the garden, how they had lain together close as two hands in prayer in the dark.

CHAPTER 21

Holland, 1945

Over the past few weeks the British Second Army and the Canadians had been slowly pushing the German line back across Belgium and Holland inch by bloody inch, and Ralph's Field Security unit followed close behind, their brief being to enter the newly liberated territory and weed out collaborators, restore something like order and justice.

In the bitter cold of a February winter's morning, Ralph fastened the strap of the steel helmet under his chin and pulled on thick, leather gloves. He kicked the motorbike stand away and stamped down on the pedal, glad to hear the engine spluttering into life. He'd had to strip the motor down twice the day before. The first time he'd reassembled it he'd found a mysterious surplus part. The bike still smelled strongly of oil. He checked that the map was there in its canvas holder. No such thing as a signpost left in Europe. The map was printed in pastel blues and greens on a square of silk, flimsy as a scarf he might buy from Liberty for Alice, but it had already saved his life once, when he had strayed into German-held territory, the scrap of silk the only means to find his bearings and return to safety.

He began to pull out, but saw Dusty loping over from the half-ruined farmhouse holding up a letter, a bacon sandwich in the other hand. Ralph killed the motor.

'Thought you might want this. Though can't think who'd write to you.' At twenty-two Ralph was the youngest in the unit by several years and came in for plenty of ribbing about his constant letter-writing to Alice.

He smiled broadly. A letter from Alice always made the day better. But taking the envelope he saw that it was Mama's writing on the front and his face froze. Mama's funeral had been a year ago, on a day almost as cold as this. He'd watched the coffin being lowered into the ground. But now here was a letter from her, as if she'd sat down and written it to him just a few days ago. He began to take his gloves off, his hands fumbling to open it.

'Aren't you gone yet, Colchester?' yelled the commander from the farmhouse door. 'You've thirteen billets to find. We'll be in Gennep before you are at this rate.' Ralph stuffed the letter inside his jacket, his arms numb and unfamiliar as he held the handlebars. He steered the bike out onto the road, hardly noticing where he was going.

He'd blamed Max Gardiner for Mama's death. After Mama left Spain to join Ralph in England, Max had broken her heart by having an affair with the crass Spanish girl who was their maid. Mama had never been strong. After his betrayal and the humiliation, not to mention all the money worries and the loneliness, she had suffered a stroke and died.

Max had turned up at the funeral. Ralph hadn't seen him by that time for over two years. The man looked ill, his face thinner and sallow. He'd placed a cold hand over Ralph's, the papery skin leaving an unpleasant sensation as Ralph pulled away. A look of hurt in the old man's eyes. Physically being near Max now gave him a feeling of revulsion. But Max had persisted, wouldn't take the hint. At the gloomy little reception after the funeral service he'd suggested they meet up at his club, now that he was back in London for a while, when Ralph next had leave.

'I don't see what we'd have to discuss,' Ralph told him. Walking away he saw a woman whom Mama had known slightly in Spain and huddled into conversation with her. From the corner of his eye he could see the old boy standing alone by the buffet table, as if stumped by what to do next. He looked pathetically out of place in his old-fashioned, Spanish-cut suit, but Ralph steeled himself against any pity. He was aware of being unkind, a quality he didn't know he possessed, but it was beyond him to quell it.

And that had been the last time he'd seen Max.

The strange thing was, only two months after Mama passed away, Max had also died. A stab of regret for the Max of his childhood, but that was all Ralph allowed himself. It seemed as though the matter was now closed. No need ever to think of Max again.

But now, a letter from Mama, as if none of the past few months had happened, all the feelings of grief and anger bubbling up again, fresh and new. He tried to concentrate on the road ahead. Winter light flickered through the tree trunks lining each side, a February wind slicing across the claggy flood plain. He pulled his scarf higher over his frozen jaw, swerving round a pothole at the last minute. Dangerous to let your mind wander in a place like this. Safer in the end if he pulled up and read it.

He stopped. Tore open the envelope. Saw the letter had been forwarded by Mama's solicitor.

He read it through twice, utterly floored by the contents, and yet everything finally making sense. All those little things that he knew he shouldn't ask about but that had remained stored at the back of his mind, finally clicking into place.

'I'm sorry, darling one, so truly sorry,' Mama had written. 'It was to protect you. No one would have been able to receive us if it was known you were the child of another woman's husband when you were born. I so wanted you to know the truth. And Max has always loved you dearly. In spite of his faults he does care for you deeply. Please try and forgive me. Please believe me, darling one, I so wanted to tell you.'

His father wasn't Robert Colchester.

His father was Max Gardiner. Max was his father.

He crumpled the letter back inside his jacket. Angry. Feeling like he'd been taken for a fool. And so typical of Max that, even at the funeral, he hadn't had the courtesy to mention the small fact that he was his father.

A long line of army trucks passed by, heading towards the Reichswald for the final push across the German border, pulsing waves of grit against the bike. When they'd gone he pulled back onto the road. Made himself focus on the spire of Gennep church in the distance.

A week earlier Gennep would have been a pretty Dutch village of neat cottages and pollarded trees. Now smoke billowed in dirty clouds across mounds of rubble and demolished houses. Railway lines bucked and rose up in the air. A thick, dirty smell of broken buildings and sewage. No sign of anything living.

Tensely listening out he pushed the bike past the half-demolished church and parked it in front of what was once a draper's, filthy shirt collars and ripped sheets scattered across the floor. Upstairs he found a room that you might sleep in at a push, the sky blinking through holes between the rafters, but he'd need more than this.

Down a side street he saw people clearing rubble. Over the entrance to a low building was stencilled the word 'Café', a smell of chicory coffee coming from the door. A leathery-faced woman who looked as though she might have survived several wars was half heartedly cleaning the bar, behind her a wary blonde woman. He negotiated with the old woman for several more billets and to use the kitchen as the unit's cookhouse. Satisfied that the army was going to pay for the privilege she fetched a glass and a half bottle of brandy.

He asked for a coffee instead, anything made with hot water. Waited to see what she would bring. He'd been assigned to Field

Security partly because he spoke several languages passably well, Spanish of course, French and German from school, but his Dutch was still rudimentary. He pulled off his gloves and sat down at a table, letting his cheeks burn in the warmth. He may as well wait there for the rest of the unit to show up. If you kept quiet, waited, people always had things to tell you. It was the surest way to know where to start looking.

Sipping the ersatz coffee he was aware of the envelope there in his pocket, wanted to get it out and check it through, as if he might have misread it, but there was a growing noise of tramping feet outside. Ralph moved swiftly to the doorway and peered out, his heart beating fast. A double column of German prisoners was shambling along the road, dazed and filthy, Allied soldiers with rifles spaced along them. One of the prisoners, rags tied round his head against the cold, grinned and gave a thumbs-up.

The blonde woman from the back of the cafe had also pressed into the narrow space of the door next to him, a child of about ten clinging to her. The woman let out a stream of Dutch swear words in reply, then shooed the child back inside. Like most children he had seen in Holland the child was horribly thin and etiolated. The Dutch had sabotaged the railways. The Germans had retaliated by imposing a starvation regime throughout Holland. The woman slumped down at the table. She wore a summer frock with two cardigans buttoned across it, her chemically yellow hair too bright against the pallor of her flesh. In spite of the cold she had bare legs; men's socks, wooden clogs. She looked so ill that Ralph pushed the hot drink towards her. She took it in both hands, staring into the steam.

'Pigs took everything across the border. Every last scrap of food, shoes, the bicycles, even the baby's prams. And the men, all the men were rounded up. Nobody knows where they've been taken. But I can tell you where you can find that pig of a mayor. He knows.'

As soon as the rest of the unit arrived Ralph briefed Dusty on the information about the town's mayor and then helped unload the truck, glad that there was no chance to sit down and try to think about what Mama had asked him to do.

The horn of the jeep sounded. Dusty was calling for him to bring the recce map, Arthur already sitting at the wheel, waiting to go. They drove through a scrubby birch forest rimed wih frost. Ralph thought back to Christmas leave, when Alice had agreed to marry him as they walked through snowy woods, the powdered crystals cold on his face as they brushed under the auburn fronds of birch twigs.

And now? Now that he had been given so much unwanted knowledge, what was he to do with it? And what was he to tell Alice? Was he still the same person that Alice had agreed to marry?

He tamped down his anger as the jeep stopped in the small hamlet. The mayor's building, with its torn red flag, overlooked the deserted square. They found the mayor inside, burning papers in the drawing room fireplace, black ash mounding round the sheaves of paper like a small version of the razed townscapes outside.

He was genial, happy to accompany Dusty and Ralph to the schoolroom in Gennep where Field Security had installed headquarters, ready to be as helpful as possible. He took his place on the chair, sizeable and fleshy; in charge; oozing the lazy softness of a man who might well flare into menace if asked to exert himself beyond a reasonable level. A self-satisfied face you could happily smack with an open palm, but that wasn't the way it was done, Ralph reminded himself, shoving his hands into his pockets.

Dusty led the interview. Where had he learned such fluent German? In another life he was a salesman for a soap company who'd travelled widely in Europe. He had a deferential stoop and untidy hair. A bumbling manner that made people let their guard down before they realised how sharply Dusty had worked them.

The interrogation – that was the word for it now – lasted till two in the morning, with all the usual unpleasantness. After hours of insisting he had no idea what they were talking about – then indignantly explaining he'd had no choice but to round the men up – the mayor indicated on the map the area in the forest where the men might have been taken.

It would take another three days before they were found, each precisely shot in the back of the head.

In the small hours the mayor's secretary was brought in, scared and shaking. She was young and plain. Clearly mesmerised by the mayor. Ralph leaned back against the whitewashed wall as she backtracked on her story, then went off in a different direction, finally confessing her role in organising the round-up of men involved in sabotage. She was crying now, explaining to Dusty that she'd had to follow orders. They had to understand. What was she supposed to do?

Dusty led her away while Arthur typed up the last of the report. How pitifully young and lost she looked.

'Couldn't we make an exception this time? She's obviously been played by that man,' Ralph heard himself asking Arthur. Just this once, couldn't she be left to go home?

Arthur didn't look up. He had dark, oiled hair. A bland face. He'd never said what it was exactly that he did before the war. A lawyer or an architect perhaps? Hard to say. The war had washed away so much of their old selves, left them like so many brown pebbles turned over on the beach, their features smoothed into something new; army men.

'You know as well as I do, old boy, locals would mete out justice in their own sweet way if we didn't do it. And then there's no end to it.' Arthur passed a hand over his forehead. 'Nothing will settle down till justice is done, and more's the point, is seen to be done. Only way to make them understand no one can come knocking on the door in the night. Draw a line and make a new start.'

'Well, it's a rotten business we're in,' said Ralph, longing to get out of the schoolroom and the overused air.

Arthur wiped his forehead once more. 'Okey-dokey.' He pulled the last page of the report from the typewriter with a tearing sound. 'Let's get this lot turned in to Security and then see these palatial digs you've scouted out for us, Ralph.'

Dusty and Ralph escorted the prisoners, now in handcuffs, to the lorry. It was the first time the mayor and the girl had seen each other, and she fixed wide, wet eyes on him. 'Maurice?' she said.

'Stupid bitch,' the man muttered in Dutch.

Ralph felt his arm fly up, felt the crack of bone on bone as his fist hit the mayor's chin and he stumbled, fell to his knees, the blood spreading from his nose, covering his chin and chest. Dusty moved swiftly to hold Ralph back and then pull the man up.

'Give us a break, Colchester, and cool down, will you?'

Ralph put his hands on his knees and breathed deeply. It hadn't been the mayor's face he'd been taking a swing at. He knew that – and he had to get a handle on this anger. Looking up at the stars in the anthracite sky he let his breathing fill with the cold air, in and out, let reason return.

As they drove back in the twilight the mayor's sly, inscrutable expression stayed with Ralph. How could anyone really know a man like that, what he was capable of under the charm? With a stab he thought of Max. Max who had spent the war years in Madrid, being wined and dined at the British Embassy, German officers everywhere, all hand in glove with Franco. Max had never really explained why it was that he'd failed to come home and volunteer to do war work, instead staying on to count beans at the Madrid bank. What had Max really been up to? And the most puzzling thing of all had been the fact that someone, somewhere had decided that Max should be granted an OBE shortly after he came back to England. For what? For staying out of it? For pushing money around in an oak-panelled office in Madrid? Nothing about Max from those years made any sense.

★ ★

'Habitable's not the first word that comes to mind,' Dusty said as they pulled a third mattress into the upstairs room of the draper's. They dropped it on the floor and a cloud of dust rose up. Ralph unrolled his bedding and sank down, too tired to unlace his boots.

Lying on his back he finally allowed himself to take out the letter. He read it through once again but the message was still the same. He was illegitimate. He didn't belong to Robert Colchester one bit. A prickling of something like shame across his skin; he was Max Gardiner's little bastardo.

'Here, old boy. Stop going through your love letters. Get some of this in you and get some sleep,' said Dusty. He had a bottle of ration whisky and was emptying it fast. He passed it over as a nightcap. Ralph took a swig, then another.

He crumpled the letter into the inner pocket of his kit bag. His eyes sore with dust, his body aching, he pulled off his top clothes. He took the leather photo wallet from his jacket pocket and stood Alice beside his bed on his kit bag; Alice punting on the Cherwell, the sun haloing her fair hair as she smiled mischievously, her presence in the room a balm. The other half of the photo frame showed a formal picture, taken in a studio. It had been her present to him once they got his call-up date. Her fair hair was brushed and back-lit; she wore pearl earrings and lipstick. She gazed up intently at the corner of the picture, carefully following the photographer's instructions. He watched her for a while. Then he lay back onto the bedroll with a feeling of sinking, heavy enough to sink down into the earth below the house, into a deep oblivion.

In the morning a forest of light shafts dazzled through the gaps above him. It was hard to wake up. The grimy mattress and rough army blanket seemed wonderfully warm and comfortable. Freezing winter air was coming in through the broken windows. He could hear birds fussing on the roof. Sparrows perhaps. When had he last heard birds? He looked over at his photos of Alice, reached out a hand and drew the photograph frame onto his chest. He put a kiss on the cellophane cover.

Dusty was attempting to shave with a mess tin of water and a steel mirror. A mile or so away the heavy artillery guns started up again. Dusty jumped and nicked his chin. You never got used to it. Ralph dragged his shirt and underclothes under the blankets to conserve the warmth there and began to dress.

In the cafe where he had housed the NAAFI they found the taproom quiet, sounds of pots banging through the doorway into the kitchen, the smell of army sausages and bacon overpowering the thin scent of old beer. Two dishevelled beds were lying in front of the tiled stove that heated the bar room. A woman's yellow hair showed above the blankets; next to her the little girl was curled up asleep.

In the kitchen the orderlies seemed to be sharing a suppressed joke. They glanced over at Ralph.

''Ad a good night's sleep then, Sergeant Colchester?'

Laughter from the boy stirring a large pot of baked beans.

'And you men? Slept well?'

'Bit noisy here at times, sir.'

Dusty came in, the smell of whisky evident from his morning nip. There was a slight tremor to the flame as he lit up the first Woodbine.

'You've billeted the cookhouse in a knocking shop. Cook says there was a right noise going on in the room next to his.'

He coloured. How could he have missed it? A chump really. 'Well, we'll have to move out. Bad for the men I know and . . .'

'Leave it,' said Dusty. 'We've only another night here all being well. The men will have to restrain themselves.' More laughter from the boy stirring the beans.

'If she's got it you've had it, Parker. You remember that.'

Two girls appeared in the kitchen, thin and bony, pale cotton dressing gowns belted round their middles. They looked like nice girls, the sort who might well work as secretaries or behind the counter in a corner shop, capable and level-headed. The war had made them all take up unexpected careers. Ralph felt horribly sorry for them. They nodded enthusiastically at cook's gruff offer of breakfast and took their loaded plates into the bar, adding more bread from the tray as they went. Soon the little girl and her mother appeared.

'Here you are then,' said cook, piling their plates up. The little girl stuffed more bread in her pocket and they hurried away to eat.

The day was taken up by assessing the numbers of Polish workers brought over by the Nazis for coal haulage along the canals. They were now destitute refugees, with no means of getting home other than to walk. They lived in squalid dwellings made from turf bricks, corrugated roofs leaking rain into their sleeping areas. The men crowded round Ralph, listless then threatening. They wanted food, shoes, soap, money to go home. They clamoured round him, asking him in their broken German to listen and write down the names of their relatives. A man with pale skin rusted with freckles was holding a knife that he passed from hand to hand as Ralph spoke, trying to reassure them he'd do something. Down in their subterranean turf dwellings it felt as if they were sinking into the mud, forgotten. The smell of mildew and other rot was overpowering.

Ralph could not believe their conditions and spent the day running around on the bike trying to get someone to take an interest in them, but came up with nothing but some sacks of potatoes from army stores and a pile of forms to fill in from the Red Cross. The local population had closed ranks, fearful and suspicious of them, inured to pity.

He got back, haunted by such wretchedness. Swathes of displaced people everywhere, so many of them wandering across Europe, looking for anything edible, for a map to find their way home, for shoes.

And if he were to set out for home? Where was that now? There had always been the idea of returning to Valencia where he was born, or his father's family home in London. Not now. Now there was only a moving forward. Towards Alice and their future. Perhaps Dusty was right. The trick to surviving all this was to simply concentrate on the next task, the next moment, on the future.

At twilight the heavy droning of planes filled the sky once again and he realised with a sinking heart that they were in for another night of nerve-shredding explosions. From the billet in the draper's he watched allied bombers passing in layers towards Goch and the other German towns, battalions of stiff wings against the deepening evening sky. One pale star.

The shuddering bombs began to sound across the flood plain. A few days later Goch was taken.

★ ★

Arriving at Goch late one winter's afternoon, they were silent. All that was left of the small, German town was its name and the smell of rotting sewage; smouldering fires burning among the mounds of black mud and churned debris; the sharp chemical stink of cordite from shells. It was hard to see how one was supposed to restore order and justice to this nothingness, this razed landscape.

The vacating army HQ had been leading operations from underground cellars which they now handed over to the Field Security unit. The CO was clearing away his papers from a small table covered by a lace cloth.

'Make the most of it,' he told them. 'Once we're over the Rhine we'll be sleeping in muddy slit trenches.'

The cellar smelled wet, a faint memory of potatoes or apples. The barrel-shaped roof was just about high enough for a man to stand up at the apex. They kept the oil lamp burning all night. Without it the place felt like a coffin.

The first thing Ralph did was to stand the leather-bound photo wallet up on the crate next to his mattress so that Alice could watch over him. All night lumps of plaster loosened and fell in papery clouds of dust as the guns pounded. Dusty reached into his bag for the last of the whisky ration, held the bottle up to the light to show only an inch in the bottom. Several days till the next allowance.

Ralph turned towards Alice's photo. If he could just feel her cool arms round his neck for a moment, her head on his shoulder. If he could just talk to Alice about the letter. He could see her serious little face, her head on one side as she listened to what he said.

'It is your decision, darling,' Mama had written. 'Only please think before you say things that you can never unsay again. Why give Alice a burden she doesn't really need to know about? Some secrets are bad things, yes, but then there are the secrets we need to keep, to protect a family. Darling, I have to tell you, if you must burden Alice, then her mother may see it quite badly if she knew you were born illegitimately.'

How could he not tell Alice? He and Alice had always shared every last thought and feeling, every idea and hope, the good and the bad. But if he told Alice, then Alice must tell her mother – everything magnified and pored over. He saw himself drinking tea in the garden with Mrs Hanbury. 'Of course, funny thing is, turns out I'm Mr Gardiner's little bastard.'

When Ralph had fallen in love with Alice he had also fallen in love with that afternoon in the summer garden, the family seated under the rose trellis as if they had always been there, and always would be. It wasn't the Hanburys' way to let things fall apart as Mr Gardiner had, leaving a wake of lumpy chaos behind him. In spite of all the awful fuss her father had put Alice's family through with his affair, somehow it had been arranged that calmer waters had closed over the matter, and nothing more was said. Since then Alice had become rather prickly and tender about things being done correctly. His heart felt pinched when he pictured himself telling Alice, the dismay on her brave little face as she struggled not to mind a further seedy layer to his story.

If he should lose Alice?

The vibrations of artillery fire from the massive cannons would probably continue all night. No hope of sleeping. He found a new sheet of paper from his writing case and began a letter in the dim lamplight.

Darling Alice,

New digs in a cellar and all cosy here with a lamp so that I can write as long as I like. Haven't been able to write for a couple of days as we are kept busy doing housework and clean-up as the army advances ahead of us.

A few nights ago managed to hear Bach's *Magnificat* on the radio. Did you hear it too, sweetest? When this is all over let's make sure we always have time for music. For the things that matter.

Dearest one, looking at your face now, smiling at me from the photograph, it is the one hopeful thing here, the only thing that makes me believe this will be over one day. I don't want a grand sort of life when this is over, just to be with you and have the chance to live simply and honestly and do something useful to lessen the stupidity that overrules everything at the moment.

I don't mind where we live, but it would be so marvellous to find somewhere in the country, a garden, an apple tree, and a dog of course. A collie dog. Do you like collies? Or maybe we'll end up in a place in London, there's always so much life in that city. Not in the suburbs, never buried somewhere in all those horrid identical semis. That wouldn't be us. Out in the country, yes. A good honest place, with plain, solid Georgian furniture we'll scout out from junkshops. When we are married. I so love saying that.

I'm going to go to sleep now, darling. And soppy fool that I am, I'm kissing your picture – until I can kiss you. Until I can touch and hold your dear face again.

Your own Ralph

It was the shortest letter he had ever written to her and he was exhausted – exhausted by all the things he had not written.

From the very start, that first evening walking side by side through the orchards of Yarnton Manor with the stars clear overhead, they had talked and talked about everything and anything, a conversation that had flowed unimpeded through all their time together, through his home leaves and their letters. But now, what would be the good in going on about Mama's indiscretion? Mama was, as everyone knew, sweet and good and so kind. Was it fair to now trumpet that she had borne an illegitimate child while still married? Illegitimacy, that louche indicator of suspect character and bad blood; such things did matter, like it or not, and especially back then.

Of course, it went on all the time. No great surprise there. But one did penance. One covered it up. The far greater sin was to flaunt it in people's faces shamelessly; that was what people simply couldn't tolerate. Really, what would be the good in raking it all up now and scattering every sordid bit of underwear over the Hanburys' lawns?

The truth was he had no intention of thinking about Max again, certainly not as a father. Max had given up that right long ago.

He stared at Mama's letter lying there next to Alice's photograph. It wasn't so much a thought as a gathering realisation in his solar plexus; a sensation that his body knew what he should do. For Mama's sake, for Alice's sake. The common-sense thing. There was no good in looking back, nothing to be gained.

He picked up the letter and held it away from the bed. Flicking open his lighter he set the flame against the bottom corner of the paper. Dusty moved in his sleep but did not wake. Turning the letter slowly Ralph watched a wavering red line move over the paper. The black ash followed behind quickly, lifted, disintegrated, and there was nothing left but a lingering smell of smoke.

★ ★

For the next two weeks they were unable to move beyond Goch, even though the guns continued to sound relentlessly along the Rhine, day and night.

Ralph and Dusty were sent out in the fifteen-ton truck to process a list of Nazi officers who had surrendered in a small village some ten miles north and left the problem of where to put them. They drove through a wilderness of blasted farmland, the fields pitted with gun dugouts like giant lumps of turf kicked up on a rugby field.

The German officers were loaded up in the truck under armed guard and taken to the vast holding pen that was little more than a field surrounded by a wire mesh fence, thousands of German prisoners milling around in droves. But returning that evening Ralph and Dusty got hopelessly lost. The headlights of the truck had been smeared with mud to dampen down the brightness and gave little clue as to what lay before them in the fading light. The truck hit a crater and veered into a ditch. They began to dig it out, the guns booming in the fields either side of the road, hurrying now, as night was closing in fast.

'Better hole up here,' said Dusty, spotting the shape of a ruined farmhouse. As they took their packs in, there was a shuddering boom and the building jumped. Ralph wondered if they had taken a hit. The house shuddered a second time, then a third. It was right next to a massive gun firing towards the east. Nothing they could do about it now.

They opened ration tins and ate in the darkness, the gun next to them one voice in a deep cacophony of explosions and noise.

Covering his head with his army blanket Ralph put his hands over his ears and hoped for sleep. He made himself concentrate on lists of German vocabulary. He would need those subtleties of the language to unpick the Nazi command from the fabric of the small German towns. It turned out that his odd, nomadic upbringing had been just the thing intelligence was looking for. Living in Spain as a child, with long holidays in Nice with Mama's friends from the French Embassy, he had spoken Spanish fluently and French passably. He'd also gained a pretty good grasp of schoolboy German, courtesy of a German tutor in Spain – an ardent admirer of a certain Adolf and his party.

Once Ralph got his call-up papers at Oxford he had found himself sent to an army base stranded out in the foggy sandbanks of Anglesey Island. It was a holding camp where men were being constantly assessed, observed, scrutinised and studied for character faults. He found out that a fair few of the men were there for potential rehabilitation following theft, fraud, or illicit contact with other men. Everyone seemed pleasant enough, ordinary or cultured even, but you could never be sure of the person you were talking to in the mess in the evening; you wondered if there was a story they didn't want to tell. Disquieting to know that he was included among them.

He'd passed all the tests and interviews and was assigned to the Intelligence Unit. He was the youngest in his cohort by a good ten years. He was known as the one with all the languages. Dutch had been a problem of course; mistakes sometimes occurred – the cafe in Gennep with the rooms of half-starved girls.

At first dawn he awoke from a drowse and realised that the blasts had stopped. The sudden benison of silence. His whole body loosened. Then he heard a scuffling in the loft overhead. Suddenly fully awake he listened out intently. There it was again, a faint shuffling above them. He shook Dusty, signalling for him to be quiet, and pointed overhead.

The entrance to the loft was in the adjoining barn where a ladder led up to the granary. His heart beating a retreat Ralph climbed up the ladder, cursing each creak, the safety catch of his pistol off. He called out in German, then Dutch, but there was no reply. He slowly inched his head up above the granary floor.

A small whimpering sound. Someone crying. Sounded like a girl or a child. Ralph glanced back at Dusty and they made their way over the granary boards to a wooden partition. Behind a stack of straw bales a small boy was pressed up against the granary wall. From the rings of dried urine on the mattress it seemed that he had been hiding there for some time.

A sigh whistled out of Dusty's lungs. He put his pistol away. Ralph crouched down. 'Hello, old thing. Hungry?' He tried phrases in German, Dutch, Flemish, but the boy kept the same grimace of distress.

After a scuffling chase Ralph managed to catch hold of him and carried the child's hollow weight down the ladder, pressing his legs against his chest to stop them from kicking. In the light their catch looked even less viable, smeared with dirt, smelling of wee. The guns started up again and the child failed to respond, a dull glaze over his eyes.

'Perhaps he's deaf,' said Dusty. 'Or gone stark raving mad. Who wouldn't with that thing going?'

'Doesn't look good for the little chap,' said Ralph, glancing around at the cold mist lifting from the fields. No sign of any family in any of the farm buildings.

The child ate half a bar of ration chocolate. He retched and then finished the bar. Greedy for water he drained the cup filled from the tap twice. He had dark, curly hair, shaggy and uncut, sallow olive skin. There was nothing to do but put him alongside them in the front seat of the truck and take him back to Goch. From there he could be transported on to the displaced persons' camp. Ralph would ask Peggy, the unit's Dutch interpreter, if she could get something out of him before they dropped the child off. He wanted to pin some details to the child; he was aware of the chaos that ruled in the rapidly filling camp, a Babel of languages and dazed people fleeing the bombardment: French, Poles, Belgians and Dutch trying to return home from forced labour or prison camps, a whole continent of people trying to remember who they had once been, holding out photos of a son, a wife.

Towards the end of the day Peggy was able to give them some details while the child, now washed and fed, slept on Ralph's bedroll in the cellar.

'Says he's been in that loft for a couple of years. The farmer's family hardly spoke to him, but they left him food every day. After the guns started they all disappeared. He won't tell me his name, says he's not supposed to tell anyone that. So it looks to me like a Jewish couple must have asked the farmer to hide him before they were deported.' She shook her head.

'Poor little bugger,' said Dusty.

'I'll take him back with me to Gennep,' Peggy offered. 'I'm closer to the refugee camp; they can pick him up in the morning.'

The sleeping child was wrapped up in his blanket and carried to the jeep. For some reason, hearing the child moan as he was lifted and carried up from the cellar into the cold afternoon light, Ralph thought of coming home from a picnic at the beach, the feeling of being carried into the house half asleep, years ago, as a child in Valencia. More came back to him with a stab of longing: an afternoon as he sat with Mr Gardiner at a cafe table outdoors, the scent of oranges, the sun through the leaves of a tree, the sparrows darting for the crumbs in the dusty, straw-coloured earth. Mr Gardiner was drinking coffee, immaculate in a cream linen suit and a white panama. He had a white handkerchief in his breast pocket, his gold wristwatch catching the sun as he lifted the tiny coffee cup.

With his beautiful enunciation and manners Mr Gardiner was the epitome of a perfect English gentleman abroad. Everything about him was correct and to be emulated, and Ralph was his pupil. Ralph liked to walk around Mr Gardiner's dressing room when he was away from the house. On the dressing table was a chest containing rows of bottles with lotions and pomade. It had drawers with ivory-handled implements: nail buffers, cuticle pushers, silver scissors, tweezers. There was a chrome rack of pressed linen suits and white shirts. In the carved Spanish dresser the drawers were neatly packed with boxes of collars and collar studs, with braces and sock garters with gold suspender clasps.

As they sat together in a cafe at the end of a walk, Mr Gardiner would sometimes tell Ralph a story about a person he knew; usually there was a lesson in there to be noted, about the way people were. He thought back to that afternoon in Valencia, how Mr Gardiner had looked around the square, leaned in closer and started to tell a story about his mother. Russian soldiers on horseback had swept through her town one night with their cudgels, leaving lines and lines of Jewish families laid out on the cobblestones, wrapped in sheets. She was the only one of her family to escape the pogroms. Fleeing to London at sixteen, she had married an English baker and slipped out of her Jewish identity to become entirely English.

'Technically you see, old boy, that makes me Jewish.' Mr Gardiner had held his finger to his lips. He explained it was a secret kind of story, only for Ralph to know. He had never understood why Mr Gardiner had burdened him with his secret. Ralph hadn't even understood then why it was a secret. He was keen to leave the cafe and walk home past the toyshop and its magnificent Meccano display.

But now, as he watched the sleeping child being carried away, and as the news of the systematic destruction of Europe's Jewry was becoming unbelievably and horribly clear, Ralph was beginning to understand that behind Mr Gardiner's English perfection and his secretive nature lay something urgent and anxious. There was a danger in being other, in being outside the fold.

He remembered then how the swallows had shrieked like wet fingers on glass, how the frozen lemon sorbet had been so cold that it hurt his hand as he held the bowl and listened to Max. For the first time it came home to him that that family lined up on the cobblestones, wrapped in sheets for shrouds, they were his family too.

The sleeping child was laid along the back seat of the jeep, and Peggy tucked the army blanket round him. He slammed the door, gave her a wave, and watched the jeep disappear into the evening gloom. Feeling heavy and weary he turned back to go underground into the cellar. When all this was over they'd make a better world. The fear and the bombs and all the terrible things he had seen would be gone. He would stand and look up at the clear night sky, nothing but stars and the moon, peace and silence soaking into his soul.

He saw himself walking home one morning, Alice at the door of a cottage in a dip of the hills, the scent of the blue woodsmoke rising above the trees – and he saw the children that would walk with them along the country lanes.

And they'd never look back.

CHAPTER 22

Gairloch, 1981

Sarah's room looked out over the gardens, and beyond them the sea. A door at one end opened out onto the set of stone steps leading down to the garden, an area of heathland that had been cultivated into some kind of order, blending at the edges with the wild grasses and heather, only a wire fence round it to keep the sheep from eating the tufts of flowers between the rocky outcrops. Placed on a cliff promontory the garden seemed to open directly onto the sea and the sky.

Her room had a sloping roof, the upper part of a converted byre, where the breath of cows had once collected under the rafters, the smell of hay and of ammonia and dung. The old walls were whitewashed in chalky lime, cool and damp to the touch, thickly built of rocks and mortar. When there was no wind, when the sea was calm, the room she was in held a profound silence that soaked into her body, relaxing nerves and sinews, unknotting the twists in her stomach. She could feel her breathing slow, her throat loosening. The grief was still there. Nicky's absence was a constant; but the rest of her life would continue now, cold and under rain.

The sister had recognised her, by a miracle, as the child who had visited the retreat all those years ago, holding the hand of her father. She and her parents had stayed there for a few days one summer, attending the twice-daily services of the convent matins and vespers, then walking along the long, empty beaches.

She'd written down her request to stay. She asked the sisters to tell Nicky and her family that she was safe, but no other details. After a couple of days something clasped at the base of her throat started to uncoil, and she had begun to talk, a few words. But she couldn't pick up the phone. Talk into it and tell them. That was too hard.

It would always be too hard.

She worked outside most days, weeding the vegetable beds placed on the slope out of the wind. Or she worked in the small poly tunnels set in a crook of the bay where the sisters grew kale and parsley and other crops that wouldn't survive in the open, not this far north.

She didn't join the sisters in the chilly stone chapel, though she could hear their trebles and contraltos as she worked, their slow harmonies that breathed in and out through the offices of the day, one body respiring slowly in sleep. Then she would stop digging and let the sounds reach her, plaintive and regretful. Even at night she might wake and catch their fluting chants, a vigil like the waves.

Sometimes, standing in the garden looking out over the shifting light on the water, she thought of the chaos of wedding things that had been abandoned at Fourwinds and she twisted inside with the guilt that she'd let it all go on for so long.

And her parents?

Too much white noise. She picked up the spade again and worked until she was too tired to think any more.

She was short of clothes. Short of money. She went into the nearby market town and bought shoes from a charity shop, a woollen jumper; it was cold this far north. As she walked over the pebbles by the sea the shoes slipped, hard and a little too loose, each faintly worn into the shape of someone else's foot, her clothes failing to keep out the evening wind rising from a sea metalled with the last light.

It was part of the routine of the order that you talked with a sister once a week, no set topic. The nun had very soft cheeks, like a faded peach, bad teeth and a kindness that could make Sarah feel weepy if she didn't check herself. One day, on some mad impulse – the courage of sharing secrets with strangers – Sarah had ruined the nun's day by letting it all spill out. Why had she done that?

A few days later she came to Sarah. 'Will you think about telling them?' she'd asked her, upset, teary-eyed.

Sarah had stared at the nun. Shook her head. She realised then that she couldn't stay for ever. She would have to leave sooner or later. Nowhere that she belonged.

If she let herself think of home then she saw her father, his clear certainty that the world was new and resurrected, and she was its brave inheritor, receiving this better world.

But she knew other things.

CHAPTER 23

RAF Kirkham, Blackpool, 1948

Peter and Duncan sat over cups of dark brown tea in the NAAFI canteen.

'Wouldn't you know it. I bet the buggers aren't going to let us go till midnight. I'll be all night getting back to Glasgow at this rate.'

Duncan took a cigarette from a packet of Woodbines and offered Peter one. He struck a match, a faint whiff of brimstone, and passed the box to Peter. 'And I've got my Doreen waiting for me back home. You finally going to tell me who you've got waiting for you just now, eh Peter? I ken you're holding a candle for someone.'

Peter shook his head. 'I'm going to be concentrating on my studies. No girlfriends for me.'

The canteen was warm and steamy from the tea urn on the side table, a smell of boiled cabbage and potatoes lingering from the six o'clock supper. Everyone had left except for the group of thirty men in civvies waiting to get the all-clear for demob. Peter had felt inside his new suit jacket two or three times to check his ticket from Kirkham station was safely there. New shoes and a new raincoat folded over the back of the canvas chair, new trilby on the canteen table. Peter moved it away from the tea spills.

'You going to come up to Glasgow to see us then, Peter?'

'Aye, maybe. I'd like that. And you come and see London. We're allowed guests at the students' lodgings.'

'Maybe I should – come down and check up on what you're up to. And remember, when you're done with that fairy story book of yours, I've always a spare copy of *Das Kapital* ready, for when you see the light.'

Peter smiled. They'd argued long and heatedly about the way to a better world, and could now recite each other's points of view verbatim. Now there was only the living to do, Duncan off to the shipyards in Glasgow and a passion for the trade unions, Peter leaving to study for a parish and the good news of salvation. Behind them the skills acquired in two years at RAF Kirkham; how to buff the steel blade of a 1914-issue bayonet with wire wool and spit; how to drill in snow for three hours with the wet soaking up to their knees; how to spruce up the army base for a visit from top brass, whitewashing every single thing in sight including the coal pile.

The double doors swung open. Commander Webb came striding in holding a sheaf of papers. 'Here we are, and it's thank you and goodbye to MacDonald, Donoghue, Needham, Maynard . . .' Not waiting for him to finish the list Duncan took the peak of his trilby in his forefinger and thumb and settled it on his head. He winked at Peter and cocked his head to the door. Minutes later they were walking out of the base towards Kirkham station.

★ ★

As Peter sat in the train compartment, the smell of the new cloth from his suit sharp in his nostrils, he had a persistent thought in the back of his mind: Maudey had said Alice might have moved to London. He gazed out at the early light reeling off the flat Midland fields. Shards of brilliance scattered over an expanse of water. He shut his eyes and saw Alice descending through the banks of asters and summer daisies.

Maudey had only heard indirectly how the Hanburys had sold the house and moved to London, through an old friend in the village. The

Hanburys had not given her any forwarding address. When Maudey had told him that, it had given Peter a horrible feeling, as if he and Maudey were a contamination to be sealed off. He placed a cheek against the windowpane and closed his eyes. He wondered what Alice would have to say if she heard he'd got into university; he pictured her face opening up with surprise. She'd grasp his arms in that way of hers. 'I knew you'd do it, Peter.' Well, there was no way to tell her that now.

The day he got the letter of acceptance to the university he'd sent a telegram to Maudey. Gave her the fright of her life, she told him. To her mind the only reason to send a telegram was because someone had died. But she was unspeakably proud of him, Peter training to be a vicar like Father Marston at the church she and Albert had attended since their baptism.

It was Maudey's brother, Albert, with his dour but kind ways, who had shown Peter a framework for the feeling that had come to him of something inexplicable and numinous. On the night Peter heard Ma had died the world had dipped and the ground given way. And yet someone, or something, had stayed near, comforting him. He was sure of it.

He'd put it away as a child's fancy; but later, as he was picking potatoes at threepence a bucket in an empty field on a hilltop near Baxendale, smarting from being dismissed from the Hanburys' house, bitter and lonely and with all hopes of the grammar gone, the tractor ahead had stopped for a moment, the farmer wiping his neck. The day was silent except for the faint beating of the wind on his ears. Across the miles of hard mud the sky was wide and white, oppressively vacant; but here was the strange thing, it was no longer empty. He stood by his bucket for a long time, attentive and puzzled, seeing the same place, yet a different place.

He'd wondered if other people knew about this — something

beyond the sky and the mud. Then the tractor had started up again, the engine choking, and he had bent to carry on picking up the potatoes in its wake.

In Albert's gruff and home-hewn faith, Peter had recognised a language for such things: Albert's mornings began with the Bible open on the table; the old miner's head bent before the evening meals in the tiny cottage parlour with the clock chiming on the mantelpiece and the smell of boiled cauliflower and coal smoke. His father had left him abandoned, but Peter began to understand that there was another Father who had stayed with him, a presence glimpsed and not glimpsed, but there, beyond the surface shimmer of things: *Our Father in heaven.*

On Sundays, wrapped in the faded spice of communion incense, Peter would watch Father Marston spread his arms like a white bird and lead the prayer of dedication. He wondered if he should tell the priest that he'd been called to serve in the same way, but he knew Father Marston would laugh.

In the mining offices – lucky to get a job in the offices and not have to go down the pit, a boy like him – he'd sat all day adding up long columns of figures. He spent the evenings at night school, studying English and history. And he wasn't sure how it would happen, but so long as he kept educating himself, so long as he kept learning, then one day he would apply for university, like Alice had said.

He thought that two years stuck in the army for National Service would scupper any chance of studying further. He'd smoked and sworn and dated girls at dances, and the privileges of being a man seemed a fair exchange for a child's fancies about being a man of God. Anyway, the truth was, for someone like him, choices were small in number, pruned off as the years closed in. Peeling a mountain of spuds for taking an unauthorised leave to slip out to a dance in Blackpool, he'd looked down at his tobacco-stained fingers, the skin crinkled and swollen by the potato water. He'd thought of a dream where he sat in a university library surrounded by books and wrote essays on poetry and God. He could feel the smooth fountain pen moving in his fingers, the flow of words unfurling on the paper. He'd shaken his head and laughed at himself.

Sometimes, standing at the bar waiting for his dark pint of bitter in Kirkham town, he'd seen shadows of Dad by his side, tipsy and bragging, a small man who was made for bigger things, ridiculous and pitiful in his delusions. He'd been too weak to stand up to Ivy, who had made it clear to Peter that he shouldn't bother coming back to visit now she was running the house.

One evening, sitting in the Nissen hut chapel for compline prayers, a vigil he kept up like a visit to an ailing friend, he'd sat on after the service in the gloomy barrel-roofed hut for a long time. The padre started to snap out the lights. One candle in a red glass lamp left hanging above the altar. The spiced smell of incense recalled the lad who had seen something more beyond the flat earth of the potato field, seen the light beyond the white sky. Now he felt his chest closing in, the smallness of the air he was allowed to breathe. The padre, a bloke with a thin moustache and a cut-glass voice, sat alongside him, making the bench creak, and asked him if there was anything he wanted to talk about.

So he had told the padre about his laughable idea that he had a calling to be a minister. He waited for the padre's condescending reply. The padre nodded slowly, as if agreeing. Peter's heart sealed over a little more with something hard, like scar tissue. Then the padre told him about a London university where they had a degree course, for men like him with a cobbled-together education. It wouldn't be a full degree as such, but he could study theology and train for the Church. If he was willing to work hard and cram for the exams in any spare time, then there might be a way.

At Watford Junction the door of the train compartment slid open and a woman in a neat green suit entered, holding the hand of a small girl in a woollen pixie hat. Peter stood up to help lift the woman's suitcase into the netting of the overhead rack. She thanked him shortly and sat down on the opposite seat, near the door. She got out a book. The child crept along the seat to look out of the window.

'We're going to see my granny,' the child said. 'Where are you going?'

'I'm going to university.'

He noticed the woman's eyes flick over him, reassessing him.

'Why?' the child persisted.

'To learn to be a vicar.'

'Don't bother the gentleman, Catherine,' her mother said.

When the train pulled in at Euston he helped her get her suitcase back down. The woman thanked him.

'Do you need a hand with that?' he said, nodding at her case as they got off the train. 'Which way are you going?'

At the taxi rank he waved them off. Feeling reckless, and sure he'd be destitute as a result, he opened the door of the next taxi and gave the address of his hall of residence in Victoria.

The taxi dropped him off in front of a red-brick building. Across the road was a square with the iron railings still missing, bare rectangles of earth from wartime vegetable plots. There was a nostalgic fragility to the air, the summer over, but fresh with a new season to be savoured. Enormous plane trees filled with shifting green light overhead.

In the lobby, beneath a stained glass window, an elderly porter behind a desk searched for Peter Donoghue on a list. Yes, he was expected. Peter realised he'd been holding his breath. The man shuffled over to a board of hooks and fetched down a key. He pointed up at the stairs. 'Two floors up, on the left.'

The sound of a choir grew louder and louder as Peter walked along the corridor, the din of trumpets and voices coming from inside the room with his number on the front. He tapped on the door, then tapped again and finally turned the handle. A man a few years older than Peter was sitting beneath a mullioned window. He jumped up and came through trails of tobacco smoke. He shook Peter's hand hard.

'You must be Peter.'

'Aye, Peter Donoghue. Pleased to meet you.' They had to raise their voices above the music.

'Fred, Fred Baxter. Here, let me shut Elgar up for a minute.'

He wore a wide-shouldered tweed jacket, hair oiled back from bald temples, tortoiseshell glasses. Peter noted the regimental tie, a tiepin holding it flat against his shirt. His bed was made as neatly as an envelope. His books and possessions lined up and in order.

'Stow your things here, old boy,' he said glancing over Peter's cardboard suitcase and pointing to a chest of drawers.

Peter placed his things in the chest: his three shirts and his sleeveless pullover. He put his comb and washbag on the top. Fred had disappeared to fill the tin kettle. He came back and set it to boil on the small gas ring. Opening the window he fetched in a milk bottle from the ledge, sniffed it and then poured it into teacups.

'Would you like the music again?' Peter nodded and Fred replaced the gramophone needle onto the disc.

'Girlfriend?'

Peter shook his head.

'That's the spirit. Nothing worse for the mind than a girlfriend.'

Fred poured the boiling water onto the tea and put the lid on with a decisive click of pottery.

'They've put out a spread downstairs, rock cakes, bread and jam. Then you've got registration, but why don't I take you out for a bit of a recce this afternoon? Get the lie of the land.'

★ ★

London had the battered magnificence of an indomitable elderly businessman setting out for work each day in a gaberdine coat that had seen better days. The masonry of some of the grand buildings was pitted with shrapnel scars. Every so often they passed a shop where the windows were still boarded up.

Keeping up a fast pace Fred delivered a stream of information – the best place to buy cheap cheese, when to see the Changing of the Guard, where to buy second-hand textbooks. He spoke like a cinema newsreel, his voice clipped, resolutely cheerful and chipper. A voice to get you through a war.

'There's the old girl,' said Fred as they walked towards the dome of St Paul's, its shape rising up at the end of a gulley of tall buildings. As they came nearer, the shops and offices ended abruptly and they came out onto a wasteland of broken walls and weeds that washed right up to the steps of the cathedral.

Everyone had seen the pictures of the Luftwaffe firestorm, St Paul's surrounded by towering flames – a miracle that no bombs had hit it. But it was still a shock to see the cathedral marooned among acres of cleared bombsites. Stringy weeds had taken over the ground like a cheap version of the countryside. Fallen masonry marked where buildings had once stood. Two office girls sat with their backs against a tombstone, eating their sandwiches, almost lost in the tall, straw-coloured grass.

Peter followed Fred up the cathedral steps. Inside its whispering gloom they were met by a man in white robes, stepping out of the shadows. It took a moment to register it was a painting. The man was holding a lamp with a greenish light, paused in the act of knocking on a bramble-covered door: Jesus knocking on the door of the soul.

They skirted the blocky pillars in silence, their footfalls echoing flatly as they walked towards the centre where the gold mosaics of the dome twinkled above the gloomy greyness of the building. The organ was playing a fugue by Bach that Peter recognised. He could feel the vibration of the bass notes like an itch in his chest bone.

'Fancy a climb up there to the dome?' said Fred. 'For a shilling you can go right up the ladder and stand inside the cross on top. Best view in London.'

The ladder inside the cross was surprisingly humble and workman-like, as if left there for repairs. Peter reached the murky Oriel window and scanned the view, the city spreading all the way to the horizon. Miles and miles of streets and buildings faded into a brown haze; Jerusalem, battered and bruised. If he squinted he could just make out the black sticks of the cranes and the docks beyond Tower Bridge. Somewhere out there, towards the East End, would be the parishes where he was going to work while training. He knew them already; the raggedy children playing in the streets, the men looking at the pittance in their pay packets. He saw himself opening doors for them out onto new possibilities, onto new lives. Redemption and hope.

Back again on the ground, standing with the weight of the building floating above, he felt humbled and chosen, lost for words.

Fred was engrossed in an inscription on a tomb, hands clasped behind him as he read. He turned from the tablet beneath the grand alabaster figure and looked rueful as he wandered back over to Peter. 'Of course, for someone like you, Peter, a chance like this is going to be a step up and a step out.' He put a firm hand on Peter's shoulder, gave a small shake as if testing the strengthening of his resolution, and then began to walk towards the portico doors.

Peter stopped in his tracks. But that wasn't it at all. How to explain the impelling sense of a calling, to serve others? He followed Fred back outside to the cathedral steps, where the weed-strewn bombsites reasserted themselves, the wind gritty. There was a yellow cast to the sky, a smell of soot in the air.

'D'you mind if I cut here? Got to meet someone, you see. You can find your way back to the halls?'

Peter nodded. He watched Fred run down the steps, coat flapping open, heading away through the derelict sites.

As Peter tried to find his way back to Victoria his eyes flickered over the faces coming towards him along the streets. There was no good reason to think that Alice would ever walk past, but he couldn't stop himself checking the oncoming faces all the same. Women in tired coats and small hats over resigned expressions; men in drooping macs or three-piece suits stretched out of shape with wear.

Cutting back up past a heap of bricks and rubble at least two storeys high he got hopelessly lost. He found himself on the edge of Trafalgar Square where smog the colour of weak tea was beginning to thicken, a cloud of pigeons whirring up around him in the yellow gloom. He realised that he must be near the bookshop in Charing Cross Road where they sold second-hand student texts. Locating the shop's frontage he pushed open the door and was taken into a warren of bookshelves.

The second-hand section was on the top floor. He climbed the narrow stairs and turned into a passageway between shelves of romantic poets. At the far end a girl in a gaberdine mac was taking a book down. She opened it and smoothed the page flat. She was so absorbed that she did not notice him there at the end of the narrow space.

Two things occurred to him. Firstly she was beautiful, a high colour in her cheeks, glossy black hair in thick waves. The second thing that struck him was the expression on her face, hungry, her lips compressed and rueful. He recognised immediately the feeling that went with that expression. It was the other devastation left by the war, the hunger for the things you couldn't have now, the cold winds that blew through half-demolished lives.

She read on for another line or two. Then, with a swift movement, she raised the flap of her bag and slid the book inside. Peter stepped back behind the stacks. What should he do? Surely he ought to ask her to replace it. Or he should run down to the cash desk and warn them to stop her before she left.

But he didn't move. A small book to fill a gaping hole. How strange that he should feel he knew why she had done it. When he stepped forward again she was nowhere to be seen.

It was almost dark as he made his way through the murky streets, oddly wistful to think he would never see his little book thief again.

The following lunchtime Peter was standing in the green and pink marble halls of the main building beneath a handwritten notice that promised a glittering evening at the theology faculty ball, selling not many tickets, when he saw a girl with dark hair crossing the hallway. It was her. It was the thief from the bookshop. Seeing the notice about the ball she paused and then came over to read it.

Peter found himself flustered, but she calmly studied the notice. She hesitated, asked if she could buy two tickets. He heard a low voice, carefully proper vowels. Her cheeks pinker than ever as she hunted for the money in a small leather purse, determined to find enough. Handed it over, triumphant. He watched her dark hair flowing down the pinstripe cloth of her jacket as she walked away. He was surprised to notice that he was a little jealous of whoever was going to have the other ticket.

★ ★

He didn't spot her at first. He didn't feel like asking anyone to dance. Then, queuing up with Fred for the buffet at ten o'clock, he finally saw her. Took him a minute to realise it was her. Even against the effort people had made for the Michaelmas ball, she looked glamorous and rare, as though Vivien Leigh had stepped down from a poster for a film. She wore a long yellow silk dress, bare shoulders, her hair piled up above a slender neck. Peter took an empty plate and moved down the buffet table, trying to keep up with her solitary quest to see how much she could balance on her plate: slices of ham, cold potatoes in salad cream, bread and butter. Haughty in her film-star dress she carried her plate out of the double doors to the terrace that looked over the Thames.

Fred looked abandoned when Peter excused himself, but there was nothing Peter could do. He had to keep the girl in his sights. He found her on the balcony, seated on a folding chair with a group of other girls. Behind them the dark Thames was wavering with the pathways of light reflected from the windows.

'May I join you?'

She looked around at the lack of chairs. Peter fetched another folding chair and manoeuvred it into the space between her and the balustrade. He sat down and balanced his meal on his knees.

'Hope you don't mind if I say how nice you look in that frock.'

She looked down at it and frowned. 'I shouldn't have bought it really. Now I've got no coupons left for anything else; can't afford to eat half the time.' She took a forkful of cold potato, ate it with relief in her eyes.

'I think it was worth it. You look like Vivien Leigh in that dress, only prettier.'

She burst out laughing. 'So what are you doing here then? I mean, what are you studying?'

'I'm reading theology.'

'You mean for the Church?'

He nodded.

'Oh,' she said. He could feel her drifting away, unsure of him now. The band started a Glen Miller tune, 'Little Brown Jug'. The music made him feel suddenly bold.

'Would you like to dance?'

'Don't mind me, I'm sure,' said the friend next to her.

She put down her empty plate, smoothed out her dress and followed him back in to the dance area in the main hall. They had an awkward tussle to get the proper hold and she giggled.

They had to shout out bits of information above the band's trumpets and saxophones. She lived by the sea. She was called Patricia and she was eighteen. She'd lost her father in the war. She was on a county scholarship, enough to manage on – if she was sensible.

He had no idea what to do when a jive started to play, but she knew how it went. She slipped under his arm, spun round and was back in his arms again. They stood up for every dance. By the time the slow part of the evening came, with the waltzes and smooching dances, they seemed to have travelled a lifetime together.

After the ball was over, in the small hours of the morning, he walked her home through the silent city, the first hint of a red-eyed dawn breaking at the edge of the darkness. She lived miles away. She took off her strappy heels – they were borrowed and rubbed her ankles – and she walked barefoot on the pavement. He gave her a piggyback over a short cut she knew through a bombsite and found the remnants of a garden blooming in the carmine-hued morning. He stopped and picked a bunch of sooty-hearted anemones for her.

Her digs were in King's Cross. You could hear the frightened lowing of the cows in the slaughterhouse yards nearby. She stopped in front of a building that was still bomb damaged and boarded up on the top floor.

'Well, goodnight then.' He took a tentative step closer and then he felt small arms go round his neck, a soft mouth nuzzling his cheek. When she took her arms away he didn't want her to stop.

'Shall I see you again?' he said. 'Soon?'

She thought about it. 'Tuesday, lunchtime. Where you sold me the ticket.' Then she looked up at him, her eyes open and serious. 'I know you saw me. I know you saw me take the book, and you must think I'm such a bad person. But don't you feel it sometimes; don't you think what's the point in being good any more, after all the awful things that happened?'

'But you've got to believe that there's a plan in all this,' he replied, earnest and convinced. 'That the future's going to be so much better.'

She frowned up at him. 'I suppose you would say that. But it's nice, the way you say it.' She looked at him ruefully. 'So, d'you promise me then, Peter Donoghue, that everything will get better?'

'I promise.'

'Perhaps I'll see you then. Tuesday.' She put her head on one side and stepped through the door, closing it slowly.

★ ★

It seemed a risk that he might burst with happiness before Tuesday lunchtime. He waited in the green marble hall, groups of students coming and going. No sign of her. By two o'clock the hall had emptied, just a few stragglers running up the stairs, late for lectures. And still no sign of her. He missed his own lecture. By three he saw that she wasn't going to come.

No one had heard of a Patricia with long black hair. He didn't know her surname. No sign of her friend anywhere. What had she said she was studying? Had she said English, or Latin? How could he not know? He walked back to her house, relieved to recognise it again. He was sure that she'd be there.

'Looks like she's done a flit, that one,' said the landlady. 'Owes me me rent too. When you find her tell her I want paying.'

Where could she be? As Peter made his way back to his room he cut through the bombsite once more and stood and looked at the anemones growing up between the bricks, the black pollen on their petals. He had to find her again. He already knew that he loved her.

CHAPTER 24

Barnstaple, 1949

After her mother's funeral it rained for two weeks, washing away any memory of the summer. They gave Patricia her old vacation job back at the telephone exchange. Everyone assumed she would stay home now. So, her first week back at the switchboard, she was there on the night of the Tenmouth flood; she found herself trying to put people through, their voices shrill and desperate as the river rose up in the dark and drowned the whole of Tenmouth village.

In the early hours of the morning she pushed her bike home in the moist dark, her arms shaking. She kept thinking: she had been the last person to hear those voices, before the flood carried them away into oblivion.

The house was in darkness when she got back. She went upstairs and stood outside her sister's door, hoping for some feeling of company. Queenie was asleep, her fourteen-year-old shape thrown across the top of the bed covers, still in all her clothes.

Down in the kitchen Patricia turned on the light. She put a match to the stove and stood next to the blue flame, feeling its small heat. Her mother's drab pinny still hung on a nail, the pink and grey flowers washed and washed to shadows. The pile of condolence cards on the edge of the dresser, each one bordered in thick black ink.

She picked up the kettle to fill it. The lino made a tacky sound as she moved, pulling at her shoe. She should mop the floor; that was what you were supposed to do. A quick flash of anger, because what she was supposed to be doing was sitting in the library in London, studying her Latin poetry; untangling pentameters to see the shape of a tall figure as he walked up from the sea. How the girl looked up and saw his comely shape against the water, how she suddenly saw that she would love him.

She heard the creak of footsteps coming down the stairs. Queenie came in.

'He was there again, Pat, down in the street. He stopped and looked up for ages.'

'Don't be so soft. You're imagining it.'

'Whoever he is he knows we're on our own.'

'How does he know that, unless he knows us? Makes no sense. Now get you to bed, and this time get in your nightdress.'

'Pat.'

'What?'

'Your accent's come back.'

'I told you, Queenie, I'm not Pat now. I'm Patricia.'

'You won't go back to London, will you?'

Silence. Then, 'I won't go back.'

Patricia pushed the side-door bolt in place, checked the front door was locked, all the windows firmly shut. She lay listening to the dark for a long time, but as soon as she slept the front door was standing wide open again, even more thick dark creeping in like wet breath. She woke abruptly, her heart pounding; she could feel the damp air coming in from her dream. Then she had to go down to check the door was really locked.

In the morning the sky was dense and white across the window; she had to make herself get up. Queenie was in the doorway.

'Pat, I bain't got no clean underthings left.'

'Well, you got to get and wash them then,' she said, in that final way that Mum had, hard at the edges, shifting and molten with old grief on the inside.

'Look what I found,' said Queenie. 'In Mum's bag.'

It was that letter from Dad, the last one, folded round a brown photo of two small girls, waiting all Christmas week for him to never come home. He'd been missing in action. Then declared dead. The photos found on his body.

'Someone's got to get the shopping.'

She was still in her slip. It was October, but the weather had turned muggy and unseasonably warm. She pulled on a dress. Outside she put Mum's wicker basket on one handle of the bike.

In the covered market she looked for cheap things: the stewing end of mutton, pearl barley to make it go further. She had Mum's long purse, both her and Queenie's ration cards.

Outside the row of butchers' shops were chairs with huge bowls of clotted cream, crusted with buttery yellow on the top. She knew that taste, sweet, unguent and healing as ointment, but she hadn't got the ration points. And suddenly she was empty and poor, envious of a younger self holding on to Dad's hand as he said yes, get some cream to their mum, and the butcher ladled it up. To have on blackberry pie, like eating summer with cream on it.

'Three dozen people gone at Tenmouth then,' the woman in front was telling the person next to her. 'Nothing they could do.'

Patricia put the scrag end in the basket and walked out and almost collided with Mr Stanhope. He was there in front of her in his long, tweed coat, grey hairs sprouting in his nostrils.

'Ain't you coming to see us then? Mary's in there.'

And against her will she was back in the narrow haberdasher's shop, Mary, his wife, yellow and sour and ill behind the counter. The same close smell, odours of camphor and formaldehyde from the rolls of cloth. The narrow passages behind the desk where he pressed close, because she'd given in once – and then she was trapped; listening to his words, the old words that kept coming back like a dark tide. 'You won't get no other job. I know what you're like now, don't I? But then, a girl like you always thinks too much of herself, see.'

Out on the pavement in the air again Mr Stanhope was pressing a bag into her hand. 'It'll fit you,' he said. 'And she bain't got long to live now. You'll never get enough at that exchange to keep the house.'

'I knows it was you there, out in the street. You keep away.'

But he laughed.

On the bridge she stopped and when no one could see, ripped the paper open. A nightdress in slippery rayon, an ugly beige colour. She was standing on the bridge, the one in the poem that won the prize at grammar school and got her the scholarship to London, the poem about the places you leave behind. She was standing on the bridge and she was holding the nightdress, like an old skin. She held it away, out above the water. Thought of the restfulness of never waking, there under the cool water. She let the cellophane package slip from her hands, watched it track through the air, suddenly taken and tossed by the water. The roar of the weir loud in her ears.

★ ★

The wicker basket cut into her bare forearm. She had to wait for Queenie to pull back the bolt on the back door.

'I wasn't afeared,' Queenie said. 'But you was a long time gone. What we 'aving for our tea then?'

'How should I know?' snapped Patricia, slipping Mum's apron over her head. 'You could 'ave at least washed the potatoes.'

She ran the water hard into an enamel bowl in the sink, the crackle of the metal vibrating. The branny earth rose like a scum and she swilled it round. 'Leopold Bloom always carried a potato,' she said.

'Is he your boyfriend in London then?' Queenie asked.

'Ain't got no boyfriend.'

And she thought of her yellow dress, how she had danced with a boy once till the orchestra played the last song and she'd thought that perhaps something was beginning.

'Your accent's come back proper,' Queenie said. She looked into the basket. 'Oh, you ain't bought scrag again, 'ave you? It don't cook.'

'Scrag is cheap,' shouted Patricia. 'So just you shut up.'

And she thought, I sound like Mum. The back straps of Mum's apron moving as she kneaded the bread dough, shouting to get up them stairs. The girls reluctant to leave the crackle of the coal fire, Queenie feeding in kindling sticks. Mum coming out, incandescent, a slap across Pat's face. Queenie already running. Dad just a letter now. Nothing to help Mum now.

She'd thought, When the time comes, Mum and me, we'll make up. There'd be an understanding. Something completed.

And then it was too late.

★ ★

She'd spent far too much of her scholarship money on the yellow satin dress. Yards and yards of material. She was waiting, sitting out on the balcony over the water, too shy to go in the room, sure she'd dressed too posh for someone like her. He asked her if she liked to dance. There'd been a moment, one arm round her waist, one arm leading her through the music, an odd feeling, as if she recognised him. His hair was not washed under the brilliantine; and she knew him already, the effortful self care of growing up lonely in the war, the missing fathers, the missing mothers.

He walked her back to her lodgings, past the bombsites. He found a patch of anemones growing among the rubble mounds.

'This was a garden once,' he said. He picked her a bunch of

the deep red and purple flowers, the pollen shedding from their centres.

Then she was on the train home. She and Queenie cycling up the hill to the hospital as fast as they could, feeling her calves would burst. They still got to the hospital too late.

★ ★

Supper was finished. Her feet were sticking to the lino round the cooker again. Tack, tack, tack as she carried the pans to the sink, Queenie rolling a pen across the table, her head on her arm. The condolence cards waiting to be answered.

'We should get and clean this bloody house,' said Patricia.

It was starting to go dark, but she got out the mops and the rags, swilling water over the floor, clashing the bucket round the kitchen. Loud knocks ricocheted down the stairs as she went at them with the hand brush. Hammering the broom along the hallway, hitting all the walls. She made Queenie strip their beds and fill the copper. They threw the rugs over the washing line to beat at them, and she noticed how it had gone dark. They had to set the whites to boil in clouds of wet steam, washing until past midnight. And still she would not let them go to bed. Vim and the sting of bleach as they scrubbed down the bath, the lavatory. Scouring the cooker with sugar soap, their hands bright red and sore now, moving every pot in the cupboards. Hanging out the white sheets to flap in the dark. Polishing the black windows with balls of newspaper. When it was starting to get light she said they could go to bed.

The warmth of the autumn sun shining in woke her. She was still in her clothes on the top of the eiderdown. Queenie came in, her blonde hair pushed up on one side, a funny grey look to her skin.

'We'll go for a swim,' Patricia told her, suddenly sorry. 'Like we used to.'

They took the bikes down to Saunton sands, late in the afternoon now. Miles along the lanes, past the cottages with the woodsmoke caught in the apple trees. Everything far away, feeling remote as they wheeled past. Through the acres of dunes, the green peaks like waves of hills at first then resolving into sand. They came to the wide beach, stretching away for miles, the immense flat sea, the silver light mercurial over the grey surface. There was no one else in sight.

They put on their costumes under towels, ran down to the sea. She tipped up in the water and let the cold salt sea go in and out of her mouth. The water was too cold for swimming really, but she couldn't register the cold; she knew it, but couldn't feel it.

As they towelled their cold limbs dry Queenie said, 'I could, Pat, I could go and live with Mrs Wells. And you could go back.'

'But you'd be by yourself then.' If she wasn't looking after Queenie, who was she now?

They rode home without speaking. Patricia floating away from herself, watching how she pedalled through the tiredness, her body numb and exhausted. Queenie whimpering to keep up.

They ate bread with a heel of stale cheddar that had broken out into a sweat. Chewing in silence. The day almost gone now, Queenie's face fading into the darkness. No one bothered to put the light on. This was how it would be now. This was how it would always be.

Someone was knocking hard on the front door, like a sudden burst of gunfire. Then it stopped. They sat and waited. Jumped when it started up again. They crept out into the hallway, standing back in the shadows. The top of a man's head was moving away and then coming back close in the glass. But he was knocking again, urgent, insistent, the glass in the door rattling. On and on. He'd have all the neighbours out. Her heart beating fast and sickly, Patricia unlocked the door.

A familiar outline against the streetlight. Smelling of evening air. A sudden shock, like a punch, seeing him there.

'Patricia?' he said. 'I'm sorry, I don't know why, I panicked and I had to make you open the door. I didn't know if something had . . . You remember me, don't you?'

She stared at him. Her face white, she took a step back, and then she was sitting on the bottom step holding onto the banisters, looking up at him, sobbing. 'It's you,' she said. 'Peter.'

He was standing with the door open, the streetlight behind outlining his shape in pale light. And that was what she remembered, that was what she always said to Queenie later, how all the future had come flooding in with him, with Peter Donoghue, through the open door.

CHAPTER 25

Birmingham, 1966

Sarah was walking close to the side of the pram and wondering who had knocked all the buildings down. The last time she and Mum had walked this way there had been narrow rows of terraces; but now, for miles and miles, all you could see was a frozen sea of bricks, wooden beams sticking up here and there like shipwrecks. The tarmac roads had been left in place like a map running through the rubble so that you had to turn left, turn right, but the houses were gone; demolished – which Mum said was a good thing. She said the old slums had to come down.

'What's a slum?' Sarah asked.

'Like Mrs Fancott's house,' Mum said.

Sarah thought of Mrs Fancott's old house, the ancient lady smiling and shrunken in her armchair with her wobbly head and the blanket of crochet wool squares. In her old house three pots of geraniums sat in a row on the windowsill; you passed them on the way to the outdoor privy. There were rings of green round the terracotta pots, and the leaves matched the flowery patterns on her yellowing net curtains. Sarah thought about how she'd never known that Mrs Fancott's house was a slum. She wondered if Mrs Fancott had minded.

So that was why Mrs Fancott had to live high up in the giant tower now, with a clonking rubbish chute next to her door. Burnt breath came out of the grey metal flap if you lifted it. The windows in Mrs Fancott's new flat had no patterned nets; they were full of sky and clouds. Up on the fourteenth floor it was just the wind blowing round the windows to keep Mrs Fancott company.

But Mrs Fancott had agreed with Mum; it was good she was living up there, because she didn't have to go outside to the privy. It was much better in the flat. Mum and Dad said it a lot, how things were getting better. Not like before, when there was a war. Although, looking around now, Sarah wondered for a moment if they might have had another war, while she was off at school with a fistful of hot plastic crayons. The acres of rubble looked like one of the black and white war films they showed on the telly, men in helmets hiding in shattered houses, shooting each other to the music of an orchestra.

They didn't usually walk in this direction; it was because of the new baby, Charlie, who was sleeping inside the big black pram with wheels as big as a bicycle. He was small and snuffly, but he had the power to make everything around him alter. With him came boxes of powdered milk and glucose, and measuring spoons and bottles, and buckets with lids on and piles of white towel nappies, and bunches of giant safety pins, and Johnson's baby powder, and a different kind of mummy, who only half listened and didn't answer you very well. Sarah still hadn't got a satisfactory answer about school.

'So can I walk to school by myself next week?'

'I don't think so, Sarah.'

'I'm the only one in my class who doesn't.'

'Yes, but they've lived here longer than you.'

'We've been here months and months. I know the way.'

'Perhaps,' said Mum, blind to how silly Sarah felt, being treated like a baby when she was almost eight years old. The tarmac was hot through the thin rubber of Sarah's plimsolls. She hadn't wanted to come, but Mum said she wasn't old enough to stay in the house by herself yet. She pushed at the bow on the side of her head; the ribbon was already slipping down so the hair was flopping over her eye again.

The clinic came into sight, a new building on the edge of the rubble. It occurred to Sarah that clinics sometimes involved injections. But Mum said no, no injections today. They had to go to the clinic so they could weigh the baby. Besides, Mum told her, like it was a lovely surprise, they were going to give Sarah free orange juice at the clinic. Which was something they never used to do. Before. In the old days. When Mum was little and they had turnips for apples and no bananas.

'Did you go to the clinic with your mum?'

'It was different. You had to find a shilling to see the doctor then, so people put off going.'

Sarah waited, but Mum's lips were pressed together in a line. 'Before' was one of those grown-up things you weren't supposed to ask about. Bits of interesting information came through, about bombs and old coats for blankets and missing parents; you were handed a few fragments of jigsaw, and that was it.

At the new clinic it was blue and shiny and the nurse knew exactly what everyone should do. Mum and Sarah had to wait on a row of chairs and when the nurse called out, 'Mrs Donoghue,' Mum had to undress the baby so he could be weighed. Then they gave Sarah a brown bottle to take home, thick, heavy-feeling. The clinic orange juice. With vitamins.

And all the way back Sarah was thirsty and looking forward to tasting the clinic orange juice, which was better than ordinary oranges, more special and delicious. They stopped at the corner shop at the end of the last few rows of houses. Sarah pushed open the shop's door, setting off its jangly bell, and breathed in the smell of damp cardboard. There were paper sacks folded back at the top like shirtsleeves to show the white potatoes. And when they came out Mum was saying, isn't it a shame, and how she'd miss old Mr Stoke's shop when his street got demolished.

Back home Mum bumped the pram up the front steps of the vicarage and parked it in the cool hallway. She motioned to Sarah to come in the house quietly. The baby was still sleeping, enclosed in its own smell of powder and of the plastic lining of the pram, a faint whiff of wool and something sickly. Sarah could hear voices behind the study door. Daddy was home, but they weren't allowed to go in because he would be having a meeting with someone from the parish.

The study door opened and Daddy came into the hall, in his familiar blue jumper and the black shirt with its funny white dog collar. Mrs Stewart followed behind, a small and wide Jamaican lady in a navy suit and a white hat made of glazed straw folded into a ball of neat origami points.

'How is that baby?' she cried, going towards the pram.

'He's still sleeping,' said Mum, but Mrs Stewart ignored her and went over and peered into Charlie's pram. She stroked the baby's face and made an interesting noise like a happy hen. Then she turned and patted the white handbag hung over her arm, as if she had something good in there.

'And don't forget now, vicar. I'll make sure you get a good rate, every time. Leave it to me. And we will see you there tonight. You all invited. You'll see how well I'm running things for you.'

'What did she mean, she'll get a good rate?' Mum asked Dad after Mrs Stewart had left. Dad followed them through to the kitchen, looking pleased with himself.

'It's the Jamaican christenings; they do like to celebrate with a big party afterwards. She says I haven't been charging nearly enough for the church hall and she's going to manage all the bookings for me from now on. Isn't that kind of her? She wants us to drop in on

Saturday and try a piece of the christening cake. And she's promised to make sure that from now on it all stops by eleven thirty.'

'I don't know, Peter. There's something, well, rather pushy about her.'

'Mrs Stewart? She's very good-hearted.'

'I don't have a good feeling.'

'People will live up to what you expect from them.'

But Mum shook her head.

A shaft of sunlight was making a bright line on the orange Formica of the kitchen table, warming the knobbly crimplene of Sarah's dress. Mum carefully poured the gloopy liquid into the bottom of a glass, added water and stirred. She handed the glass to Sarah proudly and watched as Sarah sipped the special vitamin juice – which they'd never had before when Mum was growing up.

The clinic's orange juice had a funny rubbery taste. Not nearly as nice as old-fashioned oranges. She pulled a face and held out the glass for Mum to take back.

'Honestly, Sarah. It's to make children grow up strong. Fancy wasting vitamins.'

Dad, big and shambly in the sweater that Mum had knitted, went over and took a big sip. He nodded. 'Quite pleasant really. If you drink it quickly.' He put it back down.

Sarah trailed him back to the study. 'I can walk to school by myself, can't I, next week, Daddy?'

'I'm sure you can,' he said absent-mindedly.

★ ★

The next Saturday Aunty May, who did the cleaning, came to sit with the baby, and Sarah was allowed to go down to the church hall to see the party. Just for a while. Mum had been sitting under her electric hair dryer and had fresh new curls, and her face was pretty with dusty powder on her cheeks, a white top in daisy lace and a swing-out skirt. She held Sarah's hand as they walked down. Generally there was something interesting going on at the hall; jumble sales where Sarah was allowed to sell from behind stalls piled with old trousers and dresses; or Christmas fêtes with knitted toys and musty jewellery and cakes for a penny; or bingo games for the old folks who would slip her Rich Tea biscuits between their gnarled fingers; or harvest fish and chip suppers followed by sing-songs and flickering reels of Mickey Mouse films.

The scuffed church hall with its empty stage and blue velvet curtains always smelled of stewed tea and dust. Today there was a band crowded onto the stage. With the curtains drawn against the evening light the hall was a cave of darkness pulsating with a happy, trotting beat and trumpets. In the gloom Sarah could make out people dancing, stepping side to side, bending back and forth like they were hard at work. Sweetie appeared from between the forest of arms, in a white dress with white ankle socks. She was hopping and dancing to the beat and showed Sarah the right way to move her arms, stiff and in and out, like shooing cats away. Sarah caught sight of old Mrs Stewart through the dancers, stepping back and forth, her handbag still over her arm. And there was Sweetie's mum in a green satin dress that moved and shone with her. Later she saw Mum and Dad smiling and doing a little waltzy dance like the prince and the princess in a story. At that moment Sarah's chest was full up and bubbly and she was there and she was Sarah, and everything was as right and as happy as a round new egg.

★ ★

The baby had finally fallen asleep. It had come away with a popping sound, its head weighted against Patricia's arm. What was the matter with him that he had wanted to feed on and off almost all day?

Inside her cardigan Patricia could feel the dress, and the bra beneath, crackling from a wet patch that had dried out. She smelled of soured milk. More washing. There were nappies soaking in a bucket in the scullery. Washing still out on the line that should be fetched in. And what time was it? The clock on the kitchen mantelpiece said almost four thirty. Sarah should be back by now. A flutter like a passing shadow in her chest – that she quickly quelled because it was silly to worry.

For the past week Sarah had been allowed to walk to school by herself; after all, at eight she was certainly old enough and it was a very straightforward little walk, down the road of tall red bricks of once grand families where the old vicarage was placed, across a road and along the recreation ground with its iron swings and then through the modern council estate along the lines of new terraces, their doors painted in batches of primary colours.

Carrying Charlie carefully out into the hall, almost holding her breath against waking him, Patricia laid him down in the navy coach pram, sliding her arm from underneath him as if she were laying down a doughy layer of pastry on a pie. Quietly she opened the front door and stood on the top step, looking along the street, but there was no small figure walking slowly towards the house, dawdling as Sarah always did, no Sarah stopping to talk to the cat that slept on the front wall a few houses down. Patricia closed the door and the sound of traffic in the distance faded.

She would never have chosen to live in this house, in this area. The move into the new vicarage couldn't come soon enough. The woman who lived in the other half of their tall Edwardian semi was decidedly strange; she had dark red lips painted bigger than their edges and black glasses elongated at the ends like joke eyebrows. Late each afternoon she scuttled out of the front door, her shopping bag held defensively in front with both hands. If Patricia said hello she would startle and greet her back like a denial. It was Peter's theory that the poor soul drank.

The bottom half of next door was let out to a busy Sikh dentist. You could hear the high-pitched whine of the drill through the wall when the house was quiet. Patricia had popped round to say hello when they first moved in. His turban regal and his whiskers majestic, he was standing next to the dentist's chair that had been bolted down in the middle of a sea of faded blue linoleum. The smell of rubber and antiseptic cloves made her keen to leave. It took a while to explain that there was nothing wrong with her teeth; she had merely come to introduce herself and say hello.

They had visited other prospective parishes. In a wind-ruffled garden somewhere near Oxford the vicar's wife had served tea on a rug on the lawn, next to curving beds filled with flowers she tended herself. A red setter sat close by and she fed him biscuits as she answered vaguely about what she did in the parish; in fact it seemed a novel idea that she should do anything but exist in a dream of flowers in her garden. Her children were boarders at a good school somewhere.

But Peter had decided that he should take the most challenging parish he was offered and so here they were, and she was proud of him for that. She couldn't yet share the fullness of his vision – she did feel tempted by free places for clergy children at little boarding schools – but she loved the man and she loved his faith that all would be well, and all manner of things would be well – in the end. Seen through Peter's eyes no one was past redemption; seen through his eyes, the scarred industrial townscape around them was already passing away, changing to a place that was better and new.

She put her hands round the tops of her arms. The tall hallway felt chilly even at the end of a late summer's afternoon. Under the line of coats she could see Sarah's discarded summer sandals, worn into the shape of small feet. Patricia glanced down at her watch:

twenty to five. She decided to straighten the sitting room, but found herself standing in the bay window overlooking the street. Anyway, whatever you did to the room, it was still a depressing place, high and cold. A draught from the marble fireplace. The previous vicar had been elderly and single, with poor eyesight. He'd spent his last years camping out in the sitting room. Now, with his furniture moved out, ghostly outlines of his missing pictures stained the flowered wallpaper. The parquet floors were so unpolished and ingrained with dust that they were almost beyond repair. In the new house she wanted fitted carpets, lawny expanses of swirling designs that she'd seen in *Homes & Gardens*. A teak sideboard.

They were supposed to be there for just a few months while the new house was being built on a site near the church, a house that would be compact and sensible and modern. But there had been a problem with the foundations and the date for moving had receded further and further away into the future.

Along with the house they had also inherited Cyril, the curate. He lodged up in the attic rooms on the fourth floor, with a bathroom that should have been condemned and a small cooker where he made his own meals – cans of soup mostly, a loaf of white bread. It was quite awkward not knowing when he would quietly slip through the house on his way out, pausing with an expression of forbearance if she crossed him on the landing in her dressing gown or, once or twice, an old nightgown.

She felt sorry for him. Such a lonely life he'd constructed for himself. She encouraged him to come down and share a family meal each week, though she had to practically lay a trail of breadcrumbs at first to get him to come out of his room. Last time she'd walked all the way up to the top of the house to fetch him down, making sure the smell of the casserole with dumplings was wafting up the stairwell as she held the door to his room open.

She went back into the kitchen. Ten to five. What could Sarah be doing that would take her so long to walk home? And then with a burst of relief she realised what must have happened: Sarah would have wandered in to play with Denise. She ran lightly up to the top floor. Cyril came to his door with that dazed air of someone being called back to the world. Yes, yes, he could keep an ear out for the baby. But if it woke? He looked helpless with panic. She was already down on the landing below, whispering up to him, 'I'll be no time, ten minutes.'

She ran quickly down to the recreation ground and the council estate on the other side. Denise's mum asked her into the long shared passageway between the houses. She gestured at the twin-tub washer thumping and a cage of mice on top of a rabbit hutch mixing smells of soap and damp bedding straw. Sarah wasn't there.

Feeling hollow Patricia walked rapidly back towards the house, trying to think where else Sarah might have gone. She stopped and looked up at one of the houses that had been divided into flats, and then she ran up the steps and pressed long and hard on one of the doorbells. After a while Sweetie answered. Yes, Sarah was there, she said in her liquorice-flavoured Jamaican accent. Patricia felt herself sag with relief.

It was a small, thin flat, three dark rooms set like a corridor. There was a blanket pinned up across the middle room to curtain off where someone slept. She had to push through, the blanket catching on her shoulder with a surprising heaviness. There was a nylon underslip on a chair, the thick smell of spices and cooking oil as Sweetie led her into the back room with a small kitchen area.

By the open window a man was sitting and smoking a homemade cigarette. There was music on the record player, something with an urgent, running beat. He took off his hat to Patricia and nodded. The curls of his hair were tight and oiled like machine parts. Sweetie had gone. No sign of Sarah.

'She been playing here no trouble,' he told Patricia. 'Sweetie, you wan fetch her?' he yelled.

There was the sound of someone coming in through the front door and Sweetie's mother appeared, still in her nurse's uniform.

'How come you are here, Mrs Donoghue?' she said, sounding happy and a little anxious. 'Sweetie aks your little girl round to play, then?'

'I'm so sorry. She shouldn't bother you like this. Sarah knows she should come home straight away.'

'It's no bother,' said Sweetie's mother, her speech slow and sunny, filled with a dignity that she kept somewhere high up where no one could get at it. She was tall and beautiful, with long, full cheeks. 'Him always here to look after these kids till I get home.'

The man by the window nodded and retuned to looking at the view, sipping from a glass.

'Probably best if Sweetie comes to play at our house. I'm very happy to supervise. If she tells you first, of course.' Looking round to locate Sarah.

Sweetie was back, winding herself round her mother's waist like a cat. 'Can I go? Can I? Sarah says I can go and play.'

Sweetie's mother gave Patricia a shy glance.

'Tomorrow? Can I?'

A pause.

'Hey. Don't pester Sarah's ma.' Sweetie's mother rubbed a hand over the child's hair, springy as moss.

'Of course, tomorrow,' said Patricia.

Then Sarah slid into the room, humming, and the two girls put their arms along each other's shoulders, cheeks side by side.

Patricia had questions on the way home. Sarah said no, the man wasn't Sweetie's dad. She didn't know. He was an uncle?

As soon as Patricia had tugged the child in the front door she delivered a firm, instructive slap through the back of Sarah's dress.

Straight home. She was not allowed to go visiting people unless she had permission. Did she hear?

Yes.

Louder.

Yes, Mummy.

★ ★

Saturday morning came in hot for September. Patricia looked down on the garden at the back of the house, a tired-out lawn with a curving border of ashy city soil. There was an overgrown sycamore tree, its oily leaves gritty with dirt, shading the light away from the window, and along the brick wall a row of pollarded ash trees whose sawn-off branches had regrown straight up like broomsticks.

At the bottom was a rickety fence bordering the garden of another large Victorian house, rented out to men who had come from the Punjab to supply the night shifts at the iron and steel works. It was a neglected, parcelled-out place; the landlord had painted the map of pipes running down the back of the house in odds and ends of paint – grey, purple, lime green and blue. In the middle of the worn-away lawn was a blackened spot where someone had lit a fire at some point. French windows stood open onto the garden, a greying net curtain floating in and out. Someone moved the curtain aside and a woman in a green sari came out in bare feet. Behind her Patricia caught a glimpse of unvarnished floorboards.

She turned back to the room and swooped on the bed, shaking the sheets, folding them smooth, tucking the blankets in tight. She gathered up clothes, put them away or separated out washing and headed downstairs. A wail went up from the crib and she was back at square one, weighed down on the edge of the bed with a hungry baby, the damp nappy creeping out from the elasticated plastic pants and smelling of ammonia, the answering crackle of electricity in her breast while the baby latched on and closed its eyes. And where was Sarah? She listened out for the hum of a song sung under the child's breath. She thought she heard a bump and clatter of something dropped, or feet running across the floor upstairs. Sarah playing.

Charlie clean and settled back in his crib, she glanced out of the window and noticed that a flame had now sprung up in the middle of the lawn. She moved closer to the window. The woman was squatting down in her flimsy sari, her thin limbs arranged to accommodate a life without chairs. She was fanning sticks into a neat blaze. By her side was a shallow bowl. She dusted her hands together and then picked out something that she began to pat deftly, moving it from hand to hand in a clapping motion, patting the dough into a growing disc shape. She put the delicate round on a plate and then began the next one. A child came out and sat next to the woman and began to help her cook the bread on a pan over the flames. Patricia straightened the bed covers, picked up the washing, but was drawn to the window again to watch this romance of a woman cooking on a fire in the garden, the bangles on her arms glinting in the light. Another girl had joined them, sitting cross-legged on their dirt lawn, chatting away, a firmly built child with a neat, pale brown haircut.

Sarah!

Patricia clattered downstairs, ran out into the garden. At the end of the fence was a broken plank, pushed to one side, which explained how Sarah had got through. She could hear Sarah's voice, loud and innocent and instructive. She peered through the gap and called Sarah's name until she turned.

'Come in now, Sarah,' she called pleasantly.

Sarah looked back at the fire, at her friend, reluctant.

'Can't I stay?'

'No,' Patricia shouted, much louder than she intended.

Sarah stared at the house as they walked up to the back, her face mutinous and clouded.

'You don't go wandering into a stranger's garden.'

'But it's Tara. She's in my class.'

'You play in the house, or you play in our garden, where it's safe. Honestly, Sarah, I despair. Go up to your room and stay there till I say you can come down.'

She had to talk to Peter. He was in the study, but there was no sound of the typewriter clacking like a conscientious prayer. She envied the sense of purpose that surrounded Peter, and wanted, just for a while, to sit quietly with him and recall the smell of opened books, gaze at the neat piles of notes and papers and magazines on an oak desk; to recall peaceful, monastic days in the university library, the sense of achieving and completing things. She wanted to sit where an inky smell sharpened the room's air; the Gestetner printer could turn out a hundred copies or more of Peter's thoughts in the parish newsletter.

Her own thoughts were vague and tended to run dry in the sands of the arid afternoon. The early Church fathers had named, from their monastic, desert cells, the nine deadly thoughts; and the most feared of all was Accidie, the noonday demon of apathy that could descend and bleach away all faith and hope. She had never been big on belief in the first place. Sometimes she needed to sit near the warm solidity of Peter's purpose so that she could keep on believing that there was a point to her day's circular, repetitive tasks. She opened the door a little way.

Cyril was enthroned in the armchair and Peter was leaning forward listening and nodding. Cyril had that pinched look that he had when going through another crisis. With his pale blond hair and startled blue eyes he tended to look even younger than he was, which was what, twenty-something? Shortly after they arrived, just before Christmas, Peter had been forced to talk him down from the side of the railway bridge at midnight, Cyril ready to jump as trains sliced by underneath.

She closed the door quietly again and retreated. She felt a twinge of guilt. It was hard to know how poor Cyril was going to cope really when he could no longer live with them, once they moved into the new house.

She had cold lamb in the larder. It would be shepherd's pie then. She took the mincing grinder from the cupboard and clamped it to the edge of the table with its screw attachment and began to feed the lamb through. She added a Bisto cube and mashed the boiled potatoes on the stove, straining the cloudy water into the sink, the steam frizzing her hair and making her face damp. Meat and two veg, and a proper pudding. She would bake a rice pudding in the cooker under the shepherd's pie. As a girl she had watched her mother wrap bundles of breadcrumbs and minced offal inside webs of some animal membrane that hung between her hands like glutinous lace, working it snugly round the faggots. Endless odd substitutions for food.

Always the sense of well-being when Patricia knew the oven was filled with good things, cooking steadily; a sense of living in a better world, a place of plenty for her children. Feeling almost peaceful she climbed upstairs to check on the baby. She felt heavy and itchy and ready for him to feed.

She had left the bedroom in order, but she walked back in to find the bed quilt strewn with her underwear and odd garments rifled from her drawers. The rubber girdle had escaped its cardboard tube and lay like some internal organ dissected and drained of blood. The smiling lady on the tube looked manically happy, flaunting her tiny, nipped-in waist – lying of course about just how much the thing hurt. Suspender belts lay tangled with a couple of bras. Nylon stockings sprawled across the quilt like the demarcation of a body in a crime scene. A tipped-up box of buttons and hooks and eyes and elastic were sprinkled over a flesh-coloured corset and yellowing underskirt. On the dressing table her lipstick and powder compact had been left open, balls of blush-stained cotton wool trailing across the glass top like small clouds at sunset. Patricia felt a rising outrage; wanted to find Sarah and say something about her trespasses, but looking down at the sad audit of womanly trials jumbled across the quilt, the anger drained away. All this would come soon enough.

From the bottom of the wardrobe Sarah had sprung what she was looking for – pretty, dressing-up clothes. The stiff net of a wedding veil rose up from the open wardrobe door in a cloud. The silver slingbacks had been walked across to the window and abandoned.

Round the dressing-table mirror were pinned postcards from Queenie who travelled the world as a holiday rep. A snapshot of a tanned Queenie in capri pants and a sleeveless top on a glorious beach dotted with straw parasols. Patricia unpinned the latest postcard, from Malta. As usual she studied the short and cheerful message for signs that Queenie was doing well, for any hint of problems. Care of the travel firm Patricia sent back long instructive letters on health and men and rainwear and eating properly. Recently the firm's manager had proposed to Queenie. He seemed ideal, it was true, but you could never be too careful. Patricia wanted to meet him and check him out thoroughly before she gave Queenie her full blessing.

Turning back to the chaos in the room Patricia began gathering things up from the bed, and then she thought: a moment, just for a moment. She pushed the tangle of underwear to one side and curled up on the bed. She closed her eyes. In seconds Patricia was fast asleep.

She was woken by a loud rapping on the front door. Masculine voices that she couldn't place. The baby crying. Sarah's feet pounding up the stairs. 'Mummy, there's some policemen want to see you.'

She could hear Peter talking to them down in the hall. She put a hand to her hair to check for signs of her afternoon nap as she came down the stairs carrying Charlie on one hip, flushed and feeling guilty, the two policemen staring up at her.

★ ★

Later she asked poor Cyril, who always needed cheering up, if he wouldn't like to join them and share the shepherd's pie. And by the time they sat down to eat it had become a funny story, with Cyril the audience; how Mrs Stewart had been charging double for the rent of the church hall, pocketing the difference. She'd also been selling cannabis. Christening parties were a general euphemism for an evening with beer and dope and other things – all hosted by the church. The police had cautioned Peter to take more care next time, not be so easily taken in.

The food on the table, they folded their hands and Peter said grace. She watched him, his eyes closed, and thought again how she had married a good man. And as he opened his eyes and she handed a plate to dear old Cyril to pass down to Sarah, she thought that sometimes it was a good thing that she was a little less ready to trust than Peter, because, really, when you had children you could never be too vigilant.

It was a story they were still telling three years later in the new house, in the fitted kitchen with its runs of shiny melamine units and the plate glass windows, Cyril still part of the family, since there was plenty of room really. They had sat in front of the black and white TV set, Sarah and Charlie cross-legged on the carpet, and watched a startling transmission of men in space suits, placing their feet on the surface of the moon, brilliant white figures against a night sky making giant, leaping steps; the vision become reality.

The world had been rebuilt, and it was good.

CHAPTER 26

Leeds, 1976

Sarah spotted Sally through the afternoon fug of the student union bar and waved at her. Sally came over and kissed Sarah and Laura on both cheeks, full of apologies for being late, trembling and wired as if she was on something. Which of course she was: Professor Cartwright from the French department.

Sarah noted Sally's new haircut and a wool skirt that swung out with gypsy romance over leather boots too expensive for a student. Sally perched there on the edge of the banquette, her eyes filled with a bemused, self-referential fog. She didn't seem able to get anyone into focus.

'I know. It's crazy. He's so old,' she kept saying. 'But then, he's so, you know.'

Sarah and Laura nodded as if completely knowledgeable about the kind of life that a creature like Sally might live, flying high and bright in her new metamorphosis – and dangerously close to burn-out it seemed, never still for a moment, sipping or tapping, and then standing ready to go for ages, the hem of her skirt trembling, her eyes darting about as if she thought she might be observed.

'You must promise not to say anything. Ever,' she said. 'He could lose his job.' She sounded desperately worried, and a tiny bit pleased.

After she left they picked up their pints. Bog standard scruffy students with greasy hair and bad jumpers. Tattered sleeves pulled down over hands. Not a man between them. In the gloomy afternoon light of the JCR bar, without the glamour of darkness and strobe lights, the acres of cigarette burns and black chewing-gum blobs were plainly visible across the dirty red carpet.

'God. Wouldn't like to get myself into a mess like that,' Laura said, setting her pint down judiciously.

Sarah nodded, made a glad-I-escaped-*that* grimace. But even so, Sally had left a resonance behind in the smoky air, live and disturbing. Sarah tipped up the last of her pint. 'Best get going. Seminar on Chaucer.'

'Later?' said Laura. 'Come round and we'll make toast.'

Sarah headed towards the brick and glass block that overlooked a windy concrete piazza, a deserted area designed to act as a villagey meeting place but which always felt like a stake-out. She hurried across to make her five o'clock in the Parkinson. Arrived late, but she was still only the second one there. No lecturer, just the skinny boy with a Marks and Spencer jumper evidently bought by his mum. They exchanged a brief smile and Sarah dumped her bag down on the table near him. They had formed a bit of an alliance over the past few weeks. They sat and waited.

Loud voices were approaching down the corridor, the door was flung open and a boy came scudding in, holding his hands up for self-protection as another boy thumped in and shot a rugby ball at him.

'Got you, Nicky, you old tart,' he yelled, raising both his arms in the air. 'I am good.'

'Oh shut up, Andrew,' said one of the girls coming into the room behind them, her voice beautiful and bored. Cami, or was it Ros? She settled wearily onto a chair, brushing her mane of blonde hair up higher in a languid move. Trying not to look, Sarah noted a delicate grey Fair Isle sweater and a peasant skirt with an inch of perfect white rustic lace round the hem. Sarah quashed any longing with the cruel knowledge of what that must cost in French Connection. She folded the stretched mohair jumper over her hands, a find from Oxfam.

'Don't you boys have time to shower?' the girl with blonde hair drawled.

'Disgusting,' said the girl next to her.

'What's the matter, Cami, don't you like my manliness?' said Andrew, moving nearer and pulling open the collar of his rugby shirt to show an oily chest with sparse hairs. The girls squealed, not unhappily.

Nicky lobbed the ball back at him, hard into his chest and Andrew doubled up. Andrew tackled back, thumping him with a driving right shoulder into the partition wall. The ball shot across the room, scudding Sarah's folder off the table. It crashed onto the floor, the hinges cracked open, and a term's notes spilled across the carpet.

There was something humiliating about having to get up and scrabble around for her papers. Nicky appeared at her side for a moment, a pink face, a musky smell of sweat. He started gathering up sheets in the wrong order. 'Sorry,' he mumbled. Then the ball hit his shoulder and he was off.

The lecturer came in and order resumed. The boys sat down, flicking open files. The lecturer started attacking the board with a clicking chalk, everyone racing to keep up as she compensated for lost time.

'You've all read the Yeats?' she said, dusting off her hands. They all had, except for the boy in the jumper. He raised his hand apologetically. The lecturer passed over him with a grunt.

That was one thing Sarah had noticed about these exotic people. They turned up with assignments completed. They turned up with pens. They didn't intend to mess up. At the sixth-form comprehensive essay assignments had appeared over the horizon like perverse trials – that you might or might not complete, depending on the will of the fates.

She'd heard Cami and Ros discussing recipes for zabaglione for a dinner party they were giving. A dinner party? What was zabaglione? The boys talked about what they'd do next, a law conversion course, the banking milk-round applications; no sense that things might not work out. Sarah hadn't thought about what would happen at the end of the degree.

'OK Nicky, you read.'

Nicky cleared his throat. He was seated opposite in the horseshoe of melamine-topped tables. He stood the book at arm's length, sprawled across the table and began reading, throwing himself into it, serious and concentrated. His face was beginning to lose its raised pinkness, the freckles rising again to the surface of his skin. He had dark amber hair, the sort of colour you'd suspect came from a bottle if he were a girl. As he read there was a catch to his voice, as if the words affected him. Sarah thought of a clarinet. That was it. His voice had a sort of musical tone.

O how could I be so calm,
When she rose up to depart.
Now words that called up the lightning
Are hurtling through my heart.

At the end he raised his eyes above the book and smiled at Sarah. She flicked her fringe out of her eyes and looked away. She didn't want to give him the satisfaction of approving his flirting practice.

At the end of the seminar the lecturer had a notice to give out. 'Don't forget, there are still places for the poetry symposium in Bradford. One of our lecturers is speaking, Dr Jackson. Does anyone think they might like a place?'

Only Sarah raised her hand, blushed.

★ ★

'Dreadfully sorry about what happened in there.' He caught up with her as she left the room. 'I hope your folder's OK. Your notes and everything.'

She shrugged.

'I liked what you said about Yeats by the way. Good point. Do you like Yeats?'

'Yes, actually.'

'Me too. My friend at school, his people have this place in Yeats country. A sort of old castle.'

'Great,' said Sarah.

'You should come next time we go out there. You'd like it.'

Sarah looked up at him. It was the sort of thing people like him said. Not meant. No answer expected. Sarah didn't really understand these boarding school types, who passed along the uni corridors in groups, their little worlds encased in an invisible barrier made from antique panelling and expensive violins.

'You've got some mud on your face.'

He touched his cheekbone. 'Oh heck. We ran out of time to shower. You must think we're such pigs. Where is it?' He dabbed his hand over his face.

'No, there.' She pointed towards his cheek.

The group in front had stopped.

'Hurry up, Nicky,' the blonde girl called out crossly. 'We're going to the Feathers.'

'Sorry,' said Nicky, flashing a smile and breaking away. He ran to catch up, still rubbing at his cheek with his fingers.

Back at the Jacksons' where Sarah rented a room in their upstairs flat, she made herself a Nescafé. Hers was all gone so she had to borrow a little bit of Eloise's. She thought about Sally again. The poor man who might lose his job. There were no more spoons in the drawer, so she fished one out from the jumble in the washing-up bowl and rinsed off the baby purée. Then she drained out the murky water and began to run in hot. Squeezed washing-up liquid over the dishes.

Winston would be back soon, and she could see how he would like to be able to come in and sit down and not have to start in on all the dirty dishes that his wife had left behind as usual. Eloise always made a grand entrance into the little flat with the baby buggy and her irritation and her busy activity around the small Jackson baby. She always left behind a war zone of discarded plastic bibs and cereal packets and mangled baby clothes.

When Sarah first met Eloise Jackson she'd immediately liked this woman in her stripy ethnic sweaters and hair tied up in a band of scarves. The whole house was linked up in a sort of commune system, with weekly meetings. They shared bills and a sitting room downstairs and sacks of pulses and had a rota for growing vegetables in the back garden.

'The family is a unit of repression,' Eloise told Sarah as she explained the system, showing her a small wedge of a room in the attic. 'Fine if you're a man,' she said, glaring at her husband. 'So much oppression that's happened in the past, it's all come from people being forced into a mould, in the context of family.'

Her husband nodded. Sarah was surprised to find later that the Jacksons also had their own sitting room, a privilege no one else had. 'After the baby you see . . .' said Eloise. 'Well, I . . .'

'To spare the other poor devils from the racket this little one makes,' said Mr Jackson, patting the denim sling that Eloise wore on her front, a hot little tuft of the baby's hair appearing above it.

Sarah saw herself getting good with small babies. She imagined the Jacksons' warm gratitude when they went out in the evening and she babysat for them. But she soon learned that Eloise Jackson was hopelessly and totally consumed by one relationship, and she was not letting anyone near her baby – especially not the person she kept finding in her kitchen, undisguised annoyance on her face each time.

Sitting down at the kitchen table to leaf through the paper – yesterday's copy of the *Morning Star* – Sarah spotted a scrawled note held down by a sauce bottle. Written in failing biro the words were sometimes nothing more than almost invisible scratches on the paper: Sarah. Mother called. Call her back.

A tight feeling in Sarah's stomach. She folded the paper small and put it in the bin by the sink, pushing it down under a bread bag and some curling potato peelings. She meant to call. She would. What had it been, four weeks since she'd rung home?

Eloise was out. Probably at the feminist playgroup where she took baby Jackson twice a week, always returning indignant and fired up with copies of *Spare Rib* magazine, lecturing Sarah about letting men walk all over her. Sarah wondered if Eloise had noticed that she'd never brought a boy back to the flat. She thought of the shy boy with beautiful long black hair and pristine black motorbike leathers who came to her philosophy lecture. He'd asked her out on a date. In the end she'd said no.

Sarah took her coffee and wandered through to the sanctum of Eloise's sitting room. The sanded floorboards, long porridge-textured curtains falling in unhemmed folds on the floor. Huge palm plants, a round paper light shade, so low and oversized that Winston kept banging his head against it. She sat on Eloise's futon for a moment, flicked through one of her baby magazines – 'How to keep your marriage fun after baby arrives'. You had to invest in new knickers and an expensive nightie apparently, cook a candlelit supper. Well, she'd seen a lot of that lately. Eloise's grey underwear drying in the bathroom, her monstrous feeding bras, old tights and knickers looming through the misty room like chopped-up ghosts as you lay in the ancient bath. She shut the magazine.

Sarah couldn't help feeling a bit sorry for Winston at times; the way Eloise treated him. Anyone could see how he adored that baby, but Eloise was like a guard dog. The moment he held the child she was all over him, telling him how he was doing it all wrong; he was jiggling the baby's head all wrong. And he was a beautiful child. A smile like he was chewing half a Dutch cheese, wide and gleeful. Fine nutmeg skin and tight black curls on his tiny melon head. He was going to grow up to have Winston's tall build and neat face.

Sarah heard the front door bang, Winston's long strides coming up the stairs. She didn't move from Eloise's futon since he wouldn't mind. He looked in and smiled.

'She's not back yet,' Sarah told him.

'She's taken Thomas to demonstrate breastfeeding at the NCT,' he said.

'OK.' Sarah didn't know what the NCT was, but could imagine.

'So, I'm cooking. Do you want something?'

'Sure.'

She followed him through to the kitchen, her hands in her back pockets, and watched with some anxiety for him, as she knew Eloise stocked mostly dried pulses, soya, mung, aduki, lentils, and they were always forgetting to soak them the night before. It took hours to cook dried beans if you didn't soak them. An empty fridge except for expressed milk in pots and apple purée.

He crouched down, still in his coat, opening and closing cupboard doors. Then he stood up. 'How about chips? I'm paying.'

'Wow,' she said.

So they set off down the street. Sarah didn't look at Winston as he tried to make enough for two servings out of the small coins in his hand. You could see him struggling against it, but he was always in free-fall when it came to having to spend money. As a part-time junior lecturer he was paid almost nothing of course, and that had to go round the three of them.

'I work in the bar Fridays remember,' Sarah said. 'I'm a rich woman. My turn to get the chips.'

'We'll go Dutch,' he said, as if confiding a small truth.

The chip shop had a long, Edwardian front window, elegant really for a chippy. It always felt to Sarah like she might be queuing up with the ghosts of mill girls who'd just come streaming out of the factories in flickering hoards, blankets round their shoulders, clattering wooden clogs. The chimney stacks rising above the hills of red-brick terraces were smokeless now, and gaggles of students had taken over most of the back-to-back terraces, but old Leeds lingered on persistently in the stones and in the air, in damp cellars smelling of coal, where entire families once slept between mill shifts, in cherished rosewood dressing tables and the inlaid wardrobes that stood on the pavement outside crowded junk shops – going for nothing – a work basket filled with someone's half-finished lacework.

They waited in the aromatic steam, not talking, Sarah reading the faded poster about fish until it was their turn to have the wet chips plumped on the counter and soused with vinegar.

They walked home picking hot chips out of the ripped newspaper. The lamps were starting to come on, orange against the dark blue sky. Winston remarked on how Sarah was shivering. Asked if she wanted his jacket. Sarah thought again about Sally and what she could do to her poor professor and his family.

When they got back they found Eloise home and not so much in a bad mood as incandescent.

'She's the size of a house,' she was yelling. 'Huge. Expecting his twins. At any moment. And he's gone off with some beanpole who's willing to wrap her legs round him. What is wrong with men? She's just destroyed.'

Then she sniffed. Saw the almost-finished chips in their hands.

'Oh Winston, honestly. You know the smell hangs around. At least put the papers straight outside in the bin. She took the baby from under the folds of her Indian smock, adjusted something. The baby had fallen asleep during his feed. She glared at them to be silent and took him through to the bedroom.

They gave each other a glance of commiseration, about how tough it is to be a new mum, how they understood.

Winston followed his wife through to their bedroom.

★ ★

Sarah ran a bath as quietly as she could in the tiny, antiquated bathroom. She could hear the sound of the news on their TV as she lay in the rapidly cooling water. It was a small cast-iron bath with chalky enamel, layered and uneven, the cold metal draining what heat the geyser on the wall had been able to come up with. She lay with her white knees bent out of the water, imagining she was warm, watching the red light of the heater through the rising vapour, the line of Eloise's tights and underwear through the misty room. Under the window there was a blossoming of black mould spots that even the draughts from the sash window had failed to ventilate away. The cold puckered the flesh across her breasts into goose pimples. She scooped warm water over her chest and thought of Winston in the kitchen late one night. He was heating milk at the stove. His head was bent, the back of his neck exposed.

Shivering, she towelled off her narrow, white body and wrapped her hair in the damp towel. Pulled on a long T-shirt with a drooping neck and went back into the kitchen to make cocoa.

She jumped. Winston was there – as if her thoughts had conjured him up – sitting at the table marking papers. He looked up and smiled at her when she came in. He wore a vest. The hidden places under his arms shadowy and intimate.

'Can I make you a drink?' she asked, showing him the cocoa tin. He shook his head and carried on marking.

Sarah reached up to get a mug from the cupboard. She felt a cool draught round the back of her leg and yanked down her T-shirt with the other hand. She glanced at the table, but Winston was writing hurriedly, frowning.

Sarah rinsed out the pan, left it to drain and started sipping at the hot cocoa, holding the mug in both hands. 'Oh, I've booked for the poetry symposium, in Bradford.'

'Excellent news.'

'You're speaking?'

He nodded.

'Night then,' she said.

He looked up at her. And she caught a look of startled longing in his eyes – like when he was counting through change, when he really wanted to get something, but knew he couldn't afford it.

'Sarah's just going to bed then,' he called out heartily to Eloise in the sitting room.

'Oh yeah, night then,' said Eloise as if she couldn't be less interested.

★ ★

Once a week that term Sarah had a lecture from Winston. Modern poetry. Everyone said he was a fantastic lecturer. Everybody came out of his classes in love with modern poetry and also a bit in love with Winston. He wasn't only brilliant about Eliot and Pound and Hughes and all that lot, Sarah found that he was also into a lot of unexpected stuff, Romanian and Caribbean poets. And he had a thing for Patten and Henri and the sixties Liverpool poetry scene. Where he and Eloise met as students.

Sarah found a seat as near to the front as she could. Winston was standing in front of the huge whiteboard at the bottom of the auditorium. The class was full, rows of students in the stepped seats, listening to Dr Jackson as he walked up and down holding a slim book open in one hand and stroking the air with the other to mark the rhythm. Sarah was feeling ridiculously proud of him, feeling as if Winston were her secret.

Someone sat down on the chair alongside her, a mess of books and folders sliding onto her lap. He leaned over to gather them in. It was Nicky, the boy from the seminar. He gave her a big grin but she frowned at him. Winston was reading a snippet from McGough and she wanted to hear it. It was a poem about a priest in a fish and chip queue, wishing he were buying supper for two people as he quietly waited in the vinegary air for his lone portion. Sarah felt her heart starting to beat hard, like she'd just had a message from the other side, something portentous and meaningful. He was reading it for her. She thought of them, standing together in the queue, in the aromatic vinegary air. Knew she was being silly. Then Winston glanced up to where she was sitting; he'd known where she was sitting all along. He'd read it for her. He'd meant it for her.

The banked-up students were laughing at his next reading, Adrien Mitchell's Batman poem, but Sarah was still floating above them, everything feeling hyperreal, waiting for when he'd be putting his books away in his briefcase. And she would go down and say . . .

'After this,' she heard someone whisper. 'If you'd like. We could go to the Feathers.'

'What? Sorry.' She shook her head. Nicky had been speaking to her.

'If you'd like to go to the Feathers. A drink.'

She shook her head again, annoyed that he was speaking over the lecture again. Winston was announcing the symposium on modern poets at Bradford university the next weekend, saying they could come along and hear him if anyone was interested. But the room was already starting to chatter over him, people standing and making plans in little huddles for the evening.

By the time she made her way through the students to the bottom of the stairs, Winston was gone. Must have left pretty quickly.

Laura caught hold of her sleeve. 'Did you hear about Sally?'

'What's happened?'

'It's awful. She's had some kind of nervous breakdown. Has to go home for the rest of the year.'

'How do you mean?'

'There was a huge fight at our place last night. The wife of her old professor bloke came round and she was screaming and pulling Sally round by the hair. He's suspended, and now Sally can't stop crying. It's awful.'

'God, that's terrible. Poor Sally.'

'I know. But look, her room's free now, you see,' said Laura. 'I don't suppose you want to move into our house share? It's horrible, but we're good fun, and at least you can get out of that freezing attic and away from weird Eloise.'

'I'm sort of committed until the end of the term, rent agreements and things.'

'Well, let me know. Better get off to the library. I've got to do three years' catch-up work before finals.'

Sarah turned and headed back to her digs. She wasn't being strictly accurate; if Eloise had heard Laura's offer she would have immediately given Sarah a get-out from any rent agreement. Eloise, it seemed to Sarah, would have been happy if everyone left, including Winston.

Back at the house Sarah walked into an empty kitchen. She liked the shabby calm of the room, of finding herself alone there. Then she realised she could hear crying coming from Eloise's sitting room. Eloise was on the sofa, working her way through a box of tissues, her eyes red and swollen-looking. She didn't seem to mind when Sarah went in, sat down by her on the futon.

'Are you all right?'

Eloise waved a crumpled ball of tissue around in the direction of where baby Jackson was slumped out in his pushchair, asleep. She began crying again.

'Oh, Eloise,' said Sarah. She put her arm round her. She could feel her shaking with muffled sobs, and there was a sour, tired smell coming from her, of old milk and stale clothes.

'He never sleeps,' Eloise said, pointing at the child.

'He's asleep now.'

'Yes, but he'll wake up,' she said with passion. 'He wakes up, and then it all starts again. Just when I start to sleep, then he wakes up again.'

Sarah felt a thin but bracing wave of pity break over her. She saw again the friendship that she had imagined when she first met Eloise.

'Let me watch him. You go and get some sleep, a proper lie down in your room, and I'll watch over him.'

Eloise looked greedily tempted, but her eyes swivelled back to baby Jackson.

'I promise I'll come and get you the moment he stirs.'

'Well, perhaps. OK then,' she said, and headed out of the room, her eyes still fixed on the baby to check that he hadn't seen her escaping.

Sarah took possession of the futon and got a book of poetry from her bag, but silence had fallen over the flat, an atmosphere of sleep like a fine gas. After a few stanzas she felt her concentration beginning to blur. She got up and went and checked on Eloise, peeping through her half-open door. Eloise was sprawled on her back across the unmade double bed, her jumper rucked up to one side, an arm thrown above her head. She was snoring. Sarah smiled at her work, and felt a tender protectiveness for Eloise.

Sarah slipped back to the sitting room still smiling. But the balance of peace was shifting. The baby was making small kicks and jumps in his sleep. Now Sarah was tensely on the edge of the futon, waiting in anticipation of the ack-ack noise that would announce baby Jackson awake. Already. There it went.

Then Sarah had a moment of inspiration. Winston was always taking the screaming child out in the buggy and returning eventually with a sleeping baby; the baby could not resist the soporific movement of wheels over bumpy pavements. So in her mood of solidarity Sarah committed herself to go the extra mile, and carefully bumped the buggy down the flight of stairs and out of the front door.

The Victorian municipal park was stunningly boring with its triangles of lawn and tarmac paths, but it suited the mission. She walked all the way to Headingly in her new mood of generous service, and after a while noticed that the light was going in the overcast sky. A shuffling and then a cannonade of snorts meant the baby was well and truly awake again.

By the time Sarah got back to Chestnut Grove the baby was set in a rhythm, shuddering with sheep-like sobs. She saw Eloise, white-faced, up in the widow. Eloise thundered downstairs, unstrapped the infant from the buggy and gave Sarah a look of hate before bearing the child away.

'For God's sake, we had no idea where you were,' she yelled. 'I want you to move out. I can't have this.'

Winston was at the top of the stairs, holding the door as Eloise bumped past him. He came down and got the buggy.

'I was just trying,' Sarah said, and then she found she couldn't say another word. She was crying and blubbing and Winston was putting his arm round her shoulders, half picking up the buggy with the other hand.

'She – we were just a bit worried. Maybe a note?'

Sarah nodded her head. 'I'll pack my things.'

'Hey.' He turned her face in his hand, a very soft hand. 'Hey. She didn't mean anything. She always says stuff when she's mad, but she doesn't mean it.'

★ ★

Sarah stayed in her room, only coming out to make toast when she thought she heard them going to bed. But Winston was still in the kitchen.

'You OK?' he said.

'Yeah, fine.'

'Tea?'

'Why not.'

They were whispering.

'Looks like you're the only one of my students who's coming to the Bradford poetry symposium.'

'Well, they'll be the ones missing out.'

He smiled.

'Night then.'

'Sleep well.'

Sarah slept terribly. Or sweetly. Depending on how you looked at it. She was woken by a vivid dream, the weight of a long, tender body weighing down her own. When she woke she felt bereft.

She saw him clearing away his duvet from the sitting-room sofa. Eloise was in the kitchen; gave her head a little flick as if shaking something away when Sarah came in, but she made no mention of the pushchair incident. Sarah gathered that Eloise had come round to letting her stay.

'You haven't been helping yourself to coffee, have you?' Eloise said, as she held a spoonful of rice mess in front of the baby.

'No,' Sarah said. She hadn't taken it without meaning to replace it. But she was too embarrassed to explain, especially being put on the spot like that.

As she was going out of the front door for her early lecture, Winston came running down the hallway stairs, his jacket flapping.

'I'll give you a lift in.'

'You don't have to,' her eyes going to where Eloise was sitting above them.

'Don't be silly. I'm going in anyway.'

Sarah gave a quick brush to all the rusk crumbs on the front seat and climbed in. She watched his arms turning the wheel, thumping it down with force, watched the long side of his neck as he strained his head to see behind and a luxurious feeling of being cared for came over her as she sat beside him, like a maid with her knight. Winston smiled at her, pulled out into the traffic.

'Got you a train ticket for next weekend,' he said. 'I got the cheap deal, so I picked one up for you too.'

'Wow. Thanks.'

'And Anne Ralphs is speaking on Frost.'

'I love Robert Frost.'

Sarah noticed that her heart was beating faster again.

★ ★

At the station Sarah settled up with Winston for the train ticket. Insisted. He said he'd managed to get two rooms at a place that wasn't too dear. Sarah nodded. Said thanks. They got on the train and sat down side by side, facing backwards. It was a Friday night and the train was very full. There were people standing in the aisle, pressing up against the seats. By the time they pulled into Bradford Sarah had slid down, sleeping with her head on his shoulder, and stayed there when she came to. When she couldn't bear the crick in her neck any more she made like she was just waking up, and Winston, acting as if it was completely natural that she should have slept like that, beamed a smile down at her.

She'd imagined the hotel as atmospheric and romantic. It was even more run-down than the Jacksons' flat: a boarding house with a reception desk crammed into a narrow Victorian hallway, a loud TV on a shelf above it and a noticeboard full of rules in several languages. A man who seemed to have slumped on the stool several years ago kept breaking off to shout in Greek at two kids playing on the floor.

'Room 5. You can go up, but I dunno,' he said, 'that cleaner, she slow.' He looked at the TV as he spoke.

'But didn't we book two rooms?' asked Winston. The man stared at him, shook his head, and Winston blushed.

They had to go up three flights of stairs. Doorways opened onto life crowded into small rooms, washing drying on radiators, children sitting listless on a bed.

They found the room. Winston unlocked the door and they stood and looked around. The bed was unmade, someone's sheets still on and trailing on the floor. The carpet was covered in bits, in screwed-up, ripped paper. Looked like it hadn't been hoovered in years. Empty baked bean cans and beer bottles overflowed from the bin.

Sarah was trying to think what the smell was. Old dishcloths? A little girl came and stood in the doorway. She was Indian, plaits and a tunic dress. She held on to the doorpost, swinging round it, staring at them shyly. There was shouting from a woman's voice down the corridor. She grinned at Sarah and ran away.

'It's for the homeless,' he said. 'Must be being used for council overflow for the homeless.'

Sarah had made her mind up. 'Let's go to the hotel by the station. And I've got money in my account so I won't hear of you saying no.'

The reception area was filled with plastic plants and mirrors and low lighting. Sarah paid for a room with two single beds. It was much dearer than she thought it would be, so two separate rooms were out of the question.

Long corridors of turquoise carpet. Two chocolates, one on each pillow of the two single beds. The walls were covered in swirling turquoise and lime flowers. The same flowers swarmed over the bed covers.

They had dinner in the restaurant. They both had steak and chips and black forest gateau. The Irish coffee afterwards was too frothy and sweet. Together with the sweet white wine it made Sarah's head woozy. Walking back along the corridor, he held her hand. The woody smell of Winston's aftershave, the musk from under his arms.

In the room someone had turned the sheets back. Winston picked up the chocolate on his pillow and began to eat it. He offered her the other one but she shook her head. He put it down on the dressing table and stood in front of her. He took a step closer and placed both arms round her, leaned his head down on top of hers. She could feel the prickle of stubble through the hair on top of her scalp. She thought how she would tip her face up, begin to kiss him.

He began to place small kisses along her parting, on her forehead, his shoulder in her face, his hands hot and trembling as they pressed into the tops of her arms, gripping too hard. She turned her face up, let her lips travel over his chin. She felt repulsed by the uneven, stubbly male skin. There was a smell of wine and chocolate on his breath, and that slightly unwashed odour from beneath his jacket. What she wanted was to breathe cool air, breathe freely.

'Stop.' He didn't seem to have heard. 'Stop a moment. Wait,' getting angry now. She pushed his arms away, stepped back, gulping in the air of a stuffy hotel room, rubbing the places on her arms.

He looked astonished. 'Sarah?'

'I don't want to do this,' she shouted at him, unspeakably angry now. 'What d'you think you're doing?' She might as well have slapped him.

'But I thought.'

'You thought. You're married for God's sake. It's disgusting.'

He dropped his head on his chest, the guilt and the shame arriving all in one package, just for him.

'I'm sorry,' he began. 'I'm sorry. I thought.'

They took it in turns to use the bathroom, slid into their beds and said goodnight. Then they both lay tense and silent in the noisy darkness of the town, the diffuse street glow through the thin curtains.

Long after his breathing became heavy with sleep Sarah still lay awake in the dark and stuffy air. She felt cold tears down the side of her skull. She lay, mourning how Winston's sweet weight and long limbs had moved through her dreams. And later, as she began to go down into sleep, she found another feeling, spiteful and triumphant – because he shouldn't have done it, should he? Because he had got what he deserved.

She remembered the boys she had flirted with, encouraged, in the union bar after a couple of drinks. How she had liked to see that look in their eyes, when innocent and hopeful and close they had asked her out, wanted to walk home with her, and she had made them feel small and stupid, laughed and told them to push off.

She opened her eyes wide into the darkness and realised in that moment what she had done: she had chosen Winston, because she knew that it would end this way; she'd wanted to leave him smarting; she'd known that in the end she would stay safely alone, sleeping in a single bed.

She cried then, because she understood that it wasn't in her to want anything else. Romance, falling in love, someone had buckled the tracks a long time ago; trying to set out to those places now was always going to take her somewhere she didn't want to go.

She thought about leaving first thing in the morning and missing the symposium. But here was the thing: just how much more was there still to be lost? Angry now, she determined to stick it out and go to it, enjoy the poetry and writers who would be there, lose herself in the intensity of other people's worlds.

In the morning she and Winston took turns in the shower, hearty and polite as if there had never been any other agenda to their camping arrangements. Went down to a breakfast of tinned tomatoes and watery scrambled egg. The consolation of toast and marmalade.

He said, 'I'd better get going.'

She nodded. 'I'll follow on. You're speaking, so.'

She was relieved when he left, the horrible intimacy over. As soon as she got back to the Jacksons' she was going to ask Laura if she could still move into Sally's old room. She saw them toasting slices of bread in front of the gas fire.

She walked down to the drab modern campus on her own, and the wind picked at her. She was damp and cold in a drab city, and this would be her life, walking alone, all those sweet destinations overshot.

In the glass foyer of the entrance she spotted a familiar figure and froze. What was he doing here? Wondered if there was another event going on, something mindless and sporty. She hoped to sidle past him into the lecture theatre, but as she handed in her ticket at the desk Nicky turned and saw her. His face lit up.

He chugged over, clean and uncomplicated and handsome. 'Hi. You're here. Worried you'd bailed. You said you were getting a ticket in the Yeats seminar, so I thought, good idea.' He seemed under some misapprehension that she'd be pleased to see him there. He smelled of fresh air from the wind outside. She couldn't read his expression as he half laughed and steered her into the gloom of the auditorium – she shifted away from the warmth of the hand that he had placed in the small of her back.

He found them seats near the front and sat down alongside her, pleased with himself, his left knee jigging and making the row of seats vibrate gently. Just the two of them, since they were in fact really early, alone in the banks of empty seats. And she wondered for a moment, could it be possible, had he really come partly in the hope of meeting up? But she wasn't his type, nothing like the Camillas and the Cassandras in his little group.

She looked sideways – and yes, he was completely handsome, dark red hair that always made her stomach flip, clear cheeks, flushed with pink today, a fine mouth. Then they had to stand to let others into the row and he took her elbow, made her jump, and he laughed about that. He carried on holding her arm, his hand warm and homely and oddly comforting, and out of nowhere she found that she wanted to cry.

CHAPTER 27

Gairloch, 1981

She had fallen in love. She had gone ahead with planning the wedding. But it had been wrong of her. The marquee. The bloody cake. The frock. All the guests. And then she'd heard that he'd be there. Leading the wedding service. And everything crumbled to ash. A taste of ash in her mouth. She was fooling herself. She should never have let it go so far.

Now, as she sat far away in the white room that looked out over the sea, she knew that she must tell them. She owed them that. And she knew that it would hurt them.

Always the taste of bitterness and ash round her words. That never went away, no matter how far she travelled.

CHAPTER 28

Fourwinds, 1981

As soon as the letter came, a short note for Nicky, saying Sarah was sorry – no apology for Alice – Nicky began trying to trace where Sarah was staying through the postmark on the envelope which was for an isolated region on the West Coast of Scotland. Nicky found only one retreat centre listed in directory enquiries. He was triumphant, excited. He went into the study to call them and closed the door.

Alice waited outside, but after a long silence, no further sound of Nicky on the phone, she opened the study door and went in. She found him holding the receiver, the dial tone droning on. She took the receiver from his hand and replaced it in the cradle. He looked at her as if startled awake.

'Some woman answered. Said Sarah doesn't want any visitors. She wouldn't come to the phone.' He got up, his face angry and confused, and collected his car keys from the hallstand. 'I'm going out.'

'You won't do anything silly, will you? You won't try and drive up there, not in the state you're in?'

'She doesn't want to see me. Why would I go there if she doesn't want to see me? I don't know why she has to be such a bitch.'

He left. The front door banged shut.

Standing in the hallway she could see the wretched wedding cake still sitting on the side table in the dining room, a faint yellowed tinge to the icing. Ridiculous that it was still there, but no one had had time to dispose of it or even begin to make a decision about who might use it. So many little details to unpick, the salt in the wound.

Ralph was in the sitting room.

'Nicky called the place where she's staying, but she wouldn't speak to him.'

'That's it?'

'That's it.'

Ralph had poured a glass of white wine and was drinking it standing and looking out over the garden. Alice carried on telling him what she thought about the phone call. He listened in that half-attentive way he had, nodding.

'Perhaps I should at least give the bloody cake away to someone who could use it,' she suggested.

He didn't reply.

'Or throw it away,' she said, a little louder.

He turned round, puzzled. 'If you think so.'

'You think I should throw it away?'

'Throw what away?'

He obviously hadn't been listening. Even with the wedding disaster there was something new in Ralph's distant mood that she couldn't account for.

Of course, there was work. In the morning Ralph was due to take the early train to London. Over the past few months he'd been going up regularly for meetings with clients. Very dull, he always told her. She hadn't paid much attention, not with the wedding preparations being so all-consuming. But watching Ralph now, hardly aware she was in the room, she felt a deflated sadness, an anxiety, a premonition of a race she was about to lose. There was something about this trip that he was hiding.

While Ralph was getting ready for bed she passed through the rooms downstairs, checking windows were shut, the doors locked.

Nicky was still not home so she left the hall light on. In Ralph's study she paused, looking around the shadowy room. The light from the hall shone dully on the leather cover of a diary left on his desk, a ribbon marker inside it. It wasn't the sort of thing she did; they never opened each other's letters, but she picked the little book up, slim and supple in her hands. It fell open at the ribbon marker. She saw the names of clients he was due to see the next day, two large companies, nothing unusual there. But on the next page was a note in faint pencil: C 4:30. Frowning, she held it towards the light, but there was nothing further to be gleaned. She closed the book and put it back down on the desk, prickling with unnamed fears, something ominous just out of sight.

She'd been so worried for Nicky, trying to convince him that a heart could always heal. But that wasn't really true, was it? The blood so vital to a body, the breath that inflates the lungs, how easily they could be pinched off in a moment, by a word, by the closing of a door. There were some blows that a heart could never recover from. She felt a tight pain at the base of her throat. Had she already lost Ralph?

CHAPTER 29

London, 1981

The taxi dropped Ralph off outside the Bloomsbury Hotel. A sudden shower had raised the smell of wet dust from the pavements. He hurried for the shelter of the portico. Inside he asked at the desk for Charlotte Gardiner. A man in a tailcoat showed him through to a long gallery lined with high bookshelves filled with the sort of ancient leather volumes no one is ever likely to read. He passed an old gentleman taking a sip from a tumbler with eyes averted. At the far end he saw a woman rise slowly from one of the leather armchairs, her shoulders still stooped as she held up a tentative hand in greeting.

Her face was thickly creased, the hair dark grey, but Ralph recognised the direct gaze and wide mouth of a young Tom Gardiner in Valencia. He wondered which of the children in the photograph on Mr Gardiner's desk would have been Charlotte. A lifetime ago.

They shook hands, the flesh over the back of her hand papery.

'Ralph.'

'Charlotte, how do you do? And am I right in thinking you're the eldest daughter?'

A shadow of pride passed over her face, mixed in with resentment. He was, after all, the child of the usurper.

'I still am. But take a seat, won't you? And might I get you something to drink? Coffee? Perhaps you'd like something stronger?' Charlotte signalled to the waiter.

Ralph settled down opposite her. 'I was very pleased to hear from you. I didn't realise you had my number.'

'I didn't. I saw the wedding announcement and worked out how to contact you from that.'

'Well, I'm very glad you did.' Ralph smiled.

She looked down at her hands quickly, and he understood that she had tracked him down reluctantly.

'How is Tom? I thought perhaps he might possibly be here today.'

A shadow passed over her face. 'I'm so sorry. Of course, you wouldn't know. Tom passed away, just over a year ago.'

'Tom died?'

'It wasn't unexpected in a way. We'd understood for a long time that he had a weak heart, and yet one manages to forget unpleasant things. It still came as a great shock.'

They sat in silence as Tom's memory ghosted through the gallery. The only sound the muted traffic filtering into the cloistered room, the light from the tall windows obscured by the folds of net absorbing the grey of the London air. He covertly studied her, his half-sister, and yes he could see it there, a faint likeness round the cheekbones, but there were none of the shared mannerisms that might denote family. She was a stranger really.

Charlotte turned to her handbag, fussing with the clasp, searching inside for something. She finally closed it with a snap, and held out a thick envelope.

'After Tom died I found instructions for this to be given to you.'

Registering her brittle tone he took the envelope and slid out an old notebook. It was covered in red Moroccan leather, gold patterns tooled round the edge, worn away next to the leather tie.

'Tom must have found it among Father's effects after the funeral. I think he had intended to pass it on to you, but for the last few years, especially after his wife passed away, and with his health not being what it was, understandably things got on top of him. Then I wasn't sure how to find you – until recently.'

'Thank you, Charlotte.'

He opened the front cover and was taken aback to read the inscription: 'To Ralph, from his father.' There was also a piece of folded notepaper tucked inside. He opened it out and began to read. The date was for several years earlier.

Dear Ralph,

I see that this book is intended for you. Thought you were such a capital little chap when I visited you back in Valencia. Wish things had been different so we might have got to know each other a bit better over the years.

Important thing now is that you read this book of Pa's. I found it locked away in the safe in his Madrid flat. I talked to a pal from the foreign office to see how much of this stuff rang true with him, and he confirmed it most probably is, but of course it's going to remain officially classified for many years to come. He thinks there were scores of people in on it during the war, but since then not a soul has spoken about it – with Franco still in power there could be reprisals for those involved who still live in Spain. Must be one of the war's best-kept secrets. The folk at the Madrid Embassy and their pals must have saved thousands of lives. Anyway, you must read it for yourself.

Strikes me that if Pa took the risk of writing this down, he must have been jolly keen that you read this one day.

See you soon I hope, old chap,

Tom

Ralph could hear the boyish rise and fall of Tom's voice. For a moment he caught a whiff of something sweet again, a memory of sneezing on the sugar on the churros; how he'd pretended to himself that night as they walked towards the lights of the film show, two brothers walking with their father. The taste of the fried dough had been spiked with a sharp longing, wishing so hard that Max was his real father – guilty with disloyalty.

'Have you read this, Charlotte?'

'It seems Tom didn't feel that I should see it, apparently, but I did read it, yes.' A sharp twist of the mouth for a second. 'And if it's meant for you, you should have it.'

'I'm very grateful to you, Charlotte. I hope we'll keep in touch in the future now.'

'Ralph, I appreciate meeting you today. I do, sincerely, but there it is, you see: I was brought up to think of you and your mother as the imposters. It hasn't been easy over the years.' She smiled at him sadly and rose from her seat. Ralph followed her cue.

'Goodbye, Ralph. I do wish you well. In the end I think we both suffered, in ways not so dissimilar. I'm not sure that anyone ever knew that man, not really.'

Ralph watched her make her slow progress between the club chairs, frail in her navy suit. When she was gone he sank down in his chair again.

It had always been so hard to know who Max really was; so many blank unknowable spaces, handed down as part of Ralph's inner territory, made it difficult to get one's bearings at times. But perhaps the answer, the coordinates to Max's soul, were here, inside the worn red notebook.

He rubbed a thumb over the leather, evoking a little of the spice of Max's cigars, and a memory came to him of Max, seated a little apart from the rest of the room, watching through those long, narrow eyes as he nibbled at the side of his finger. Ralph looked down at his fingers and he saw the ragged edges of bitten skin.

CHAPTER 30

London, 1981

Ralph couldn't bear to take the notebook out and glance through it while he was in the taxi, a fear that it might be lost if it wasn't firmly pressed inside his jacket pocket. In his hotel room he took off his mac, thumped down against the headboard and untied the leather fastener. Inside, the pages were crammed with Max's handwriting, small and dense, wilfully difficult to read.

Ralph turned to the first entry: Madrid, June 1940. He thought back. He would have been at the boarding school in Hampshire then, the summer before he went up to Oxford.

The first entry was for the day that Max and Lily moved from Valencia to Madrid, the Spanish civil war over, the Second World War almost a year old and the newspapers in the UK filled with the dismal news of the defeat at Dunkirk.

Madrid, 10th June 1940

Glad to say that Mama's very happy with the new apartment. And a nice spare room waiting for you, when we can get you out here from England again – once this wretched war is over. Mama's desperately hoping to come and see you in England soon but it's impossible to get on a flight out unless you're top brass these days. I know how very much she'd love to be back home with you, and I'm so grateful that you are loaning her to me right now, old chap.

You see, this promotion to the bank in Madrid is something I've felt obliged to take, without being able to entirely spell out the reasons to your mother, but she's such a brick, never complains. And it's not really something I can explain to you in a letter that might go astray right now. So I've decided that I'm going to keep this diary for you, Ralph, then whatever happens, you'll know what we were up to – and how very much we are missing you.

Coming into Madrid on the train from Valencia it was terribly sad to see the old girl so reduced. Huge areas of the old barrios all but destroyed.

Talk about swank. Hillgarth sent the embassy car to meet us at Atocha station. There are very few cars on the road now since it's so hard to get petrol. The old red trams are still clanking along, and there are carts drawn by donkeys. People look pretty derelict and hard up, the war years written on their faces.

Smatterings of bullet holes in the garden walls here and there along the paseo de Castellano, but otherwise those grand old mansions look remarkably untouched. Our apartment is just off the paseo and I must say really very civilised, spacious even. Consuelo got here ahead of us a couple of days ago and has been charging around the place checking that all the rooms are ready, which was a godsend as Lily had to lie down in a darkened room soon as we got here, poor dear. The train gave her a frightful migraine.

I met up with Hillgarth at a place on the paseo. You may remember him from the embassy crowd in Valencia some years back, handsome chap, dark hair. It would have been at one of those picnics in the park – seems like another century now. He was posted here as the new British naval attaché a few weeks back.

Found him at the bar, where he'd already ordered champagne cocktails, speciality of the house. It's a rather smart little place called the Embassy Tea Rooms. It acts as a very British establishment in the afternoon – a little bit of England for the homesick – and then the set from the embassies roll in for cocktails in the evening, along with some of Franco's generals and some of the high-ranking bureaucrats from the government – and all very strange to be sipping away at our champagne when there's a couple of Wehrmacht types in uniform standing at the bar. No one appearing to pay them any attention – but of course everyone is.

Glad to find your mama was fast asleep by the time I got back to the apartment, hoping she'll be feeling much better tomorrow. Doing my best to look after her for you, old boy. Pretty late now as I add these notes, three in the morning if you must know, and I'm sitting at a new desk that I had made in Valencia. Got it delivered here last week. There's a very clever hidden lever that opens a panel where one might slide in a couple of rather private documents – and now this diary too. You'd never work out it was there unless you knew the trick.

The thing is, dear boy, who knows what will happen in the future with this beastly war on, or when I will next see your dear face – or when we will sit and chat over a cup of hot chocolate made just the way you like it. At least keeping this diary gives me a feeling of being a little more in touch with you. I expect you're fast asleep now, certainly hope you are in fact. Dear Ralph, how we do miss you.

Ralph paused, taken aback, a little pit of longing in his stomach to hear the old affectionate Max. He read the last couple of lines over again. But then Max had always been a smooth talker. Wasn't it actions that counted? He shook his head and read on.

11th June

Walked up to the Ritz hotel this morning for a meeting with Hillgarth and Sir Hoare, the new ambassador to the British Embassy. He's only just arrived in Madrid and Hillgarth wants me to help fill him in a bit on this and that. As it is, Hoare's convinced he'll be shot at any moment and has apparently asked to keep a pistol about him at all times. And he won't let the embassy plane go back to London in case he needs to jump on it and get out of here. Needs his nerves calming somewhat. Of course, all that's over now in Madrid. All the skullduggery here goes on behind closed doors in a very civilised fashion.

It's beginning to get awfully hot here in the afternoons, with none of the sea breezes that you get in Valencia, but this morning the air was still pleasingly cool, the cedars and the palms along the paseo de Prado blowing under the bluest sky as I walked up to meet Hillgarth and Hoare. People about on errands as if the war had never happened.

And funny to think I was walking along the same stretch of the paseo we'd seen in a newsreel in Valencia of Franco's victory parade only a few weeks before. He does like to put on a good show, Franco, his guard of Moorish troops very dashing, all white cloaks and veils like a little regiment of Valentinos. Dapper as a film star – and getting a little plump Lily thought. Bed sheets hanging from all the balconies, 'Viva Franco' painted on them in big black letters, crowds bristling with everyone saluting madly.

And right behind Franco a fleet of very expensive-looking cars – the German Condor Regiment – the very same men who bombed Madrid into submission on Franco's behalf. Of course, the Nazis think they have Franco in their pocket now. But we'll have to see about that.

Of course, we know now that Spain was merely the Luftwaffe's target practice for what was to come: Poland, Holland, Norway and Denmark, Belgium and France, and now our boys on Dunkirk beach. Hard to believe, our British troops driven to the very edge of the sea. And of course, only thanks to our men back home they got back safely. (It's not being shouted about in the papers, but a hell of a lot of the men fighting the vanguard have been left stranded in France, huge numbers in German prison camps.)

So many unknowns now. If Spain decides to go into the war on the side of Germany? If Britain falls? Nothing to do but wait it out and see.

One thing certain is that Spain hasn't got any money left after the wretched civil war, not a bean. So if we want Spain to stay out of the war then it's going to be about keeping a squeeze on her coffers – a financial war, as Hillgarth terms it.

So I met up with Hoare and Hillgarth in the palm court at the Ritz. The whole place all newly painted, white and gold. You'd never guess that a few months ago it was a military hospital. They've had to billet Hoare there since there's nowhere else up to Lady Hoare's requirements in this war-damaged city but I doubt that anyone's pointed out to her that the Ritz is also the favourite watering hole for all the Abwehr spies crawling over Franco's government offices, mostly with his permission.

Shook hands with Hoare and then we took him for a stroll to the Retiro Park. Gangs of men in aprons there restoring the park to its former glory on Franco's orders, and gangs of skinny children in bare feet playing in the dust, asking for pennies, not looking well fed one bit.

We walked up to the ballustrades around the lake where there was no one around to eavesdrop. Do you remember that lake? I took you there once when we visited Madrid. You sailed your boat. One hears the splashes of carp snapping at flies but never quite sees them.

Hillgarth wanted to know what I thought of a chap called Juan March. I told him what I knew: he's a stunningly wealthy shipping magnate who used to come into the bank in Valencia flanked by two of his henchmen. Known as The Pirate since he looks the part, dark and swarthy, and because he practically runs the seas around Spain. Very keen not to have the Nazis seizing control of the Mediterranean.

You see, now that France has fallen, it's critical Franco doesn't let the Germans take their troops down through Spain and cut off the Med completely. So March has contacted Churchill with a plan. He's offering to bribe some of Franco's generals to make sure that Spain stays neutral – using British money, but fronting the deal as if the money comes solely from him. The British government can't be seen trying to bribe the Spanish generals directly or that will shatter Spain's so-called neutrality and give the Nazis every reason to simply invade Spain.

Anyway, Hoare didn't like it. He suspects that March will simply keep the cash, a small matter of some ten million pounds, and scarper with it. And it is true that there's nothing we can do about it if he does.

I told Hoare that I thought March would most likely pass the money on as bribes as promised if it was going to help keep Nazi fingers out of his business. It's certainly an open secret that March doesn't like Franco very much, a lot in fact.

So the money will be sent from London and through a series of international transfers and various bank account switches. I'll have to make it appear as if the bribes are really all March's own money.

So there you have it, that's really why I'm staying here and not coming back to England with you. I can't tell you this now, dear Ralph, as I write this, but am hoping you'll read it and understand – one day.

Lily so desperately wants to be with you, dear boy, but bless her she's decided to stay on here with yours truly. She is such a wonderful person. I do love your mother awfully, you know. And to be honest there's little chance of her getting on a plane back to England the way things stand. But if she really can't bear it, if it all gets too much, I'm going to ask Hillgarth to get her home on one of the embassy flights. God knows he owes me one.

Your mama and I talked about you for a long time today. You see, Ralph, we did ask ourselves if we shouldn't tell you certain things at this point. Of course, if you are reading this, Ralph dear, then the war will be over and – if all goes well – I will have had a chance to sit down and talk with you, tell you face to face certain things – explain why we never told you outright that I am your father. And so very proud to be so. Perhaps by then I'll have taken you out for your first English pint, walking home with you in an English spring. And I hope you will have forgiven me all those shabby little reasons why we couldn't tell you the truth before – that must seem so pathetic now. You see they loomed so impossibly large when you were born.

I only hope that one day you will forgive us, forgive me, and always know how very much I do care for you, dear Ralph, as your father.

Ralph decided that he needed something strong to drink. He found a small bottle of Johnny Walker and poured a measure. He'd had no idea that Max had been involved in such high-level negotiations. He'd thought Max had stayed on for the easy life that Madrid offered, the well-paid post at the bank. But Max, it seemed, had been living a double life. What else had been going on that Ralph didn't know about?

13th June

Hillgarth dropped by today. He came to ask a favour of course. And I must say, when we heard what's going on, we were only too glad to do any thing that we could.

It's not only the servicemen stranded after Dunkirk who are trying to escape from France down through Spain. According to Hillgarth, Churchill's been getting some dreadful reports through from the Poles. Unspeakable things happening to Jews in Wehrmacht countries. Hard to believe, in this day and age, quite frankly. The upshot is, Churchill's asked the embassy to quietly expand its newly created special evacuations operations to including any Jewish refugees. Now that the Swiss border's closed, we'll be their only route out.

But you see it's all going to have to be done directly under the noses of Franco and his Jerry friends here, who are going to mind awfully if they find out. Churchill's suggestion is that Hillgarth use people one would never suspect, such as ordinary people like Lily and me!

I have to say it was all a bit of a shock, hearing how desperate things are for Jewish families. Even for the children. I felt frozen, as Hillgarth talked, chilled to the bone.

My mother was a Jewess from Pinsk – your grandmother, Ralph, though of course you never knew her. I wonder if you recall me telling you about her once. She was a remarkable lady. I didn't even know she was Jewish for many years. She converted. Never admitted that she was Jewish to anyone. It was her secret.

But once, at Christmas, when Mother had had more sherry than was wise she began to tell me very strange stories about her home in Pinsk. Sitting by the fire, it sounded too frightening to be true, a Grimm's fairy tale of bears and wolves that came out of the forest. She told me about Cossacks on horses, who rode into town at night with sticks and clubs and left behind bodies wrapped in sheets, lined up on the cobblestones – entire Jewish families dead.

She was the only one from her family who survived that night, hiding away in a cupboard. She left for England, taken into a neighbour's family.

The next morning, the effects of the sherry gone, my mother denied she'd ever told me any such story. I asked my father and he told me to put it out of my mind, for her sake. So I did. After all, in modern times in Finchley, we slept safe in our beds. But it still left me with some dreadful nightmares.

So you see, after Hillgarth left, I must say I sat in utter shock. I couldn't believe the things he'd told us. It felt as though time had moved backwards, as if the wolves have come out of the forest again; bodies lined up on the cobblestones. Children even. It's simply too dreadful what men can do.

I thought of my mother then, and for the first time I think I understood just why she had always been so insistent on our Englishness, the English public school she sent us to, as if she were weaving a magic cloak that would protect us from harm.

And I understood this: it won't serve you well if I tell you outright that you are that valiant lady's grandson right now, not till all this madness is over. My dear boy, if this wretched war drags on you could be sent over to France in a year or so's time. Much better if you don't have the burden of hiding the knowledge that you're partly Jewish, not until some kind of sanity returns to Europe. Which pray God it will soon.

When war is over, one afternoon, sitting over a good lunch in a restaurant in Piccadilly, we'll talk. If you knew how the thought of that time to come does my heart good, dear boy. Until then, I am sending all a father's love and I will read and reread the letters that you send, dear Ralph.

Ralph's back had gone stiff sitting against the headboard. It was terribly late, but he didn't want to stop, astonished to hear Max's voice so clearly through the pages of the diary.

He walked around the room to uncrick his back, taking in what he had just read. Ralph had always seen Max as affectionate, yes, but ultimately indifferent, and later, worse than indifferent: a man who had never cared for him enough to come out and tell his son, face to face, that he was his father. But now he glimpsed something new, a powerful underwater current in Max's affections, a current so deep that its ripples barely showed on the surface: the profound drive of a father to protect his child.

He sat down on the edge of the bed and picked up the diary again. Rubbing his thumb over the diary's worn cover he thought of Max tying the leather fastening each time, slipping the book into some hidden place. Storing up his secrets so that he might pass them on to Ralph. He wished Alice were there with him to share this. He badly wanted to call her. So much to tell her. But at two in the morning she wasn't going to appreciate that.

He opened the diary once more.

27th June

As Hillgarth likes to say, it's always the things under your nose that are hardest to see.

So once again, Lily and I are heading down to the Embassy Tea Rooms to meet with Hillgarth and some of his chums. Lily reckons you could honestly think you were having tea at Simpson's in the middle of London once you are inside: decent English crockery, silver teapots, and proper scones and jam. The owner is a Margaret Taylor, the widow of a Dutch diplomat who opened the tea rooms after she saw the embassy wives had nowhere respectable to go – other than the sort of bar that might end a lady's reputation. She's Irish aristocracy, wears beautifully tailored dresses that are really the thing Lily tells me. And not a bit someone you might suspect of running a safe house for servicemen escaping from France.

She does however have a most alarming gaze, I can tell you. Sees straight into you.

So over the past few days we've joined the embassy crowd and all their hangers-on in the most unlikely operation to assist escaping soldiers and airmen. No one suspects for a minute that such a snobbish and pampered bunch might be risking their skins – for no other reason than they want to do the decent thing, help out a fellow in a fix. Hillgarth's recruited a whole gang of the embassy wives – butter wouldn't melt in their mouths so you'd think. He's also roped in lots of his contacts among the old Spanish aristocracy, all of them completely irreproachable and supposedly Franco's greatest allies, but they haven't hesitated to donate food stamps and clothes, and even open their mansions to help the tide of truly desperate refugees arriving from Marseilles.

And the whole thing goes on around the tea rooms with its string quartet, and its waiters in white jackets – and I have to say, goes on right under the noses of the Wehrmacht officers who naturally frequent the tea rooms since they prefer only the most upmarket places.

It goes like this: in the early hours of the morning, while it's still dark, the refugees turn up at the back door of the Embassy Tea Rooms, having made their way down one way and another through safe houses in the Pyrenees. They're generally in a pretty sorry state I can tell you, looking like just another little queue of down-at-heel people asking for work as they wait to be let in. Madrid is full of such scenes.

Then once through the door, they're taken upstairs and hidden in Margaret's apartment above the tea rooms, or sometimes down in the cellars. Margaret has heaps of donated clothes ready so Lily tells me – but only the best clothes mind you – the sort of thing you might wear to go out to afternoon tea at the Embassy Tea Rooms.

Then, once they're rested and fed and dressed in the smartest of suits and dresses, they discreetly make their way into the tea rooms – where Margaret shows her elegant guests to their table – and where their dear friends from Madrid are expecting them for afternoon tea.

Perhaps they don't speak much, perhaps you might notice that they watch and follow the way that their Madrid hosts handle afternoon tea a little anxiously. But then no one does notice. What possible subterfuge could be going on around English teapots and scones, and with Spanish and German officers only a few tables away?

They always leave by the front door. Margaret often accompanies them out onto the street and waves them goodbye. She'll call out, 'So lovely to see you. Do come again soon, dears. Give my love.'

It's a heart-stopping moment the first time it happens and you walk out with your guests. I thought Lily might well faint, she looked so pale as we headed for the door, both of us trying to appear perfectly calm. But honestly, no one bats an eyelid as we leave.

We walk with our guests for a few streets to where Hillgarth has the embassy car ready, his personal chauffeur waiting to drive them to Vigo or Gibraltar. Or sometimes one might go with them to Atocha station and see them onto a train. If it's getting late, they'll come back to the apartment and then leave the next day.

We've done it several times so far. Two men from the Highlanders regiment who'd escaped via Marseilles. Then a Jewish Austrian couple, who'd been living in France until it fell. A Czech couple. I think they were Czech.

Ralph, I can't tell you how proud I am of your mama. She really is the most amazing person. You know she's always been prone to bouts of poor health, not strong, but she won't let that stop her.

I do ask myself if it's right to be committing these things to paper, but I promise you, I am scrupulously careful. A moment's flick of the hand and the diary is hidden away in the compartment, entirely undetectable. Not even Lily knows. Life in these times is so unpredictable that I have to leave something behind that will let you know what we lived while we were apart from you, how much we thought of you, and how brave your mama has been. Hillgarth's taken a sealed letter from me to keep in the embassy files. I said it was to be passed on to you – should something happen to us.

But I'm counting the days till all this is over, when we'll be back with you in London. My prayer is you never have to read this, that there will be no need. I will tell you all myself, man to man.

25th July

Ralph, you wouldn't recognise Lily.

As we walk down to the tea rooms again, the faint summer scent of Lime trees in the evening air, I have to look twice at this slight woman at my side, nothing but fire and determination, her eyes glittering with tiredness, but she won't give in. And I wonder where she's learned this subterfuge, my own timid little Lily.

But then, of course, it's not the first time she has risked all, and been prepared to play a part if she has to. I do know just what Lily can endure for those she cares about.

Our little jaunts don't get any easier, I have to admit, no matter how many times you go through it. Takes strong nerves – and some downright cheek. But it all passes off smoothly. We share a tense hour over tea with our new dearest friends – glad that the string quartet in the corner has a marvellous ability to muffle the conversation around one, Lily chattering on, though I know her heart is hammering in her throat. Sometimes there's a child with them. That really breaks your heart, to think of all the others who haven't escaped – and makes one more determined.

Now that Switzerland is closed, the Madrid underground railway is the only viable route out of the axis for Jewish refugees. So Churchill's told Hillgarth to increase the activity in evacuations as much as is possible, do whatever he needs to. It seems all the best families are in on it now. Quite the thing. And no one breathes a word.

Each time it happens, dear Lily seems a little thinner, a little more worn. Some evenings, by the time I've helped her to bed, raised her feet up onto the mattress, she's already falling asleep.

I said to her, 'Lily dear, you don't have to do this. Do you really want to take more risks?' But do you know what she replied? 'But what would we tell Ralph, if we knew we hadn't done all we could?'

And she's right, dear boy. One day, I want to tell you what we did to play our part, for a better world. For the world you will live in.

Ralph was filled with longing for the affectionate man who had once been such a vital part of his life, and with all the feelings that he hadn't let himself admit for years. He missed Max, missed him terribly.

But why hadn't Max let him know all this himself? Ralph was partly to blame, he knew that, the way he had pushed Max away at Mama's funeral and refused to even open any letter from Max.

Then Max had died so suddenly and so swiftly after Mama had passed away. When Ralph had got the news in the barracks there had been a WREN officer there who had meant kindly but misunderstood, telling Ralph how people deeply in love often went swiftly together, couldn't live without the other. At the time he'd shaken his head at that – she'd got it so very wrong – but now he wondered. And he saw that Max must have surely been intending to talk to him and tell him, was waiting for the right time, but his sudden death had robbed him of that chance.

Ralph took a shuddering, almost involuntary sigh and realised that a deep love for Max had never really left him; it had simply been tamped down hard, somewhere deep inside his chest.

16th *August*

Such a long time since I've had a chance to sit down and write in this little book. Long hours trying to broker a new deal with Spain through the embassy bank. Spain's completely bankrupt in effect, so, for the right amount, they've agreed to sell their entire stock of wolfram ore to the allies – if we outbid everyone else. There's no other source of wolfram in Europe, and it's vital for arms manufacture. But there's nothing the Nazis can do now that Spain has agreed to quietly sell the whole caboodle to us. Means it's only a matter of time before the Nazis run out and that will affect their ability to expand into Russia or Africa this winter certainly.

The real headache however has been this deal with March. He's got several of the generals in his pocket all right, but the money to pay their bribes has had to pass through the US banks in Switzerland to help wash away the British connection, and since they can see it all going to a Spanish recipient the US has blocked the whole ten million — we can't tell them outright what the deal is about, you see.

Hillgarth and Hoare are frantically trying to get the funds unfrozen. In the meantime, March has stumped up half the cash from his own funds, to stop the generals turning on him and throwing him to the dogs. Frantic negotiations to try and get it all sorted. I'm getting very little sleep.

I've told no one about this except this little book. Not even dear Lily, who has enough to think about. Even when we're alone, we rarely speak of what has happened during the day. There will be a time for talking openly, one day soon.

The light was beginning to show through the shiny fibreglass fabric of the curtains, making the bedside lamp unnecessary. Max let the diary rest on his lap.

That was why Max was given an OBE. For the first time it made sense. All the secret deals that Max had brokered so that March could keep the generals from letting Franco think it was a good idea to let the Nazi troops roll down through Spain. And the deals to stop wolfram ore going into arms manufacture so that Hitler had had to scale back his plans to expand. This was what Churchill's government were thanking him for when they made him the award. Quietly, unassumingly, without ever making a song and dance about it, not even a hint, Max must have saved a hell of a lot of lives through his work. And even more than that, there was all that Lily and he had done for the fleeing refugees and escaped prisoners.

Ralph picked up the diary and read on.

23rd September

We've had a visit from a Wehrmacht officer today. Came to the flat. Very friendly. Impeccable manners. Walked around looking in all the rooms, admiring the splendidly appointed accommodation. Rather pointedly menacing in his manner to be honest.

Not sure if they are on to something about the bank or there's word about our guests, but I don't like it. If they took me in for questioning, I think I could cope, but Lily is another matter. I know about their methods.

So there's a place come up on a flight out and I'm making sure Lily's on it. God willing, you'll see her in a couple of days. She's torn in half. Longing to see you but she's crying next door, tells me she's not going each time I go in. But she has to. It's not safe.

'But you'll come too?' she keeps asking.

I told her that I'd love nothing better, but I can't. So much depending on the transactions going through the bank to keep Spain lined up with the allies. I know I have to stay and see it through. We drove out to the airport at Barajas late afternoon. We talked a long time before your mama left. We asked ourselves whether she should tell you now. Decided the right thing is to tell you only when this is over, my own dearest boy. In time. I held her for as long as I could before she had to go, waited, watching her plane lift into the sky and then I stayed and watched it until it disappeared.

I seem to have taken to praying again, for you both to be safe.

19th January 1941

It's been a long and hard winter so far. But today, a letter from you got through. How is Oxford? I'm sure you will ace your exams there, dear Ralph, in the years to come.

How the days do drag with no Lily. Consuelo has really stepped up to the mark I must say. She gets the flat ready for the ashen-faced guests I still bring back every so often. Thousands have gone through the Madrid safe houses now. It doesn't stop.

Consuelo works like a trooper, always ready with whatever one needs.

Ah, but it's so empty here in the apartment without you both, my dears. I wish so much I could jump on a plane and come and see you for a few days, but flights to England are now cancelled indefinitely. I know it's so important not to lose hope, to keep looking to a better day, a brighter dawn. But it's hard. One *sees no end to this war. Quite when it will be over no one can say, or how things will end. Perhaps in a few months the situation will have changed enough for me to take leave and see you both at last.*

I take my meal in the kitchen these days and sit talking with Consuelo. Warmer there than in the chilly dining room by myself. Share a few glasses of wine.

Dear boy, how you and your mama are so very missed.

After that there were no more entries, but Ralph could fill in the rest of the story, from news that had arrived in letters from Mama's friends in Madrid over those following months.

At the beginning of 1942 Consuelo had appeared in the Embassy Tea Rooms dressed in one of Lily's old coats, a fox fur stole clipped round her neck. Max had looked hunted, embarrassed, but Consuelo hardly seemed to notice or care, her cheeks rouged, triumphant and reckless. No one spoke to Max after that. He was given the cold shoulder, not so much for sleeping with the maid, but for rubbing everyone's noses in his bizarre little scandal.

His post at the bank had been affected; new blood brought in to look at things in a different way, they said. After the scandal he'd caused they wanted him out, but still needed him for the long nights of covert deals and brokering that Max had taken on to keep Spain out of the axis. By the time Ralph had gone up to Oxford, Lily and Max had agreed a divorce.

At the time Ralph had seen nothing but fault in what Max had done. No excuse for it. But now he saw another Max, alone, wanting to come home so very much but having to hang on in Madrid; the long evenings in the lonely flat; the war stretching out till God knew when; and then a bleak moment of weakness, taking a little comfort where he could find it – not seeing how it would unravel everything.

Then a few months later, while Ralph's unit was in Holland, a telegram had come announcing that Lily had died. That was when a cold hate towards Max began to simmer in Ralph's chest. He'd adamantly blocked any attempt of Max's to get in touch with him after that, even at Mama's funeral, vowed to never forgive him. And a few months after the funeral Max was also dead. Ralph had not gone to that funeral.

But now he didn't so much forgive Max as found that he saw all Max's imperfections and weaknesses spread out before him like the autopsy of a damaged heart. The bitterness he felt towards Max and Consuelo drained away. And for the first time he saw the logic and fear and perambulation that had led Max to keep silent.

A feeling of calm came over Ralph; there had been a shift inside, an untying of something wound tight: he had stopped being angry. Ralph closed the small volume. So much to take in, everything about Max and Lily now seen from a different angle, all their secrets and strenuous efforts to help those in a desperate situation revealed.

Heroes, you could say that. They were heroes really.

But most of all Max's diary was a letter from a father to a son. For years, even after he had been told Max's secret by Mama, the memory of walking with Max and Tom through Valencia had been of a child longing to walk with his father, believing he never would. But now he saw his small hand firmly held in the large, rough palm of his father, his childhood years held in the gaze of his father's concern.

And he was bursting to tell Alice. The story wasn't finished, not until he had shared it with Alice.

Ralph blinked twice, slowly. For the first time he let himself see how the years had let a distance grow between them, and he saw for the first time how he had wanted and even engineered that. What had he been thinking? Had he really been so wasteful, so stupid? For what? Those years were gone now. He couldn't go back and change it.

It was as if that small boy from Valencia was now sitting beside him, watching him, wondering why it had mattered so much that he should hide himself away like that. Why? The closeness that Alice and he had shared on the day they'd moved into the damp and tumbledown cottage, he wanted it back. He wanted Alice back – if it wasn't too late.

It was still ridiculously early, but he began to stuff his things haphazardly back into his case. A brief splash of water on his face. The night attendant on the desk was a little grumpy to have to process his bill at such an hour. Out in the deserted street Ralph hailed down a lone taxi and asked to be dropped at Euston.

He counted off the stations as the train neared home. Watching the passing fields and blurred townscapes through the window, those indistinct shapes from the past that he had lived with for so long began to materialise into forms that he could finally see with clarity. Yes, there was the stultifying heaviness of Lily's silence, her shame at his illegitimacy, her fear of being cast out; but with Max he also recognised an altogether darker garment, made from the terrified pulse in the throat, from the close, hot breath of the shadow of death passing over a people as Lily and Max had walked home through the streets of Madrid with a couple of desperate refugees. An old tattered coat made from the stories that Max's mother had told him by the fire one winter, its lining sewn from stories of pogroms and men with clubs. For the first time Ralph clearly understood the heft of fabric that had weighed down his own limbs; a coat of fear and silence, worn by instinct, without question, how it had silenced and isolated him. Well, no more.

Another hour and he'd be with Alice

CHAPTER 31

Fourwinds, 1981

Around ten in the morning the taxi dropped Ralph off at the top of the drive that led to Fourwinds. The morning had opened out into crisp sunshine. He wandered along the drive and over the lawn, exhausted, but home. He came to the wooden bench and sat down, spreading himself out to simply look at the old place.

. That was how Alice found him when she came out to peg up washing. He was sitting and thinking, still in his crumpled mac, the suitcase and briefcase abandoned on the lawn. She stopped dead, and then walked slowly towards him. She saw immediately in his face that something had happened.

'Why didn't you tell me you were coming this early? Ralph, what is it? What on earth's the matter with you?'

He pulled her down to sit by him.

'What is it?' She ducked her head slightly, bracing herself for what he was going to say.

He placed an arm round her shoulders. 'There's something I have to tell you.'

She began to cry softly. 'Who is she?'

'What do you mean?'

'You're seeing someone. Who?'

He pulled back. 'But why would you think that? Alice, how could you think that?'

'I know there's someone else, Ralph – someone your loyalty lies with, because it isn't me. I know that. Tell me her name.'

'Alice, I promise you.' He had grabbed onto the tops of her arms. She saw a look of horror on his face. 'There's no one else. No one.'

She shook her head, her eyes open wide to take in every detail of his expression, to read the truth. 'Do you promise me?'

'Of course I do. But I don't understand why you'd even think that.'

'Because I never know. Because you never tell me what you're doing any more, what's in your head.'

'Oh Alice.' He circled his arms round her back and pressed her against his mac. She let herself crumple against him, shaking with sobs.

It was a long while before she stopped crying. Eventually she sat straight and blew her nose. He placed a red notebook on her lap. 'No more secrets.'

With a frown of incomprehension she opened it and began to read. After a couple of pages she skimmed more than read, but she got the gist. She stopped and looked up at him. Excited.

'So Max was your father. Did you know that?'

'I'm so sorry. Ma told me in a letter I received just after she died. I wanted you to know, but . . .' He stopped.

Alice stroked his face with her hand and sighed. 'Oh Ralph. When I met Max at Lily's funeral, when I saw you both standing side by side, that was the first thing that struck me. Darling, it was hardly a secret.'

They talked for a long time. He showed her the important parts of the notebook. Read out passages. The whole of Max and Lily's secret life inside its pages.

Alice was aware that her hair was a mess, her nose red, but there wasn't time to think about that now. She took odds and ends from the fridge and the larder and they ate out in the garden, a late lunch, or an early supper. It was as if time had slipped, the cool of the dusk around them. The comforting warmth of her body at his side as they sat and looked over the Dove plain, the glint of the river across the checkered fields.

'What's got into you couple of love birds?' Nicky was back, walking across the lawn towards them, hands in his pockets, not shaven. He looked so tired in the fading light. His face slack, the expression rubbed away. Eyes without any real hope. Alice felt a stab through her heart then, because Nicky didn't have this. And she knew she'd been at fault. Hadn't she pushed at Sarah to get the wedding into shape? Pushed her away perhaps. Failed her. Just as she had failed Peter.

She bit her lips together. Well, not again. Not this time. Not if there was something she could do about it.

CHAPTER 32

Birmingham, 1981

Patricia woke too early, the sun sharp through the gap in the curtains, making her eyes feel sore. The phone was ringing. And immediately she was back in the same unfinished thought: a silent Sarah, so far away. What had happened to make her disappear and cut herself off so completely?

The phone carried on ringing, the day starting to crowd in. Someone with a question about the confirmation service that morning perhaps, about sandwiches in the church hall. She pulled herself up out of bed. Down in the hallway she picked up the phone. The clock on the wall said six o'clock. Who would phone at 6 a.m.?

And then she knew.

'Sarah?'

'Mum. I'm sorry. It's too early.'

The shock of hearing Sarah's voice again after so many weeks. 'No, no, it's not too early.' Patricia could hear the hysteria in her own voice, bright sun on shattered glass. 'Never too early.' The silence again. 'Darling?'

'It's just, I have to tell you now. If I don't do it now, I don't know if I can.'

Patricia thought: It can't be worse than what has already happened. She would look back and remember how she had stood with the phone in her hand and thought: At least we will understand what has happened now. Things will begin to get better. We can begin to mend things.

She waited again in the silence, not wanting to scare Sarah away. She thought how Sarah's bones had felt so fragile when she hugged her shoulders as a child, a rabbit caught and held, waiting to flee.

'Sweetheart?'

Sarah began to talk. The phone melted in Patricia's hand. She twisted it back into position, her hand filmed with greasy perspiration. Was she mishearing? Misunderstanding?

'When? When?' she heard herself saying. She was aware that the hallway was buzzing loudly, or was it inside her head?

Sarah talked, haltingly, in bursts, Patricia still grasping to understand. The world had flipped over. Nothing was as it had been before. The one thing Patricia had known she had done well was to protect her child with great vigilance. Yes, with too much vigilance at times – she had known that – but it was a skill learned from hard experience, in the years after mum died. She had always been on the lookout for danger like a wolf sniffing the night air. She had learned what people were like, how men could be – in those days when she had been alone. And yet, in plain sight, in their own home, someone they trusted, someone they had loved and helped, had reached in a clawed hand and ripped the heart out of everything.

She was stunned. It wouldn't sink in.

'But are you sure, Sarah?' she heard herself saying, stupidly, even as she knew it was true. 'How?'

'I'm going to put the phone down now, Mum.' Sarah's voice had gone slow and almost slurred, exhausted. 'Tomorrow. I'll ring you tomorrow. Mum, you'll have to tell Dad. Please. I can't do it. And Mum. Will you tell Nicky? Tell his family. They'll let it all drop when they know.'

The line went blank. 'Sarah? Sarah?' she called into the dull buzz.

She put the phone back, missed and settled it clumsily as if this was a new thing, to put a phone back in its cradle. She was standing in the hall; she was wearing a nightie, and her own child had been alone and frightened and assaulted as she slept in the same house. She hadn't seen it. She who had eyes for such things – because she knew, she knew the hard way – she had failed to see what was happening.

She thought of Cyril's sweet and boyish face, how he had blossomed with Peter's help, how good he was with the children, and she felt sick and hot with anger and disgust.

'Who was it?' Peter was at the top of the stairs. There was stubble on his chin, grey in the early light from the hall window. In his pyjamas, his hair dishevelled, he looked suddenly frail: the old man he would become one day. She shook her head, no words yet, his face puzzled because she didn't reply. She went up the stairs, nearing him. At the top she took his hands in hers. She could smell the staleness of night on his breath. She was hollow inside, her stomach turning over.

'It was Sarah.'

A gleam of hope in his eyes. 'Why didn't you call me?'

'Sarah wanted to tell us something. Something about Cyril.'

'Cyril? About him taking the wedding? But I've already contacted him. Told him it's been cancelled.'

She sank down on the wide step of the half-landing, holding the newel post. 'Are you all right?' he asked her. He crouched down beside her, concern in his face.

She felt her numb lips and tongue forming words. She heard the harsh, foreign words and she watched his face, his reactions, as if from a long way away. She watched the world open up in front of Peter and his startled tears; and they rocked together on the step, the chasm at their feet. Then he was up, treading back and forth along the hallway, furious. He slammed a fist into a door. She heard the wood splintering. They stood looking at the damage in the sharp light of a summer morning. He was nursing his hand, a jagged dent in the door. He turned wide startled eyes on Patricia.

'That was it. That was it. I told her Cyril could step in and take the service. She shivered – I saw her give a funny shake; I didn't know why – and then the next day she was gone.'

He thumped his hand into the door a second time.

'Stop it.'

Patricia pulled him to her and put her arms round his arms. 'I know. I want to kill him. But we've got the day to get through. The morning service. We'll get through that. And then we must sit down and try and work out what to do to help Sarah. That's all that matters now.' She paused. 'Oh God.'

'What?'

'Alice rang yesterday. She's coming by this afternoon with Nicky to pick up a box of his things. I said I'd post it, but she insisted on coming.'

'Today? They're coming today?'

She nodded.

He shut his eyes.

One thought going round and round in a loop in the front of the mind. In the kitchen she dropped a plate. Trying to pull out of the garage Peter forgot to put the car into reverse; she saw what was happening but couldn't stop it as the car bumper thumped into the wall. They sat, looking at the bricks, silent and frozen. Peter manhandled the gears clumsily and pulled out backwards into the driveway, paused to pull out into the road.

'Stop,' said Patricia, her hand on his arm. 'The veils. I forgot the veils.'

She ran back into the house and came out with a pile of ironed cloths with dangling tapes. Laid them on the back seat.

The church was full for the confirmation service. Peter stood on the threshold and tried to focus on the morning. The building felt like a place he had never seen before, its purpose obscure and ridiculous. He found the bishop already in the vestry, robing for the service, lifting a gold stole over the white surplice and gold robe, vestments from the high Roman church in the third century still worn almost two thousand years later. Why?

Through the doorway the children and teenagers were milling around, expectant and excited by the attention. Patricia handed out the veils to the girls, helped tie them under their hair at the back. The boys in white shirts, lining up in twos ready to go through into the service. Music from the organ pipes playing them in.

At the moment of confirmation Peter stood alongside the bishop, whispering the names of the children to him as they came forward in pairs to kneel and have hands laid on their heads, confirmed by the Holy Spirit. Seeing the large red hands, the white hairs on the backs of the fingers, lying on the head of a child, he felt his heart panic and skitter, the blood in his ears klaxonning danger, and he couldn't remember who the next children were, lost his place on the list, and the bishop waited, glanced over as Peter hunted through the names, the children's eyes puzzling up at him. There was cold sweat round his collar.

And later, lifting the communion cup to a woman's lips, he was shaking, shaking with anger. Anger with God. Standing in his priest's robes, holding out the comfort of the communion cup he understood for the first time the heft of no longer believing, how it felt to wait alone in a dark world after God had turned his back and left.

Disrobing in the vestry after the service, hanging his white surplice on a wire coat hanger, the silver damask stole draped round the empty shoulders, he asked Bishop Fraser if he might stay for a word, before they joined the families for the lunch set out in the church hall: plates of sandwiches under cling-film wrap, the smell of cut cress and hard-boiled eggs seeming to waft into his thoughts and make his empty stomach turn over with nausea. Peter closed the door and the bishop waited. The words in Peter's mouth were like hot coals. He felt small and shabby and foolish – and fearful, his head pounding. The bishop's friendly, pastoral demeanour had turned to concern.

'Peter? Sit down, dear man. Are you ill? Patricia?'

He shook his head. His ears rang as if he had just registered the impact of an old blow.

'It's Cyril.'

'Canon Prior?'

Peter felt the chair take his weight as he thumped down. Heard the groan from his lungs. As clearly, as dispassionately as he could, Peter told him how Cyril had abused their trust. Several serious assaults on a child and later a rape. A string of death threats over several years to buy that child's silence. He watched the bishop's face, grave and stunned, disgust and disbelief passing over it like shadows.

Confidential. It would be confidential, the bishop told him. But there would be an enquiry. The police. And then they had to join the cheerful families in the church hall, the din of chatter and chinking teacups, and Patricia like an automaton sliding portions of damp quiche onto paper plates.

Going back in the car Patricia put her hand on his arm. 'It will be all right, won't it? It will be all right? Sarah. In a way we can't see yet. It has to be.'

And he realised then that she was relying on his faith. She was coping, because she still believed that he would think like that.

★ ★

At four o'clock they heard a car pull up in front of the house. The bell rang and Patricia jumped. Peter was already going to open the door. She heard Alice's contralto tones, warm and friendly. Nicky's deeper voice. She went out to greet them and showed them into the sitting room. The guests sat down, side by side on the wingback sofa, Nicky leaning forward tensely, his elbows on his knees and his hands clasped. On a side chair sat a cardboard box with some vinyl records, books, a scarf and a jumper folded on top. Nicky didn't look at it.

Patricia set out tea things, passed round a plate of digestives. She saw the biscuits were chipped and crushed at the edges. She hadn't noticed when she had slid them out of the packet onto a plate. She felt her cheeks hot, tears prick her eyes. As they chatted about the journey, the weather holding, she could see that Alice had picked up on their preoccupied distraction, and she realised that Alice was uncomfortable, interpreting it as animosity. Which wasn't right, because she wanted more than anything for things to be mended between Sarah and Nicky. She'd imagined meeting with Alice again, how she would once again tell her how sorry they were for the ruined wedding, for all the trouble. She would tell them how they knew Sarah cared deeply for Nicky. She had so wanted to reassure Nicky that they were ready to do anything they could to set things right.

Nothing she could say to explain why she and Peter were frozen and stiff, unless they began to unpack the whole stinking mess. It was as if she were watching a spiteful wind spinning things further and further apart.

A silence in the room. Patricia had crumbled one of the biscuits onto her plate. Nicky sat looking washed out and bruised, the blue tinge to his pale skin, the rusty freckles unnaturally pronounced against his whiteness. Alice placed her cup in its saucer with a clink and put them down on the small table by her chair. She looked around the room and leaned forward.

'Since all this happened, I realised how much pressure I've been putting on Sarah, on Nicky. One has these little demons poking you with their pitchforks to do things right. I want to do everything I can to say sorry, to help sort this out.'

Patricia and Peter stared at her blankly. Then Peter looked over at Patricia. The glance of a man being carried further out by an unstoppable tide.

'It's OK, Mum,' Nicky said. 'Look, I just wanted to ask you both if you'd heard any more. You see, I'm thinking of driving up there and speaking to her. I know she's said not to, but I can't believe she'd mean that. I've got to speak to her face to face. I can't leave it like this.'

'Nicky, there's something we must tell you. Sarah has asked us to tell you something in confidence. She wants you and Alice to know, to understand.' And so Peter began to tell them what had happened to Sarah, a great weariness and sorrow almost stopping the words, but he carried on. When he had finished speaking Nicky sat as if slapped. Then he seemed to shake himself awake, stood up. 'We should go to her. Drive up.'

'She's asked us not to go and see her,' Patricia said. 'We don't feel we can force her to see us. Not until she's ready.'

'I can't leave it like this. I have to see her. You don't object, if I try?'

'I think perhaps she might see you,' said Patricia quietly.

Nicky left quickly, ran down the steps to the car. Alice glanced around the room. She stretched forward and grasped Peter's hand. 'I'm so sorry.' Then she moved swiftly to catch up with Nicky.

Peter and Patricia could hear them talking outside on the pavement. The car started up and drove off. A few moments later the doorbell rang. Peter found Alice on the step.

'He wants to drive up, alone, so I've let him take the car. I think they need to talk. One way or another they must talk at least.'

Peter nodded. 'Let me drive you back.'

'I don't think you should drive anywhere, Peter. Look, you're shaking. I can get the train.'

'At least let me call for a taxi.'

The box of Nicky's things was still there on the chair after she had gone.

★ ★

Patricia and Peter stood in the garden that evening, the disappointing town garden that no one had had time to tend, not with so many things to do in the parish. So much given up for the good of others. In faith.

Like the thief, the con man, the trickster, he had crept into their lives, his intentions hidden and smiling, and stolen and betrayed. And they had never once put up a guard or even imagined such an evil heart.

They hadn't seen. How could they not have seen?

CHAPTER 33

Birmingham, 1981

At eleven that night Peter had to walk down to the church. The day before one of the old choir members had passed away after a long illness. He had asked to have his body lie overnight in the church in the old way, instead of at the funeral parlour. There being no family members left, the new curate had done the first few hours of the vigil and would now be waiting for Peter to take over.

Peter unlocked the side door into the silent building. The curate stood up and immediately left, a new baby at home. The door locked again. The church was barely lit, the glass in the stained-glass windows now black with night. The coffin stood on trestles in front of the sanctuary. Above it a red votive light in its brass holder hung down from the roof on a long chain, moving slightly from some unseen draught.

Peter slid into a wooden pew and let the silence sink round him. Alone in the church he began to pray. First the Our Father, a prayer so familiar it was embedded into the very synapses and neural pathways of his mind – the only prayer given straight from the mouth of God's own self, his Son.

Halfway through he stopped. Forgive us our sins as we forgive those who have sinned against us.

The words dried up. But he had to say it; it was central to his faith. All men could receive forgiveness, through the cross. He believed that.

But now the words froze; now there was an exception. It would be easier to lift the stones of the church than to forgive something so unforgivable.

All he wanted now was revenge, recompense, he wanted restitution for all that had been taken from Sarah. He could kill the man. Wanted to kill him. He fought against it, tried again to say the words. His head, too heavy to hold up, slumped in his hands. After the war, through all the years, hadn't he worked tirelessly, in faith, to build a better world, a world based on love and God, based on hope and forgiveness? But he hadn't been able to rebuild the human heart. That was the error in the plan.

He knelt down in the transept, but his limbs were still too heavy. He lay down along the terracotta tiles, cold stone against his sweaty face. An hour he lay there, maybe two. Waited. Waited to feel God the Father there.

And nothing came. No one came. No answer.

He got up, with difficulty, his joints stiff, and sat back down in a pew, the wood creaking. The red votive light above the coffin still eyeing him. He should say the prayers for the dead.

On the wall behind the altar the plaster effigy of a half-naked Jesus watched, while Peter began to recite from the prayer book into the silence. God had gone from the building, left it dark and empty, but he read on. And the wounded man behind the altar, his bones broken and twisted, listened. The wounded man. Who spoke forgiveness out of ashes. Who let himself die and rot three days in the dark. Nothing but a hope to say that that man would ever rise again from the dead, walk from the tomb.

Peter put down the book. Looked at the plaster statue. Even as he wanted to shout obscenities, even though it felt like it would kill him, even though he felt sweat break out over his back with the effort, willing himself against his own will, he said the words. He said, 'You are forgiven. I forgive you.'

Felt his bones disintegrate, felt something crack and break open – something small and new beginning.

CHAPTER 34

Gairloch, 1981

Nicky got out of the car and looked over at the group of steadings, holding on to the door carefully since the wind felt strong enough to wrench it back. He walked along the track, the sea glinting in the distance, and saw three women in blue skirts and cardigans working in a garden sheltered by hedges of green plastic netting and bushes. He shaded his eyes, but none of them had Sarah's slight build, or her way of moving. She must be somewhere inside the low, white buildings. One of the women began walking down the track to meet him.

Sarah had gone. She hadn't wanted to leave a forwarding address. 'I think she might have gone to look for work in a town down the way,' the woman told him, exquisitely sympathetic.

Back in the car Nicky sat dazed and unsure what to do next, the wind thumping on the car body so that it rocked every so often. Then he started the engine and began to drive back the way he had come.

He had no address or any information about where she might be, or even if she was there, but he stopped in the small cluster of houses by the sea shore that the woman had called a town. He walked around the deserted streets. The strand of sand along the shore was empty. At the far end large brown fishing nets were draped over standing poles, marking insubstantial rooms of transparent netting. Facing the sea, next to a small grocer's store, was a café with a steamed-up window.

At the counter he waited for his order, turned and looked around the room for a table where he could sit undisturbed and think. The café was half empty. There was a woman in the corner, sitting with her back to him, slowly stirring a cup of coffee. Her dark hair was lank, she wore a baggy oatmeal sweater and a navy parka hung on the back of the chair. The defeated posture was nothing like Sarah, he didn't recognise any of the clothes, and yet his heart was racing. He paid for the coffee and carried it over.

He stood by her table. She looked up. No change in her dull expression; perhaps it became a little more guarded.

'Can I sit down?'

She nodded. 'I'm sorry you came all this way.'

'Of course I came. Sarah, I had to find you.'

She went back to stirring her coffee. Her eyes on the shoreline through the window. She looked tired, uncared for, someone down on their luck.

'I've a shift at three, in the shop next door. I'll have to go.'

'I'm so sorry. So sorry, about what happened. Why did you never tell me how hard it's been?'

She flinched.

'I'm sorry. I didn't mean to . . .'

She looked vague, scanned the room. 'You want me to tell you all about it? I can tell you. But you won't want to hear it.'

'Tell me. Please.'

She lowered her head, a side-to-side movement, a tired negative.

'You can tell me.'

'I don't think so. There's not really any point.' Her eyes went to the door. Then she jumped as Nicky slapped a hand on the table.

'No point in explaining to me why you left? You think I can accept it, just like that? I love you, Sarah. You owe it to me to make me understand what happened here. Because I can see no reason why you left. And unless you make me understand, then I am staying here by your side. I won't accept it, not unless you make me understand.'

She sat in silence, watching him, and he held her gaze. Then she sighed and she gave him the details, reciting them without emotion, the facts medical, unpleasant. Looked down at her hands.

'You do ask yourself why it should change you so much. I've thought about it, and I think it's because, someone like that, they don't care if you live or die. A few times I really thought he'd go through with it – that I'd die. Walking to church he'd whisper threats. Now, just being in a church building makes me panic.

'And you can't tell anyone, you can't tell anyone who you really are, what you've become; it's too shameful. So you're alone. You're afraid, and you're alone.'

'I'm so sorry.' He could feel tears cold on his cheeks.

'Then when I was thirteen we moved, and I thought it was over. I thought I could forget.'

He stretched his arm across the table, closed his hand round hers. She looked at it sadly. 'I'd better go. I'll be late for my shift.'

He held on. 'Come home with me, Sarah.'

She pulled her hand away. 'Look, I have to go.'

'Please.'

'Don't, Nicky.' She picked up her bag and began to leave.

Out on the pavement he caught up with her.

'Nothing's changed, Sarah. I know what you've been through now, but nothing's changed. I love you just as much.'

She folded her head down on her chest, her eyes shut.

'I love you, Sarah.'

She gave a sigh, a quiet sound of loss and tiredness.

'Come home with me?'

He waited, nothing but the sound of the sea, the cold wind. Saw he might lose her, if she started walking away.

Then she nodded slightly. The faintest nod, just once. He moved closer and put his arms round her, relief flooding through his body. For a long time they stayed like that, leaning together on the pavement, swaying slightly.

'Let's go home.'

They went back to her room to gather up her few things and then went out to the car parked in front of the curve of sand round the bay. He opened the door, but she didn't get in.

'I think it will take time, Nicky. I think I'll need to talk to someone, and I don't want to hold you to something, if you think it's not working out.'

'It's a new story, now. Not the old one. You get to write a new story. And I'll be there with you.' She thought about that. She put her hand on the curve of his cheek softly.

She slid into her seat. He ran round, got in, slammed the door, and they began the long drive home.

CHAPTER 35

Fourwinds, 1993

Alice was awake ridiculously early, as she often was now. But she felt well, her body cleared of last night's aches and nausea. The little canvas tent was full of sleep, the breath of the children mixed in with the smell of crushed grass. The sun through the canvas was too bright to let her doze off again.

She slid out of the sleeping bag, got her towel and then undid the nylon zip at the front of the tent, hoping its complaint would not wake the grandchildren, or Ralph who had found a night under canvas difficult, and was now out cold, his grey hair peeping grudgingly from a nest of sleeping bag.

Outside she zipped it up again carefully – they'd sleep for another hour or two – and then slid her legs into damp wellies, rolling her pyjama bottoms over the top. The air was cold on her bare scalp, the sun spreading carmine and orange over her hands, lighting up the dewfall, everything delineated with the clear intensity of a new morning.

Barely five o'clock, no one else about. She walked down through the paddock that ran along the side of Fourwinds. A low sun dazzled through the hedges, transforming the field of autumn grasses into a sea of light flecks, the tents here and there, rising up like small islands.

It was for the grandchildren that they'd agreed to spend the night under canvas. Ralph had cited what the doctor would have to say about that, but Alice had said they were going to camp, even though they had a whole perfectly good house right there. And it wasn't cold, the summer lasting well into September, like a gift. All the same Ralph had insisted on collecting layers and layers of extra bedding for the tent and had dragged a foam mattress down from the loft.

The gathering of students who'd first sung together that weekend at the beginning of the war, had continued to meet each year at Yarnton. And after Daniel had passed away and the Yarnton estate was sold, the gathering moved to Fourwinds. Over time people began to bring children with them, and now grandchildren. This year it was going to be a work by Britten, *Noye's Fludde*, for the children.

She walked to the end of the paddock and down through a gap in the laurel hedge, into a small, secluded garden, the dark laurels and the sweet box hedges screening it on three sides. To the west a gap in the hedge looked out over the Dove plains, the hill falling steeply away beyond the fence.

And there it was, sunk down in the middle of the lawn, its rim level with the grass, two chrome taps standing up incongruous among the green. Nicky had installed the bath there a few months ago. She smiled to think of him lying out under the stars, a glass of wine in one hand no doubt. It was so like Nicky to do things his own way – and then make you wonder why no one had thought of it before.

It was the same with the barn that now stood in the lower paddock beyond the laurels; that had also been Nicky's idea. After the great storm had taken down several of the oaks along the top field, it was Nicky who'd suggested letting them dry out and then building with them. He'd constructed the barn in the old medieval way, entirely without nails; no one in England had built anything like it for a thousand years. Inside was the large, warm space where Nicky and Sarah now lived with the children.

Nicky and Sarah and Ralph had all raved to her about the bath in the garden as something almost Zen; the night sky clear and sharp with stars; the quiet; the pool of candlelight in the middle of the lawn; the steam white mist against the darkness. She'd meant to try it. But then came the visits to the hospital, and no one had mentioned it as a good idea after that. She had started to think in terms of things she wouldn't do any more.

But awake so early and feeling perfectly well, she'd thought why not? Why shouldn't she? Today she would do something for the first time.

She had to swill a little mud from the bottom of the bath. The water was hot as she filled it, the steam rising. It would cool quickly. She pulled over a garden chair and folded her clothes and the towel on the seat. She stood shivering, the cool morning breeze slipping round her white skin, over the marble pucker of the scar across her chest. The laurels cast a long shade over the lawn, a burst of orange sunlight through the leaves. There was a line of sun on her arm, but failing to promise any real heat.

Holding on to the chair she stepped down into the bath, carefully lowered herself into the water and lay down, the grass at eye level. She stretched out, her head lying against the rim, her light frame buoyed up as if she might float away. She watched her white body lengthen and retreat like a mirage under the water, making strange bends where her arms and legs passed from air to water. She shut her eyes and let the warmth rock her until the momentum of her disturbance settled. She felt the stillness all around, the birds' watery song in the air, the smell of autumn leaf mould from the laurel hedge. She lay unmoving, her body long and white, the earth by her face, the tang of the soil in her nostrils. The sudden cry of a bird gunning through the hedges.

Someone was coming along the path. The crunch of gravel. Ralph was calling her name. She sat up with a sudden rush of water and the cold came in like a pressure. She gasped.

He helped her stand up, her skin running with rivulets, wrapped the towel round her pale, amorphous body.

'I didn't know where you'd gone,' he said.

'You shouldn't worry.'

'I do,' a little angry now. 'I do worry. If you'd fallen.'

'Ralph. Darling, I'm fine. But what have you done with the children?'

'Inside.' He nodded at the barn, its roof just visible beyond the laurel hedges. 'Come on, old thing, I'm taking you in too, so you can get warmed up.'

★ ★

When Ralph had woken and found Alice gone he'd struggled up, unbent his limbs after a night on the floor and walked round the tent outside to see if he could spot her returning. The noise had the children awake and up, asking where Granny Alice had gone, ready for the next adventure. He took them with him to the main house first, curtains still drawn, no one up, then decided to try the barn. No sign of her there either.

Feeling an undeniable anxiety now, a shadow of dread, he settled the children with bowls of cereal at the table. Where on earth could she be? And then, by some instinct, a feeling for the way Alice thought, he hurried out to the paddock. Alice lying motionless in the water. He'd lurched forward, a burst of relief to see her sit up in a rush of bathwater.

Ralph made sure she was safely installed on the red velvet sofa, a blanket tucked round her legs and a mug of hot coffee on the table nearby – still feeling a bit cross with her. She was looking drowsy now, her head wrapped in a bright scarf, leaning against the sofa's back.

Agnes and Ben in pyjamas and muddy wellies were singing and chattering with the energy of small children at half past six in the morning. The barn was filled with the light flooding through a wall of windows, the living space busy with all the usual clutter that went with two children, bookshelves and toys and scattered clothes.

Nicky and Sarah's wedding had been a simple affair – three years after the wedding that never happened. Sarah had worn a shift dress sewn from a length of white Indian muslin bordered with small gold embroidery. Carrying roses and orange blossom from the garden, and with a beaming smile, she'd walked down the middle of the old church on Peter's arm. She and Nicky, facing each other, made promises learned by heart. Family and close friends walked to a small reception in the hall next to the church, sandwiches and quiches made by ladies in the village. Queenie, who now owned a teashop in Devon, had arrived with a two-layer chocolate wedding cake as her gift, made by the baking genius who did the scones and fairy cakes in her kitchens.

Sarah and Nicky had settled for a while in the US, but every so often they talked about coming home, perhaps to a village near Fourwinds. Then the storm and the oak trees, and the idea of the barn had taken root.

At one end, beyond the sofas, was the door through to Nicky's office where he ran his thriving architect business. Sarah was busy with the children most days, or travelled into town twice a week where she worked as a counsellor in a hospital clinic. You forgot what energy the young had. It had been a relief to hand on the running of the festival to the next generation, to the three boys and their wives. Especially now.

When Alice had finished her snooze, knocked out as she was by the hot water and the brisk morning air, they should walk over to Fourwinds and see how things were going with the rest of the family. And perhaps there'd be news. Perhaps Melissa would have called, left a message.

At the far end of the barn rows of masks of animals and birds were lined up on decorating trestles. Ralph took his coffee over and picked up the red sequinned mask of a bird of paradise. Strands of red down curled from the ends like eyelashes. Agnes followed him and picked up a dove's mask. She put it on, her blue eyes looked out through the eye holes, her serious gaze among the feathers uncanny. He thought of angels.

Footsteps came down the wooden staircase from the loft area, Sarah in a striped dressing gown, her hair in a messy ponytail.

'You're here, and up so early. Who woke who up?' She laughed and looked at Agnes in muddy wellies and a bird mask. Took the mask away and let Agnes rest her hand on her side as the child kicked off her boots. Agnes wanted to be picked up and Sarah carried her over to the sofa where Alice was opening her eyes.

'I'm cooking bacon rolls. How does that sound?'

'Lovely, darling.'

'And for you, Ralph?'

He nodded. 'Yes please. I'll lay the table. Want to help me, old man?' Ralph and Ben put out eight plates, bowls, cutlery.

Nicky came clattering down the stairs, and then Peter and Patricia. Patricia wore her hair as a short silver cap, half-spectacles on her nose. Agnes immediately brought a book over for her to read a story, having detected Patricia's weakness in that area as an off-duty headmistress, and the two of them sat turning the pages at the breakfast table, as orange juice, bacon rolls and ketchup circulated.

Sarah and Nicky studied the food roster, his hand resting on the small of her back in that easy way they had of being together, discussing deliveries of bread rolls and beef burgers for the evening meal – a giant barbeque on metal half-drums.

Ralph got up to fetch the coffee and more milk, but ended up standing at the window, looking up towards the shared drive.

Alice half opened her eyes. 'Don't worry, she'll be here,' she murmured. Even with her eyes closed Alice had a rare talent for knowing what he was thinking. 'What time did she say she was arriving?'

'She didn't give a time. Said as soon as she could get here.'

'She'll be here.'

There were a lot of rehearsals in the morning. The children waited behind the barn in their costumes, ready for their cue to come running out. Kept getting it wrong. The woolly tights and jumpers they wore were too hot in the sunshine.

For the first time Alice wasn't playing her violin. You had to commit to the rehearsals, and the way things had been, well. But it was fine as Mark's wife, Parthivi, a doctor who also happened to be an excellent violinist, had stepped in. It was nice to just sit and listen. Ralph sat with her under the shade of the open-sided marquee that had been erected ready for the audience, half listening to God commanding Noah to do something, Noah complaining back in an aggrieved baritone. You had to concentrate to really follow the words. The text was a medieval mystery play as old as the church next door, the story older still by thousands of years. But the continuity felt soothing. He thought of Britten wading through his flooded house on the Suffolk coast, taking in the news of all the people who'd been lost the night before in the roaring sea tides, the first bars of the music coming to him as he slopped over to the piano. He'd included parts for beginner recorders for the children and the old sea hymns that were sung with such fervour in the churches along the coast. It was an opera the whole village could take part in.

Alice had been half drowsing again in the warmth. She murmured and opened her eyes. 'Is she here?'

He shook his head.

Tom's granddaughter, Melissa Gardiner, had got in touch with Ralph out of the blue. Could she come and visit? She was travelling on a gap year and had decided to drop by and check them out. When she'd suggested visiting on the day of the performance Ralph had immediately said yes, come then, not wanting to put her off in case she didn't manage to come at all.

'And there's something I have to give you,' she'd said on the phone. 'Something from Aunt Charlotte.'

★ ★

They were clearing away the soup bowls and the remains of the bread from the lunch tables that had been set out on the flagstones in front of the house when Alice put down a water jug and tapped Ralph's arm. He looked up. Nicky was walking across the lawn, a rucksack on one shoulder. By his side was a girl with the same shade of auburn hair, the same lean build, both of them talking eagerly. Ralph and Alice exchanged a glance.

Melissa wanted to know everything about everyone. Ralph felt her eyes reading his face as they chatted, and watched her studying the children for clues of belonging when Agnes and Ben insisted on taking her hands and leading their prize on a tour of the plywood Noah's ark.

Alice made sure the girl had some lunch and then Melissa sat turning the pages of the photo album that Ralph had fetched from the study, pictures of Max in Valencia, Ralph as a boy. Melissa was thrilled, full of questions; she hadn't seen any pictures of her great-grandfather from those years.

'Oh yes, and I've brought something to give to you,' she said. It took a while to find it somewhere in her rucksack. Triumphant, she handed Ralph a slim, black box like a stubby jewellery case. Inside was a medal on a red twill ribbon: Max's OBE.

'Tom wanted you to have it. It says so there, in the note inside. When I said I was coming to see you Aunt Charlotte went and found it somewhere in her desk. She said to tell you she was sorry she'd hung on to it for so long.'

Ralph nodded. He couldn't speak for a moment. The idea of Tom writing the note, intending the medal to reach him, made him feel intensely grateful and close to Tom, who would realise what holding the medal represented to him. He now understood how valuable Max's work had been, the lives Max and Lily had saved.

Ralph took it from its box and laid it on his hand.

'What is it?' asked Ben. 'Is that a soldier's medal?'

'In a way. It shows that your great-grandfather did some very brave things. I'll tell you all about it, but later.'

The director was calling for everyone to get ready, checking off names on his clipboard. Sarah took the children to get into their costumes. There were some last-minute instructions for Ben because he was playing the mugs, an instrument devised by Britten. Hung in a row from a wooden frame, the mugs made just the right earthy, ringing notes for raindrops when tapped lightly with a drumstick.

A roll of the kettledrums and the performance was beginning, the children hidden away behind the barn now, waiting for their cue; the choir's penitent and mournful refrain beginning to rise and sink with the solemn heaviness of the sea; Noah arguing with God; then the fun of the ark being assembled. Mrs Noah, drunk and rolling, refused to get into the ark and had to be carried in, Ben tapping out the first drops of rain as the storm began to rise and the kettledrums crashed.

And suddenly here they were, the children, dressed in their animal masks and costumes, transformed into birds and gazelles and lions, running two by two into the ark with their fluting calls of 'Kyrie kyrie, kyrie eleison'. And with them the ecstatic, mad brass band of resurrection trumpets and drums and cornets.

Alice leaned across to Peter. 'You know, this would be a nice send-off for a funeral. A rather good ending.'

Peter squeezed her hand. 'An ending and a beginning.'

She blinked twice. 'And a beginning.'

The animals all gathered in, Noah's beard now a bit lopsided as he raised his staff, a final roll of drums, and everyone stood up to sing the old sailor's hymn 'Eternal Father, Strong to Save'.

Afterwards, the ark safe on dry land, and all of them eating sausages and burgers from paper plates, Melissa delighted by everything and everyone, they watched enormous flowers of light exploding in the night sky.

Alice said to Ralph, 'You'll keep on doing this, won't you, holding the festival here? Next year?'

He looked up from his plate, his face caught in the exploding light and he didn't move for a while, his hand spearing a sausage and said, 'Yes. Yes, I will.'

And later she lay down on the picnic rug in the darkness, suspended on the earth's flank among the wealth of stars. Agnes lay down along her side and Ben came and rested his head on her arm, and she felt the weight of those small bodies pressing her in place for a little while longer.

'You know, the sky isn't flat,' she told them. 'If you look carefully you'll see it's deep, made of layers and layers of stars, like frogspawn. Beautiful frogspawn.' Then Ralph lowered himself down next to them with an 'Oof' and they lay and looked up at those stars, so huge and white and, surely, so very, very close.

Acknowledgements

I am indebted to Jenny Hewson at the RCW agency for bringing this book to publication and also to the wonderful editors Anna Hogarty, Maddie West and Sara O'Keeffe at Corvus.

In researching the work of British refugee intelligence in the Second World War, I read Duff Hart-Davis's book *Man of War: the Secret Life of Captain Alan Hillgarth*, and Donald Caskie's *The Tartan Pimpernel*. Thanks also to the National Archives in Kew through which I was able to read the correspondence between the Madrid embassy and London from 1940, information that had been classified until recently. Thanks to Patricia Martinez de Vincente whose discovery of her father's diaries from Madrid in 1940–41 alerted me to the incredible work of those in and around the Madrid British Embassy in saving many lives. Her father's story, not included in this book, is told in *La Clave Embassy*. Very many thanks to the Embassy Café in Madrid who warmly welcomed us and shared photographs of the café from the Second World War years.

It was due to the research for this book that I uncovered a surprising family link to a smuggling ring that helped some 20,000 Jewish refugees and many Allied prisoners of war escape from Occupied France through Spain. After France fell in 1940, there was no longer a viable Swiss route out of Europe for Jewish refugees, so Churchill quietly asked the British Embassy in Madrid to do all it could to set up an escape route through Spain. They came up with an audacious secret operation that was carried on under the noses of the pro-Nazi regime. There was no extra manpower available in terms of secret agents, so it was operated by the employees and expatriates around the British Embassy community, helped by the sort of Spanish upper class you would never suspect of acting against Franco's policies. But act they did – to save a lot of lives. Many people were involved and yet all kept the operation secret, and because the same Franco's regime continued in Spain until the end of the seventies, no one spoke about it even when the war ended. It was very moving to uncover the bravery of people like my husband's grandparents, William and Louisa Gentry, who carried the details of their exploits to the grave – apart from a cryptic comment or two that only make sense in retrospect. So I would like to dedicate this book to all of the people around the British Embassy in Madrid in 1940–1945 who did so much to help save so many lives at a time when most routes out of occupied Europe were closed to Jewish refugees and escaping prisoners of war.

I was greatly helped in developing the book by Deborah Cohen's book *Family Secrets: Living with Shame from the Victorians to the Present Day*; also Brené Brown's book *Daring Greatly*.

Many thanks to the tutors on the Oxford Creative Writing diploma, especially Antonia Logue-Bose, Kate Clanchy, Jane Draycott, Frank Egerton, Clare Morgan and Tim Pears. Very many thanks to fellow writers on the course: Marianne Allen, Neville Beal, Alastair Beck, Sarah-Jane de Brito Martin, Sue Cox, Stephanie van Driel, Suellen Dainty, Pauline Fiennes, Nick Harries, Brian Harrison, James McDermott, Karen Pomerantz, Margaret Keeping, Peter Saxby, Nageena Shaheen and Fred Volans.

I would like to thank the tutors on the Royal Holloway University of London Creative Writing MA: Susanna Jones, Jo Shapcott and

Andrew Motion, and the wonderful tutor group: Emma Chapman, Tom Feltham, Carolina Gonzalez Carvajal, Kat Gordon, Lucy Hounsom, Liza Klaussmann and Rebecca Lloyd Jones.

All characters in this book are fictional, but are set in carefully researched times and places referencing the last century. A huge thank you to my parents Frank and Joan whose stories and anecdotes informed the fabric of the war years narrative, and also to Hazel and Douglas, especially to Hazel who was such a wonderful archivist of how it felt to live through those years. Endless thanks and love to Josh, Hugh, Kirsty and George for all their encouragement and support during the years when this book was evolving.

READ ON TO DISCOVER MORE ABOUT

Return
to
Fourwinds

Q&A with Elisabeth Gifford

1. What compelled you to write Return to Fourwinds?

The generation that lived through the Second World War wanted to look forward to a better world for the sake of their children, so their wartime experiences were played down or hardly spoken about in the family. In their seventies and eighties, my parents and many in their generation became more interested in handing down diaries and letters, and it was amazing and rather wonderful to be able to see what they had experienced. For me, this led to a more general interest in the nature of secret keeping between family members – what sort of secrets we keep and why. I read Deborah Cohen's book *Family Secrets* on how the types of secrets families feel compelled to keep has changed over the past century, as has the notion of what we consider shameful. I also looked at how some secrets are kept through a desire to protect others, and what the personal cost of that may be.

It was only through researching this book that we finally found out why my husband's grandfather was given the OBE during the Second World War. He was involved in activities in wartime Madrid that had to be kept secret in order to protect lives and national security. I took my husband – his grandson – to see places in Madrid such as the Embassy Café where his grandfather had been part of a ring of people who smuggled Jewish refugees and stranded servicemen out through Spain after France fell in 1940. An equal impulse in writing the book was to record something of the character of that wonderful wartime generation for the next generation.

2. *There are a lot of deep themes in the book. What do you hope readers will take away from the story?*

The linking theme is having the courage to risk showing who we really are to those we love. While writing the book I came across Brene Brown's books and TED talks on wholeheartedness. They were a great help in clarifying why I was writing *Return to Fourwinds*. For various reasons, several of the characters in the book hide themselves through fear of rejection. Their situations in the story may be more extreme than many we experience in daily life, but we all still experience the burn of social shame and want to put on a 'good face'. We may not be as hung up on class issues as Alice is in *Return to Fourwinds*, but we still have pressures from magazines, TV and school exams to be and live a certain way, and push our children to achieve and conform to certain ideals. Risking being honest and open about who you are and respecting the difference in others is the basis for a loving and intimate relationship.

3. *How did writing* Return to Fourwinds *differ from your experience with* Secrets of the Sea House?

I wrote the two books in tandem over two writing courses that I did in Oxford and London, so the books do have some similarity in themes. But they are also very different stories. One is a love letter to Scotland and the Hebrides, and the other forms a sort of love letter to Englishness in all its variations and permutations. I wanted to examine and celebrate the uniqueness of both places. In *Return to Fourwinds* I wanted to celebrate and hold the various time frames and English locations as being part of a whole, so that if you plotted all those points of experience with authentic detail, then you would come up with a sort of 3-D shape that might describe a portrait of English experience at a certain time span of history. And, of course, part of that experience is that people live abroad for a while, or move to England from other cultures.

4. What character do you identify with most in the novel, and why?

I have to say that I identified with all the characters! One of the best things about writing, and reading other novels, is the chance to see the world through someone else's eyes for a while and experience a life you'll never live. So while I'm writing that character, I try and see through their eyes. I especially enjoy writing about characters in the past as it has the exciting element of time travel.

5. Return to Fourwinds *sweeps through locations and times. Did you travel to any of the destinations within the novel for your research?*

I included places that I knew well, or knew from quite vivid family accounts, such as my father's experience of the Manchester blitz, or memories of my great grandmother in her tiny Devon cottage who had a broad country accent and called me 'my little maid'. I wanted to take a close look at how people lived in an actual place and time so I needed locations where I could access a lot of detail. As a child we moved around to various parishes with my father's work and got to experience life as part of different communities, from a hard-up council estate to a well-heeled country village. Of course, the book ends in 1980 so it doesn't include experiences from the last three decades, but I hope it still carries a way of looking at a society that can hold lots of variations with equal respect, from the new to the traditional – it's all part of the mix. And that vision of equal respect is as important in a country as it is in a family for everyone to thrive, and to keep the cohesiveness of a group that, at the end of the day, you hope will be there for you when you need them. I'd love the next generation to have enough of a vision of community to keep the NHS going, for example.

6. Can you tell us a little bit about what you are working on next?

The next book is a true story about a remarkable man called Janusz Korczak, who cared for 200 children in the Warsaw Ghetto. He was famous in Poland for his books such as *How to Love a Child* and *The Child's Right to Respect*. His works are still quoted by the NSPCC and the UN. He believed that children needed to be studied individually and understood for who they were and the stage they were at, whether three or thirteen. He also advocated that adults should apply the same rules to themselves as they do to children, with mutual respect and no violence. He was a sort of Polish Lewis Caroll and a well-loved national figure. He was also Jewish. In August 1940, the Nazis swooped in on all of the ghetto orphanages in Warsaw and marched away 4,000 children to the trains for Treblinka in the space of a single day. Dr Korczak was offered the chance to escape but he refused to leave his children and died with them in Treblinka. The story focuses around Misha, one of the orphanage workers, and his wife Sophia. They were among the one percent to survive the Warsaw Ghetto and continued to teach and spread Korczak's ideals after the war.

Reading Group Questions

1. What did you think were the central themes of the novel, and how did they resonate with you?

2. The narrative takes us on a journey from Valencia and the English countryside to the post-war slums in the north. How does the author evoke a sense of place?

3. 'How easy it was to wreck a life, with a careless word...' Explore how both Ralph and Sarah feel compelled to keep the secret of their past in order to protect those that they love.

4. Sarah abandons her fiancé Nicky and vanishes without a trace on the eve of their wedding. How did this affect your response to her as a character, and how does this change as the novel progresses?

5. We often put our best face on for the world. With reference to Alice and Ralph, what might happen in a relationship when people do not feel able to be open and vulnerable with each other?

6. All families were affected by the war years in the last century, and many people report a reluctance to talk about the experience of that painful time. Do you relate to this in your own family history?

7. Has what people feel should or should not be kept secret within a family changed over the past century?

8. Fourwinds itself becomes a character in this book. How important is the concept of home to the characters in the novel?

9. Did anything surprise you during the course of reading this book? Did it alter any of the views you currently hold?

10. Were you satisfied with the ending of the novel? What do you think it is trying to say?